A KILLING KINDNESS

Camellion was just in time to see three helmeted KYP troopers coming through the windows. The Death Merchant almost felt sorry for them. *Almost.* Because his finger was already squeezing the trigger of the Beretta, spitting out 9-mm projectiles. The first goon was hit above the nose, the bullet bursting his brain and blowing out the back of his head. A tenth of an eyeblink later, the second trooper—he was swinging around—was stitched from navel to neck. The third member of the trio fared no better. Two slugs bored a lethal tunnel into his brain. A slight smile curved across Camellion's mouth. He knew the Cosmic Lord of Death was laughing insanely—only a split second from claiming more victims.

DEATH MERCHANT series:

APOCALYPSE

Joseph Rosenberger

A DELL BOOK

Published by
Dell Publishing Co., Inc.
1 Dag Hammarskjold Plaza
New York, New York   10017

Dell ® TM 681510, Dell Publishing Co., Inc.

ISBN: 0-440-10160-3

Printed in the United States of America

April 1987

10 9 8 7 6 5 4 3 2 1

WFH

And behold a pale horse, and he that sat upon him, his name was Death, and hell followed him. And power was given to him over four parts of the earth, to kill with sword, with famine, and with death, and with the beasts of the earth.

The Apocalypse of St. John
the Apostle 6:8

This book is dedicated to the
real "Fox"—
J.J.A.

Book One

Book One

Chapter One

I

One Sunday afternoon I spent a whole year in Los Angeles. This is worse. Always bored with traveling, Richard Camellion wished he could be back in Texas at his *Memento Mori* ranch in the Big Thicket instead of being cooped up inside a Pan Am jetliner, which was preparing to land at Ellinikon International Airport south of Athens—or *Athinai,* as the famed Greek capital was called in English.

What annoyed the Death Merchant most was not that he had to go to Greece. His irritation arose from his agreeing to undertake the mission with a total neophyte, a man whose probable only experience with "spies" was motion pictures he had seen on television. Bunk! Camellion doubted if Nicholas Notaras ever watched television, unless it was a science program on the Public Broadcasting System. He probably didn't even read fiction. Scientists as a whole lived their work.

Camellion glanced at Notaras sitting next to him. Even now, when he could be flying straight to his own death, the physicist had his pudgy nose stuck in *Scientific American.* Camellion felt sorry for the man. Notaras had been submerged in academia for so long that, in the Death Merchant's opinion, he didn't realize the extreme danger in which he was placing himself.

The Death Merchant, gazing out of the window, didn't regret his decision. Success meant $150,000—tax free. If he failed, all the money in the world wouldn't matter. He would be one of the Mute People ruled by the Pale Priest, in that Far Country from which no one ever returns. The money was another irritation. *I could just as easily have asked for $250,000. Grojean would have paid it!* Camellion had not demanded more money because that would have made the overall situation more difficult for Courtland Grojean. The chief of the CIA's Clandestine Division had offered $50,000 more than Camellion's usual fee, saying "See here, Camellion. You are the only one I can send to Greece. This project requires a man of your experience and particular talents."

Camellion knew he was only kidding himself about the money involved. In view of what was at stake, he would have paid the CIA to undertake the mission! The United States was also *his* country. The free world was also *his* free world!

Sifting through the carefully indexed files of his mind, Camellion wasn't overcome with enthusiasm when he recalled his surprise at learning he would be working not only with agents of the United States' Office of Naval Intelligence but also with expert operatives of SIS, the Secret Intelligence Service of Great Britain, and with foreign field specialists of the French SDECE—the *Service de Documentation Extérieure et de Contre-Espionnage*—the French "CIA."

Well . . . fudge! It was about time France and Great Britain did something to help themselves and lent a helping hand to Uncle Sam, who was doing his best to protect *them* as well as himself. Especially France. Ever since France had pulled out of NATO, back in the late sixties, she had insisted on doing things her way and had formed her own ICBM missiles defense force against the Soviet Union. By agreeing to help the Americans and the British, the French not only proved the international scope of Operation Zeus but helped to emphasize the seriousness of the situation.

The Death Merchant's mouth became a tight line. It had been more than a surprise when an ONI officer had given him the fantastic details regarding Tesla's magnifying transmitter. Incredible!

Even more mind-boggling was the progress the Soviet Union had made in transforming Nikola Tesla's notes into a workable transmitter. The danger could not be minimized or rationalized away. Should the Soviet Union succeed in its experiments, the Kremlin's ruthless killers would actually be able to control the world's weather. And the terrible danger was that the nation which discovered the secrets of weather modification and/or control could rule the world!

And do so without firing a shot!

Listening to the sound of the turbojets deepen as the pilot changed the fuel mixture, Camellion glanced again at Notaras, who was still absorbed in *Scientific American*, and reflected that the physicist was, in a sense, right and proper for at least half the job. He was second-generation Greek. He could speak and read Greek idiomatically. His was a brand-new face. The KGB and the Greek KYP couldn't possibly know him. That's why ONI had wanted him: because he was an unknown.

Notaras had not made any discoveries, not even a minor one. He had not written any important papers.

In the world of American science, he was a nobody. However, he did possess a doctorate in theoretical physics and had a thorough knowledge of integral and differential calculus. He'd be able to evaluate the equations in any notes or papers pertaining to TMT —Tesla's magnifying transmitter. Notaras might not be able to put the entire formula together, but he'd be able to separate truth from fiction, provided Professor Stefanos Paspyrou could be found and kidnapped and his research papers acquired.

But Camellion considered it poor strategy to take Notaras with him, and he had said so to Grojean.

"They might call you the Fox, but you made a mistake on this one," Camellion had said, deliberately smirking a little. "Why saddle me with a greenhorn professor when you want me to blackbag Paspyrou? Once we bring him and his notes to the United States, the government can get the best scientists in the country to go over his papers. And we both know he'll talk—by the use of drugs, if nothing else."

Grojean had folded his hands on the desk. "I agree with you. Having Notaras go with you isn't my idea. We're cooperating with ONI, remember. Sending Notaras with you was ONI's brainstorm, and the deputy director of intelligence okayed it. Another thing, don't call me the Fox. I don't like it any more than you like being referred to as the Death Merchant."

Camellion thought of his own identity. He also was a nobody. Only one man in the world knew he was the Death Merchant. That man was Courtland Grojean.

As the aircraft lowered and swung around for the final approach, Camellion leaned closer to Nicholas Notaras and whispered, "How many more American science magazines did you bring aboard in the carry-on bag?"

Notaras blinked several times and his mouth opened slightly. "This one and *Science Digest,*" he said. "Why do you ask?"

"Leave them on the plane," Camellion told him. "I don't want any science magazines with us. We're businessmen from New York. Our only interest is in importing Greek knickknacks for Triangle Importing and Exporting Company."

"You're the boss."

"Remember what I told you," warned Camellion. "Think before you speak. Do not—I repeat: do not—mention one word about the mission anytime, anywhere, unless I mention it first."

"I understand," Notaras said obediently, like a little boy.

An hour and a half later, after the big jet had landed and Camellion and Notaras had gone through Customs and were in a taxi headed for the city, Camellion's impression of Athens was that of a congealed sea of cement covering all the visible lands from the mountains to the Saronic Gulf. From afar, thousands of white cement housing units, most two to seven stories high, appeared as so many tombstones densely packed together in a haphazard sprawl.

The two men were miserable, and not because of Operation Zeus. July is always hot in Greece. The temperature was almost 90 and the cab was not air-conditioned. Their shirts were plastered to their backs, and their summer suits were soggy with perspiration.

The ride was normal for Camellion, who had ridden in Greek cabs before. It was a nightmare for Notaras, since the Athenian cabbie was indulging his natural passion for speed. He had to. Greek drivers are among the most aggressive and competitive drivers in Europe, with any pedestrian, or any other car, qualifying as their quarry. Tailgating was considered a mark of courage. To be passed by another car was considered an unendurable affront.

The Death Merchant had seen it all before, but Notaras was as excited as a ten-year-old visiting Disneyland. As the taxi passed through Syntagma Square, they saw that hundreds of people were seated in open-air cafés that spilled out on the sidewalks and ranged around the orange trees and fountains in the island center. There hours were minutes to those who might care to sit in idleness, sipping drinks, or spearing melon slices, or merely watching the passing parade: the elite of Athenian society arriving at the Grande Bretagne Hotel; elderly sponge peddlers festooned with their wares; macho Greeks on the prowl for unchaperoned girls; lottery sellers with their tickets flying like pennants on banner-style poles. Now and then Camellion and Notaras caught sight of the bravest of all men in Athens—waiters from one of the great hotels who, with trays held aloft, ran across a minefield of nonstop traffic to serve a special customer at a table on the square's center island.

In the distance they caught sight of tourists clicking their cameras at pleat-skirted *Evzones,* the presidential guard stationed on either side of the Tomb of the Unknown Soldier.

Camellion and Notaras were not surprised at the cab driver's friendliness. Greeks are the most talkative and gregarious people in all of Europe. After all, Greek is the only language in which the word stranger, *xenos,* also means "guest." In spite of the cliché "the Greeks have a word for it," they don't have any equivalent of the English word standoffishness. They will talk to anyone about anything and at any time.

This driver—he introduced himself as Savvos Konstantopoulous—rattled on like a wound-up Zorba, talking about everything and jumping from one subject to another. He said that the English were the worst tippers in the world and that all Germans were Nazis, then started on Athens, saying that the city was very unhealthy. "I tell you, Athens is doomed. That's why the birth has fallen. It's due to air pollution. Do you know that eighty-two percent of the women in Athens have no interest in sex because of air pollution? I tell you, it is fact."

Amused, Camellion wondered how and by what logic the cab driver had managed to arrive at such an alarming statistic, but he knew better than to ask. Anyhow, by now the taxi was close to the Royal Olympic, one of the less expensive hotels, the kind that two businessmen in the importing and exporting business would choose. Deluxe hotels, such as the Grand Bretagne, the King George, the Athens-Hilton, and others were for the wealthy and for tourists staying in Athens only a short time.

Soon the cab was pulling up to the Royal Olympic. . . .

Camellion and Notaras first turned up the air conditioner and unpacked, after which the Death Merchant looked at his wristwatch.

"Nick, I suggest you phone Mr. Pappas and let him know we've arrived," Camellion said. "We can meet with him tomorrow."

He watched Notaras, in shirtsleeves, go to the small writing desk, take out a small notebook from his pocket, pick up the phone, and give the number to the hotel's switchboard operator.

After four rings, a woman answered in Greek. "Pappas Importing and Exporting Company. Miss Sofoulis speaking."

"My name is Nicholas Notaras. Mr. Camellion and I have just arrived from New York. I should like to speak to Mr. Pappas."

The woman's voice became more friendly. "Oh, yes, Mr. Notaras. We've been expecting to hear from you and Mr. Camellion. One moment, please."

Almost immediately a male voice came on the line, one that was deep and businesslike, forceful and confident.

"I am Joseph Pappas. I trust, Mr. Notaras, that you and Mr. Camellion had a pleasant flight. I'm sorry I couldn't meet you at the airport."

"We understand, Mr. Pappas. We've read your letters to Mr. Cornwell, the president of our company. We're especially interested in your Greek gods collection. I am sure we can arrive at a wholesale price agreeable to both of us. As you know, most of our outlets in the United States are mail-order gift houses."

"Neh, I agree. We won't argue about price." Pappas laughed. "At least not too much." There was a short pause. "Would the two of you care to meet with me tonight, Mr. Notaras? I'll be working late."

"It's already four-thirty," Notaras said. "We're pretty tired from the long flight. How about tomorrow?"

"Would eleven o'clock tomorrow morning be convenient? By the way, are you sure you can find us? I assume you will rent a car at your hotel and drive?"

"Eleven o'clock is fine. Don't worry. We'll find your company."

"Fine. I'll see you and Mr. Camellion tomorrow morning. Good-bye, Mr. Notaras."

There was a click at the other end of the line. Putting down the phone, Notaras translated the conversation into English for Camellion. By that time Camellion had made up his mind that there was something not quite right about the Greek-American physicist. He became puzzled when Notaras turned on a pocket radio and motioned for him to follow. Notaras carried the radio into the bathroom. Once both men were in the bathroom, Notaras turned on both faucets in the sink and whispered, "Mr. Pappas said we could have met him tonight. I told him we were tired because of the flight. I didn't want to apear anxious in case our phone is tapped. I guess that was all right?"

"For an amateur, you learn fast," Camellion said, smiling. "Turning on the radio and the water taps is an old trick to defeat a bug."

"I saw it on television," Notaras explained. "I think it was a James Bond movie."

"Let's shower and change and have dinner," Camellion suggested.

By six-thirty, Camellion and Notaras had dined on *arnáki* and all the side dishes that went with young lamb, and were back in their two-room suite. They had spread out a large tourist map of Athens on the rug of the sitting room and were studying it, the Death Merchant sipping coffee, Notaras alternately sipping retsina and—of all things—unsugared tea.

Pappas's office and warehouse was at 2761-K Ramicus, on the southern edge of Kaisariani, a suburb southeast of Athens.

"We shouldn't have too much difficulty finding Pappas's company," Notaras said, "if the cab drivers don't kill us."

"We'll have to start about eight-thirty," Camellion said. "The morning traffic will be sheer murder. I'll drive, since I have an international driver's license."

On his hands and knees, the Death Merchant took another swallow of black coffee and smiled when he saw the notes on the margins of the map, printed in the neat, precise hand of C.C. Buntlow, who was called the Ozzard of Wiz by other ONI agents. Most men could relax with a drink and enjoy sports. Not Buntlow. He amused himself by reading the Encyclopaedia Britannica.

Remember, Buntlow had printed, *NEH means "yes" in the Greek language. Greek is the only Indo-European language that begins the affirmative with the letter "n."*

There were other notes on the side of the map.

The people of Athens have developed a specific vocabulary for various periods of the day which has to do with their philosophy of not being rushed through life. Keep in mind that *MESIMERI* does not mean 12:00 noon but the start of the siesta time. This *MESIMERU* can be anywhere between 1 and 3 P.M., the actual time depending on the schedule at one's place of employment. The "little afternoon," or *APOGEVNATAKI*, comes after the siesta. This is a one-hour period in which one gets back into the swing of things. The *APOGEVMA* is considered the second half of the workday and may continue until 8 or 8:30 P.M., after which comes the VRADAKI, or "little evening." This is the time to prepare for the VRADI, the evening proper, which begins about 9 P.M. Dinner, at the earliest, is taken about 9 P.M., but usually an hour or two later. Night, or NICHTA, begins after midnight.

"We ate early, didn't we," Notaras said, picking up his pipe and tobacco pouch.

"It really doesn't matter," Camellion said, seeing another notation on the big map: *"Do not forget the*

Greek gods figurine collection, or Mr. Cornwell might fire the two of you."

Clever, clever, clever. A precautionary measure, in case the map was lost or read by the wrong people.

II

The desk clerk smiled and handed the keys and the receipt to Richard Camellion. "The license number is on the paper," he said in his most professional manner. "The Volkswagen is in the hotel parking lot. I'm sorry the air conditioner on top doesn't work. Do have a nice day and enjoy Athinai, gentlemen."

The drive to Kaisariani was not half as miserable as Camellion and Notaras had thought it would be, despite the heat, the honking of horns, and the fumes from factories and traffic. One of the ONI agents had told them that Athens still qualified as one of the most exciting cities on earth. Exciting? The agent should have said as one of the most noisy and confusing.

Driving southeast on Venizelos Street, Camellion had the impression that the buildings, of all sizes and shapes, were nothing more than characterless cubes of various colors of brick and concrete and stone. It was obvious that tourism was the city's main industry, with such trappings as gaudy-fronted discotheques, clip-joints, strip clubs, pizza parlors, and adult bookstores.

Such commercialism seemed almost sacrilegious when one looked at the hazy Acropolis towering over the city. It was this massive limestone stronghold, whose plateau and periphery contained one of the world's most spectacular concentrations of great works of antiquity, that was the true heart of Athens and the main magnet of the tourist industry that brought Greece almost $1 billion a year, roughly one-third of all its foreign exchange.

Once the Death Merchant reached the edge of Athens, he made better time, for at this hour of the smoky morning more traffic was coming into the city than going out. By midmorning he was driving the Volksie through Kaisariani, a suburb as dull as Athens, its buildings a hodgepodge of mediocre architecture.

Nick Notaras, looking at the partially folded map, kept Camellion posted on the route. "Go two more blocks, then turn right on Peridis Street."

Camellion drove five blocks on Peridis and made another right turn onto Ramicus Street, which was actually a road that turned and twisted into the countryside. Soon there were fields on each side of the road and small thickets of myrtle and oaks and beech trees. Here and there was a house, almost always in need of paint and repair.

"It doesn't look right, but I'm certain we're on the right road," Notaras said calmly. "We couldn't have made a wrong turn."

"We could have, but we didn't," Camellion said, his face stone, his eyes darting from left to right. To the left, he noticed "2973" on a brick building not too far from the concrete road. "We have only a short distance to go."

"I hope so," Notaras said. "It's already as hot as the inside of an oven."

"Get used to it," Camellion muttered. "We still have to drive back."

The Death Merchant let up on the gas slightly, feeling vaguely uneasy and at the same time on guard. He and Notaras could be driving into a cleverly set trap, even though the Central Intelligence Agency and the Office of Naval Intelligence were almost certain that Pappas was a member of the Delphi Circle.

Ahh, there it is. The sign to the left was six feet long and three feet high, and was set on two steel poles in the ground, the black letters, both in Greek and in English, against a white background: 2761-K. PAPPAS IMPORTING & EXPORTING CO., LTD. WORKS OF ART. NOVELTIES. JOSEPH PAPPAS, OWNER.

A quick flash of the future, as clear as a three-dimensional photograph, came to the Death Merchant as he was turning onto the asphalt drive. The 50-megaton hydrogen bomb would explode 1,200 feet over Athens. Instantly a million people would be vaporized by the heat that, for a nanosecond, would reach the temperature of the interior of the sun. Another million would be flash-burned; and as the mushroom cloud boiled upward into the blue Athenian sky, the 600-mph wind, spreading out from the epicenter, would kill hundreds of thousands more five to fifteen miles from the blast. The firestorm and radiation would follow.

It would be the same in Rome, Moscow, New York, London, Warsaw, Los Angeles, Tokyo, Leningrad, Chicago, Berlin, Tel Aviv, and in other major cities of the world.

As he was turning into the asphalt drive, Camellion —and Notaras—saw that the office warehouse was in reality a large villa that had seen far better days, a rambling two-story structure that, with typical neo-classical features, had Doric columns in front and balustrades and pediments above the windows. The roof was edged with *akroteria,* decorative tiles in the shape of palmetto leaves. Decaying stone lions guarded the villa's entrance. However, the grass was neatly cut and the rose bushes trimmed. On one side of the grounds, beyond a stone fence, was an orange grove. Weeds and a few thorn trees were on the other side.

A small Greek Korisa, a four-door Subaru, and a Mazda RX-7 were parked to the right. Camellion parked next to the Mazda and looked at his watch: 10:46. Pleased with the time he'd made, he got out of the car and with Notaras walked up the dozen stone steps.

The interior was as weather-worn as the exterior, including the front desk behind which was a woman. The desk could have used several coats of varnish. The woman wouldn't have won any beauty contests. But the office was air-conditioned.

"Good morning. May I help you?" Miss Sofoulis's smile was as sexy as her voice. The trouble was that the smile and the voice didn't match the rest of her. Too much of her bulged in the wrong places. Her skin was drab and her black hair was done all wrong. Swept back into a bun, it accentuated her round face, and with her shape, she should never have worn a blouse with horizontal stripes.

Notaras pulled off his sunglasses. "Good morning. I'm Nicholas Notaras. I spoke with you yesterday." He indicated the Death Merchant. "This is Mr. Camellion. He's the other buyer from Triangle Importing and Exporting Company in New York."

Anna Sofoulis smiled again. "Mr. Pappas is expecting you. Take the door to your left."

"Thank you," said Notaras. She had spoken English and he had replied in English. He and Camellion walked across the room, opened the door, and went into the next room, a large area filled with cardboard boxes of various sizes. On shelves on the walls were hundreds of items—shiny brass Elefsis horses; Ionian jewelry; gold-toned wires fastened together to make chokers, bracelets, and clip-on earrings; and thousands of souvlakia skewers topped with bronze animal figures. Hanging on long metal racks were Thalassa kaftans of light sea-blue cotton and Edessa sweater jackets.

A big-chested man with hawklike features was sealing a carton with wire strapping. He turned and looked questioningly at Camellion and Notaras. They sensed he was not Pappas.

"We're here to see Mr. Pappas," Nick said in Greek. "Are you he?"

"Ochi. He's in the next room." The man inclined his head toward a door and resumed his work.

"Efkharisto," Nick thanked him. He and the Death Merchant walked across the area, opened the door, and stepped into the next room. A man was seated on a stool, sandpapering a large rolltop desk. He was doing a good job. The grain of the oak was already showing.

"Mr. Pappas, I'm Nicholas Notaras," Notaras said pleasantly. "This is Mr. Richard Camellion. He's the other buyer from Triangle."

To the Death Merchant the moment of truth had arrived. John Peponis had given Professor Fiorino a recognition code to be used by anyone who might contact Pappas. Should Pappas not give the first part of the recognition phrase, Camellion and Notaras would know that something was very wrong in Greece.

Pappas put down the block of wood with sandpaper wrapped around it, got to his feet, and probed Notaras with intense black eyes. Built like a baby bull, he stepped forward and held out a large hand.

"I'm George Joseph Pappas," he said, pumping Notaras's hand. "Call me Joe. I hate the name George. It was the name of my grandfather, and he was a mean old bastard."

Pappas shook the Death Merchant's hand, his grip like a steel band. "I was expecting only one buyer from Triangle," he said slyly, looking from Camellion to Notaras. "Tell me, Mr. Notaras, do you enjoy eating *imam baildi?*"

"I have never cared for dishes with Turkish names," Notaras said carefully.

Pleased with Notaras's reply, Pappas turned to Camellion and said in Greek, *"Christos anesti"* ("Christ is risen").

"Alithos anesti o Kyrios," Camellion replied promptly, "The Lord is risen indeed!" completing the identification code between the three.

Sizing up Joe Pappas, Camellion felt he would be a tough nut to crack in any free-for-all. Shorter by half a head than Notaras and Camellion, both of whom were an even six feet, Pappas was much wider and thicker than either man and weighed in the neighborhood of 240 pounds. Perhaps forty, he was nice-looking, his ink-black hair, combed in waves, matching the thick eyebrows that went straight across his forehead. His long sideburns curved almost to his chin. He wore a bright-green polo shirt, open to the waist, dark-green slacks, and leather sandals.

"Good," Pappas said in English. "Now that we know who we are, we can get down to business. But not here. Come with me."

He turned and walked quickly to another door. Following, Camellion remarked, "The desk you were working on. I wasn't aware you exported antique furniture."

"I don't." Pappas opened the door and hurried into the room, adding matter-of-factly, "Finishing old furniture is a hobby of mine. If I didn't have a hobby, I'd drink myself to death."

The three men were in a very large room in which cardboard cartons were stored flat. There were also large wooden packing crates, their tops open. The room had a high ceiling and at one time must have been a banquet room, judging from the large chandelier hanging from the middle of the ceiling, from which paint was peeling.

Crossing the room, Pappas picked up a short aluminum ladder and placed it to one side of the dirt-caked chandelier. He checked the ladder to make sure it was on solid footing, then climbed to the tenth step. He reached out and turned—counterclockwise—the decorative metal knob in the center of the chandelier's cut glass.

Camellion was not surprised when one of the high stacks of flattened cardboard cartons began to rise slowly from the floor. The stack tilted back as a square section of the floor lifted.

Nicholas Notaras's mouth hung half open, and he stared at the opening.

"Just like a James Bond movie, isn't it?" Camellion said with a smile.

"Wait up here," Pappas ordered. "I'll go down and turn on the lights."

The Greek felt his way down the steps, and soon the darkness below was replaced by a soft yellow light. Notaras and Camellion went down the steps and saw that Pappas was standing in front of a small refrigerator at the end of the small, low-ceilinged room, whose walls were unpainted concrete blocks. The floor was also concrete.

Pappas pulled on a curved hook on the wall, and the trapdoor and flattened cardboard cartons closed silently.

Pappas opened the refrigerator and took out a bottle of Metaxa brandy. "What will you have to drink, gentlemen?"

"Coffee," Camellion said, giving Notaras a quick look.

"I wouldn't mind a cup of coffee about now," Notaras said.

Pappas turned and frowned. "Coffee! I'm not running a restaurant," he said good-naturedly. "All I have is booze."

"I'll have a beer," said Notaras.

"Nothing for me," Camellion said, his eyes taking in the round oak table and the four matching caned-seat chairs, the grain of the wood showing through the clear high-gloss varnish.

"I had to take the table apart to get it through the opening above and down the steps," Pappas explained, a hint of pride in his deep voice. After placing the bottle of brandy on the table, he went back to the refrigerator, took out a can of beer, pulled the tab, and returned to the table. He placed the can of beer on the table and waved a hand toward the chairs.

"Be seated and we'll get down to business," he said, his voice mild and patient. "You Americans want something from me. What is it?" He tossed a hard look at Camellion and Notaras as he sat down.

Camellion and Notaras sat also, facing Pappas across the table. The Greek hadn't said anything definite, not a single word that could be incriminating. Camellion could only conclude that Pappas was still not satisfied, still not convinced. Or he might suspect his visitors were from the KYP, or else Pappas was the enemy and was waiting for Camellion and Notaras to incriminate themselves.

"Mr. Pappas, your—"

"Call me Joe!" Pappas snapped.

"Very well. Call me Richard. He's Nick." Camellion was just as blunt. He folded his hands on the table, looked straight at Pappas, and gave him the facts. "A certain Greek in Rome mentioned your name to another man in Rome. The second man was a very respected Italian. He passed the message along to other people. That's why Nick and I came to

Greece. That's why we are sitting here." Camellion's voice became sharp. "But if all you're going to do is spar with words, Nick and I might as well wave good-bye and return to Athens."

Pappas, grinning like a Cheshire cat, was getting ready to go to work on the brandy, right out of the bottle. He took a long swallow, then put the bottle on the table, his expression softening.

"The two of you were seen getting off the plane at Ellinikon, and you were tailed to the hotel," he said. "We know you are who you claim to be. However, I must tell you that I'm in the dark about why the American CIA should send its people to contact me. I assume you are from the CIA."

CIA! A vulgar expression, a dirty combination of letters, in Greece. A calculating look crossed the Death Merchant's face. At length he said, "We're not from the Central Intelligence Agency. Even if we were, we wouldn't admit it any more than you would admit being one of the leaders of the Delphi Circle."

Pappas scooted his chair closer to the table. He said, "Eleven weeks ago I was informed by certain people that a highly placed member of the Delphi Circle had conveyed a certain message to Professor Vincente Fiorino. At the time no one knew if the professor would pass on the message. It was not until after I received the first letter from Mr. Cornwell, the president of Triangle Company, that we suspected that Professor Fiorino had gotten word to the Americans. For that reason, I—we—suggested to Mr. Cornwell that he send a Triangle buyer to Greece. There is one more thing I must tell you so that you will have a better understanding of my position."

"But you said you didn't know what we wanted," said Notaras.

"My contacts did not tell me why the Americans would contact me," Pappas said, emphasizing the "why." "I was only given the proper recognition phrases. I was also told that whoever made contact with me would give me a full explanation. You see, you two know more about what is going on than I do."

Pappas's black eyes raked over Camellion and Notaras as he studied the two Americans. It was obvious to Pappas that Camellion was the leader. It was he who made the decisions. His features were average, his mouth firm, his dark-brown hair cut short, military style. Quick-moving and well built, he weighed about 175 pounds. As far as Pappas could see, there wasn't an ounce of fat on him.

It was Camellion's Holland-blue eyes that intrigued Pappas. They seemed to have a life of their own, as if some alien intelligence were lurking behind those two windows in the head, something terribly remote and distinct from mankind, something suggestive of ancient and unhallowed cycles of life in which the world of matter had never played a role.

Nicholas Notaras was tall, broad-boned, and slightly heavy around the middle. Relaxed and affable-looking, he wore his black hair long and looked younger than his forty-one years until one noticed the prematurely graying hairs at his temples or the mature depth of his hazel eyes. Pappas had the feeling that Notaras had an easygoing nature and preferred to think the best of everyone and most situations.

Notaras is an idealist, thought Pappas. It was different with Richard Camellion. The man with the unusual blue eyes was pragmatic, a realist who would not let the morality of the moment hinder him in any way.

Camellion did some fast thinking. The answer had to be very tight security within the Delphi Circle. The Greek revolutionary organization wasn't taking any chances. He was aware that Pappas was waiting for him to reply, his grim countenance framed in expectancy. Tell the full truth to Pappas? Yes, but in bits and pieces.

The Death Merchant said tersely, "We assumed that you were one of the leaders of the Delphi Circle. Since you apparently are not, we can only wonder why a highly placed member of the Delphi group would mention your name to Professor Fiorino. I would say that's a reasonable question, wouldn't you, Joe?"

"Let me explain something," Pappas said in a low, persuasive undertone. "The Delphi Circle draws membership from all levels of Greek society. The KYP hasn't been able to smash us because we operate in small eight-member cells. There are also cells of two and three persons. It's a matter of security."

"You still haven't answered my question," Camellion said.

"The two- and three-member cells are key cells," continued Pappas, acting as if he hadn't heard Camellion. "In my case, I'm the major communications link between Delphi's enforcement group and the various contacts of the planning committee. I hope that will give you men a clue to why my name was given to Professor Fiorino."

"This enforcement group," said Camellion. "What is its function?"

"Bombings, assassinations, raids on armories—you understand," Pappas said with equal briskness. "Supposedly, military rule in Greece ended in December of 1974. Officially it did."

"Don't tell me that the generals control the government," Camellion said, sounding as if he wanted to argue. "Papandreou and his government are in firm control of this country, and his government is strictly socialist."

"Very true, my American friend, but the socialism we have today in Greece is one that is married to the military. At the heart of the military is the KYP, the Greek Central Intelligence Service. General Nikos Cyatorus, the director of the KYP, is more communist than socialist—a genuine lover of the Soviet system."

Nick Notaras interjected, "But the Delphi Circle is socialistic!"

"We favor the Panhellenic Socialist Party, which is pure socialism untainted by communism," explained Pappas, sounding to Camellion as if he were talking down to Notaras. "The Delphi Circle is against Premier Andreas Papandreou and his watered-down version of socialism. We're against the communist members he has in his cabinet. Let me tell you, the communists are gaining more and more control through the United Democratic Left, which has ten seats in the National Assembly. We will use any means available to destroy them."

"Terrorism!" Notaras said in a flat voice. "The Delphi Circle is a terrorist group."

Pappas finished lighting a cigarette. "Yes—in the same sense that American colonists who dumped British tea into the Boston harbor were terrorists."

"We didn't come here to discuss politics," Camellion said, looking with unsmiling eyes at Notaras. His gaze jumped to Pappas. "Joe, I'm sure you've heard of Professor Stefanos Paspyrou. He's a professor of physics and quantum electrodynamics at Athens University."

"Who in Greece hasn't heard of him!" Pappas couldn't conceal the look of incredulity on his face. "Professor Paspyrou is involved in whatever this is about?"

"He is—right up to his eyeballs," Camellion said. "But let me begin at the beginning, starting with a scientist before our time—Nikola Tesla. I'm sure you've heard of him."

"He was an American inventor." Pappas crushed out his stub of a cigarette. "I believe he did a lot of research in communications back in the 1920s."

"Yes, and in the field of high-tension electricity." Speaking slowly and precisely, the Death Merchant then gave the very interested Pappas a rundown on TMT, Tesla's magnifying transmitter.

"Tesla's MT device was based on his conviction that unlimited, undepleted energy could be drawn from the earth's atmosphere and that this force or power could be used to make and control the world's weather. But he never built the transmitter. He died in 1943."

Camellion then gave Pappas a short history of Soviet weather modification experiments, including how the American National Security Agency—NSA—had traced long-impulse waves to Riga, Latvia.

"This was in 1976, eleven years ago. Radio communications around the world were disrupted by some mysterious influence. Intelligence services still believe that this influence was caused by waves originating at a small Tesla magnifying transmitter in Riga."

Pappas's expression was uncertain. "How does Professor Paspyrou fit into all this? Are you saying that he's working for the Russians in Latvia?"

"No, not in Latvia," Camellion said. "The message that was delivered to Professor Fiorino was that Professor Paspyrou is right on the brink of solving the secret of Tesla's magnifying transmitter. There's more, and all of it is bad news. The KYP has kidnapped Paspyrou and has taken him to some island to complete his experiments. We're not sure where the island is. It might be in the Adriatic, or in the Ionian

Sea or the Mediterranean. The capper is that we're convinced the Soviet KGB is behind the scheme."

Pappas belched and a look of pure hatred flashed in his eyes. "I've no doubt that the KGB cockroaches are being assisted by General Cyatorus," he said, almost in a snarl. "That sadistic son of a bitch has always been in love with Marxism." His thick brows became a questioning V. "But why should the KGB and the KYP keep Paspyrou in Greece? Why not take him to the Soviet Union?"

"We don't know." The Death Merchant shrugged. "That's another answer we still have to nail down."

"Are you sure the information about Paspyrou is correct?" Pappas moved the tips of several fingers over one of his long sideburns.

"All we can tell you at this point is that the information came from a very reliable source—from the member of the Delphi Circle who passed the information to Professor Fiorino in Rome. I won't give you his name. If your people had wanted you to have his identity, they would have told you. I presume they will when you check to verify our story. At the moment, we have to work on the premise that the information is correct and act accordingly."

Pappas gave a low chuckle. "Do you two still insist you're not in the CIA?"

"If we do represent any intelligence agency, it's not the CIA," Camellion lied. He didn't like the faint mocking quality in Pappas's voice, but he couldn't blame the man. "It doesn't make any difference. I don't make the final decisions. Neither do you. When you confer with your people, I'm sure you'll be told to work with us toward the common goal of finding the island where Paspyrou is being held. Our second job will be to rescue him."

Joe Pappas considered Camellion's words, his fingers drumming an accompaniment to an inaudible melody. He finally said, "I trust that after the rescue, Paspyrou will be taken to the United States, so that the U.S. can make the world dance to its special tune of weather control?"

Again that sneering tone that irritated Camellion. This time he let Pappas know that he didn't like it.

"Listen, Joe, I don't give a damn if the world ends in a shout or a whisper, or in fire or ice or in another flood," Camellion whipped out savagely. "We're only doing our job. You do yours! I suggest you get word to the planning committee of the Delphi Circle—the sooner the better!"

"Naturally." Pappas didn't seem angry or insulted. "I'm convinced that Delphi intends to give its help or the information would never have been passed to Professor Fiorino."

Notaras spoke up, his tone petulant. "Then why all the doubts on your part? Or could it be that you're still not sure about us?"

Pappas smiled. "The enforcement section of the Circle doesn't have the means to locate the island. Even if we could, we don't have the arms for an all-out attack. We don't have ships. What you are asking is impossible. Or is that part of your function, to supply the necessary materiel?"

Camellion told him, "The equipment will be there when it's needed. I don't know how it will be supplied. We're waiting to be contacted."

Puzzled, Pappas rubbed his jaw. "Your function was only to contact me?"

"I'm a physicist!" Notaras spoke right up, much to the consternation of the Death Merchant, who would have liked to hit him. "If and when we rescue Professor Paspyrou, it will be my job to decide which papers in his lab are important and to evaluate them. Of course, first we have to find the man."

A huge smile—a toothy smile—spread across Pappas's face. He laughed then as if enjoying a very funny joke.

"We're two of a kind, Nicholas Notaras," he said. "We both have taken on extracurricular work. I used to be a marine biologist at Athens University. I was fired when the generals openly controlled the country. I've never tried to be reinstated."

Neither Pappas nor Notaras expected Camellion's question. "Your receptionist and the man upstairs packing boxes. They are part of your network?"

"Why do you ask?"

"Your security is our security."

"The man is Gregory Sofoulis. He's half Turkish, which is the main reason he is willing to work for the Delphi Circle. The Turks would hate the Greeks if Jesus Christ ruled from Athens. The truth is that I'd trust Gregory with my life. I have, several times."

"And the woman? Her name is also Sofoulis."

"Anna is his daughter. I will give you a tip. Don't make a pass at her, or Gregory will slit your throat. Any man who fucks his daughter will either end up her husband or a corpse. Don't ask about the other enforcement members. You men will meet them at the proper time, if that time ever comes."

"I'd just as soon not know," Notaras said agreeably.

Camellion thought about the half-truth he had told Pappas, about their waiting to be contacted. They were, he and Notaras, by either ONI or the SIS. He had only neglected to mention that they were also scheduled to meet a young woman named Melina Arnaoutis. An ONI agent had given Camellion full instructions for contact just before he and Notaras had boarded the plane for Greece. He was to meet the young lady that very night, in a discotheque called the Pepper Pot.

"I'll contact my people this afternoon," Pappas said with a sudden show of candor. "All I can do is pass on your information and wait for the results. In the meantime, you will want to establish your cover as buyers for Triangle. I suggest that tomorrow the three of us go out and see what the handicrafters in and around Athens have in the way of good bargains."

"We could start with the collection of Greek gods," Camellion said good-naturedly. "Or don't they even exist?"

Pappas laughed lightly. "The Greek gods exist. They're a lot of fake marble junk, but they're great sellers, especially Zeus. He's the central figure. Athena also sells well. Don't ask me why."

Noticing how Notaras had turned his head and was studying the refrigerator, Pappas said, "Something is wrong, Nicholas?"

"This room was meant to be secure from the authorities, or you wouldn't have built it," Notaras said.

"Yes, that is true." Pappas frowned slightly.

"Suppose a KYP agent put his ear to the floor upstairs," Notaras theorized. "He would be able to hear the refrigerator when it's running and deduce there was a room underneath the floor. Maybe he couldn't hear it with only his ears, but suppose he used an amplifying device?"

"I haven't given much thought to it," said Pappas, giving Notaras an odd look. He ran his tongue slowly around a fleshy lower lip. "But it's not likely that a KYP agent will be putting his ear to the floor." As an afterthought he asked, "Do you want another beer?"

Chapter Two

In spite of the lateness of the hour, Courtland Maddock Grojean didn't look like a man who had already put in a fourteen-hour day. His lavenderation tie—an exuberant show of carnations on hand-woven Italian silk—was knotted snug against his neck and lying straight on his pinpoint Oxford cotton shirt, which looked neatly pressed.

The chief of the CIA's covert section wasn't even aware of the hour. He didn't have a job. He had a life. That life was the CIA. Day and night he lived his work, and he was constantly looking for new methods and techniques to improve the efficiency of his agents.

There were few noises in the soundproof office. There was only the steady sound of the electronic air cleaner and the ever lower humming of the in-place IPMS monitoring system, the most sophisticated bug detector-locator available in the world (even the East Germans didn't have better equipment). The IPMS system continued to operate even after Grojean locked the two steel doors to his office. After the doors were locked, only he could unlock them, first by pressing in sequence the buttons of the combinations, second by voice command, by saying "Grojean. Open." The electric relays were encoded with his voiceprint.

A single fluorescent light burned over the massive desk, its soft glow illuminating a dark-red plastic file lying next to an electronic cypher device. The words OPERATION ZEUS were in black in the center of the cover.

Grojean studied the sheets lying on the desk, each marked *Most Secret*. He felt rather guilty when he thought about Richard Camellion. In the past that lean, mean Texan had performed miracles, always making the impossible possible and succeeding where others had or would have failed. Operation Zeus was a different matter. The Death Merchant would be sitting down in a game in which all the players would be using marked cards.

It had begun when the Rivkin-Hagberg Foundation, a think tank connected to the Massachusetts Institute of Technology, had received secret word that Professor Stefanos Paspyrou, a world-famed particle physicist at the University of Athens, had made some fantastic discoveries regarding Tesla's mysterious magnifying transmitter. The information had been given to the R-H-F people by one Vincente Fiorino, a sociologist and historian and a member of the Club of Rome, the celebrated predictions society that, in 1972, had startled the world with its publication of *Limits of Growth*.

Dr. Fiorino had obtained the information from John Peponis, a Greek diplomat at the Greek Embassy in Rome. Peponis, an economics attaché, didn't know the nature of Paspyrou's discoveries. He did know that Paspyrou was on the verge of solving the riddle of TMT and that special agents of the Greek KYP had kidnapped the scientist and were holding him on some remote island off the Greek mainland. There was a well-equipped laboratory on the island, set in a series of underground bunkers the Germans had built during World War II. Worse, Soviet scientists were on the island, helping Paspyrou with his experiments.

The CIA and the National Security Agency, which had been apprised of the situation, knew that for any number of years the Soviet Union had been desperately trying to unlock the secrets of TMT. Soviet scientists had made progress. In the winter of 1976, Soviet physicists and climatologists managed to change weather patterns so that Europe and North America experienced the worst winter in one hundred years.

The Soviet Union, however, got more than it had bargained for. The experiment backfired. Russia also had a terrible winter, Moscow itself being so cold and ice-shrouded that a hundred-year record was broken.

Sitting there at his desk, Grojean recalled how, eleven years ago, American scientists had speculated on the mistakes the Soviets could have made. One thing the Russian scientists might have failed to calculate properly was the various flows of the world's oceans.

Weather generally moves from west to east in jet streams above the earth. In theory, weather modification could be accomplished by regulating the movement and the motion of the electrically charged particles in the upper atmosphere, which would result in changing the direction of the jet streams.

Nonetheless, any such redirection of the jet

streams would have to work in concert with the directional flow of the various ocean currents. For the planet as a whole, the oceans are the "master regulator," the great stabilizer of temperature, a "savings bank" for solar energy, receiving deposits in seasons of excessive abundance and returning them during periods of want.

Without the world's oceans the planet would be visited by unthinkably harsh temperatures. Earth would be perpetually cold, with 100 degrees below zero being "normal." The reason is that the water that covers almost three-quarters of the earth's surface is a wonderful absorber and *radiator* of heat. The oceans can absorb a great deal of heat from the sun without becoming "hot," or they can lose much of their heat without becoming "cold."

One fact was clear. The main goal of the Soviet Union was complete control of the world's weather. They hoped to reach this goal with a Tesla magnifying transmitter, a device that would send out a stream of invisible charged particles.

The frustration of Grojean and a dozen other people in the CIA and in NSA—not to mention scores of American scientists—was born of their awareness that Soviet progress had not been due to any superior research. Soviet success had been achieved because of American stupidity, procrastination, indecisiveness, and naivete.

The United States and the Soviet Union even had an agreement not to use weather modification against each other in times of war. Still considered a joke in the diplomatic community, the agreement was signed on May 18, 1977, and was known as the Convention on the Prohibition of Military or Any Other Hostile Use of Environmental Modification Technique.

The United States had faithfully lived up to its end

of the agreement. To have done otherwise would have been "immoral" and "unethical." Realists knew how the Soviet Union would honor the agreement, which explains why the treaty was a riot of laughs in the diplomatic community.

Even more incredible was that the United States had signed the agreement with full knowledge that the Soviet Union was already conducting numerous weather modification experiments. The evidence was there. It had been checked and double-checked by the CIA and by NSA.

Grojean's eyes scanned the sheets.

ITEM: Early in 1974 the National Severe Storms Forecast Center in Kansas City noted a strange shift in the jet stream wind patterns. This unexplained change of direction caused an inquiry by the CIA which, in August 1977, prepared a classified working paper entitled *A Study of Climatological Research as It Pertains to Intelligence Problems.*

The CIA weather experts reported that a climatic change was taking place and that it had caused major economic problems in the world. The study had been declassified and released for publication in 1975, but all information pertaining to Soviet weather modification experiments had been deleted on the recommendation of the U.S. State Department. The State Department suggested that the United Nations let the International Council of Scientific Unions and the World Meteorological Organization investigate the problem.

The Union Nations didn't act on the problem. *The Soviet Union objected. . . .*

ITEM: The world's largest electromagnet was delivered to the Soviet Union in June of 1977, with the permission and the blessing of the Carter administration. Scientists realize that a tremendous magnetic field is part of TMT.

ITEM: President Carter and his administration also arranged—in the name of "peace"—for the Soviets to have a giant $13 million computer for—of all things—"weather research"! Known as CYBER-76 and manufactured by Control Data Corporation of Minneapolis, the computer had been the most powerful available to the Soviets at the time.

ITEM: In 1981 one of NSA's LINK-3 satellites detected what was later described as "manmade and man-generated patterns" over large parts of western Russia, Finland, and northern Turkey. French scientists stated that the patterns had dispersed as suddenly as they had arisen and that such patterns were neither normal nor natural.

ITEM: Tesla's last known assistant was Arthur H. Matthews, who had retired and was living in Quebec, Canada. Canadian authorities reported that an "unidentified" Soviet scientist spent several months in Quebec, interviewing Matthews about Tesla and his methods.

The Canadian secret service hadn't even bothered to notify the CIA. The information came to the Agency in a newspaper, in the February 1, 1977, issue of the *Los Angeles Herald Examiner,* in an article written by Stephen M. Aug of the *Washington Post.*

The CIA had immediately contacted the Canadians. How could they have known the man was a Soviet scientist if they couldn't identify him? The Canadians replied that Matthews had told them!

Disgusted, Grojean returned the papers to the file, got up, walked across the office, and locked Operation Zeus in his private safe. He set the self-destruct-by-acid buttons, then went into the tiny kitchenette and put on water for tea, all the while wondering if more could have been done under the circumstances.

The Rivkin-Hagberg Foundation people had known what to do with the information they had received from Vincente Fiorino. It was obvious to them that John Peponis expected the Americans to take action, since he had even given the name of a contact in Greece, an importer and exporter in Athens—Joseph Pappas, a member of the Delphi Circle, a revolutionary group doing its best to overthrow the government of Socialist Premier Andreas Papandreou.

Julius George Hagberg had given the CIA a full report. The CIA had notified NSA, and a high-level conference was held in Washington, D.C. In attendance had been Hagberg, four high CIA officials, including Grojean, two members from President Reagan's staff, and several top officials from ONI.

The CIA was very weak in Greece, mainly because of an exposé-type book written by a renegade Company agent. In it he had named all the CIA case officers in Athens. The result was that the chief of station and four other agents had been murdered.

At the conference, various possibilities had been discussed. There had been agreement on two points: (1) At all costs, the Soviet Union could not be permitted to build a fully operational Tesla magnifying transmitter, and (2) the operation would have to be an international effort. France and Great Britain would have to be told of the horrible danger facing the West.

There was another possibility: Suppose John Peponis had lied? Suppose all of it was a setup to make the United States look like a war monger?

Three weeks later another meeting had been held. This time, officials of France's SDECE and Great Britain's SIS had been in attendance.

It had been agreed that the CIA would send one of its most experienced field agents into Greece. In this case, the operative would be Ralph Buntline, who would travel under the name of Richard Camellion. Grojean had not mentioned that "Richard Camellion" was an on-contract agent.

The how and the why had been next on the agenda. "Richard Camellion" would have to have a legitimate reason for going into Greece.

The CIA owned numerous proprietary companies throughout the world and in the United States. But the three in Greece had been closed for some years. Nor did SIS or SDECE own any cover companies in Greece.

Courtland Grojean had supplied the answer. The CIA had a proprietary firm in New York that was perfect: Triangle Importing and Exporting Company, Inc.

Why couldn't Richard Camellion fly to Greece as a representative of Triangle? By so doing, he would be able to make contact with Joseph Pappas, who also had an importing and exporting business. The KYP wouldn't suspect a buyer from an American importing and exporting company. Unless Joseph Pappas was working for the KYP or the KGB. Or unless Pappas was suspected and being watched by the KYP. . . .

The president of Triangle Importing and Exporting had sent a letter to Pappas Importing and Exporting Company, Limited, to inquire about the kinds of exports available and listing the items that Triangle could export to Greece. It had to be assumed that Pappas knew what was going on or would take the hint and realize that American agents were trying to make contact with him. If so, he would reply and, hopefully, suggest that Triangle send one of its people to Greece to look over what he had to offer.

Joseph Pappas had done just that!

The British and the French did have small networks in Athens, but few of their people were trained field agents. The Americans did have one ace on their side. Camellion would be able to get help from an ONI "street man," Arzey G. Holcomb. While the CIA network in Athens had been dismantled, ONI's apparatus was still intact and functioning, even though it was small. In fact, ONI had only seven "street men" undercover in Athens; four were native Greeks. Arzey Holcomb, the head ONI agent in Athens, would keep in contact with Richard Camellion through a Greek girl who would act as a courier.

There was still the complex problem of the possibility of duplicity on the part of John Peponis or Joseph Pappas, or possibly both men. But if the KGB or the KYP was conducting some kind of enticement operation and Soviet scientists were helping Professor Paspyrou build a Tesla magnifying transmitter, why should they try to lure American intelligence into Greece by telling the truth? On the other hand, why tell a lie when the truth would serve as well?

Courtland Grojean spoke quietly, offering his plan, a solution that surprised everyone.

"Surely we can't expect any scientist to sacrifice his life," the Deputy Director of Intelligence had said. "That's expecting a bit too much.

"The man who might go with Camellion wouldn't have to be a scientist," Grojean had continued. "He would only have to pretend to be one. We could give him a fictitious background and not even let Camellion in on the secret. Provided we can find such a man. I doubt if we can."

Such a man was found, with the help of the Rivkin-Hagberg Foundation—one of their own people, a computer analyst. For nine days he was briefed and instructed on what to do, what to say, when to say it, and how to act.

On the tenth day Grojean introduced him to Richard Camellion.

Grojean had sugared his tea and returned to his desk when one of the telephones on his desk rang— the green phone that could only receive calls within L-Building. The caller was Jason Skarett, his chief assistant.

"I assumed you would be working late, sir," Skarett said, "and I was anxious about the situation. The cafeteria was closing up, but I managed to get ham on rye and liverwurst, and, of course, coffee."

"All right, Jason. Come on over," Grojean said. "A bite to eat would be welcome about now."

Waiting for Skarett to enter the first outer office, Grojean turned on the television monitor. Skarett often reminded Grojean of himself when he had been a green kid in Intelligence, right after the Korean War.

Later, as Grojean and his assistant were eating, Skarett said, "We should hear from Holcomb by tomorrow night or Friday afternoon."

"Friday night at the latest," Grojean said, cutting a sandwich in half with the blade of a pearl-handled knife. "I should think that the KGB would order the KYP to move at once, should it be a setup."

"We could lose Camellion; he's a valuable man." Skarett wiped a bit of mustard from the corner of his mouth with a paper napkin. "He always has a bag full of tricks, but he's not superman," he added, taking another bite of the ham sandwich.

"No one is indispensable," Grojean said. "We have to know the truth. It's better that we find out early in the game rather than later, after we might have been sucked into believing God knows what."

Skarett finished swallowing. "Notaras is the man who deserves a lot of credit. How long does he have —I mean, if he returns to the U.S.?"

"From six months to a year, a year and a half at the most," Grojean said. "As soon as we hear from Holcomb, we'll have Triangle send a telegram and tell him to come home, provided he and Camellion are still alive. . . ."

Chapter Three

Colonel Boris Malenkova, walking on the beach with General Gregor Shchors, was not interested in the soft moonlight bathing the island of Miskos. Malenkova's only interest at the moment was learning enough about the island so that he could prepare a defense, should the island ever be attacked.

The twenty-eight-year-old Soviet Spetsnaz commander would rather have taken his 150 men to Afghanistan, where they could have practiced kill tactics on the native savages. Instead, he and his men had been sent by submarine to this insignificant speck of nothingness in the Aegean Sea.

General Gregor Shchors was saying in a business-like voice, "As I told you this afternoon, Comrade Colonel, the island is only six kilometers long and three kilometers wide. For all practical purposes, one can say that the surface of Miskos is composed of only three mountains, the tallest of which is 381 meters. On the east and the west and the north the mountains slope directly into the sea. It's only on the south that there is a beach. That's why this island was never turned into a resort. I would suppose that's why the Germans, forty-five years ago, chose Miskos as a supply depot and a submarine base."

Shchors looked over his shoulder and saw that Major Valeri Fedchenko, Malenkova's aide, and Major Sergei Diamov, the head of the KGB on the island, were only a short distance behind. And behind them were two Spetsnaz commandos, Vitmorkin machine pistols holstered on the belts of their slacks. Uniforms were not worn on the island.

General Shchors continued: "The Germans did more than enlarge the caves on the south side. Their engineers used explosives to hollow out a portion of the base of Mount Posso, the mountain on the west whose slopes drop directly into the sea. The German engineers—"

"Very clever of those Teutonic brutes," commented Malenkova, who had always secretly admired the Nazi SS not only for its efficiency but also for its total ruthlessness. "The submarines we were on were completely submerged as they entered the opening, weren't they?"

"I was coming to that," General Shchors said crisply. He disliked being interrupted. He disliked Colonel Malenkova even more. There wasn't anything personal in his antipathy; it had nothing to do with Boris Malenkova the man. It was what he represented. All Spetsnaz were nothing more than sadistic barbarians, even though they were necessary. The entire world, especially the United States, was working to destroy the Soviet Union. "The Germans blasted a passage to the sea twenty-five meters below the surface of the Aegean. That made it possible for their submarines to remain submerged and enter the passage into the base of the mountain without being seen. Inside the base, they built six submarine pens and constructed a series of bunkers, which we enlarged. Dr. Paspyrou and twelve of our own scientists are building the magnifying transmitter in the bunkers. I can assure you, Comrade Colonel Malenkova, we are very well protected."

An athletically built man, six feet two inches tall, with sandy hair, cut short, gray-green eyes, and sharp features, Malenkova was quick and to the point with his reply.

"All of the Aegean is a vast pleasure area. There are many, many boats. What security measures are in force at present should some yacht drop anchor, say just off shore to the west, and scuba divers start poking around? With modern closed breathing diving systems, twenty-five meters is not all that deep."

"Let us sit down; we have walked far enough," said General Shchors, pointing to some flat rocks jutting up from the sand just ahead. He glanced at the much younger man and smiled. "You needn't be concerned about scuba divers finding the passage, swimming inside, and surfacing to discover the submarine pens and the bunkers. A rock wall blocks the passage thirty meters from the inside. Our technicians raise the wall when a submarine is about to enter, then lower it after the submarine has passed. That is why it took our people six years to prepare the island. Not only did they have to construct the wall, they also had to enlarge the pens to accommodate our modern submarines. And as I have said, the bunkers had to be enlarged. Even now there is construction work in progress."

Shchors sat down on a flat rock. Colonel Malenkova sat down to his right. Very soon, Major Sergei Diamov was on a rock to his left. Major Valeri Fedchenko and the two Spetsnaz guards took positions on rocks to the right of Malenkova. To the south, in front of the men, waves broke on the rocks. The breeze, cool coming from the sea, was so gentle it wouldn't have disturbed a sleeping baby.

Malenkova lit a cigarette and blew smoke out to-

ward the sea. "What about this beach and the caves
to the north?" He stared out over the moonlit water.
"People could drop anchor out there, come ashore,
and do what they damned pleased. How are the
caves protected?"

"Some have come ashore, Comrade." Major
Diamov, the KGB boss of the island, spoke up. He got
a good deal of pleasure from the expression of amaze-
ment on Malenkova's face. "Only last week ten people from an American yacht came ashore and spent
an entire day on this very beach. Do you know why
they didn't discover anything and why we were not
concerned about their presence?"

"I am sure you are going to tell me, Comrade Major Diamov," Malenkova said coldly.

Diamov was even less of a fan of Colonel
Malenkova and his Spetsnaz commandos than General Shchors, but for different reasons. Diamov and
his thirty-three Department-V agents considered the
island their own private preserve and its security
their responsibility. They didn't need elite fighters of
the Soviet General Staff poking around and suggesting all kinds of changes.

General Shchors and his people, all scientists, had
never presented a problem. Although Shchors was a
member of the *Kah Gay Beh*'s Directorate-T, the
Scientific and Technical Directorate, his rank carried
little weight and even less authority. He was Gregor
Shchors, Ph.D., from the Lenin Institute of Science
and Technology in Moscow. His total realm of authority lay only in developing the device that, in
theory, would be able to change much of the world's
weather.

Weeks ago, on learning that Spetsnaz would be
coming to Miskos, Diamov had sent a radio report to
General Viktor Chebrikov, the chairman of the *Kah
Gay Beh*, stating that Spetsnaz were definitely not

needed on the island. He also pointed out that while there was ample room to house the Spetsnaz, feeding them would present a problem and necessitate more trips by the supply submarines. Security demanded that food *not* be brought from the Greek mainland.

General Chebrikov replied that he had already conferred with General Feliks Vladimir Aleksandrovich, the director of the General Staff's Main Intelligence Directorate, the *Glavnoye Razvedyvatelnoye Upravleniye* (the *Geh Eh Ru*—Soviet military intelligence). The *Spetsalnaya Naznacheniya*—special-purpose forces, or Spetsnaz—were attached to the *Geh Eh Ru.* General Aleksandrovich had agreed to lend a hundred Spetsnaz to be sent. However, Major Diamov would still be in command of all security on the island, and while Colonel Malenkova would not be directly under his command: "He will not be able to erect any kind of security measures without your approval, Comrade Major Diamov."

Politics! It was the bitter rivalry between the giant *Kah Gay Beh* and the smaller but still very effective *Geh Eh Ru.* As a matter of pride, Chebrikov could not possibly allow any KGB officer to be placed under the command of a *Geh Eh Ru* Spetsnaz. At the same time, it would not be proper to make a colonel in the Spetsnaz subject to the orders of a major in the KGB.

"Yes, Colonel Malenkova, I am going to tell you," Major Diamov said with an extra touch of politeness. "We don't care who explores the caves. What could they find? There is an entrance from the rear of the largest cave to a tunnel that leads down to the bunkers in the base of the mountain on the west. That entrance is blocked by a rock wall. Its weight is enormous and it can only be moved electrically. I trust I have answered your question?"

"Not quite!" Malenkova continued to stare out at

the sea. "There's the remainder of the island, the east and the west and the north sides." He turned and stared at Diamov. "There may not be a shore on those sides, but the mountains can be climbed."

"We have ultrasensitive sound sensors around the mountains," Diamov said authoritatively. "Even if someone were foolish enough to climb one of the slopes, it wouldn't matter. They wouldn't find anything. The exception would be the top of Mount Posso. A freight elevator connects to the top of Mount Posso. But climbers from any side would never reach the top, or for that matter the tops of the two other mountains. Rock slides would kill them first. We would make sure of that."

General Shchors stated, "The magnifying transmitter will be made operational from the top of Mount Posso. That's why it is of special importance."

To the right of Malenkova, Major Valeri Fedchenko leaned out, turned his head, and looked at Shchors and Diamov. Like his boss, Fedchenko was young and at the peak of health. The difference was that he had a round face, a chubby nose, and a head of thick dark-brown hair.

"Won't that be dangerous, exposing the device to aircraft?" He sounded startled. "And won't passing ships see the machine?"

"Come, come, Major! You underestimate us," Shchors said, chuckling. "The magnifying transmitter is nine meters tall, but it will be under a camouflage netting that will appear from the air to be part of the mountain. The netting is being made by experts right now in the Motherland. Only the very top of the transmitter will protrude from the net, less than a meter."

Colonel Boris Malenkova took a last puff from his cigarette, dropped it to the sand, and crushed it out with the tip of his shoe.

He looked from Diamov to Shchors and sounded more friendly as he said, "I was told in Moscow I would be briefed completely on the magnifying transmitter. I do know that the principle of its operation is based on the American Tesla's theory that the earth could be used as a giant conductor of electricity and could be made to respond to electrical vibrations of specific frequencies."

"It's far more complicated than that," General Shchors commented. He placed his hands on his knees and moved his upper arms back and forth, stretching his neck and shoulder muscles. Only a few months from fifty-eight, he suffered slightly from arthritis. "We proved Tesla's theory was correct some eleven years ago. We built a giant transmitter in Latvia. To save time, let's say it was half a radio transmitter and half a magnifying transmitter. So that you won't be confused, let me add that a magnifying transmitter does not 'transmit' like a radio transmitter. It more or less projects what could be called an invisible beam.

"We used extremely low frequency radio pulses on a frequency of thirty-one point five Hertz and were able to cause giant standing 'waves'—or troughs—of electrified air in the Rocky Mountains in the Western Hemisphere, between Alberta, Canada, and the state of New Mexico in the United States. We also managed to affect the El Niño current off the western coast of South America."

"Positively amazing!" Malenkova sounded awed. "And you say you did it with ELF radio pulses?"

"Not in the sense that you might be thinking," Shchors said sternly, as if he were reprimanding a student. "It's far more than ELF signals. Much of it has to do with the manipulation of the earth's magnetic field. This means that, to accomplish our purpose, we direct tremendous amounts of electromagnetic energy at specific regions.

"We conducted more experiments in 1977 and by generating standing waves manipulated that part of the earth's magnetic field which resides at the edge of space up in the ionosphere. During November of that year, we created a super-giant standing wave along the ionosphere from the western tip of Alaska to northern Chile in South America."

"There were some mistakes," Major Diamov said mildly.

"No, not true mistakes." Shchors was becoming irritated. "We were venturing into unexplored scientific territory. We had no way of anticipating the 'airquakes.' Sounding like explosions, these 'booms' were first heard off the northeast coast of the United States in December of 1977. They were the result of releasing concentrated electromagnetic energy into the jet stream above the planet as we established terrestrial electric resonance."

Diamov persisted . . . like a matador taunting a bull. "I was referring to the 1978 experiments in Latvia."

Gregor Shchors frowned and chewed for a second on his lower lip. "Ah, yes. . . . We did succeed in dropping a very cold winter over Europe and over the U.S. and Canada. Unfortunately, there was a backlash of electromagnetic energy. We also suffered the worst winter in a hundred years. But our 1981 experiment was very successful. By the way, Colonel Malenkova, it was in 1980 that the *Kah Gay Beh* learned that Dr. Stefanos Paspyrou was experimenting with Tesla's magnifying transmitter and had actually made more progress than I and Dr. Sarvar Chuchkin of the Leningrad Institute."

"I was thinking about the airquakes," commented

Colonel Malenkova. "Didn't they make the Americans suspicious?"

"The Americans should have thought something was wrong off their coast," Shchors said. "When the airquakes went off they triggered thousands of smoke detectors in the northeastern section of the United States. You see, the detectors reacted to ionization, to a rapid change in the electric charge in the air."

Major Sergei Diamov leaned back and braced himself by putting his hands on the rock. "The truth is that we don't know if the Americans were suspicious over the airquakes. We did learn that President Reagan gave orders years ago for U.S. scientists to pursue research in weather modification, and we suspect that with their excellent equipment, they could have traced the standing waves in the 1977, 1978, and 1980 experiments conducted in Riga, in which case their satellites would have searched for the installation and possibly have found it." Diamov turned and smiled broadly at Colonel Malenkova. "Don't get the idea that American satellites can photograph this complex. It's inside the mountain. There isn't anything to photograph."

"I'll tell you something else, Comrade Colonel. Those damned Americans won't be able to find the electromagnets and our power source either with their snooping satellites!" General Shchors rubbed his hands together with the relish of a man who has just scored a winning point. "The magnets are underground, sixty kilometers north of Moscow!"

Having lighted another cigarette, Boris Malenkova exhaled and looked up at the moon. "I was going to ask about the electromagnets and the power source. I knew you couldn't have brought the magnets from the Motherland or obtained that much electric power from the Greek mainland."

"Not very likely," said Shchors. "There are thirteen magnets. The largest weighs sixteen metric tons."

"The idiot Americans even gave us one in 1977." Diamov smirked. "For 'peaceful weather research'!"

"The power for the magnifying transmitter will come from Moscow," said General Shchors, whose scientific discipline was particle physics. There were notes of pride in his voice. "Let us say that the power is broadcast! How does that strike you, Comrade Colonel Malenkova?"

Malenkova didn't let his astonishment register on his face. "I suppose you're going to tell me next that the electromagnetic power can be 'plucked out of the air' by a special receiver?"

"In a sense, yes. But not in the conventional way that a radio receiver is used. Even the principle is different. Part of it is endothermic—a chemical reaction in which heat is absorbed. The energy of a charge has a lot to do with it. This is represented by E equaling one-half QV, given in ergs, when the charge Q and the potential V are in electrostatic units. For the energy distribution, we—"

"Dr. General Shchors," interrupted Major Diamov, "I am sure that Comrade Colonel Malenkova is not interested in the technical aspects." He turned and looked at Malenkova. "As far back as 1930, Tesla succeeded in lighting two hundred light bulbs at a distance of thirty-five kilometers—and without the use of wire to conduct the electricity. We use the same principle to broadcast power from Moscow."

"It was that part of the project that delayed us for many years," Gregor Shchors said quickly, as if racing to catch up with the conversation. "We had to solve the problem of transmitting the energy without wires and do so without creating standing waves and airquakes. There was also the problem of what can be described as 'feedback.' That problem, too, has been solved."

Malenkova weighed Shchors's words carefully before commenting. "I'm curious. How much power will the magnifying transmitter have? I suppose that would be difficult to explain to a nonscientist?"

"Try to imagine a trillion-trillion volts of electricity —all of it perfectly controlled—and a billion bolts of lightning strikes, all of it without any sound or flashes," Shchors said. "Such a mental picture would come close to describing the power of the magnifying transmitter. That's what the device does: It *magnifies* power."

Malenkova considered for a moment. "None of that explains the precise nature of the experiment. I mean, when the device is made operational, will you and your people be trying to change the weather in any specific corner of the world—and why did we need Professor Paspyrou?"

Shchors said simply, "There will be snow this year in September in the United States." Again he moved his arms and stretched his shoulder and neck muscles. "There is also mathematical indication that the transmitter could possibly be used as a death ray. Keeping this in mind, we are going to try to affect the ozone layer about the planet, but only in a very tiny section."

The Spetsnaz officer's eyes widened. He dropped his cigarette on the sand and crushed it out with the heel of his left shoe. "Wouldn't that be very dangerous—tampering with the ozone layer?"

"Noooooooo," Shchors replied thoughtfully, as if he weren't sure of his answer. "Picture the surface of clear water in a large bucket. Now move a finger very slowly through the water of only one portion of the surface. The same effect could be applied to what we will do to the ozone layer. We will barely stir it. Professor Stefanos Paspyrou? He supplied the missing equations we needed to make the transmitter functional. He doesn't like helping us, but he knows he doesn't have a choice."

Major Diamov had sized up Malenkova as a ruthless bureaucratic climber. Nothing wrong with that. In the Soviet *Nomenklatura,* who wasn't ambitious? It was the nature of the system. You were either one of the cannibals or you became one of the eaten. Yet Diamov still despised Boris Malenkova. The man was a narcissistic egotist who thought the universe revolved only around him.

Diamov got to his feet. "Comrades, I suggest we return to the complex," he said. "It is not wise to get too far from the caves. I also suggest, Colonel Malenkova, that you pay more attention to matters of security."

Malenkova's eyes flashed in resentment. "What do you mean?"

"What brand of cigarettes are you smoking?"

"Red Star—why?"

"Should anyone come ashore, find the cigarette butts and analyze them, they could learn the cigarettes were manufactured in the Soviet Union, don't you agree?" Diamov said very politely. He didn't want to order the Spetsnaz officer to pick up the butts. He could refuse.

"Yes, you are correct, Comrade Major Diamov," Malenkova responded with an equal measure of courtesy. "It was a mistake on my part, a very bad mistake."

Immediately Malenkova stooped and began searching the sand with his fingers, much to the consternation of Diamov, who knew that Malenkova had turned the tables on him.

As the group walked back toward the caves,

Diamov continued to castigate himself for opening his big mouth. They were close to the caves when Malenkova said in a mild tone, "Tell me, Comrade Major. How is our intelligence in Athens—if you are permitted to tell me? I'm sure the American CIA is trying to reestablish its network."

"The CIA is always making the effort in Athens, for all the good it will do the Americans," Diamov said. "I'm not privy to what is going on in Athens or in other parts of Greece. Our *rezident* in Athens is a good man and is in firm control of the situation. I do know we have an agent placed securely within the ranks of the other side."

"How does General Nikos Cyatorus of the KYP fit into the picture? Does he know what is going on here on Miskos?"

"Cyatorus only knows we're conducting weather experiments. I don't know the exact amount of money Moscow paid him. A substantial amount was banked for him in Switzerland. We also promised him to assassinate Premier Papandreou at the proper time and assist him in installing himself as premier!"

Colonel Malenkova laughed. "And the fool actually believes such nonsense? I never would if I were in his place."

"Cyatorus is so power-hungry, he can talk himself into believing almost anything."

The walk continued in silence, Diamov thinking of how Malenkova had said "I," as if his own position were next to God's! Diamov was convinced that if Malenkova could love himself more, he'd turn into a married couple!

Chapter Four

I

The arrangements had been made. Joseph Pappas would meet Richard Camellion and Nicholas Notaras for lunch the next day at their hotel. The three of them would then visit various handicrafters from whom Pappas often bought merchandise—makers of jewelry and statues, workers in copper and brass, people who made dolls wearing Greek costumes.

As soon as the Death Merchant was in the car and pulling out of the drive, he said casually to Notaras, "I'd like to know why you told Pappas that you're a physicist and came with me to Greece to evaluate Professor Paspyrou's papers. Didn't I caution you to think before speaking?"

Notaras was startled by Camellion's tone. "I don't see any harm in what I said. Mr. Pappas isn't going to tell anyone." He turned and looked at Camellion. "You trust him or you wouldn't have given him any information. So what's the big deal?"

The Death Merchant turned the Volkswagen onto Ramicus Street. "In this business you never reveal to a friend anything you would keep from an enemy. Did you hear me telling Pappas about Melina

Arnaoutis? She's none of his business. In the future, keep your mouth zippered and think half a dozen times before you submerge yourself in diarrhea of the mouth."

"Very well." Notaras put his right elbow on the window slot of the door and began watching the hot, tired-looking countryside.

Blessed with an intuitive sensitivity about men and women, the Death Merchant was convinced that Notaras was presenting some kind of false persona, hiding behind a façade of—of what? The CIA had double-checked him. The man was what he was supposed to be . . . from a good family, his background spotless, an instructor in physics at the Massachusetts Institute of Technology—Grojean had assured Camellion. That was the rub! There were times when, if Grojean had said "Good morning," Camellion would have known it was night and have gone home and jumped into bed! *He would lie to God to get a job done!*

Notaras did have an allergy and took three chlorpheniramine maleate tablets every five hours, each tablet of 20 mg. Camellion wasn't a pharmacist, but he did know a good deal about drugs. Since when did chlorpheniramine maleate come in 20-mg tablets? Or did Notaras have a special prescription?

They drove back to Athens in silence. It wasn't until the Volkswagen was on Ermou Dromos (or street) that Notaras said, "It will only be about four o'clock by the time we get back to the hotel. What are we going to do with the rest of the afternoon?"

The Death Merchant again heard that little warning bell about Notaras. *He'd have to have Alzheimer's disease to forget what's ahead!* Before Camellion could form any words, Notaras said, "I haven't forgotten your meeting with Melina Arnaoutis at the

Pepper Pot. You don't have to make contact with her until eight."

Camellion slowed because of traffic. The Greeks called themselves Hellenes and their country *Vasilion Tis Ellados,* the Kingdom of Hellas, and were quick to point out that their nation had been the birthplace of Western civilization. No one would have known it from looking at downtown Athens. The roads were thick with cars, motor scooters, and bicycles, the air thick with smog and gasoline fumes. To Camellion's left were an adult bookstore and a motion picture theater. He couldn't read the Greek words on the numerous signs, but the large photographs of naked girls spoke an international language. The movie house showed only pornographic films. Camellion smiled softly to himself. Socrates and Aristotle would do handsprings in their graves if they could see what Athens had become in the twentieth century.

"By the time we shower and change into clean clothes, we'll be able to eat an early dinner," Camellion said, trying to sound friendly. He felt rather guilty for having chastised Notaras, who, after all, deserved a lot of credit. He was risking his life by coming to Greece.

"When do you think ONI or the British or the French will make contact?" Notaras asked absently.

"I have no idea," Camellion murmured. Looking into the rearview mirror, he saw a Greek driver trying to tailgate him. "It will be soon, and they'll make the first move."

Even the Death Merchant—forty-six minutes later —was surprised at how soon that first move was. As soon as he and Notaras entered their suite, they saw the note that had been slipped under the door. Notaras picked it up, took it out of the envelope, and read it out loud. " 'Come to the bar downstairs and have a drink. I'll be at the end of the bar—cream polo shirt, cream slacks. Short beard, no mustache. I'll be pretending to be slightly drunk.' It's signed 'A.E.C.' " He handed the note to Camellion. The words had been printed with a ballpoint pen, and he saw the tipoff sign—at the ends of the last sentence was a period with a circle around it. The note was from Arnold Everett Cahill, a British Secret Intelligence Service agent. Even if Cahill hadn't given a description of himself, he would know the man from photographs the Fox had shown him.

Camellion looked at Notaras and put a finger to his lips. "He must be another buyer. I don't know him, do you?" The Death Merchant quickly shook his head.

"No, I don't know him," Notaras said, watching Camellion tear the note into tiny pieces.

The Death Merchant started toward the bathroom, to flush the note down the white throne. "We'd better go down and meet him before we change. We don't know how long he's been waiting—whoever he might be."

"If you don't mind, I'll stay up here," Notaras said, following him. "I'm somewhat nauseated; it must be the heat. I'll take a shower, then lie down and have a nap."

"It's fine with me," agreed Camellion. He opened the bathroom door, relieved that Notaras wouldn't be going with him to the bar. At least he wouldn't be able to flap his jaw before thinking. It was bad enough that the damn fool had read the note out loud, even though it wasn't likely that the rooms were bugged.

Camellion dropped the pieces of paper into the john and flushed the toilet.

II

The air-conditioned bar was comfortable, with only five men at the bar and half a dozen couples in the green leather booths. Camellion spotted Cahill at once. The Britisher was at the north end of the bar, his feet draped on the rounded chrome sides of a stool, a glass of beer and drachmae bills and coins in front of him. Slightly to his left was an ashtray full of cigarette butts.

Camellion sat down on the leather stool next to Cahill and ordered a glass of Santa Helena, a mild wine, from the bored bartender. Under ordinary circumstances, the Death Merchant never drank alcohol. He didn't like the taste and was afraid he might acquire the habit, his fear based on the fact that his uncle had died an alcoholic and that for thirty years his father had been a hopeless drunkard. Camellion knew the same weakness was in his own genes.

The Death Merchant saw Cahill watching him in the glass behind the bar. Of average height, Cahill could have been forty. He wasn't a big man, weighing perhaps 165 pounds, but he was well muscled and would have given the appearance of robust good health if he hadn't been sitting like a big frog—hunched over the bar—on the stool and if his shirt and slacks hadn't looked as if he'd worn them for three or four days.

An aquiline nose emphasized his strong profile, and high cheekbones gnarled a face that looked as if it belonged to a man who did pushups without hands. His light-brown hair didn't do anything for his appearance either. It seemed that he had washed his hair and forgotten to comb it after it had dried. His chin was decorated with a short sandy beard that needed a trimming.

Cahill didn't speak until the bartender was serving another customer. "It's hot in Greece this time of the year but much colder in Peking." His voice was low, sibilant, and well modulated. He deliberately swayed slightly on the stool.

"I think the summer is milder in London." Camellion gave the first sentence of the recognition code.

"And not quite so hot in the United States," Cahill said.

Camellion completed the code. "Unless there's a very unexpected change in the weather."

"After I leave the bar wait five minutes, then come to the hotel's car park." The caution had left Cahill's voice. "I'll be waiting in a powder-blue Civic 1300 Honda. I'll be parked on the east side of the car park. We can have a bit of chin-wag, and I'll fill you in on the latest developments. Okay, Yank?"

"Five minutes after you leave. I'll be there," Camellion said.

Cahill suddenly sat up and slapped his left palm down on the bar, the sharp sound making the other people there turn and look at him.

"I say, how about some service at this end!" he slurred in a loud voice.

The bartender, a young, overweight dude with *komboloia*—worry beads—around his neck, walked to the end of the bar.

"Yes, sir?" he asked in an overly friendly voice, while his eyes revealed disgust.

"Two shots of ouzo. No ice." Cahill's words were a pronouncement.

As soon as the bartender placed the glass of ouzo in front of Cahill, the Britisher handed him a 600-drachma bill. "Keep the change," he said magnanimously. "Your service is excellent. By God, I am going to talk to the manager of this establishment and demand that he give you a promotion."

"Thank you, sir. Thank you," the bartender said politely, and smiled. He should have grinned from ear to ear. His tip was slightly more than $7.85.

Cahill polished off the ouzo in one gulp, hiccoughed loudly, picked up his change, slid off the stool, and stuffed the bills into his pocket. Staggering slightly, he then left the bar.

The Death Merchant consulted his Heuer wristwatch, took another sip of wine, and glanced around the Gold Room by looking in the mirror behind the bar. Cahill was a good actor. But how good a street man was he? How reliable was he when the Cosmic Lord of Death was closing in? Another thing that bothered Camellion was that he was unarmed. He didn't intend to be for long.

The bartender, passing with a drink for another customer, paused and glanced at him. "Another glass of Santa Helena, sir?"

Camellion shook his head, drained the glass, and put the change into his billfold, leaving three twenty-drachmae bills on the bar.

The Death Merchant sat down next to Cahill on the seat and closed the door, Cahill giving him the once-over with keen brown eyes behind wraparound sunglasses. The British SIS agent immediately shifted, backed out of the slot, shifted again, headed for the street, and turned on the air-conditioning.

"Don't worry, Camellion," he said cheerfully when he saw the Death Merchant open the glove compartment. "This car isn't bugged, and I'm sure a bumper beeper is not attached. I have a wide-spectrum detector in an attaché case in the boot." He let out a little laugh. "In what you Americans would call the trunk."

Camellion found himself liking the man. "If we have the time, we can stop and get some Popsicles," he offered with a smile, "or what you Britishers call 'iced lollys.'"

Genuinely surprised, Cahill gave him a brief glance. "Oh, ho! You have spent a good deal of time in Great Britain! I was told you had been about this old world a bit."

The Death Merchant changed the subject. "I'm curious about your clothes. Do you usually—"

"I was afraid you would never ask—out of politeness, you know. Politeness has no place in this bloody business. Soiled clothes are a part of my cover as a British expatriate with a fondness for spirits and tarts. Supposedly I'm from one of those fine aristocratic families and live on funds sent from home. A large check does arrive each month. At the hotel bars and various other places I'm considered a bore, a harmless pest, who's also a big tipper. Say, were you serious about stopping for Popsicles?"

Camellion laughed. "The only thing I want is to know if there have been any developments pertaining to the operation. Where are we going, or do you enjoy driving in traffic? On the road, the Greeks are worse than the Israelis."

"We're going to meet the Frenchie who's in charge of the SDECE lads here in Athens." Cahill became very serious. "First, let me tell you about the dangle operation we—we meaning SIS and your American ONI—began last night."

Speaking in a rapid and clipped tone, Cahill explained that the dangle had only one purpose: to find Professor Stefanos Paspyrou. For four and a half months Petros Makarezos, the assistant head of the Greek Ministry of Foreign Affairs, had been having a sexual liaison with a pretty young woman from the German Archeological School on Odho Street in Athens.

"She's been working for us—for SIS—the past two

years," Cahill said, then stopped the car for a red light. "I've never met her and she doesn't know I exist. How we acquired her is another story. What does matter is that she can only be trusted up to a certain point. She's a double agent. We have proof that she's also sold bits and pieces of information to the French SDECE. I—"

"Proof can be very tenuous in such cases," commented the Death Merchant, who was beginning to think there were too many strings attached to the package. "But we can't have Napoleon's conquests without Napoleon's battles. Risk is always a necessary element."

"Exactly." Cahill moved the Honda forward. "In this case we do have proof absolute. The French told us that she sold them information about German tourists she suspected of being BND agents. The Frenchies reasoned they should inform us when they became part of Operation Zeus. I hasten to add that Karen Spreitler isn't aware that we know she has done business with the French *Service de Documentation Extérieure et de Contre-Espionnage.*"

Camellion listened to the slight *whoosh* of the air conditioner. "To that I hasten to add that her true loyalty might be to the East German MfS or to the West German BND," he amplified. "SIS has tested her?"

"To be sure. So far she's been honest with us, which really doesn't mean anything. Now let me tell you what we did, my people and your people. We . . ."

Two weeks earlier Karen Spreitler had taken Petros Makarezos to see her new apartment on Kapodistrious Dromos. The Greek government official never suspected that foreign intelligence agents were setting him up, that they had spent a week in equipping the apartment with a two-way mirror behind which was a special motion picture camera that could use infrared to take photographs in the dark—sixteen frames per second. The agents also installed a long-playing tape recorder with six sensitive microphones carefully hidden in the bedroom.

Within five hours after Spreitler and Makarezos entered the apartment, SIS and PNI had enough photographs—with "dialogue"—to give "that Greek bugger enough nightmares to last him the rest of his life."

The special high-speed camera had photographed every act. The tape recorder had transcribed every word, every sigh, every moan of delight. Later the agents had made numerous still photographs from the film, every single one of them clearly showing Makarezos and Karen indulging not only in sexual intercourse but also in acts that technically were considered major crimes in many states in the United States—oral sex acts, such as fellatio and cunnilingus. Just as incriminating were photographs showing Makarezos on all fours, like a dog, on the rug in Karen's bedroom, with her standing over him—stark naked—with a whip in her hand.

The dangle operation was blackmail, pure and simple.

Cahill increased speed. He turned and flashed a smile at the Death Merchant—one of his very sudden smiles, as quick as a light bulb's being switched on. He said, "Last night we contacted Makarezos and showed him some of the photographs. We gave him a choice. We told him that either he would reveal the location of Professor Paspyrou or we would send the photographs and tapes to his wife, his two married daughters, Premier Papandreou, and other Greek government officials."

Cahill paused as he increased speed. "In addition, we told Makarezos that we'd scatter fifteen thousand photographs all over Greece. All of Greece—eventually the whole world—would learn that he was a sex pervert. Conversely, if he cooperated and gave us the desired information, no one would ever know about his sex life. We would give the photographs and film and tapes to him, but only after we had proof that he was telling the truth."

"I'm listening." The Death Merchant didn't say that he felt the operation was so full of holes it would make a pound of Swiss cheese look as solid as an iron bar. "What was his response?"

Arnold Cahill didn't reply until he had made the long, curving turn onto Athanassious Boulevard. "What could he do?" he said smugly. "The photographs were there in front of him, proving we meant what we said. Makarezos fell apart. He agreed to help us find Professor Paspyrou, but he didn't have the foggiest where the KYP has hidden him. He did say he would be able to find out, but that it would take him a week."

Hunched down in the seat and feeling sweaty, Camellion performed some rapid mental gymnastics. It was not very likely that Makarezos would report the blackmail scheme to the KYP. No man ever wanted his sexual abnormalities exposed—a fact the intelligence services of the world were well aware of.

"How was contact made with Makarezos?" demanded the Death Merchant, playing devil's advocate.

"Arzey Holcomb and one of the ONI's Greek field operatives met him in Foros Park. They were both in disguise—beards, large mustaches, skin dye, and Arzey affected an accent. Makarezos thinks they're Turks." He added good-naturedly, "Now ask me about Karen Spreitler."

"Why bother when you're going to tell me."

"Arzey gave her fifteen thousand of your American dollars, and she took a flight to Paris. I daresay she'll probably open a tart shop."

"Arnold, I—"

"Call me Arnie."

"You haven't told me why ONI and SIS chose Makarezos. Why do you feel that the assistant head of the Ministry of Foreign Affairs has access to such information, or can gain access?"

"The Ministry and the KYP are very closely connected," Cahill explained. "Makarezos told Arzey he could get the information from General Cyatorus's secretary. Makarezos explained that he'd lent her money to buy a house in the suburbs and that he'll cancel the debt in return for her telling him where the KYP is having Paspyrou build the transmitter. We gather the old fart gave her the money as part of a scheme to get into her panties and have his jollies."

Camellion made a noise of disgust. "Where's the evidence, however small, that she won't report Makarezos to General Cyatorus?" he asked.

"There isn't any guarantee. There never is." For the first time, Cahill sounded impatient and irritated. "Makarezos also told Arzey and Vyron Rozakis— Rozakis is the Greek who went with Arzey—that if she refused to get the information, he would threaten to reveal certain improprieties she had committed. She's married and it would appear that she's been sharing the beds of many high officials." His laugh was musical. "These Greeks do like a change of sex partners. . . ."

"The bottom line is that we have to sit around and wait a week or so for Makarezos to find out where Professor Paspyrou is hidden!" Camellion said. He saw that the Honda was in an area thick with nightclubs, bars, restaurants, and strip palaces. "Where are we going to meet Rene Beaufault?"

"We do have to get you back in time to meet Melina Arnaoutis," Cahill mentioned companionably.

"You know about her—obviously!" Camellion grunted. "Tonight at eight o'clock at the Pepper Pot, on Cofu Street. As you already know, she'll serve as the contact between me and Holcomb and bring messages from the U.S. Embassy straight to me."

"ONI trusts her that much?" Cahill said guardedly.

"ONI doesn't trust her at all," Camellion said softly. "As a matter of security, she'll never know the contents of any message she might carry. The printed message will be in one of our usual A7d codes. It will only be the cover message. The genuine message will be on a microdot—the last period of the last sentence. You're supposed to supply the microdot enlarger, the shortwave, scramblers, decoders, and the black box 'squirt' attachment. What about Beaufault?"

"He's waiting for us in front of a striptease establishment called The Orange Glow. I know. The name is asinine, but that's how the Greek name translates into English."

"Do you read Greek?"

"No, but I'd have a difficult time missing The Orange Glow." Cahill laughed. "I've been there five or six times. The manager is a member of the Delphi Circle. The Delphis have arms and explosives stored in the place. Three more blocks and we'll pick up Rene."

The SIS agent then told the Death Merchant what he already knew: that Rene Beaufault had been in Greece for nine years, was a citizen of the country, and operated a service for tourists, taking them to rubberneck at the ruins of the Delphi Oracle at Delphi, to Olympia, where the first Olympic Games were held in 776 B.C., and to numerous other ancient ruins considered supremely historical.

"We already have one shortwave and all the necessary attachments," continued Cahill. "Rene has everything hidden in a false closet in his apartment. I have a transceiver for you and Joe Pappas in the boot. The microdot equipment is in the boot too."

The Death Merchant turned and stared at the British agent. "In the trunk of this car?"

"Oh, it's not that bad of a kick in the balls," Cahill said dryly. "Remember what you said about Napoleon? Besides, I have my own secure garage. The automobile will be safe at my place. The only danger is if some wild Greek bashed us from the rear."

The glints in the Death Merchant's eyes sharpened. "Pappas will be meeting me and Notaras at our hotel tomorrow at noon. I suggest you meet us at his place at four in the afternoon. Then you can transfer the radio and the microdot equipment into his warehouse. He has a secret room that would do fine. The antenna would be a problem, but I can work that out."

For the time being Arnie Cahill didn't speak. He was too busy looking from left to right. On both sides of the street was a glass and electric jungle of neon signs and posters, garish advertisements for entertainment—booze, food, girls, sex.

"Yes, this is the block," Cahill said at length. "Meeting at Pappas's warehouse at four is a splendid suggestion."

"What's your own radio setup, yours and Beaufault's? I assume you use the transceiver stashed at his apartment."

"Yes, we do. We have all the augmentation necessary for scrambling, coding and decoding, and squirt effect. Ahh, there's Rene. . . ."

Cahill drove another 120 feet, swung the Honda to the curb in front of The Orange Glow, and stopped.

Rene Beaufault walked over to the car and climbed in the backseat.

III

"The safe house on Stazoukis Avenue is the only one we have," Beaufault said. "For all the good it would do us. The KYP or the *Asfaleia* would close in so fast, I doubt if any of us would have much of a chance."

"We would hardly be as well off as God and France, would we?" joked Cahill. "The weakest link in our whole chain of networks is the Greeks working for us. In all three services, they have passed numerous tests. I still cannot trust them completely. It's psychological. I've never liked Greeks. They're too prone to think emotionally."

Watching several bikini-clad girls dive into the large tear-shaped swimming pool, the Death Merchant took another sip of *mazi-omi,* an orange-flavored noncarbonated drink sold by park vendors, and thought of the telephone number Grojean had given him: the safe house that, if necessary, would be provided by ONI. *No, don't give Cahill and Beaufault the number and the recognition phrases until you've conferred with Holcomb. . . . The matter is not that pressing, not yet.*

"Camellion, you haven't inquired how we contact Holcomb," Cahill said lightly. "I should suppose you were told before you left America."

Camellion stirred the two straws in the paper container half filled with *mazi-omi.* "Holcomb and his wife have a nice cover. The little tourist shop they operate on Akadimias is a perfect setup. It's an easy matter for either one of you to drop by his place of business once or twice a week."

"And just as easy for you to do the same," Beaufault said quietly, a large question mark in his voice.

The Death Merchant nodded understandingly. "ONI isn't playing some kind of game with either SIS or SDECE regarding contact with Holcomb," he explained. "I won't make personal contact with him because I'm a direct link to Joseph Pappas, who is a high muckitymuck in the Delphi Circle. Should the KGB or the KYP tail me to Holcomb's shop and later to Pappas's warehouse, they'd tie the three of us together. Frankly, I feel such caution is ridiculous."

"You do?" said Beaufault with some surprise.

"If the KGB or the KYP is tailing me, they've already seen me with Pappas and possibly with the two of you," Camellion said. "In that case, they'll eventually follow one or both of you to Holcomb's shop—or you, Arnie, tomorrow when you come to Joe's warehouse. The blunt truth is that it's impossible to operate with just 'brush-by' contacts or meetings in out-of-the-way places."

Beaufault offered, "The American intelligence services have always been too cautious. The SDECE is even more timid, and at times this safety factor has worked against us."

For a moment there was silence, except for a loud slurping sound as Cahill finished his *mazi-omi*. An hour ago he had driven to Sophocleous Park, one of the largest parks in Athens that had a public swimming pool. But he hadn't driven to the park so that he and Camellion and Beaufault could mentally remove the bikinis from the girls splashing in the water. In summer, Greek businessmen often drove there and spent time watching people—including half-naked girls in the pool—while they conducted business in a relaxed environment. "It's the Greek way," Cahill had said. "No one will pay any attention to us."

Now Cahill remarked with a thin smile, "I suppose both of you realize that even if we can pinpoint Professor Paspyrou, our chances of freeing him are almost nil. Even with our combined forces and the help of the Delphi Circle, we won't be an army."

"We don't even have any guarantees that the Delphi revolutionaries will help," Beaufault said. He was not a young man—he had to be fifty—but he gave the impression of being strong. At least six feet, he was trim and had a lean, olive-complexioned face with languorous brown eyes, black hair parted in the middle, and sensuous lips. He spoke with a slight lisp, and his accent, when speaking English, marked him as a Breton, a native from the Brittany peninsula in northwest France.

"I have news for both of you," Camellion said amiably. "Wherever the illusive Paspyrou is, he's on an island. That's 'Gospel according to ONI'! There are 1,425 islands in the Aegean Sea, but only 167 of them are inhabited. That leaves us with only 1,258 to choose from." His laughter was light and short. "Any suggestions?"

Camellion could tell from Rene Beaufault's swift inhalation and from the startled expression on Cahill's face that neither of them had been given that information.

Cahill reacted to the Death Merchant's revelation like a horse with half a dozen burrs under its saddle. "Completely preposterous!" he snapped in disgust. "What we are supposed to do is impossible, at least the last phase of Operation Zeus. We're not commandos! I ask you, Camellion: How are we supposed to rescue Paspyrou with only a bloody handful of men? It's enough to give one goose pimples! In all likelihood the KYP has its *Baruzi*—its uniformed troops—on the island."

"We've picked up rumors in the past few weeks

that the Soviet Union has sent special KGB *Boyevaya Gruppa* combat killers to Greece." Rene Beaufault's undertaker's tone was not as forlorn as his eyes. At times he seemed to be a man who could relax completely, so much so that it would seem he could fall asleep in a roller coaster. Now was not one of those times. "I must agree with Arnie, Camellion. We are not a suicide squad, and I for one don't intend to become a part of one."

"Nor I!" Cahill snapped. The look of anger on his face deepened. No one had told him so; yet he was convinced that the United States had initiated Operation Zeus and that France and Great Britain were only "poor relations" who were expected to tag along. Cahill resented it.

He looked over at the Death Merchant, saw that his large paper cup was empty, and took it from Camellion's hand. He reached over his shoulder with his left hand and said to Beaufault, "If you're finished, give me the empty container. I'll get rid of the three of them."

After Beaufault handed Cahill the cup, the British agent got out of the car and started toward a trash container fifteen yards away.

Camellion and Beaufault maintained an expectant silence, and it wasn't until Cahill had returned that Camellion said slyly, "Gentlemen, in my humble opinion, I seriously doubt if ONI, SIS, and SDECE expect us to charge across some beach and rescue Paspyrou."

Cahill was quick to ask in guarded tones, "Do you have any information to substantiate that opinion? This is not the time to withhold facts."

"I'm not withholding anything," Camellion responded placatingly. "It's a matter of common sense, or you might call it deduction. The people in charge know that after we locate Paspyrou—*if* we find him

—we won't be able to grab him. We have neither the manpower nor the materiel. We know it. They know it."

Turning sideways behind the steering wheel, Cahill glanced contemplatively at Beaufault, then stared at the Death Merchant, exploring his face in detail. "That leaves only special forces and could be extremely dangerous."

Beaufault was delighted. "But of course it could be dangerous—to the Russians and the Greek forces on the island," he said heartily. "Our *Force Rapide* is very good!"

"I rather think Arnie is referring to Soviet response and political reaction after the strike," Camellion said easily, feeling that Cahill was inexperienced in how the pig farmers in Moscow operated.

"I most certainly am!" Cahill said reprovingly. "We could trigger World War III! I can't comprehend the stupidity of expecting the Soviet Union to ignore our cutting them down to size on some Greek island in the Aegean Sea."

"What would you expect the Soviets to do—complain to that useless debating society, the United Nations?" pursued Camellion. "I can just see the ivans getting up in the UN and telling the world that they were on a Greek island—"

"With a Greek scientist they had kidnapped—and on an island where their people shouldn't have been in the first place!" Beaufault inserted quickly.

"Plus getting up in the UN and admitting they had broken a weather-war treaty they had made with the United States in 1977—smashed it to bits by constructing a device that could change the weather of the world!" The Death Merchant's cold stare stabbed into Cahill, making the Englishman feel oddly uncomfortable. "I'll tell you what the Soviet Union will do. *Nothing!* There will not be one diplomatic protest. The Soviets will pretend that the incident never happened."

"I must admit you do sound sure of yourself." Cahill spoke with less defiance.

"I'm basing my opinion on other things that have happened in the world," Camellion said. "The Soviets have been hit hard before in covert strikes, not only in Africa but in South America, and in the Pacific, and even off the coasts of Cuba. I'm not just whistlin' Dixie either. I'm sorry that I'm not at liberty to discuss it."

Cahill sighed deeply. "I really don't think it matters a whit in the long run. Sooner or later a mistake will be made and the world will be turned into a sea of nuclear glass, in spite of all the covert action by the West."

"Ah, *mon ami,* don't belittle covert action," said Rene Beaufault, taking out his cigarettes. "It was covert action during the post–World War II period that saved Italy and Greece from going communist."

The Death Merchant straightened up. His voice was businesslike. "Arnie, let's get back to the hotel. I still have to take a bath, have dinner, and meet Melina Arnaoutis."

"How is Nicholas Notaras holding up?" asked Beaufault, leaning back against the rear seat. "Bringing him along was a mistake. He has to be a Neanderthal in this kind of business."

"He's a nice man and we have to give him a big *B* for bravery." Camellion defended Notaras. "Most men in his position wouldn't willingly risk their lives."

Cahill turned the key in the ignition. "Camellion, do you still want me to meet you tomorrow afternoon at Pappas's warehouse?"

* * *

They were halfway back to the Royal Olympic when Camellion turned to Cahill. "During the past few months has there been anything in the papers or on television about Professor Paspyrou or his wife and children?"

"Not a word," Cahill said without hesitation. "A year and a half ago the papers stated that he had contracted chronic myelocytic leukemia and with his family would be leaving Greece and going to an 'undisclosed' foreign country for treatment."

"A beautiful excuse," Beaufault said thoughtfully. "Friends don't pry and ask questions when they think cancer or some other fatal illness is involved."

"It figures. The professor's wife and daughters are with him on the island," Camellion said. "Paspyrou is violently anticommunist. He wouldn't be helping the Russians willingly. The KGB must be using his family to force him to work with their scientists. It would be typical of the KGB."

Chapter Five

Although the Death Merchant would have bet Damon and Pythias, his two pet pigs at his *Memento Mori* ranch, that Melina Arnaoutis would arrive at the Pepper Pot early, he didn't walk through the door of the third rate nightclub until seven fifty-five.

Dressed in a powder-blue summer suit, a Corinth coral sport shirt, and loafers, he made his way to the bar, edged in between two fat Greeks jabbering in their native tongue, and ordered a glass of Pallini. After the bartender placed the white wine before him, he turned and, with his elbows on the bar, looked over the noisy place. To one side was a small orchestra playing *Bouzoukia* music, which explained why the dancers on the floor were men, in circles of five and six, dancing precisely to the Greek rhythms.

Scattered around the large dance floor were tables packed with men and women. Toward the outside wall was a line of small booths; these, too, were filled. People in the booths as well as at the tables could clearly see the bar.

It was possible that Melina Arnaoutis would guess who he was—if she has any smarts at all in her pretty head. The Death Merchant had positively forbidden Courtland Grojean and ONI to give his photograph

to any Greek in the ONI network, though he had
permitted Joseph Pappas and Arzey Holcomb to see
his and Notaras's photo. Camellion, however, had
viewed front and profile photographs of Melina
Arnaoutis and had studied a ten-minute motion picture of her, which had been made while she was at
work. She was employed by the Greek *Karagiorgi
Servias* tourist service and was a guide at the *Akropo-
lis*—the Acropolis.

It wasn't likely that Arnaoutis would be at one of
the tables. A young woman alone—he had been told
she was twenty-eight—would be too conspicuous and
would have to fend off too many ardorous Greek
males eager for a one-night stand.

Camellion turned to the bar, drank half the white
wine, and listened to and watched the two fat
Greeks. As he did, he reflected that if most Greeks
had their hands tied behind their back, they would
automatically become mute. After finishing the
wine, he made his way to the line of booths by the
wall. Slowly he walked north, glancing briefly at
the men and women occupying the booths, just on
the chance that Arnaoutis might have broken orders
and brought along another Greek member of the
ONI network—*God help her if she has!*

There was only one booth with a lone woman, and
she wasn't Melina Arnaoutis. Disappointed, the
Death Merchant started back toward the bar, this
time letting his eyes wander over the numerous tables around the dance floor. He was not far from the
main entrance when he saw her. Apparently she had
just come in and was standing on the top of the three
steps that led down to the main section of the nightclub, looking toward the bar. She was swinging her
head around to look over the tables as he started
toward her. Then she saw him. *Uh-huh, she has the
smarts, all right. . . .* Though she hadn't known

what he looked like, her smile—before he had time to introduce himself—clearly conveyed that she guessed who he was.

"Miss Arnaoutis, I'm Richard Camellion."

She was far better looking than her photographs and the short film he had seen. She wore a long-sleeved off-white blouse with tan dots, neutral tan slacks, and high heels that made her look taller than her five feet six inches. Her raven hair, which matched her large intelligent eyes, hung down around her neck and shoulders and framed an oval face whose ivory skin was without a single blemish.

It was how Ma Nature had put her together that intrigued the Death Merchant, who was far from being a stranger to feminine pulchritude. She had a slender waistline, a flat stomach, and, in the common vernacular, was well stacked, her well-shaped breasts apparently not imprisoned by a bra. When you see two faintly dark circles outlined beneath an off-white blouse, and pushing out against dots, you can bet Damon and Pythias that the nipples are free and unconfined.

The Death Merchant had also shared enough beds with the opposite sex to know that there were three kinds of women. There were those who appeared as cold as a dead fish but became wildcats in bed. Other women looked and acted sexy but were as frigid as a 3,000-year-old statue. In the last category were those women who exuded sex and, later in bed, proved it by having orgasms almost as fast as slugs can spit from the muzzle of a MAC-Ingram submachine gun!

Camellion wouldn't have bet Damon and Pythias —or even King David, his pet rattlesnake—but in his own mind, he was positive that Melina was pure sex —*Who could turn a young man into an old man within two weeks!*

"I'm sorry I'm late, Mr. Camellion," Melina apologized in a sultry voice, her English words without an accent. "But I had to work overtime, and the taxi had a flat tire. Would you care for a drink first, or should we go straight to my place?"

"I suggest we go to your apartment," Camellion said, taking her by the elbow. "By the way, call me Richard. I'll call you Melina. All right?"

She flashed another smile, showing even teeth. "Fine, Richard." Then in a much lower voice: "But don't you want to know the recognition words?"

"It's not necessary; I know who you are."

She stepped closer, her dark eyes sweeping over his face. "I don't know you!"

" '*A man is not old until regrets take the place of dreams,*' " Camellion said. He could hardly argue with procedure.

" '*Most of us are too young to be as old as we are,*' " she replied. Again, a smile. "Now we can go, Richard."

He did a quick study of her as the taxi took them across Athens to her building in an older section of the city. Sitting close to him, she chattered away, mainly about how modern architects were wrecking Athens by constructing apartment houses that resembled cubes piled one on top of the other, and ". . . ugly office buildings without a trace of feeling or beauty."

"It started in the United States," Camellion told her, enjoying the fragrance of her perfume. "Years ago in the States, simply designed glass buildings were considered an art form. Then it occurred to architects that such designs offered the largest space for the largest number of people. The result was that this singular design scheme became more important than pleasing the people who appreciated some beauty and intricate design where they worked and where they lived."

"So typical of America," Melina said curtly. "Americans have always been an impatient people who look for quick and easy solutions. They have never understood the psychology of people who live in other countries."

So that the cab driver wouldn't hear, she leaned close and whispered in Camellion's left ear, "But America has the best form of government in the world."

In twenty minutes the taxi had pulled up to 1117 Karamikou Street. While an old building, the apartment house was well maintained. By the time Melina and Camellion were climbing the dark stairs to her apartment on the fourth floor, he had decided that she was a well-educated young woman who lived without pretext or apologies of any kind. *So what? Can I trust her completely?* ONI maintained that Melina Arnaoutis had agreed to work with American Intelligence because she favored the small and very violent Greek Democratic Party, which was against socialism in any form. *Fudge!* What she had told ONI didn't make a damn bit of difference to the Death Merchant, who wouldn't automatically trust God, even if the Creator agreed to take a polygraph test! After all, look at the mess God had made of His creation.

Melina locked the double locks on the door and motioned for Camellion to sit down. "Anywhere you want," she said. "I'm going to get out of these hot clothes and put on something cool."

She hurried off to the bedroom, her high heels silent on the thick brown rug. On the way, she stopped to turn on a window air conditioner. Camellion took off his coat, hung it on the back of a chair close to the door, walked farther into the surprisingly large living room, and looked around. The furniture was old but in good condition, the apartment spotless. At the end of the living room, to the east, was a kitchenette and dining nook, three windows over-looking the street to the south, the bedroom to the north. There was another door on the north side, evidently an outside door to the bath.

He was contemplating a two-foot-high wooden statue resting on a small table and trying to decide whether the hideous red-and-black-face thing was Greek, Babylonian, or a representation of some wrathful deity from Tibet when Melina came out of the bedroom. Barefoot, she was wearing a mint-color two-piece cotton shorts set, the shorts skin-tight and showing her long, shapely legs to good advantage.

His hands folded behind his back, Camellion glanced at Melina, then resumed looking at the statue. "A good or bad demon," he said, "and from what period in history?"

"All bad. It's from the pre-Hellenic period." She sat down on the low couch. "It wasn't until the third century before Christ that the concept of a 'good' demon emerged. As I recall, it was Hesiod who got the idea that a 'good' demon could be a person's constant companion and cause either his happiness or unhappiness. But as early as the fourth century sacrifices were being made to an *agatho,* a 'good' household spirit."

"You're very knowledgeable about Greek mythology," Camellion said.

"Not really," she said with a little laugh. "It's part of my job as guide. Tell me, Richard, do you find the idea of a protective demon strange?" She patted the couch. "Come. Sit beside me."

Camellion turned and almost smiled. "Very few things on this little planet surprise me. Actually, when Hesiod and Plato used the word *daimon,* they intended it to be synonymous with *theo,* God, and sometimes they used *daimon* with the nuance of a 'near-human.' I might add that their daimons didn't have any connection with Christian demons or devils. Lucifer and his gang were a later invention used to scare the hell out of the gullible and the superstitious."

Instead of sitting down next to Melina, Camellion walked over to the television set, against the east wall, and turned it on.

"It's too early for the news," she said, sounding disappointed.

Camellion picked up the "rabbit ears," turned to Channel 2, and turned the fine-tuning knob to its extreme counterclockwise position.

"Richard, what are you doing?" asked Melina, frowning deeply and watching him with a perplexed expression.

"I'm checking for a bug—a hidden transmitter." As he moved the rabbit ears up and down and from side to side, he explained the procedure to her. By turning the fine-tuning knob to its extreme counterclockwise position, he had brought the frequency to approximately 60 MHz. He would now watch the television screen for a herringbone pattern and listen for the feedback squeal as the 6 MHz band was swept. He would then advance to Channel 3, whose low end was 60 MHz. All television sets are 6 MHz in width. By repeating the process through Channel 6, he could check the spectrum between 54 and 88 MHz. Beginning with Channel 7 the frequency would jump to 174 MHz. By repeating the process through Channel 13, the 174- to 216-MHz spectrum could be covered.

Next would come the UHF band. Beginning with Channel 14, the low end of which was 470 MHz, he could scan the spectrum in six-MHz increments to Channel 83, which would be 890 MHz.

"It's rare to find a bug transmitting at that high a

frequency," the Death Merchant said, "but there's always the possibility of picking up a harmonic of a lower frequency."

Melina crossed her legs, an angry look on her pretty face. "There can hardly be a transmitter in this apartment," she said, watching Camellion slowly go through the channels. "As you saw, the front door was securely locked. There aren't any fire escapes outside the windows, the door to the back stairs is made of metal, and there are two steel bars across it on the inside. That door, too, is locked. No one could have possibly gotten in."

She began to swing her lower left leg back and forth impatiently, all the while staring at the Death Merchant.

"Simple locks would hardly be a problem for the KGB," Camellion said, and continued to make the sweep. Four minutes later he was finished. He turned off the television set and put down the rabbit ears.

Smiling genially as he walked back to the couch, he sat down next to Melina, reached for her right hand, and patted it.

"Believe me or not, I never once thought you might have planted a transmitter," he said soothingly, hoping to placate her. "Years ago I learned there is only one kind of proper security: that's thorough security. Suppose we get down to business."

"Would you care for something to drink? I'd like some coffee," Melina said, her abrupt change to her former friendliness indicating to Camellion that he had done a good job placating her. *Or else she's a marvelous actress!*

Without waiting for him to answer, she got up from the couch and started toward the kitchenette. Camellion followed, appreciating the way her buttocks, under the tight shorts, kept time with each other as she walked. "How do you receive messages from the U.S. Embassy and get them to wherever they are going? How do you pass them on?" he asked.

Camellion pulled a chair from the dinette table and watched Melina fill a copper teakettle from one of the faucets over the sink. The door to the rear steps was in the kitchen. The narrow door did have two bars over it, one at the top and one at the bottom.

"My job as a guide simplifies the process." She turned off the faucet, went over to the stove, and placed the kettle on the right front burner. "A 'tourist' might slip me a message in the morning. I might then turn it over to another 'tourist'—courier in the afternoon, or even the next morning, depending when he shows up," she explained, turning on the electric stove.

"The old switch system," Camellion said.

"It's not difficult," Melina said. She sat down at the table across from Camellion. "Each day of the week, except for Saturday and Sunday, there is a different recognition signal that a 'tourist'—a courier—must give me. For example, the signal tomorrow will be *'Kindness is the golden chain by which society is held together.'* Isn't that a laugh? I don't have to give a return recognition signal to the courier. I don't know him, but he knows me. I don't know any of them, but all of them know who I am." She gave a tiny laugh. "It doesn't seem fair, does it?"

It's not "fair" that I'm in Greece either! "Such a system can be more complicated than it sounds, and it can carry considerable risk," Camellion said.

Melina raised her arms so that her elbows were on the table.

"A lot depends on the size of the tour group I might be in charge of," she said. "Sometimes it takes three or four hours—sometimes longer—for a courier to get me alone and be able to whisper the recognition sign without someone hearing it. Once I know he is 'our' courier, I ask him for a light. But I don't do this until other people are around. He gives me a matchbox and tells me to keep it. I take out a match and light my cigarette. The message is always inside the matchbox underneath the matches. Later I pass the box to another courier. The procedure is reversed and he asks me for a light."

The Death Merchant leaned back in the chair, his eyes thoughtful.

"Then you never meet leading members of the network?"

Her chin resting on her folded hands, Melina looked at him reproachfully. "Richard, why don't you trust me?"

"It's not a matter of trust. I'm only being cautious. My pappy once told me that a wise man never tells a friend anything he would keep from an enemy." His tone was more informative rather than reproving.

"I see," Melina said. At no time had she lost her poise and self-assurance. She smiled. "I can't blame you for being careful, can I? When you protect yourself, you're also protecting me. I am a part of the American network."

"I'm glad you understand my position." Camellion saw that she had relaxed. "As I said, the switch system can be very involved. How do you receive the verbal recognition signals for the five days of the week?"

Melina began tracing tiny circles on the polished wood of the table with a forefinger. "Mr. Holcomb brings them to me. Sometimes he comes here and delivers them. Other times I go to his shop and pick them up. It's a system that has worked well for several years."

The Death Merchant had the feeling she was telling him a bad joke without a punchline. Imagine, the chief of a U.S. intelligence network, operating in a foreign country, actually going to the apartment of a national of that nation—a citizen who was a member of the spider web and spying against her own government! Unbelievable! Grojean has said that the ONI network was somewhat "slapped together." Perhaps. But this was ridiculous.

That left Arnie Cahill and Rene Beaufault, both of whom had told him that they didn't even know what Melina Arnaoutis looked like.

Or were they dropping in to have tea with Greek members of their network? *Fudge—double!*

The teakettle began to sing. Melina got up, went over to the stove, and shut off the burner.

"I have only decaffeinated, Richard." She looked in his direction. "Is that all right with you?" She turned and started to take cups and saucers from the cabinet.

"Certainly—no cream, no sugar. Make mine strong." The Death Merchant had the feeling that he was sitting on top of a giant time bomb ticking away.

They had moved a metal folding table, placed it in front of the couch, and were sipping their coffee when Melina startled Camellion by saying offhandedly, "Richard, you're welcome to move in here with me. It would save time in our making contact with each other. It's just an idea."

Camellion put his cup on the saucer on the table. When a woman was built like Melina, only a fairy—and not the mythical kind that tapdances on the petunias!—could live in the same apartment with her and not want to play bedroom games.

"Another agent came with me to Greece," Camellion said significantly. "He's back at the hotel. I didn't bring him with me because it wasn't necessary."

"I see," Melina said in a small voice, looking crestfallen. "I didn't know."

"Which doesn't mean I couldn't check out of the Royal Olympic," Camellion said enthusiastically after a moment's hesitation. He pretended to look around the room. "The problem might be room. Do you have enough—room, that is?"

"My bed is large enough for the two of us," Melina said provocatively, brightening up, "unless you don't want to sleep with me. . . ."

The Death Merchant chuckled. "I can assure you, I'd love to sleep with you."

"Then it's all settled," Melina said happily. "Come along, I'll show you how large the bed is." She got to her feet, glanced back at him and smiled, and started toward the bedroom. Camellion was quick to follow to a bedroom that was as spotless as the rest of the apartment.

Melina pointed to the king-size bed neatly made, with not a wrinkle in the blue satin cover. "See for yourself, Richard!" she said in a sultry voice. "Wouldn't you say there's room enough for the two of us?"

As if to prove her point, she lay down on the bed and stretched out on her back. She put her hands underneath her head, her left leg straight, her right leg raised slightly at the knee.

The Death Merchant sat down on her side of the bed, took her in his arms, and kissed her. Melina didn't resist. Her arms encircling his neck, she pressed her mouth tightly against his, her tongue pushing itself between his lips. She moaned as he slipped a hand to her back to unbutton her halter, then removed the garment and for a time lavished kisses on her breasts before moving his hands to her shorts.

"You did that well," she said softly, watching him drop the shorts to the floor, "as though you've had a lot of experience."

"It's all a part of the trade," Camellion said with a straight face. "Manual 16-G-14F-K."

His fingers went to his belt buckle. A few minutes later he was lying beside Melina on the bed, but not before he had surreptitiously looked around the bedroom to make sure no mirror was flush with the wall.

Breathing heavily, Melina pushed her beautiful breasts toward his mouth, her hands at the back of his neck, pulling him down against them. He let his tongue circle the left one first, moving the tip slowly and feeling the young pinkness rising, the hardness of the nipple exciting him. It was only a tiny protrusion dotting the much larger mound of creamy, succulent flesh.

Her desiring quickening, Melina brought her right breast to his eager lips. She began to make sounds of want, of urging, not words that could be understood but plainly expressions of rapidly mounting desire that was increasingly demanding satisfaction. She rolled and pressed her hot body against him, little gasping noises pouring from her throat. Her lips moved down through the hairs of his chest as she broke new frontiers of pleasure . . . kissing, biting, nibbling, then moving on, always downward, to elicit more pleasure from him and to increase her own. Finally, pulling away, she began to gasp more loudly. All the while her hands pulled at him, every cell of her being rising to him, her emotions the result of primordial urges that had not changed in millions of years.

"Do it! Do it! Do it to me!" she pleaded, her long fingers clawing at him.

He held both hands to her breasts and admired the naked beauty of her full-figured body as she twisted with need and thrust up against him. She pulled desperately at him, sobbing, "Now! *NOW!* Please!"

Letting his hand move down over the pulsating

softness of her belly, Camellion found her warm wet-
ness, that source of man's greatest pleasure. She cried
out at his touch, at his probing fingers. The thighs
opened; her body quivered and she reached quickly
for his hardness. Expertly she guided him into her,
giving a great sigh of relief and pleasure when she
was full. Responding, meeting his every thrust, she
began to move her hips in rhythm with his own motions, the desire in both of them increasing in proportion to the speed of their movements. Camellion
pressed his body to hers, and she held him in the vise
of her arms and legs. Her long moans changed to
short gasps that seemed to be in a race with the
tempestuous movements of her hips. Camellion,
feeling Melina growing more wild beneath him,
stayed with her by increasing his own speed. Very
suddenly her body began to jerk violently, choking
sounds pouring out of her throat against the side of
his neck. Her fingers dug deeply into his back, with so
much force that they were painful. Her legs kicked
outward, her feet stabbing air, the intensity of her
climax conveying itself to Camellion, who, seconds
later, felt his own universe explode and the flood-
gates open.

His hands under her shoulders, he held her, their
loins together in a pleasure of giving and of receiving, her breasts and abdomen flattened against him.
He remained with her, their rapture mingling, her
low moans gradually subsiding, a reluctant admission
that the Supreme Moment had come and gone. Melina went limp, gave a final long sigh, and removed
her arms from his back. Her legs sank to the bed and
straightened.

Camellion pulled out of her and rolled over on his
back. Melina turned to face him, her head resting on
her crooked arm.

"Did I satisfy you, honey?" she murmured. Her

nipples were still steel-hard on breasts that continued to rise and fall rapidly.

"Very much so—for now," he said softly.

Melina placed her head against his chest, curled up against him, and reached down to hold that vital part of him. Camellion felt her relax and the tension slowly drain from her body. Eventually her breathing became low and regular, and he knew she was asleep.

Thoughts clicked away in his mind. He would have to phone Notaras and tell him that he wouldn't be returning to the hotel until the next morning. Lying there, Camellion thought about the message he would soon receive from Arzey Holcomb: that the case had arrived from the U.S. Embassy in Athens. Where to stash the case and its precious contents was not really a problem. The safest place would be the secret room in Joe Pappas's warehouse.

Camellion was still pessimistic about Operation Zeus. There were any number of holes in the network and his and Notaras's cover-for-status wasn't all that secure. Another quick thought: *I wonder if Melina has a Bible, a revised King James's version? If not, I can always buy one.* . . .

Chapter Six

I

Joseph Pappas, driving his four-door Subaru, arrived at the Royal Olympic at eleven-thirty. He explained to Camellion, who was packing two suitcases, that he was the impatient type and usually arrived early for an appointment.

Pappas looked at the suitcases on one of the beds. "I gather you gentlemen are changing hotels," he said, his tone cautious yet curious.

"I met a girl friend," Camellion said. "I'm moving in with her."

He turned to Pappas, put a finger to his lips, and shook his head, silently telling him not to ask questions. "I'll take the suitcases with me and put them in your car. Later on you can drive me to her place."

After the three of them had left the hotel and were in Pappas's car, Camellion explained that Melina Arnaoutis was the courier who would arrange to have messages carried back and forth between "me and Arzey Holcomb, the ONI chief of the American network. My moving in with Melina will save a good deal of time."

Pappas, who was driving, grinned obscenely. "And

if she warms your bed, so much the better, eh, American? Our women love sex—often and with passion."

The Death Merchant chuckled. "When we came from the airport the cab driver told us that eighty-two percent of the women in Athens have no interest in sex—due to the air pollution."

Pappas gave a loud snort. "Those damned taxi drivers! Each one thinks he is a Plato and has a font of wisdom. That's the trouble with Greece. Everyone has 'facts' that aren't true. Fifty percent of the work done in this country is done by people who think they know everything and run in all directions!"

"And the other fifty percent?"

"By people who never feel well."

Camellion glanced in the rearview mirror and saw that Nicholas Notaras was putting another chlorpheniramine maleate tablet in his mouth—*If that is what the tablet really is!* Camellion didn't believe it was. Chlorpheniramine was an antihistamine used to reduce the intensity of allergic and anaphylactic reactions. What kind of allergy demanded twelve to fifteen antihistamine tablets a day, tablets of 20 milligrams each? None that the Death Merchant knew of. At the same time, Camellion knew a little knowledge could be a dangerous thing. He wasn't a doctor.

Camellion could see from Notaras's expression that he was not feeling well. The man was miserable. Camellion swung around in the seat.

"Listen, Nick! Why don't we take you back to the hotel?" he suggested. "Why torture yourself by coming with us?"

"Thanks. But it's better that I go along in case someone is watching our movements," Notaras said, sounding tired. "Both of us are supposed to be buyers for Triangle. We should both go with Joe."

Pappas asked, "Camellion, do you want to have

lunch first or have me take you to Melina's apartment?"

The Death Merchant told him about Arnold Cahill. "I told Cahill to be at your place at four this afternoon," Camellion said. "I know that won't give us much time to shop for merchandise, but we can pick up tomorrow where we leave off today. The microdot machine and the shortwave radio are far more important. I'll drive back with Cahill and he can drop me off at Melina's apartment."

"Okay. We eat first. There's a place close to here that serves excellent seafood. Now, about the goods you want to buy . . ."

Camellion told Pappas that all he had to do was pretend that he was buying merchandise to sell to Triangle Importing in New York. "The fact is, Joe, you won't have to do much pretending. Tack your usual profit onto the purchase price. Everything you buy you will ship to Triangle in the usual manner. Look at it as a normal shipment, with all the attendant paperwork."

"How much do you want me to spend?" asked Pappas.

"We have a letter of credit for fifteen thousand dollars," Camellion said. "Another thing, we'll go along with whatever you buy. But for the looks of it, try to get everything as cheaply as possible."

Pappas roared with laughter. He finally calmed down and told Camellion and Notaras what had sent him into gales of laughter.

"It certainly is obvious you two don't know this business," he said, still giggling. "If I didn't argue with the people who make the junk, you'd need fifty thousand dollars! I couldn't afford to look gullible even if I wanted to. I export to dozens of companies overseas and have to get the best bargains possible."

"The better the bargains on your end, the more your profit, right?" Camellion said.

"Up to a point, yes."

Lunch was excellent, except for Notaras, who barely touched his food, but drank four glasses of *kokineli* wine—rosé. They had slices of *synagrida*—sea bass—cooked in wine and onion sauce, noodles, and green salad. For dessert slices of *karpóuzi*—watermelon. By one-thirty they were on the road again, headed toward the Old City where most of the handicrafters and craftsmen had their shops.

Camellion and Notaras had expected a lot of haggling between Joe Pappas and his fellow Greek artisans. What they witnessed in the next hour and a half was a verbal knockdown and dragout, with the craftsmen shouting and screaming at Pappas (and waving their arms) and Joe screaming and shouting back (and waving his arms). When it was all over and the three of them were in the Subaru, with Pappas driving toward his place of business, he had ordered $3,214.75 worth of merchandise—"authentic Ionian jewelry," vases of all sizes, colors, and descriptions, brass elfin horses, and reproductions of pottery "of the kind found at Troy."

It was when Pappas was turning onto Venizelos Street that he said, "Gentlemen, I have been curious about something. Why do we have to bother with trying to rescue Professor Paspyrou? Why doesn't the American government just leak the information to Premier Papandreou and his cabinet that the KGB, with the help of General Cyatorus, has kidnapped Paspyrou and has him somewhere on an island? Your U.S. Ambassador to Greece could tell Papandreou that the KGB is forcing Paspyrou to help them with weather control experiments. Papandreou would act immediately.

"You don't have to think too hard to know the answer," the Death Merchant said curtly. "It's not just stopping the KGB."

"It's also more than rescuing Paspyrou," Pappas said evenly. "If the Americans told Papandreou, then the KGB might destroy all the notes and kill the professor. Even worse, Papandreou and his crowd might learn the secret of weather control. Is that not so?"

"It is. We Americans want the secret," the Death Merchant bluntly admitted as he looked at his watch —3:41.

II

As soon as Pappas turned the car and started up the drive, the Death Merchant saw that Arnie Cahill's powder-blue Honda Civic was parked to the right of Anna Sofoulis's Mazda RX-7. The SIS agent was not in the car.

"He's inside where it's cool," Notaras said. He had seemed to recover his spirits after lunch and was in a better mood.

After parking and hurrying inside, they found Arnie Cahill relaxed on a bench outside the wooden railing that enclosed the desks and the files. He was wearing a Toongabble toweling hat, a red short-sleeve sport shirt, gray chino pants, and leather sandals.

Camellion introduced Pappas and Notaras to Cahill, who then glanced suspiciously at Anna Sofoulis, who was drinking iced tea and working at her desk.

"She's one of us, Englishman," Pappas said, and reached for his cigarettes. "You could trust her with your life. I trust her with mine."

"Arnie, you did bring the equipment?" Camellion asked.

"Four suitcases in the boot of the automobile. All we have to do is bring them inside."

Camellion swung to Pappas. "Is it safe in the daylight? Could anyone be loafing around in the orange grove?"

Pappas's thick black eyebrows went up slightly. "It's not likely, but let's not take any chances." He turned and called out to Anna. "Anna, go get your father."

Anna got up from the desk and disappeared into the rear. Soon she had returned, her barrel-chested, grim-faced father lumbering behind her. He pushed open the gate in the railing and walked over to the group.

"Gregory, go outside and check the orange grove," Pappas said. "We have some important equipment to bring in and we want to make sure no one sees us."

Gregory nodded and started toward the door.

"We can all go out and have a look," Camellion said. He started after Gregory Sofoulis.

Arnie Cahill said as they walked down the steps, "I knew that you and Nick would want some arms, being Americans and all."

"I was going to ask you today," Camellion said.

"A couple of German nine-millimeter Steyrs in shoulder holsters and spare magazines. Naturally, in this abominable heat—"

"I know. We can't conceal large-frame autos without coats, and wearing coats in this heat would make us look conspicuous."

"I also brought a couple of small American pistols with ankle holsters," Cahill said in a self-satisfied tone, implying that he had solved the heat problem for Camellion. "Forty-fives. The pistols are called Detonics. Odd name, that. I have them and the German weapons in a brief bag—an attaché case. It will look very businesslike when you carry it and no one will be suspicious."

It didn't take much time to check the orange grove. It took even less time for the group to transfer Camellion's two suitcases to Cahill's car and to carry the four suitcases and the attaché case into the building.

Pappas led them to the rear, and they passed through the same rooms that Camellion and Notaras had seen previously. Once more Joe moved the ladder to the chandelier and went through the procedure of opening the carton-disguised trapdoor.

"The radio," Pappas said, replacing the ladder by the wall. "It will require an antenna."

"All transceivers do, even such sophisticated sets as a Motorola SATCOM AN/URC," Camellion said. "We can't use any radio from below without an antenna. I don't suppose there is any way we can string a long wire from the room below, up through the floor, and onto the roof?"

Pappas shook his head. "Impossible. We could, but to do so we would have to drill a hole in the floor and in the ceiling. I'll not compromise the security of the room below."

Cahill said in the tone of one imparting a revelation, "If I could get a word in edgewise, I'd like to tell you that the transceiver doesn't require a conventional antenna. It's a SATCOM AN/URC with a parabolic dish antenna. As I understand the operation of the set, one has to use it on the outside, or at least in a position where the dish is accessible to the outside."

"In that case the problem is solved," Camellion said quickly. "Joe, this is a large house. Do you have a flat section of roof? All I saw were slants from the front—and would it be safe to use the radio on the roof?"

"How would an attic with a small skylight do? The skylight opens," Pappas said. "Why wouldn't it be safe? We are a good distance from the road. It is dark here and no one is around. Here there is only myself and Gregory and Anna." When he saw Camellion's subtle expression of surprise, he added, "Gregory and his daughter have an apartment on the second floor. My own place is to the rear of this floor. Well, let's get the equipment below."

As they carefully went down the stairs, Pappas gave them a short history of the place. The mansion had originally been owned by a wealthy family and had been requisitioned by the Germans during World War II. A German colonel, his mistress, and part of his staff were killed by partisans who discovered an escape tunnel that the original owner had built.

The Greek family who had lived in the mansion had died in a concentration camp, and the house had passed through various owners before Pappas had acquired it.

"I got it cheap because of its size and rundown condition," Pappas said, closing the trapdoor by pulling on the curved hook on the wall. "No one wants a house this large. To put it in first-class condition would cost millions of drachmae. Camellion, place the suitcases on the table if you want."

Camellion nodded. "I'll check the radio to make sure all of its components are there and that the batteries are strong."

With the others watching him, he opened the suitcases and first checked the SATCOM AN/URC. He turned on the transceiver and saw that the battery strength meter shot all the way to the right, to FULL.

He then removed the various parts of the microdot device and assembled it on the table. In response to Joe Pappas's question of "How does it work?" he explained that it was nothing more than a device that photographed a sheet of paper, reduced it to a "period," and automatically devolved the film-"dot." The second part of the apparatus did just the opposite; it enlarged the microdot and projected it onto a screen or a light-color wall.

Camellion held up a small, flat case containing numerous kinds of tweezers. "The delicate part is placing the 'dot' over a period, the round point of a semicolon, whatever. It requires patience. The 'dot' is special and self-sealing. There's no chance that it will fall off."

"How do you know where to look for the dot?" asked Pappas. Then, turning to Cahill and Notaras, he asked, "Would you gentlemen like a drink? I have beer and liquor."

Notaras shook his head. Cahill choose brandy— ". . . if you have it." He continued to study the microdot machine while Notaras seemed to be fascinated by the "black boxes" of the SATCOM transceiver.

"All the messages from Holcomb to me will have the microdot in the period at the end of the first sentence," Camellion lied, figuring it was none of Pappas's business. "Nothing to drink for me."

It was a few minutes after Pappas had gone to the refrigerator and had brought a can of beer, two glasses, and a bottle of brandy to the table that Arnie Cahill turned to Camellion. "Have you told Mr. Pappas of the dangle operation?"

From the hard look Camellion gave him, Cahill realized instantly that he had asked the wrong question.

"A 'dangle operation'?" echoed Pappas. "What is that?"

"We're blackmailing a certain person in an effort to

force her to give us the location of where Professor Paspyrou is being held."

To prevent the nosy Greek from asking for details, the Death Merchant asked, "Joe, you passed along the information to your people. How did they respond?"

"The Delphi Circle is willing to help, but they don't know what they can do." Pappas's voice carried an unmistakable note of disappointment. "What we need are a hundred commandos, plus the equipment."

An expression of deep concern dropped over Cahill's slightly rubicund face. "It is my understanding that you control numerous enforcement people in the Delphi Circle," he said to Pappas.

Pappas finished taking a long slug of the brandy, then shrugged.

"Now, listen, Englishman," he said stubbornly, "you are not going to talk me into doing anything foolish. First of all, I control only one agent. He controls twenty people. I control them through him. What does it matter? We don't have boats, and we can't attack the KGB and the KYP with only machine pistols, or what the Americans refer to as submachine guns."

"Joe's right," Camellion said, his firmness and manner conveying adamantine determination. "It would be suicide to attack the island with only members of the Delphi Circle, sheer suicide."

"If we find the island," Notaras said with a sigh as he placed another chlorpheniramine tablet on his tongue.

"We have to proceed on the basis that the subject of our dangle operation will give us the necessary information," Camellion intoned. "For the moment that's all we can do."

III

There was one trait that the Death Merchant admired in Arnold Cahill: the man could drive a car as if he were a part of it. He could cut corners like a good "get-man" and zip in and out of traffic with split-second timing. Rare was the Greek who could tailgate him. As for Cahill's expertise in the craft of the business, Camellion was quick to admit that snap judgment more often than not was faulty judgment.

Cahill was saying, "Have you ever stopped to think that everything we have heard about the magnifying transmitter is the product of Soviet *disinfomatsiya,* geared to make your nation and mine and the French look like halfwits?"

"I doubt it." Camellion didn't feel disposed to quibble about probables. "The powers that be have irrefutable proof."

"It does seem—" Cahill turned the wheel, shot the Honda Civic around three other cars, and zipped back in line to avoid another vehicle in the opposite lane with only seconds to spare, or so it seemed.

"It does seem paradoxical that the Russians should engage in such a delicate experiment outside of the Soviet Union. I find it impossible to conceive of them taking such a risk. Should the Soviets actually be on some island, then surely the effort was deemed worth the danger involved."

"The answer to why they chose a Greek island might be modern electronic technology," Camellion said pointedly. "The Soviets are aware that their 1978 and 1981 experiments were traced to Riga, Latvia. Ask yourself, how could the American government possibly accuse the Soviet Union of conducting illegal weather experiments if the source of the electromagnetic energy was traced to some Greek island?"

Cahill glanced worriedly at Camellion. From the very first, Cahill had realized that the Death Merchant was exceptionally facile at shifting from one cognitive process to another and at transferring one mode of mental representation to another. Some men were like that. Camellion could shift with ease from the abstract to the concrete. Perhaps that's why Camellion is the agent in charge, thought Cahill. He looked to the left at a street sign. "I can barely read these signs. Are you sure we're on the correct route to Miss Arnaoutis's apartment?"

"I'm positive," said Camellion. "In another four blocks we'll be on Karamikou Street."

The light changed to green, and Cahill shot the car forward.

"Regarding contact between us in the next two or three days," he said. "Should Rene or I come to her apartment? I suggest we don't."

"You're right. She doesn't know that you and Rene exist. Let's keep it that way," Camellion said, one of his feet brushing the attaché case containing the two 9-mm Steyr autopistols and one of the Detonics autoloaders. The other compact Detonics was in a holster on Camellion's left leg. Nick Notaras had declined to carry one of the Detonics; his refusal wasn't a surprise to the Death Merchant.

Camellion said, "I'll give you her phone number. Should you have to phone, refer to yourself as Vito. When you see Rene, tell him he will be Nashtos."

"In theory, it will be another five or six days before we know if Petros Makarezos will give us the information," said Cahill. "I don't suppose you would want that information—whether it's a success or failure—conveyed by telephone?"

"Absolutely not," Camellion said scathingly.

"Arzey Holcomb will give me that information via microdot."

"There should be something we could do to further the mission," Cahill said. "Perhaps if you contacted your people . . ."

The Death Merchant was cold and remote. "I'll contact the home office only if and when it becomes necessary. Let's just say I'm supercautious—and you and Rene had better be. The KGB is very good. Keep in mind that cooperation is a frame of mind—like nations—and doesn't necessarily mean a course of action."

"What about my phoning the apartment?" inquired Nicholas Notaras. "She knows about me; you told her."

"Sure, you can phone, although it won't be necessary," Camellion said. "Tomorrow we'll rent a car. We'll drive out to Joe Pappas's place, then do more shopping for Triangle in his car. I'll pick you up at the hotel at ten."

"Cooperation is a frame of mind, like a country," said Cahill. "I fail to see the logic of your linking the two."

"All nations are countries of the mind," Camellion said. "There are a lot of things that give an individual his identity. Geography is one of them. You 'think' British because of British manners and customs and history. But you 'feel' British because you live in Great Britain, a nation that occupies a specific place on the map."

"I have never thought about it in that manner," Cahill said in a hollow voice.

There's a lot of things you haven't thought about, my British friend.

"Anytime now," said Camellion. "We're almost to Karamikou Street."

Chapter Seven

Life is many things. Part of it is approaching any given problem. Any problem, depending on its complexity, can be approached from many angles. Its solution can be reached in countless ways.

Camellion and Grojean and the chief of ONI had solved the problem of letting the Death Merchant know which message from Arzey Holcomb might contain a microdot. Not all of them would. Some of the messages would contain information that would not refer directly to Operation Zeus.

They solved the problem by using both a code, composed of letters, and a cypher, which is always composed of numbers. Should Melina Arnaoutis bring a message with numbers, these numbers would refer to chapter and verse and specific words in the Bible. Such a message would not contain a microdot. However, should the message contain only letters, then Camellion would know that the last period contained a microdot filled with ultrasensitive information.

It was on the third day that they had been living together that Melina came home with a message from Holcomb, the ONI's top agent in Athens. The Death Merchant had gotten in only thirty minutes ahead of her and, having taken a shower, was still in his robe.

"I'm going to take a shower," Melina said. She handed him the matchbox, then put her arms around his neck and kissed him on the mouth, her tongue twisting with his. "Would you like to go out for dinner or have me fix something here—and would you like a quickie after I shower?"

"Let's go out for dinner." Camellion paused, then added tenderly, "As for the 'quickie,' a wise man does not sample the food at a banquet. He slowly eats and savors each course."

Pleased with herself, Melina turned and headed toward the bathroom.

The Death Merchant sat down on the couch, removed all the matches from the matchbox, and pulled out the tiny slip of paper from the bottom of the inside container. The message was in cypher. Camellion went to the bookcase and from the second shelf pulled a Bible he had bought that afternoon. It took him only ten minutes to decode the message by looking at each number and thumbing through the Bible, memorizing each word as he came to it. If he had written each word on paper, the message from Arzey Holcomb would have read:

Special case arrived. Have transferred it to Sinbad. R-C: Two dead men on a hangman's tree. Reply: Without any branches. Red Apple.

The *special case* was the Death Merchant's makeup laboratory. *Sinbad* was the code word for the safe house at 8427 Stazoukis Avenue. *R-C* meant recognition code. *Red Apple* was Holcomb's code name.

Camellion refilled the matchbox, put the Bible back on the shelf, hurried into the kitchen, and stood over the sink. There he struck a match and put the flame to the small slip of paper. After it ignited, he dropped it in the sink and watched it burn until it was only a brown-black crumple. He washed the ash down the drain, then went into the bedroom, remaining in his robe, only loosening the belt. He didn't want to be completely undressed until Melina had dried herself off and was in the bedroom. Melina was a gal who enjoyed sex in a shower. Camellion didn't. He couldn't enjoy a woman with water pouring down on his head. The only other thing that he didn't like about Melina was that she never shaved under her arms. Greek women never did.

Camellion began to remove his robe when Melina came out of the bathroom, naked except for a nylon bathing cap and pink fluffy slipons.

"Was the message important, Richard?" she asked, and sat down at the dressing table. "Or shouldn't I have asked?"

"It was not very important and you shouldn't have asked."

On the fourth day after Camellion and Notaras had arrived in Athens, the Death Merchant and Melina were awakened by the telephone ringing at 5:30 A.M. Notaras was phoning from the Royal Olympic. In a sad voice he explained that he had just received a telegram from his sister in the U.S. His father in New York had suffered a massive stroke and was not expected to live. He should come home at once.

"I've already called the airport," Notaras said. "A Pan Am flight leaves for Paris at eleven-thirty this morning. I was able to get a reservation. From Paris, it will go to London, then on to the States."

"I understand," Camellion said. "You must go."

"I don't suppose I'll be seeing you before I leave,"

Notaras said. "I'm sorry that I must ask you to complete the buying for Triangle."

"Don't be. It's not that much of a problem," replied Camellion. "Half the merchandise has already been contracted for. I'm certain Mr. Pappas and I can do the rest in a week or so. As you know, tomorrow—well, today—we're going to Dháfni to look over reproductions of Greek swords and spears. On Friday Mr. Pappas and I will go to Petroúpolis to inspect those dishes he told us about yesterday. Anyhow, have a good flight, if such is possible under the circumstances. And I'm sorry to hear about your father."

"Thank you, Richard. I'll see you in New York when you get back. Good-bye."

"Good-bye—and God bless."

Camellion hung up the phone. He didn't believe one word that Notaras had said, especially about his father's being ill and about to Go West. None of it rang true.

The electrochemical circuits of his brain clicked. Grojean had not given him much information about Notaras. He had only said that the man was a physicist and would be able to evaluate Professor Paspyrou's notes. The Fox had not discussed the man's family. So! How could Notaras's sister—*If he has a sister!*—know that her brother was in Greece? *How could she know he was staying at the Royal Olympic? ONI and the CIA wouldn't have told her.*

Some of the best executives of the largest corporations in the United States were a success because they responded to gut instinct. The Death Merchant was the best "international contractor" for the same reason. That's what he did now: He followed his intuition. He didn't have a shred of evidence, yet every instinct told him that the telegram to Notaras had been sent by Courtland Maddock Grojean.

Why?

I'm being used and I don't like it. . . .

Chapter Eight

The swords, shields, and spears used by the Spartans in their heroic defense against the Persians in the battle of Thermopylae!

Camellion and Joe Pappas ordered fifty of each for Triangle Importing and Exporting, which would sell the items to people who loved to decorate their walls with ancient weapons of battle.

However, they did not drive to Petroúpolis on Friday. On Thursday, Pappas made three telephone calls to the craftsmen who made the replicas of ancient Greek tableware and learned that the wholesale purchase price was too high.

"It would be a poor buy," Pappas told Camellion. "To make a profit, Triangle would have to charge three hundred of your American dollars per set. That is entirely too much money. Believe me, my friend, Triangle would not want the dishes."

Having nothing better to do on Friday, the Death Merchant drove to Pappas's place of business in a rented FIAT Uno and spent the rest of the morning and most of the afternoon checking Triangle's orders and fine-tune inspecting the microdot machine and the SATCOM transceiver.

Camellion left the Pappas Importing and Exporting Company in the late afternoon, toying with the idea of calling Arnie Cahill. The two of them could then drive to the safe house on Stazoukis Avenue. *Okay, I'll phone from the booth in front of Melina's apartment house.*

He had only one stop to make before returning home, a health food store six blocks from Melina's apartment. Camellion had exhausted his supply of vitamin B6 capsules. Vitamin B6 was essential in removing homocysteine from the blood. Diets known to cause atherosclerosis, or "hardening of the arteries," were usually high in cholesterol and methionine. And methionine produced homocysteine. Vitamin B6 helped destroy homocysteine and prevent fatty deposits from building up in vessels and arteries.

It was 4:23 P.M. when Camellion parked the FIAT in front of a television and radio retail store, the next business west of the health food store. There were three other cars ahead of the FIAT and several others to the rear.

With an easy stride, one that concealed his caution, the Death Merchant walked into the health food store, almost certain that the clerks would speak English, at least enough to understand what he wanted. Most clerks in Athens spoke English, some very badly, but they could still make themselves understood.

The clerk, a young and dumpy woman with beautiful black hair, spoke very good English and was eager to help Camellion, who bought two bottles of 50-milligram B6 tables and a bottle of 250-milligram choline capsules, which helped destroy fat in the liver.

He left the store and started to walk west toward the FIAT Uno, sixty feet away. He was in front of the TV and radio store when he detected what appeared to be several inches of a sonics suppressor protruding from the bottom of the front window on the right side of a Nissan 200. The Nissan had parked two cars behind the FIAT while Camellion had been in the health food store.

The average man might not have noticed the few inches of the rounded silencer, or if he had, he might have hesitated, taking time to wonder what the object was. The Death Merchant knew instantly that he was staring not only at the black muzzle of a silencer, but that someone was about to try to quietly put a bullet into him. Whoever it was almost did. The silencer went *phyyyt phyyyt* at the same instant that Camellion jerked himself to his right, directing his body to the space between the front of the Datsun and the rear of the Audi, which were parked in front of his car.

Ivan Berzin, a KGB *Boyevaya Gruppa* kill-expert, had pulled the trigger of the silenced Czech CZ75 pistol twice. The first 9-mm flat-point bullet tore into the space between the Death Merchant's left rib cage and his inner left arm. The second slug passed half an inch from the outside of his left biceps. Both shots continued going east down the street, miraculously not hitting anyone else on the sidewalk. One bullet broke the glass of a telephone booth, changed course, and was stopped by the rear wall. The second slug buried itself in the aluminum frame of the booth.

An unhappy Richard Camellion, crouched down in the three-foot space between the Datsun and the Audi, jerked up his left pant leg and pulled the .45 Detonics from the ankle holster. He had gotten only an instant's look at the car containing the would-be assassin, but he had seen enough to know there were two men in the front seat and a woman in the rear. He also reasoned correctly that the three would have backups, in another car either behind or in front of the FIAT. He couldn't be positive, but he was fairly certain that the Datsun and the Audi were empty. That left the Camaro sport coupe, the third vehicle in front of the FIAT.

Well, fudge! Camellion might as well have been trapped at the end of a blind alley. He couldn't flee north into traffic without the enemy, in either the Nissan or the Camaro, whacking him out. He couldn't race across the sidewalk and into the television and radio shop for the same reason. And they could close in on him from both sides.

I'm fresh out of miracles. Now I'll have to do some hard thinking. . . .

Ivan Berzin, the Russian with the suppressed CZ75 pistol, and Matvey Avalov, the driver of the Nissan, were angry at having missed the target—and surprised. Easing out of the car, they began to creep east toward the Death Merchant, Berzin on the sidewalk close to the curb, Avalov on the pavement, a 9-mm Hungarian FEG pistol in his right hand.

In the backseat of the Nissan, Nadra Gulikov—a not unattractive brunette of thirty-one—waited, holding her hands low in front of her so that no one would see the Samopal-62 Skorpion submachine gun in her hands. She began to think that it didn't make much difference who saw the SMG. People passing on the sidewalk had already seen Berzin on the sidewalk, the CZ75, with its long silencer in his hand. They weren't lingering to see what was about to happen. Some were actually running away while others were darting into the cover of storefronts. Gulikov was uncomfortable. Berzin had never missed—until now!

In the meanwhile, Genrikh Golmenka, the driver of the Camaro sport coupe, and Leonid Shorzenko, the other man in it, had gotten out. Armed with a Beretta 92 SB pistol, Shorzenko moved west on the

sidewalk. Golmenka moved west on the road, a
Heckler and Koch auto in his right hand.

Avalov nodded at Berzin and the two rushed forward and closed in, ready to fire at Camellion, whom
they had seen duck between the Datsun and the
Audi. With their weapons pointed downward, both
KGB hit men felt like fools when they saw that the
space was empty.

They stood there stunned. The target hadn't
moved into traffic and he hadn't run south across the
sidewalk. Either way, they would have seen him.
There was only one answer: He had either crawled
under the Audi and was slithering forward or else he
was belly-wriggling west underneath the Datsun.

Their realization came seconds too late. Knowing
he had only seconds to live if he made a mistake, the
Death Merchant crawled the rest of the way from
beneath the Datsun, turned to his right, and fired.
The compact Detonics autopistol roared, the .45 FP
bullet smashed Ivan Berzin between the shoulder
blades and drove him to the sidewalk.

*You slow-witted dummies! You must be from Ari-
zona!*

Camellion spun to the left, ducked, and fired almost during the same split second that Matvey
Avalov's FEG pistol cracked, the explosion of its
9-mm cartridge mingling with the echo of Camellion's shot. Avalov's bullet missed the left side of
Camellion's head by an inch and stabbed into the
windshield of the FIAT, creating an instant hole
around which was a spider web of cracks. The Death
Merchant did not miss. His .45 projectile popped
Avalov high in the right side of his chest, brought an
"UHHHH!" from his half-open mouth, half spun him
around, and dropped him to the pavement.

Golmenka and Shorzenko, realizing the target had
tricked the hit squad, darted to the front of the Audi

and got down. In their opinion the termination had
failed. But they were not in charge. Captain Nadra
Gulikov was. There was never a plan for failure, so
Golmenka and Shorzenko kept down, trying to decide what to do. Common sense told them to flee
before the *Asfaleia,* the regular Greek police, arrived. Their training was far greater than their logic.
They waited. They knew they were damned if they
didn't and damned if they did!

If Golmenka had leaned out around the Audi and
taken a look ten seconds after he had ducked behind
it, he would have been able to kill the Death Merchant by putting a bullet in his back.

Camellion had taken the chance because he had
to, because he knew he had to move or die. Staying so
low that he was almost on his knees, he ran on the
pavement past the FIAT and the next two cars and
was soon moving along the left side of the Nissan 200
SX Turbo.

He was not entirely successful. There was a limit to
how low he could keep his body and still be able to
run. Nadra Gulikov spotted the top of his head. She
tried to swing the Skorpion to her left, but Camellion
disappeared too quickly.

Gulikov was at a complete disadvantage. She was
used to instant success. One pulled the trigger, the
target fell, the squad drove off. Not this time. It had
been total failure. Not only had the squad missed the
target, but he had actually killed two of the expert
Boyevaya Gruppa and now he was coming after *her!*
And where were Golmenka and Shorzenko?

Almost in a panic, Gulikov knew that Camellion
would have to fire through the rear window or else
come around to the sidewalk side and toss a slug
through the right rear window. She was twisting
around to look at the rear window when Camellion

fired from outside the window—twice, to make sure he would get her through the safety glass. He did.

The first bullet hit the woman just below her right eye. It bored through the zygomatic (or cheek) bone, zipped through her nasopharynx, and went out the back of her head. The second .45 slug smashed her in the right side of the neck and ripped apart the carotid arteries. Both pieces of metal made her head jerk back and forth before blood began spurting from her neck and pouring from her mouth. Her eyes rolled back in her head and she fell forward and slumped in the seat.

The Death Merchant had only three cartridges left and realized that if the last two Russians—*Or could they be KYP?*—had any sense, they would be able to turn him into a corpse. He had gotten a brief glimpse of Nadra Gulikov's Samopal Skorpion, and intended to get it. Accordingly, he looked around the right rear side of the Nissan. Nothing. The last two triggermen were still down behind the front of the Audi.

Risk it! You have to! Camellion darted forward and jerked open the right rear door of the Nissan. Nadra Gulikov's corpse had slumped in such a manner that her bloody head was hanging between her knees, her right arm twisted and still on the side of the seat with the Skorpion.

The Death Merchant pulled the deadly little SMG from Gulikov's hand and pulled back. He was just in time to see Leonid Shorzenko look around the right front end of the Audi. Camellion didn't have time to raise the Skorpion. All he could do was throw himself to the sidewalk at the same instant that the beefy-looking Shorzenko fired a round from his Beretta. The 9-mm projectile passed a foot over Camellion's head and back.

Shorzenko should have pulled back. Instead, convinced he had Camellion trapped, he jumped up and began to swing the Beretta down for another shot. It was the last and the only fatal mistake of his life. The Death Merchant's stream of 7.65-mm Skorpion slugs rained all over his parade and knocked him back against the rear of the Camaro, the buzzing metal butchering his stomach, spleen, and liver and cutting apart his spine.

In an instant, Camellion was on his feet and racing to the left rear side of the Nissan, all set to blow up Genrikh Golmenka. He need not have bothered. Golmenka's parents hadn't raised a complete idiot. Seeing Shorzenko chopped apart, Golmenka left his position by the left front of the Audi, ran back to the Camaro sport coupe, and started the engine. By the time Camellion looked around the left front rear of the Nissan, Golmenka was spinning back rubber and heading the Camaro out into traffic.

The Death Merchant raised the Skorpion pistol-style and pulled the trigger. The remaining ten 7.65-mm projectiles tore through the car's rear windshield. Three of them hit Golmenka in the back of the head and scrambled his brain. Stone dead, Golmenka slumped over the wheel. His left foot pressed down on the gas pedal and the Camaro shot forward into traffic.

Camellion ran forward and looked inside the Nissan. The key was in the ignition. He ran to the other side, slammed the right rear door, opened the right front door, got in, and prepared to drive off. He had chosen the Nissan because it would be easier to pull away in than the FIAT. He would save several minutes by not having to back out of a tight space.

The Camaro shot northeast across the pavement like some animal racing in for the kill. To avoid ramming into the left side of the Camaro, a motorist, moving north, slammed on his brakes with such force that his Korisa half spun around. Still moving at 50 mph, the Camaro shot diagonally into the westbound lane of traffic. Once more there was the screeching of rubber on concrete as two drivers, coming from the east, slammed on their brakes to keep from hitting the Camaro's right side. There were four loud crashes in rapid succession when two vehicles rammed into the rear ends of the first two cars, and several more automobiles then slammed into the rear of them.

The Death Merchant pulled the Nissan out into traffic and drove east, the odor of blood thick in the car, a sweetish odor with which he was very familiar.

I've been made! But the Death Merchant wasn't happy about it. Certain intelligence services always operate in a specific manner, and he had tangled with the Soviet KGB enough to know when he had been the target of pig-farmer hit men. The ambush had KGB fingerprints all over it. How had they made him? How had the KGB known that he was in Athens working on Operation Zeus? Whether or not they knew the name of the operation, apparently they knew he was trying to prevent their experimenting with Tesla's magnifying transmitter, and if they knew that: *They know I'm looking for Professor Paspyrou.* Did the KGB know about Pappas . . . Holcomb, Cahill, and Beaufault? He had to assume that they did. Then again, maybe not. It depended on how the KGB had learned about him and/or the identity of the traitor. Joe Pappas? Perhaps. Camellion didn't think so. More likely candidates would be Arnie Cahill or Rene Beaufault. *But I don't think they are. That leaves Melina, who knows only about me and Holcomb. Could she be the traitor?* She very well could be, but Camellion desperately hoped that she wasn't—and not just because she was good in bed. He genuinely liked her.

First problems first. He couldn't continue to drive the Nissan, not only because of the bloody corpse in the rear but because he had to assume some witness had taken down the car's license number. The time was four-fifty, and he was only a long spit away from Melina's apartment. She would be home by five-thirty at the latest. He could use her small Vislos two-seater to drive someplace and from there go by taxi to the vicinity of the safe house on Stazoukis Avenue —if he used it. There was another safe house—a CIA security house that hadn't been deactivated when the CIA network had fallen apart. Even Arzey Holcomb didn't know about that one. The Death Merchant didn't know the address. He just had the phone number and the code recognition phrases.

Where to leave the car? How to get to Melina's apartment?

Park and walk, you damn fool! How else? And you have to warn the others, but you can't use the phone in her apartment.

There was also the small matter of his light-blue slacks and sport shirt looking as if he'd crawled through oil and grease, which he had, wriggling underneath the Datsun.

After he parked a block from Melina's apartment, he checked the back of the car. The dead woman's corpse had slumped between the seats. Good. No one would see the body unless he walked over to the vehicle and looked inside. With its rear window shattered, the Nissan would quickly attract the attention of the police. Camellion wasn't concerned. By then he would be in another part of Athens.

He left the car, locked it, and started walking casually toward Melina's apartment, ignoring the curious stares of people he passed, people who were wondering how he had gotten oil over the front of his pants and shirt. He received several more stares when he reached the apartment house and climbed the stairs. The only worry he didn't have was that the *Asfaleia* would trace the rented FIAT to him. He had used forged identification, including a false name and a phony address—and international driver's license to match. He had brought all of it to Greece with him, concealed in a small leather portfolio in one of his bags.

He let himself into Melina's apartment, then went straight to the bedroom and got out of his oily clothes. In the bathroom, he didn't bother to take a shower; he washed his face, arms, and hands, then returned to the bedroom and put on an off-white broadcloth shirt and a seersucker suit that had olive-khaki stripes on a khaki ground.

Camellion didn't care for hats, but witnesses would report to the police that the "gunman" who had escaped had not been wearing one. To go with the suit, he chose a light-brown Panama straw hat with a dark-brown band. He also took an attaché case from the closet. He moved the combination rings on both sides to 9669, opened the case, and soon was wearing a leather shoulder holster filled with an eighteen-shot 9-mm Steyr GB D.A. autopistol. He put two extra clips for the German-made autoloader into a coat pocket and shoved a fresh magazine into the .45 Detonics on his ankle. Then he closed the attaché case, picked up the Panama hat from the bed, walked into the living room, sat down, and waited.

It was five forty-one when Melina came through the door, saw him sitting on the couch, and smiled. Walking over to him, she frowned when she saw the attaché case and the hat next to him on the couch.

"You're going out, Richard? We're not going to have dinner together?" She sat down next to him, an expectant expression on her face, and opened her handbag from which she took a pocket matchbox.

"This was delivered to me this afternoon. The courier whispered that I should give it to you."

"To me!" The Death Merchant raised his head and his eyes glittered. "He mentioned me by name?" He stared at her.

"Oh, no, not by name." Melina handed him the matchbox. "He said that I should give it to Andromeda. I assumed you or Holcomb was Andromeda, or would know who was. Do you?"

"Yes, I'll see that Andromeda gets it," Camellion said, beginning to remove the wooden matches from the box. Indeed he did know the identity of "Andromeda." It was his own code name, known only to Grojean, the head of ONI, several high officials in British SIS, and Arzey Holcomb.

She watched him pull the tiny piece of folded paper from the bottom of the inside section of the matchbox. "Richard, is something the matter? Did something happen today?"

The less she knows, the less she can tell! He had another reason for not telling her about the ambush. And he certainly hoped he was wrong. . . .

"Something did happen this morning, but it will work out," he said, opening the small square of paper. "I'll explain it after I get back."

He looked at the paper. DWSDGH FBB-KLOAA. Y. FDW-KPO. BLENCI. *Code!* The last period had to be a microdot.

"Listen carefully, Melina." He folded the paper and returned it in the matchbox. "I'll be gone for several hours. Should anyone call here on the phone" —he began putting matches into the box—"and ask for me, tell them I've gone to meet Contact-Four, and that they should come to 1689 Ridakino Avenue. Apartment 8-C. They will ask for me by name, either 'Richard' or 'Richard Camellion.' Do you have all of it?"

She nodded like a little girl. "Yes. They will ask for you by name. I should tell them that you've gone to meet Contact-Four. Apartment 8-C, 1689 Ridakino Avenue."

"Good, those exact words and nothing more."

"Suppose they come to the apartment? I mean, if they come here?"

"They won't." Camellion finished putting the matches into the matchbox, closed it, stood up, and dropped it into his pocket, pretending not to notice that Melina was looking up at him with worried eyes.

"One more thing. I'll need to borrow your Vislos," he said. "Do you mind?"

"Of course not." She reached into her handbag for the keys. "You don't even have to ask; you know that." She handed him the keys. "What time should I expect you back?"

"No later than nine." He bent down, gave her a quick kiss on the mouth, then turned and started toward the door.

"Be careful, Richard," she called after him.

Camellion drove several miles from Melina's apartment, parked, went to a telephone booth on the sidewalk, and dialed Arnold Cahill's number. A woman answered. "Yes?"

"This is Richard Camellion. Is Arnie there?"

"No." Her voice was low and cautious.

"Tell him I said 'Rumble-Red.' "

"Anything else?"

"No, just 'Rumble-Red.' "

The Death Merchant next dialed Rene Beaufault's number. It was Beaufault who answered.

"Rene, it's 'Rumble-Red' all the way down the line. The other side tried to kill me this afternoon—an ambush. I'm alive. They're dead. Warn everyone in your network and be prepared to run to the safe house. I've already warned Arnie. One more thing: Is it possible for you to activate some of your street people within the next half hour?"

"Within the next fifteen minutes if necessary," Beaufault said firmly.

"It's necessary. I want them to watch a small apartment house at 1689 Ridakino Avenue," Camellion said. "I want to find out if the uniformed KYP and the *Asfaleia* raid the place. I'll explain later when I see you."

"I'll attend to it at once."

"I'll contact you—or Mr. H. will—either later tonight or sometime tomorrow," Camellion said. "Good-bye."

A few minutes later the Death Merchant had dialed Joseph Pappas and was talking to him. "Joe, it's 'Rumble-Red,' " Camellion informed him. "I'll give you all the details when I see you. Do you remember where you and I and Notaras had lunch the day you came to our hotel?"

"Yes, I do."

"Meet me there as quickly as you can, but don't come up to me. Just walk by, then leave. I'll follow you out."

There was a slight pause at the end of the line. "How serious is it?" Pappas asked.

"As bad as it can get." Camellion's voice was ice. "Try to get to the restaurant as quickly as possible. It's possible the KYP have a pickup order out on me."

"I'm on my way, American. It should not take me longer than forty minutes."

The Death Merchant left the phone booth, put on his Ray Ban sunglasses. Carrying the attaché case, he walked three blocks, then hailed a taxi.

Chapter Nine

2200 hours
Embassy of the Union of Soviet
Socialist Republics

Kostyan Vasokin Muzychenko, who held the rank of major in the KGB, was unusual in many ways. Invariably, all people with red hair wished they were blonds or brunettes. Not Muzychenko. He was proud of his thick and wavy red hair. He cut his hair every week and kept his red mustache carefully trimmed.

Muzychenko was uncommon in another respect: He was an authority on the poets and poetry of the English Romantic period and knew as much about Byron, Keats, Shelley, and others as many American, European, and Soviet professors of literature.

At the moment Muzychenko was not thinking of his red hair or poetry. His sole interest was in assuring Major Sergei Diamov that the American network did not have the slightest idea where the weather experiment was to be conducted. Diamov had come to Athens from the island of Miskos the previous day.

Muzychenko was saying "We don't have any evidence that Richard Camellion and the others are even aware of the experiment to be conducted with the transmitter. He didn't mention anything about it to Comrade Rada Zavidova, not a word."

"A highly trained agent wouldn't," countered Major Diamov, who was tall and raw-boned. Lacking a sense of humor, he seldom smiled. His skin was pockmarked and his teeth uneven. "Your agent couldn't read Camellion's mind, and since the squad failed to kill him, her effectiveness is at an end. Even if Camellion and his companions don't kill her for treachery, they will notify the KYP that she's a Soviet illegal. General Cyatorus will have to take action or the Americans and whoever else is involved will suspect that he is working with us."

"It was diabolically clever the way he gave her that false address," Anastas Benediktov, Diamov's second-in-command, added. "It proves that Camellion had always been suspicious of her, or else was making a test due to the attempted termination. As soon as he left her apartment, he must have made arrangements for some of his group to watch the apartment house to see if the police arrived."

He glanced at Kostyan Muzychenko, the KGB Resident of the Soviet intelligence apparatus in Athens. "It was a mistake having the KYP conduct the raid."

Before Muzychenko could offer a rebuttal, Captain Martin Poskreko, Muzychenko's chief assistant, said quickly, "Comrade Benediktov, after Rada Zavidova telephoned and tipped us that Camellion was going to the apartment on Ridakino Avenue, all of us agreed, including you and Comrade Major Diamov, that the best course of action would be to phone Cyatorus and suggest he have the KYP raid Apartment 8-C. I suppose you must have forgotten that fact."

"Yes, that is true. We did agree," the fat-faced Benediktov was reluctantly forced to admit as he squirmed slightly on the couch. "At the time we thought such a course of action would net us the American Camellion and some of his people."

Major Diamov spoke rapidly to cover Benediktov's mistake. "The raid wouldn't have taken place if those damned *Boyevaya Gruppa* had done their job properly." Sitting at one end of the couch with Benediktov at the other end, Major Diamov looked thoughtfully at Muzychenko. "I should think you will have a difficult time explaining the failure to Moscow Center."

"To the contrary, I shall only report that the five of them failed to kill Richard Camellion," Muzychenko said suavely. He sat with his arms raised, his elbows on the rounded, padded sides of the chair, his hands folded. "Moscow insisted that I use the *Boyevaya Gruppa* squad. I didn't request the help of Nadra Gulikov and her goons. In fact, I told the Center that it wasn't even necessary to kill Camellion."

Anastas Benediktov broke in hastily. "But didn't you presume Camellion was dangerous?"

"Not really," said Muzychenko without any hesitation. "What could he learn? Why not let him run all over Athens and make a fool of himself? What happened was that Moscow Center ordered him deactivated. My hands were tied. I did suggest to Gulikov that we let Meli—that we let Rada Zavidova kill him. It would have been easy. She was sleeping with him. She could have used a slow-working poison in a drink or some other method. All Gulikov succeeded in doing was getting herself and her four people killed."

"Worse, the news of the gun battle will be all over Greece by morning," interposed Martin Poskreko, reinforcing his boss's explanation. "The Greeks will wonder why five 'West Germans' tried to kill another man. At least Gulikov was efficient enough to equip her squad with plenty of forged identification. I guess we can always use disinformation and leak terrorism to the stupid press."

"The tricky part will be our explaining what went wrong to General Cyatorus," Major Muzychenko said thoughtfully. "He's always been a nervous individual, and he's furious that the raid on the apartment on Ridakino Avenue came to nothing. Imagine, raiding an apartment and finding only a bedridden old Greek and his blind wife!"

Major Diamov, shifting about uncomfortably, said, "Let's hope that the KYP will find that damned Richard Camellion at the Greek importer's. I consider it fortunate that we were able to convince Cyatorus to raid Pappas's warehouse."

He looked up at the clock on the wall above Major Muzychenko's desk. "It's almost ten-thirty. It is still too early for us to hear from Cyatorus."

Lieutenant Benediktov eyed Muzychenko suspiciously. "We can't be positive that Camellion went to Pappas's warehouse after he left the apartment of Comrade Zavidova." He laughed. "You will certainly be hard pressed if the KYP finds he wasn't there."

"He'll be there." Muzychenko permitted himself to look and sound smug. "There is only one other place Camellion can go: That's a safe house on Stazoukis Avenue. One way or another, the KYP will get him." Pleased at the expressions of surprise on Diamov's and Benediktov's face, he said, "Yes, we know where the network's safe house is located. Camellion will need new identification, a new passport and forged visa. He will have to go to that safe station before he can flee Greece."

Muzychenko hoped that his revelation would at least force a single crack in Diamov's tough protective shell. He failed. Diamov's expression didn't change, but his eyes revealed strong concentration.

"Then you have an informer within the ranks of

the American apparatus, or—more likely—the Delphi Circle?"

"No." Muzychenko's answer was instantaneous. "We received the information about the safe house from Moscow. What matters is that we have its location. And face it, Major Diamov!" Muzychenko's voice became ruthless. "General Cyatorus has no choice but to cooperate with us. He's in too deep not to."

"What about the others?" asked Diamov, seizing the initiative. He cleared his throat importantly. "Another thing that puzzles me—and it will infuriate Moscow—is how Camellion could have escaped the ambush. Damn it! There were five of them! I can understand that he might have escaped, but he killed every single one of them! One would think he had a backup; yet witnesses reported he was alone—unless the police have ordered newscasters not to mention it."

"We are certain that Camellion and Pappas are linked to Arzey Holcomb," Muzychenko said. "We also know that Arnold Cahill and Rene Beaufault are part of the network."

"But isn't it true that Beaufault is part of the French apparatus?" Diamov asked briskly.

"We think so, but we can't be positive," replied Major Muzychenko. "French or American! What's the difference? There isn't anything mysterious about how Camellion was able to kill Gulikov and her men. He was only extremely lucky. What other answer is there?"

The overweight and prematurely bald Anastas Benediktov jumped in. "It's possible that the CIA is working with the Delphi Circle in some kind of operation that would overthrow the Greek government."

"I have the same theory," Muzychenko said modestly, "although the Otdel here in Athens doesn't have anything to substantiate such a hypothesis. I'm certain that the Americans are completely in the dark about the weather-control project."

Major Sergei Diamov gave a courteous smile. "Tell me, Comrade Muzychenko, are you going to take any executive action against Holcomb and the other two?"

Muzychenko would have liked to tell the supercilious Diamov to go to hell and get back to the damned island. He couldn't. He didn't dare. His orders from Moscow were to cooperate fully with the son of a bitch. However, the Center had also told him that all decisions on the mainland would be strictly within his province. Such had not been the case with the special-operations *Boyevaya Gruppa* squad. Muzychenko had not been able to say no. Moscow had wanted Richard Camellion dead. Secretly, Muzychenko was happy that the American had turned the tables on Nadra Gulikov and her four overly confident gunmen.

"I don't intend to do anything about them," Muzychenko said. "Why bother? Once Camellion is out of the way, the network will fall apart or creep along. Even if it doesn't, it's better to watch them. If we took executive action, their service would only replace them with new faces."

Martin Poskreko gave a meaningful nod. "The important thing for you to remember, Comrade Major Diamov, is that Richard Camellion and the CIA network, such as it is in Greece, is not a danger to the project on the island. Your only concern should be the security on Miskos."

Major Diamov gave Poskreko a long, rigid stare, as if trying to stab within the interior of the younger man's brain. The nerve of the upstart!

"My concern is the success of the experiment," Diamov said stiffly. "Automatically that entails anything the Americans might do on the mainland. What happens on the Greek mainland could affect us on the island. You did mention a safe house that Camellion and his group could use. Are you sure of the information?"

Major Muzychenko thrust out his lower jaw and a slow smile crept across his wide mouth. "We're sure. The information came straight from the French SDECE in Paris. We—"

The telephone on his desk rang. . . .

Chapter Ten

I

Hunched over the wheel, Joe Pappas turned onto Venizelos Street, the two bright beams of the headlights making a quick half-circle slash in the deep twilight as the direction of the Mazda RX-7 changed to the southeast. He had driven Anna Sofoulis's car into Athens because he felt it wouldn't be recognized as easily as his Subaru. He fed more gas to the engine and increased speed.

"I think we will be able to decode the microdot before the KYP arrives, American," he said, radiating self-confidence. "It was clever of you to give Melina Arnaoutis that address. Is there really such a number and an apartment on Ridakino Avenue?"

"I spent a few hours the other afternoon finding such a place," the Death Merchant said. "I first chose an apartment house, then went inside and knocked at random on an apartment door. A blind woman opened the door of apartment 8-C. But I'm afraid you're missing the red meat of the matter."

"Such as?" demanded Pappas.

"Unless Melina is working against us, the KGB and the KYP won't even know the apartment exists,"

Camellion said evenly, thinking of how easy it had been for Pappas to pick him up at the restaurant. "I hate to say it, but right now I'm hoping she is a spy and did tip off the other side. If she did, it will give us the time we need. That's the theory of it, anyhow."

"There is no way we can be positive what the KGB or the KYP might do." Pappas was growing agitated from tension and anxiety.

"That's true. I'm only going on the assumption that it was the KGB that tried to sanction me."

"And the KGB will want revenge for your killing its five people. Is that what you believe?"

"It's not that simple," the Death Merchant explained. "Revenge doesn't enter into it. The KGB is practical and knows that they win some and we win some. It's a matter of business."

"But they know about us," Pappas said.

"The KGB had to know about me—how isn't important. It follows that they know about you and Cahill and Beaufault. That the KGB intends to put an end to what we are doing is fact, or they wouldn't have tried to kill me. The Soviets and their KYP stooges now know we're on our guard and that we realize our days of wine and roses are finished. Even if we didn't go underground, it would be a waste of time for them to watch us. All they can do is close in, in the hope they can grab one of us and make us confess."

Pappas looked at the speedometer. They were on the outskirts of Athens and traffic had begun to thin. Yet he couldn't go faster; he had already reached the speed limit. "I guess that's it. Either we go underground or end up in the hands of the KYP," he said grimly. "It was a good try, but we failed—for now!"

A disconsolate Richard Camellion kept his eyes on the traffic. It was almost totally dark, and on each side was a moving ribbon of broken steel with bright white-yellow eyes. He hated the word failure. At the same time, he couldn't deny what had happened, what *was*. So far, Operation Zeus was as successful as a lead balloon trying to get off the ground.

"Do you and Gregory and his daughter have a secure place to go to?" asked Camellion. "If not, you're welcome at our safe house."

"We have a place," Pappas said gruffly. "Do not ask for its location, and do not tell me where yours is. My only regret is leaving the importing and exporting business behind. I had grown fond of it. We'll soon be in Kaisariani." He gave a sudden explosive laugh and glanced at the Death Merchant. "This will be a night to remember when we are old men, eh, American?"

The "soon" seemed like a short eternity. But the time did come when the Mazda RX-7 was moving on Peridis, then was on Ramicus. Dark fields flashed by, the myrtle, the oaks, and the beech trees black sentinels that no longer were neutral.

"Joe, stop the car after you turn into the drive," Camellion said. "If we hear crickets, we'll know that the KYP hasn't arrived ahead of us and is lying in wait."

Pappas nodded. "You keep saying the KYP. How do you know the KGB couldn't be waiting?"

"Any raid on your place would have to be official. It would have to be Greek police who conducted it, in our case the uniformed branch of Greek intelligence and security. That's the KYP."

In only a short while, Pappas turned into the drive. He drove forty feet, stopped, turned off the engine and the lights. There was only the darkness, a low half moon, and silence, except for some crickets and the love calls of half a dozen sex-happy toads.

Pappas started the Mazda and drove forward. He stopped again a 150 feet in front of the old mansion and turned off the lights, then picked up a four-cell flashlight from the seat, held it outside the window, and turned it off and on three times in rapid succession—"so that Gregory and Anna will know that it's us. But just in case. . . ." Pappas pulled from his belt the 9-mm Steyr autoloader that the Death Merchant had given him and placed it on the seat.

Ahead, from a window to the right of the front door, a flashlight blinked rapidly three times.

Pappas drove ahead, swung the car to the left, and parked in front of the long porch. Gregory Sofoulis, an Italian Socimi T-821 submachine gun in his hands, opened the door when Camellion and Pappas were only halfway across the porch.

The big Greek, whose face made Camellion think of a tombstone, rattled off a stream of words in his native tongue. Pappas nodded vigorously and replied, making a sweep with his hand toward the outside as he did so.

Walking toward the rear of the house, Pappas explained to the Death Merchant that Gregory had told him that Anna was on the second floor, watching the rear, and that the explosives had been placed.

"Explosives?" Camellion was instantly on extra-alert.

They came to the area concealing the secret room below the floor.

"I don't intend to leave anything standing if and when the KYP close in," Pappas said, his tone razor-sharp with determination. "We have two hundred fourteen sticks of *Zipvikidas* planted toward the center of the house—that's commercial dynamite in America. It's more than enough to bring this old wreck tumbling down."

"Presumably after we are gone!" mused Camellion, watching Pappas take the ladder to the chandelier. He added in a voice that lacked humor and was as cold as the shriveled heart of a corpse, "Should they attack before we manage to leave, we might have to dissolve with this old mansion, unless of course a wise man, such as yourself, has already planned for such an emergency."

The Death Merchant was positive that Pappas had made some kind of escape arrangements. He was too clever to be caught flat-footed.

Pappas started down the ladder, glanced at the cartons on the trapdoor that was rising upward and backward, then turned and grinned at Camellion.

"Remember the old escape tunnel I told you about?" he asked, motioning for Camellion to follow him to the steps. "Be careful, American. These steps are steep."

"Can we reach the tunnel from the room below?" Camellion asked, following Pappas down the first few steps.

"No. But the entrance is close by. It's not as easy as it sounds. The tunnel is one hundred twenty meters long and ends by a small creek that's dry this time of year. If any KYP should be waiting at the end of the tunnel. . . ."

Reaching the bottom of the steps, Pappas turned on the two overhead bulbs in their rounded metal shades. He didn't, however, bother to close the trapdoor.

"You decode the microdot," Pappas said next. "I'm going to get some weapons out." He moved across the small room to a metal cabinet.

The Death Merchant went to work. He turned on the microdot machine, sat down at the table, and took a pair of small scissors from the kit that came with the device. Carefully he cut a tiny section from the message, a section only one-fourth of an inch square. In the center of the square was the last period of the message—the microdot. Using a pair of long tweezers, he picked up the dwarfish square, opened the main plate of the device, and placed the square of paper in the circle in the center of the beam-frame. He closed the cover over the plate, then pulled down the twenty-inch-wide screen at the other end of the table.

Going back to the machine, he saw that Pappas had taken two Beretta M-12 SMGs and six magazines from the cabinet and was loading the submachine guns.

Camellion pushed the ON button and began to adjust the focus knob with one hand and the magnification knob with his other hand. Within a few minutes he had adjusted the focus so that any photograph or writing would be clear on the screen. Rapidly, Camellion increased the magnification, finally reaching 4643 power. At last, Camellion adjusted the focus knob, and there was the message—sideways on the screen. He turned the H-V-D knob and moved the plate into proper position. The message was now vertical, and as clear as fresh tar on newly fallen snow— printed in English.

Pappas gasped in surprise and, with Camellion, read:

> Mr. M. cooperated fully. The Russians are on a small island named Miskos in the Aegean Sea. A.H.

The Death Merchant stared at the message angrily. Holcomb had not even bothered to put it in code. Conversely, Camellion was elated that the network had accomplished its goal and had learned the name of the island—*For all the good it does us.* Mentally he began scanning the various factors. Even though he had warned Arnold Cahill and Rene Beaufault—and one of them was to warn Arzey Holcomb—he had no way of knowing where they were and what they might be doing. Presumably they would take refuge in the safe house at 1766 Stazoukis. Or had the KYP trapped one of them—or all three?—before he could get to the safe house?

There was an escape plan by which Camellion could get out of Greece, only he didn't know what it was.

"It's a matter of security," Courtland Grojean had told him. "If you're netted by the KYP, you can't tell what you don't know, no matter what they do to you. I'll give you the phone number and the recognition code. Should you have to go to that station, be sure to mention 'Thunderbird.' That word will start to activate the escape route."

How to get the name of the island out of Greece was the immediate problem. To take the SATCOM AN/URC transceiver and go to the roof would be cutting a large slice out of time, time that he and Pappas and Gregory and Anna didn't have—*And I won't be able to use the transceiver in Rene's apartment. That leaves only the safe house on Stazoukis. Or I can use the phone number Grojean gave me.*

The Death Merchant turned off the microdot machine, picked up the tweezers, and heard Pappas say in the pessimistic tone of a man who has been told in the morning that he has won a $5 million lottery, but learns in the afternoon he has incurable cancer and will have a grass cover and a granite pillow in six months.

"I tell you, American, I have the feeling that Clotho, Lachesis, and Atropos have to be laughing at us," Pappas said, with an added bitter half laugh that was more of a snicker. "We have the name of the island, but will we live long enough to do anything with it? And did you notice, the message did not say that Professor Paspyrou was on Miskos!"

Appreciating Pappas's reference to the three Fates

in Greek mythology, Camellion opened the cover of the plate and, with the end of the tweezers, carefully picked up the tiny square of paper from the center of the beam-frame.

"The hell with the Fates," Camellion said curtly. "Those three bitches are as dead as the glory that was Greece and the grandeur that was Rome." He took a match from the matchbox that Melina had given him, struck it, and touched the flame to the diminutive piece of paper at the end of the tweezers. In seconds the message had turned to ash. Camellion stooped and let the message fall to the floor. He then ground it into nothingness with the heel of his left foot.

Joe Pappas picked up one of the Beretta submachine guns, cocked it, and pushed on its safety. "How long will it take to go to the roof and make contact with your superiors in the United States?"

"Too long," Camellion replied, looking around the room. "We don't have the time, Joe. We could even run into the KYP coming in as we're pulling out. Do you have a hammer down here?"

"Why?"

"To smash the radio and the microdot machine."

With an instant sly smile on his small, fat lips, Pappas went to the metal cabinet and pulled out a dozen gray sticks of *Zipvikidas* taped together with black electrician's tape. From the front of the dynamite protruded a coiled fuse that could have been twenty feet or more long.

"This"—Joe held up the packet of dynamite—"will destroy everything that's down here." He placed the explosive on top of the microdot machine and began to uncoil the fuse. "You bring the flash and the machine pistols," he said energetically. "I'll stretch the fuse up the steps."

Camellion stuffed the flashlight into one of his coat

pockets and began putting spare magazines for the two Beretta SMGs in his waistband. "What's the length of the fuse?"

"Almost seven meters." Pappas moved toward the steps. "That's slightly over four minutes burning time, then—the big bang!"

The Death Merchant and Pappas had moved up the steps and were on the first floor when Gregory Sofoulis hurried into the back room, the moving beam of his flashlight announcing his arrival. For the first time Camellion noticed that he had a walkie-talkie strapped to his belt.

Without so much as glancing at Camellion, Gregory spoke in a low but excited voice to Pappas, who rose after stretching out the fuse. He replied to Gregory rapidly in Greek, who turned and ran back toward the front of the house.

"They're here!" Pappas said. "Gregory said that Anna called him on the walkie-talkie and said she thought she saw movement in back. I told him to tell her to come downstairs and remain with him in front and to wait until he hears from one of us."

"That settles our leaving by car," Camellion conceded. "How much time will we have before the larger package of dynamite explodes?"

"Five minutes from the time the fuse is lighted," Pappas said, sounding worried. "We do have a problem. If the KYP rushes us and gets inside before the *Zipvikidas* explodes, we could be in real trouble. They could find the explosives and pull the fuses."

"Where's the entrance to the escape tunnel?" Camellion asked patiently.

"In the cellar," Pappas said. "I've already cleared the opening. That's the real danger: that the KYP could find the opening and come after us. We would not have one chance, my American friend."

The Death Merchant knew there was only one

logical answer. "We have to stall them—to force those KYP goons to move with extreme caution. Here's what we'll do. . . ."

By the time Camellion reached the room in front where Gregory and Anna Sofoulis were waiting, each holding a Socimi SMG, Pappas had begun firing short bursts with the Beretta from the rear of the enormous house, running back and forth between four rooms on the north side, to make the KYP think there were many more people inside.

In the almost pitch-black darkness, Gregory and Anna stared at Camellion, who had placed the flashlight on the floor. He told father and daughter: "We must stall the KYP because of the short burning time of the fuses. We have to make the police think we're ready for them. Anna, you stay in this room and fire short bursts. Gregory, you and I will move through the other rooms here in front and trigger rounds, say a full magazine each."

"It is Joseph shooting in back, yes?" growled Gregory.

"Yes. He'll fire a few magazines, then go to the cellar. You and I and Anna will light the fuses, then join him."

Anna said with happy expectation, "If we do it right many of the KYP troopers will be trapped in the explosions."

She no longer resembled the young woman who sat behind a desk in the front office. Her long black hair was no longer fixed in a bun. She had let it down and tied it behind her head. She wore jeans and a woman's blue long-sleeve shirt.

"Gregory, it's—" The roaring of a dozen SG-510 assault rifles, from the south, cut Camellion off. Scores of 7.62-mm by 39-mm NATO-Patrone projectiles stabbed into the front of the mansion. Glass in

windows dissolved, and there were numerous ricochets as spitzer-partition slugs struck metal and other
hard objects. There was more firing from the rear,
from the north, and a dozen spotlights, mounted on
tripods, began to sweep back and forth on all sides of
the house.

"Let's go, Gregory," urged Camellion, shoving off
the safety of his Beretta. Gregory and Anna, shaken
by the thunderous blast of gunfire, noticed the
change in Camellion, a subtle transformation from
some anxiousness to total calm, to a tranquillity that
was abnormal, that gave the impression of complete
ruthlessness. Even his voice was different—mechanical, merciless. "Anna, remain here and don't try to
fire when the enemy is firing, and never try to fire
twice from the same position at any given window."

Anna dropped to the floor and Camellion and
Gregory did a postage-stamp act against the east wall
as again the SG assault rifles roared and slugs zipped
through windows already devoid of glass and thudded into the north wall.

The bursts of gunfire subsided as quickly as they
had begun, and Camellion and Gregory darted low
into the next room to the east, a few of the spotlight
beams raking across them before they could dive
down. Instantly there was another blast from the
outside and slugs sliced through the warm air, some
coming dangerously close to the men before slam-
ming into the wall.

Cursing in Greek, Gregory dropped his barrel-
shaped body by the left corner of a center window.
The Death Merchant, chain lightning in his feet,
raced to the door of the next room, calling over his
shoulder, "Stay put. I'll handle the other rooms."

He tore into the next room, which hadn't been
cleaned in years and was filled with furniture from
another time, a time forgotten except in history

books. He managed to get to a window in the southeast corner before more gunfire erupted from the KYP uniformed troopers. This time when the lag time came, Camellion leaned around the edge of the window and fired a short burst, catching a glimpse of green-uniformed men wearing ballistic helmets, darting back to the refuge of Joseph Pappas's Subaru and Gregory Sofoulis's Korisa. More chains of 9-mm slugs were directed at the KYP by Anna and her father.

Camellion leaned around the side of the window and fired again. This time several of his 9-mm slugs hit two troopers who had gotten crazy brave and were trying to get closer to the house. Darting into the next room, he was almost trapped in a hail of slugs from the next enemy blast. A SG 7.62-mm bullet burned air an inch from the back of his neck. A second projectile passed to the rear of his right leg—to the back of the knee as the leg was raised—and cut through the pant of his left leg, the metal barely touching the rear of his thigh. He flung himself to the nearest window—the second one from the east wall —and waited: *If they had any sense, they'd have used tear gas by now!*

The moment the KYP stopped firing, he raised up and raked the forward area with a final burst, his effort rewarded with several cries of pain. There was more firing up the line to the west, from Gregory and Anna.

One of Camellion's concerns was that sooner or later the KYP would rise up and attack from the east and the west sides of the house. He pulled out the empty clip, shoved a full magazine into the feed slot of the Beretta, and sent a cartridge into the firing chamber. When the firing resumed, Camellion crawled under a dozen lines of slugs into the next room. As soon as the firing stopped, he got to his feet, went to the east side door and opened it. He was just in time to see three of the Swat-helmeted KYP troopers trying to come through the windows of the east wall. One of them had a leg through a window. Another trooper was already inside and was helping the third Greek goon through another window.

A slight smile curved across Camellion's mouth, and he was positive that the Cosmic Lord of Death was laughing insanely and only a split second from claiming more victims. Camellion almost felt sorry for the three: *Well, if you'll forgive me for being brilliant, I'll forgive you for being stupid!*

The man who had his leg through the window spotted Camellion first and yelled a terrified warning. It was an exercise in futility. Camellion's finger was against the wide trigger and the chattering Beretta was spitting out 9-mm projectiles. The man who had been trying to pull himself through the window had attempted to pull back and dropped. He almost succeeded, and would have if a single bullet hadn't hit him just above the nose, burst his brain, and blown out the back of his head. A tenth of an eyeblink later, the trooper already in the room—he was swinging around—was stitched from navel to neck. The third member of the trio wasn't any better off. One of Camellion's 9-mm projectiles stabbed him in the throat and turned his voice box into mush. Two more slugs hit him in the face, tore off his nose, and bored a bloody tunnel in his brain.

Too experienced to remain where he was, the Death Merchant moved back into the room from which he had come and closed the door. He had only one magazine left and didn't intend to waste it or the remaining cartridges he had left in the Beretta. He dove to the floor in time to avoid another tidal wave of hot metal from the outside. Just to let the KYP know he was still alive and in a fighting mood, he fired off a short burst from a window in the next room, then dropped to escape more solid-core metal that thudded into the north wall. He could still hear firing far to the rear of the house and could tell from the sound it was Joe Pappas's Beretta. He could also hear short bursts now and then and knew it was Anna. But Gregory Sofoulis's weapon was strangely silent. In a few minutes Camellion found out why. Gregory was a corpse, stretched out on his back, the front of his skull opened by a bullet and a pool of blood beneath him. The big man hadn't ducked in time.

Fudge! Camellion crawled into the next room and found that Anna had moved from the window into the next room to the north and was standing by the door, clutching her submachine gun as if it were made of solid gold. It was plain to Camellion she was terrified.

"W-where's my father?" Her voice came out in a nervous croak.

"I'm sorry, Anna. He's dead," Camellion said simply, and when he saw the beginning of hysteria rising on her face, he said sharply, "And we will be too if you crack up. We have to light the fuses and meet Joe in the cellar. Lead the way to the main charge of *Zipvikidas—move!*"

Managing to control her emotions, Anna brushed a tear from her eye. "Follow me."

Anna led Camellion through several rooms and down a long hall, all the while keeping the beam of the flashlight close to the dirty floor. She stopped twenty feet from a doorway to their left and pointed with the beam to the end of a fuse that stretched ahead and moved through the doorway into the room beyond. "The explosives are in a box in the room," she said. "There's the fuse."

The Death Merchant struck a match and lighted

the fuse, for a few seconds watching the sparks rapidly eat into the length. Camellion and Anna retraced their steps and raced through the darkness to reach the fuse to the dynamite in the underground room. In moments the Death Merchant had it burning.

Anna led the way to the cellar, the two of them almost bumping into Joseph Pappas on the way. He had just left the rear of the house. "Where's Gregory?" he asked.

"He's dead," Anna said dully.

At length, with Pappas in the lead, they came to what must have been a storeroom at one time. At one end of the floor was the opening in which were the wooden steps that led to the cellar.

"Be careful," Pappas warned Camellion. He pointed the beam of light down the steps. "Those steps go down for almost seven meters. But they are solid and there is a handrail, as you can see."

After they reached the bottom of the steps, the Death Merchant saw that the opening to the escape tunnel was in the east wall. The entrance appeared to be a doorway, seven feet high and seven feet wide. He also saw Pappas open a wooden box and take out three Greek army-issue gas masks. He handed one to Anna and one to Camellion. The third one he kept for himself.

"These are necessary," Pappas said. "There could be gas in the tunnel. If—" He stopped in surprise as Camellion, who had an uncanny sense of time, started toward the entrance of the tunnel.

"We'll have to put them on inside the tunnel," he said. "The dynamite is about to blow. . . ."

II

Captain Nikolaos Frangopoulos, crouched by the left rear of Anna Sofoulis's Mazda RX-7, stared at the front of the house through a binocular-type night-vision IR scope. A career KYP officer, his record was due for review in another month, and he couldn't afford to make any wrong decisions and lose more men. Eight had been killed and three had been wounded, one seriously.

"I believe we killed all of them," Lieutenant Peter Likisis whispered solemnly. "There couldn't have been more than half a dozen terrorists in there, including Joseph Pappas and the American, if the American did come here."

Captain Frangopoulos lowered the infrared night glasses and unconsciously stroked his large mustache, a tipoff to Lieutenant Likisis that, for the moment, he was undecided as to the course of action to take. Likisis often wondered why Frangopoulos wore such a huge mustache. It was far too large for his oval face.

"It could be a trap," reflected Frangopoulos. "They might be trying to lure us into the open before they fire again. Then again . . ."

"We'll never know until the men charge, sir," the thinner and much shorter Likisis said. "None of them can escape. We can be positive of that. We have the entire house surrounded."

"Pappas was anticipating an attack; he and the others were waiting," Frangopoulos commented morosely. "We could have saved time by coming in from the front. What's done is done." He made up his mind. "Lieutenant, order the men to attack from all sides, firing as they go."

"Yes, sir." Lieutenant Likisis took the Vadis-L FM

transceiver from his belt, turned it on, and began speaking to the sergeants.

Within several minutes the attack was under way. Raking the windows with hundreds of slugs, the troopers zigzagged forward and soon were storming through the front door and the two rear doors. Others crawled through windows on the east and the west sides.

No one, least of all Captain Frangopoulos, expected the explosion. As suddenly as a bolt of lightning, there was a gigantic blast that made the ground shake as if an earthquake were about to take place. The large house gave a tremendous shudder, then began to cave in, the roof and sides falling inward.

Standing in front of the Mazda, Captain Frangopoulos and Lieutenant Likisis were staring in horror at the collapsing old mansion when *BERUUUMMMMMM!* The second explosion in the secret room roared off and sent blown-apart materials upward and outward, only to be met by tons of beams and other parts of the house already falling inward. With an enormous crash, the entire house fell in, the pressure sending clouds of dust in all directions.

"My God!" Likisis gasped, his eyes wide. "Those damned fanatics blew themselves up! Half of our troops must have been inside."

Captain Frangopoulos leaned against the Mazda, a sick feeling rising in his stomach. He tasted bile. He knew that he would never be promoted to major, not after this catastrophe.

III

With the first explosion, Camellion, Pappas, and Sofoulis, now wearing gas masks, felt the tunnel shake with such violence that they feared it would cave in. At the time they were only twenty feet beyond the farthest reaches of the house. There could now be no turning back. The cellar would be filled with tons of rubble.

The second explosion was not as cataclysmic; this time the tunnel only quivered slightly.

The three had entered the tunnel so fast that the Death Merchant hadn't had time to ask Pappas what lay at the other end and if he had made plans to depart the area.

Several steps ahead of Joe and Anna, Camellion stopped and turned around. "Joe"—he lowered the beam of the flashlight and shifted the Beretta in his arm—"how is the other end concealed? Clue me in."

His voice sounded odd, muffled, not only because of the gas mask covering his face but also because of the small size of the tunnel. The flat roof was only inches above their heads and each side almost as close, the stones covered with lichen.

"We'll come up on this side of the creek," Pappas explained. "We'll use a ladder to get to the trapdoor. It's covered with weeds. There's little chance that any of the KYP sons of bitches will be around. The trapdoor is too far from the house."

"Then what? How do we get to Athens from here?"

"The Delphi Circle agent I control lives in Kaisariani. We can reach his house before the sun rises." Pappas sounded as if the matter were settled. "The KYP will not be looking for us. They think we blew ourselves up and are buried in the rubble. We will hide out at my friend's house until we can make arrangements to move on."

The Death Merchant didn't reply. After all, you had to throw the hay down where the goats could get at it. If you can't have steak, be happy with lunch meat.

It was the time factor that annoyed Camellion. It might be another day, even longer, before he could get to Stazoukis Avenue in Athens—if he chose to go to the safe house there. He had a chilly feeling about the safe station. Since the KGB and the KYP already knew about him and Pappas, and no doubt knew about Arnold Cahill and Rene Beaufault, who was to say they weren't aware of the safe house?

Feeling like microbes crawling in some giant hardened artery and being pursued by evil antibiotics, they moved as rapidly as they could through the escape tunnel, the beams of their flashlights stabbing the darkness ahead.

The Death Merchant and his two companions were uncomfortable. Their clothes were soaked with sweat. They felt grimy, and their hot breath, coming back at them within the gas masks, only increased their discomfort. But the masks were necessary. Chokedamp worked very quickly. Odorless, such a gas could render them unconscious without warning.

Finally their beams caught the ladder and the wall ahead. The ladder, which looked new, leaned to the left and was set in what could be described as a well whose top ended twenty-five feet above on the surface.

"I'll go first, American," Pappas said. "I must cut the ropes holding the trapdoor in place. Hold the flashlight for me."

Pappas shut off his flashlight and forced it into his waistband. He put his Beretta SMG on the dry tunnel floor and started to climb the ladder, the Death Merchant's flashlight beam pointed upward and staying just ahead of him. Toward the top of the ladder, Pappas paused, took a large pocket knife from his pocket, and, with two quick motions, cut the two ropes holding the trapdoor down, severing them where they were tied to rings set in the stones of the well.

"Leave the machine pistol," Pappas called down. "It's empty."

"Go ahead, Anna," Camellion said gently. He could see that, underneath her gas mask, she was crying. She had dearly loved her father.

Pappas moved upward four feet and pushed against the trapdoor, which was made of wood and twenty-eight inches square. He was very careful not to let the trapdoor fall back, hit the ground and make a loud noise. Instead, he let it down very slowly. Quickly then, he crawled the rest of the way to the surface. Anna and Camellion proceeded up the ladder, and they too were soon on the ground next to Pappas. Only then did Pappas pull the trapdoor toward him and gently replace it over the square opening.

The half moon was much higher, and the countryside was bathed in soft light. There was a slight wind, and all was hot and humid. Down on their elbows, Camellion, Joe, and Anna peered into the moonlit night. Behind them, to the northeast, was the dry bed of the creek, a wide, shallow ditch twisting its way like a worm to the southeast.

To the southwest, seven hundred feet ahead, was the pile of rubble that had been the 125-year-old mansion. Very clearly they could see the gray-white dust that was still settling, the spotlights around the area moving over the shifting rubble. Every now and then there was a loud snapping sound from a beam breaking under weight of rubble above it. They could hear men shouting, and they knew from the way troopers were running back and forth that KYP men had been trapped inside when the mansion had collapsed.

"It's too bad we didn't get all of the bastards," Pappas hissed. He took one of Anna's hands and pat-

ted it. "Nevertheless, we've avenged the death of
your father."

The large mound of rubble that had been the
house was not important to Richard Camellion. The
three troop-carrying trucks and the two gray
Zigarkas automobiles were—damned important.
The five vehicles were four hundred feet southwest
of the Death Merchant and his fellow conspirators,
parked by the side of a dirt road that came in from
the west and began to curve to the southeast 570 feet
behind where the old mansion had stood. Outlined
against the glare of spotlights was one of the troopers
guarding the vehicles.

"The KYP used the back road to make sure we
wouldn't hear them approach," Pappas said.
"There's a patch of woods to the northeast. We'll wait
there several hours and—"

"Never walk when you can ride, and never ride
when you can fly," Camellion said quietly. "Those
KYP cars have sirens and red lights. We could leave
here and be in Athens in fifteen minutes."

Pappas jerked his head toward the Death Merchant, his glare ferocious. Then, as the possibilities
began to reveal themselves, the scowl softened.

"We'd also have to render the other vehicles in-
operable," Pappas said decisively, "including the
two-way radios."

Anna, new hope in her voice, whispered, "The
house in Athens would be a lot better for us than the
one in Kaisariani. We could save days."

"We'd take the first Zigarkas," Camellion said practically. "We couldn't keep it for any length of time.
Once we're in Athens, we'll park it and go our separate ways."

"How will you get to your safe house?" Anna
asked. "You neither speak nor read Greek."

"The numbers are the same in Greek as in English.

I'll have a cab driver take me to within three blocks of the address."

"I have a better way, my American friend," Pappas said, his eyes glinting. "First, how do we manage the guards and do it quietly? If it were only one man, but three of them! You and I can creep up, I suppose, and—"

"No! I can do it better alone," Camellion assured him. "Let me have that big pocketknife of yours."

Pappas took out the knife, then hesitated and looked at Camellion.

"Are you sure you know what you're doing? But of course you do, or you would not be doing it." He handed the knife to Camellion, who opened it.

The Death Merchant began to creep southwest, pausing every now and then and prepared to drop and flatten himself to the ground should one of the three guards walk around to the east side of the trucks. He was careful about where he stepped, gently lowering one foot and testing what was under the sole before putting his full weight on the ground. A single snapping twig could warn the guards, although he was certain that their full attention was riveted on the rescue efforts taking place around the rubble of the house.

Halfway, he pulled the 9-mm Steyr from its shoulder holster. He forged ahead as quietly as a drifting shadow. Soon he was able to proceed with greater speed, for as the distance narrowed, the weeds thinned and there was only grass, finally only dirt and dust. When he was only eighty feet from the right side of the first truck in line, he stopped, flattened himself to the ground, and looked under the three trucks and the two cars. One guard was positioned to the front left of the last truck in line. Another guard was standing in front of the first Zigarkas, his left foot on the bumper. Earlier Camellion, Pappas, and Anna had seen three troopers. Where was the third guard now? Not in the cars or in one of the trucks. The glare from the spotlights made it possible for Camellion to see that the six vehicles were empty: *Unless he's lying down on one of the seats. Not very likely.*

Camellion opened the knife, pushed the safety of the Steyr to *F*, got to his feet and moved rapidly forward, his destination the right side of the first troop-carrying Droka truck. He reached the vehicle, looked underneath it, and saw the third trooper. The man was standing twenty feet west of the left side of the truck. That's why the Death Merchant hadn't seen him.

All three guards had their SG-510 assault rifles slung by straps over their right shoulders, and it would have been a simple matter to pop off the three with the Steyr. But the shots would have warned the main force, or rather what was left of it.

The trooper in front of the first Zigarkas was the most accessible. Camellion crept northwest. He wasn't in any real danger. Should one of the troopers come to this side of the vehicles, Camellion would shoot him, then shoot the other two and run like hell back to Pappas and Anna. All three would race to the woods. The danger was that they would be tracked down because one shot would be the tipoff that they had not died in the two explosions.

He crept past the small open space between the front of the first Droka and the rear of the second Zigarkas. Faster, but with caution! He crept past the second gray automobile and the next space between the two Zigarkas. He switched on the safety of the Steyr pistol, jammed the weapon underneath his belt, and took a few steps forward. The trooper had removed his booted foot from the bumper and was preparing to light a cigarette. The man never got to strike the lighter.

The Death Merchant struck with incredible speed. His left arm shot out around the front of the man's neck. The trooper never really had time to realize he was being executed. By the time Paul Ladas's mind told him that he was being grabbed from behind, Camellion's left arm had tightened against his neck and the five-inch blade of the knife was stabbing through the lower right side of his back, the tip of the steel slicing into a kidney. The scream sliding from his throat never got past his mouth. Camellion's arm, squeezing his throat, wouldn't let it. It died a bub-bling gurgle inside Ladas's mouth. Shock pulled the shade of blackness over Ladas's brain and he sagged and went limp. The Death Merchant pulled back the dying man, dragged him to the left side of the car, freed the knife from his back, and let him fall to the ground. Then he retrieved the SG-510 assault rifle from underneath the right shoulder of the body.

Camellion ran to the second car, dropped to his knees, and looked underneath. The two other troop-ers were still in their former positions. He hurried to the space between the back bumper of the second truck and the front of the last one. The SG A-R in his left hand and the handle of the knife in his right hand, he moved toward the trooper who was stand-ing by the front left of the last Droka.

Camellion was only a second from stabbing the short barrel of the assault rifle into the neck of John Kaloudis when the other KYP trooper, twenty feet west of the left side of the first truck, happened to turn around and spot the Death Merchant. For a moment, the man froze. A yell of warning was jump-ing from his mouth as the knife left Camellion's right hand and the blade flew into his chest. With a cry of pain the trooper staggered back. His knees started to buckle. Trying to pull the SG-510 assault rifle from his shoulder, he went down.

Now warned, Kaloudis swung around and grabbed the assault rifle and tried to twist it from the Death Merchant's hands. Camellion didn't resist. He released his hold on the rifle and let Kaloudis have it, but only because he needed his hands free. Before Kaloudis had time to react and formulate any plan of attack, Camellion stamped on his left instep with his right heel and stabbed him straight in the throat with a bunched-finger left spear hand, the tips of his fingers mashing the Adam's apple. Choking, Kaloudis dropped the SG assault rifle, his hands going to his throat as if he could pull breath into his starved lungs. In an instant, Camellion was behind him and reaching for the rim of the ballistic helmet. He grabbed the rim with both hands and jerked as hard as he could to the right. Kaloudis went limp, his neck broken.

Now to wreck the radios! Camellion picked up the assault rifle, ran to the other side of the line of vehicles, and, outlined against the glow of the spotlights in the distance, motioned for Joe Pappas and Anna Sofoulis to come forward.

As soon as he saw them get to their feet and start running, he pulled open the door of the last truck, got inside the cab, and jerked the microphone and its coiled cord from the radio. He had pulled the coiled rubberized cord from the radio of the second truck and had taken the key from the ignition by the time Pappas and Anna arrived.

"Joe, we'll use the first patrol car. Start its engine," Camellion said. "Anna, pull the microphone from the radio in the second car and take the key from the ignition. I'll handle the next truck."

Before he could reach the truck and Pappas and Anna the two Zigarkas vehicles, the unexpected happened. Aris Tsirimokos, the trooper who had caught Camellion's knife in the chest, recovered enough to roll over, pull the SG assault rifle from his shoulder, and fire a short burst into the air. What had happened was that the blade of the knife had gone through part of a thick leather strap across Tsirimokos's chest, and the leather slowed it down. Only three inches of the blade had gone into his chest, and he had never completely lost consciousness. Weak, Tsirimokos now struggled to his knees and tried to aim the SG at Camellion, who promptly put a 9-mm Steyr bullet into his chest. This time Tsirimokos would not get up.

"Anna, get to the car with Joe," Camellion yelled. "I'll take care of the radios." Anna ran toward the first car, and Camellion stepped up on the rung of the truck's cab, pulled open the door, leaned across the seat, and put a bullet into the radio. After pulling the key from the dash, he got down and started for the second Zigarkas.

The blast of slugs from the now-dead Aris Tsirimokos had alerted the other troopers. By the time the Death Merchant was leaning across the seat of the second automobile, he could see spotlights swinging around toward the vehicles and troopers starting to run toward the area. He put a slug into the radio, pulled out the key, and, with the assault rifle in his hand, ran to the first car. Pappas had started the engine, and Anna was beside him, her eyes fixed in a frozen stare of fear, her face glistening with perspiration.

Getting into the rear, the Death Merchant snapped, "Get us out of here—fast." He shoved the barrel of the SG A-R through the left rear window, his lips curled back over his teeth in a snarl. He was angry not at himself, not even at the Greek KYP and the Soviet KGB. It was the total lack of information that kept hammering thumbtacks into his brain. Had Cahill and Beaufault reached the safe house? What about Arzey Holcomb and his wife? Were they safe? Had Melina Arnaoutis betrayed him and the others? Camellion didn't know. He did know that, right now, KYP troopers were trying to kill him and Pappas and Anna.

Although still quite a distance away, some of the troopers opened fire, their projectiles missing when Pappas gunned the engine and the Zigarkas shot forward. Camellion held his fire, preferring to save his rounds for that section of road that was only 570 feet from the house.

Pappas told Anna to "Keep your head down, damn it!" in Greek and, hunched as low as possible over the steering wheel, pressed down on the gas, increasing the speed to 60 mph.

Camellion spotted seven or eight troopers running south when the car was still several hundred feet from that stretch of road which curved inward toward the house, then swung outward to the northwest. Braced against the door, he began triggering off 7.62-mm projectiles at the KYP troopers, cutting down four of them before they could throw themselves to the ground. At 60 mph, it didn't take long for the car to roar past the remaining three troopers, all of whom remained hugging the ground to avoid Camellion's slugs. The car was ninety feet past the dangerous section of the road and was turning to the northwest when the firing pin of the assault rifle in Camellion's hands struck an empty chamber. He shoved the useless weapon out the window and leaned over the front seat.

"How close are we to the main road?" he asked Pappas, who had just switched on the siren and turned on the three red revolving strobe lights on the car's roof.

"Only three kilometers," Pappas said. "The main highway will take us straight through Kaisariani and on to Athens. But the nearest house is only a kilometer from where my place stood. The KYP will surely go there and telephone their headquarters."

"With the siren and the red lights flashing, we can hit seventy-five to eighty klicks per hour," Camellion said. "We should be in Athens by the time the word goes out on us." He added, "You mentioned there was a better way for me to get to the safe house than the one I was going to use. What is it?"

"I will tell you, but first I must ask a small favor of you."

Noticing the faint apprehension in the Greek's voice, Camellion was cautious. "I'd be happy to do a favor for you, provided it doesn't interfere with my mission in any way. What is it?"

"I want you to take Anna with you to your safe house."

Chapter Eleven

I

Dr. Marchenko spread out the large climatological map on the table, took another quick puff on his cigarette, placed it in an ashtray, and peered closely at Dr. Stefanos Paspyrou, who was standing on the other side of the table with Gregor Shchors.

"Let me explain," Lazar Marchenko said politely. "We know you are one of the world's great particle physicists, but Dr. Szamuely and I feel that you lack a full understanding of how the jet streams work. Climatology and meteorology are our disciplines."

Short, heavy, and bald, he motioned impatiently. "Come to this side of the table, please. We will show you how the free electrons and the charged neutron particles from the magnifying transmitter will affect the various jet streams."

"We are positive of our mathematical calculations," added Alexander Szamuely, moving forward, his hands stuffed into the pockets of his gray lab coat. In contrast to the toadlike Marchenko, the long-faced Szamuely was pencil-thin and had an enormous head of gray hair, which he dyed black. With his narrow face and long nose that curved upward slightly at the end, he made one think of a large bird of some undiscovered species, especially when he became excited and moved—flapped—his long arms wildly.

With General Shchors, Dr. Paspyrou walked around to the other side of the table. His voice was tired. "I'm not a climatologist, yet I know that a jet stream is a narrow, flat tube of air which moves more rapidly than surrounding air. I feel safe in saying that a jet stream can be compared to a narrow current in a river—moving faster than adjacent waters."

Marchenko nodded vigorously. "Yes! Yes! An excellent comparison. I should like to point out"—he raised a hand, his forefinger pointed upward—"that a jet stream must be at least fifty knots as a threshold value. We will show you on the map."

He picked up the wooden pointer and first tapped the top of the map, then the bottom. "These masses of air make up the main stream of the circumpolar whirl about both the North and the South poles. As you can see by the wavy blue lines, the circumpolar jets move back and forth between thirty degrees and seventy degrees latitude. Forget them for now. It will be the two subtropical jet streams that we will change slightly, alternating their direction of flow." The pointer moved on the map. "They are between twenty degrees and fifty degrees latitude. There are other and shorter jet streams. They do not concern us here, not for the moment."

Dr. Szamuely said proudly, "Put another way, we will change the course of both the prevailing northwesterlies and the prevailing southwesterlies at the horse latitudes and manipulate the cyclostrophic winds in both hemispheres. We will do that in the final experiment. The first experiment will be to succeed in fluctuating the macroclimate over Europe; that means the general overall climate of the entire geographic area. In the long run, we will be changing the climatic oscillation."

"It won't be until six months later that we will conduct the final experiment," Dr. Marchenko said. He paused to light a cigarette. "That six months will give us time to organize our bioclimatological system in which we will utilize indices of precipitation effectiveness in plant growth," he said, exhaling smoke.

"We wouldn't want the system to backfire over the Soviet Union," Dr. Paspyrou said dryly. "That would be a terrible tragedy, far worse than the meltdown at Chernobyl last year."

Gregor Shchors smiled. Of medium height and weight, he had close-cropped black hair and high, rounded cheekbones beneath a high forehead. His lips were pale but full and rested over a strong jawline. He knew that Dr. Paspyrou, hating them as he did, was being facetious and subtly mocking Marchenko and Szamuely, and it amused him.

Conversely, Lazar Marchenko, believing that the Greek scientist was serious, replied quickly, "Indeed it would be a catastrophe. We will change much of the macroclimate over the Ukraine and over other southern areas of the Motherland. By so doing, we will be able to grow fifty times more wheat and other grains than we do now."

"Another benefit will be our much warmer winters," commented Dr. Szamuely. "Unfortunately, the spring and the summer in southern Europe, North Africa, and the Near East will be much warmer. We estimate the mean rise will be three point seven degrees."

Dr. Paspyrou stood up straight and took several steps back from the map. "Don't forget to mention that if the final experiment is a success, within a few years the midwestern section of the United States will be turned into a desert," he said with pretended unconcern.

Marchenko's flat face, with its slightly Oriental eyes, registered genuine bewilderment. "The United States is not our concern. Our task is to increase the growing season in our own nation. The Americans are a clever, inventive people. I'm sure they'll think of some solution."

General Shchors patted Dr. Paspyrou on the shoulder and said sagely, "Think of the favor we will be doing the Canadians. Canada and the Soviet Union are on the same longitude. We will also be increasing their growing season."

"The Canadians can feed the Americans," Dr. Marchenko said with a sardonic laugh, turning to Paspyrou. "So you need not worry about the poor, starving *Amerikanski*, Stefanos."

Szamuely's dark eyes twinkled with amusement. "We will also be doing some of the Americans a favor, depending on what part of the United States they live in. There will be much warmer winters on the East Coast!"

"With summers in which the temperature will average one hundred ten degrees Fahrenheit." Marchenko snickered. "Of course the southwestern part of the U.S. will become much cooler and receive three times more rain. But the Northwest and the West Coast will become much colder."

Dr. Paspyrou, who disliked any of the Russians calling him by his first name, did not make any kind of rebuttal. There was only one way of answering a bad argument, and that was to ignore it, even if he would never be able to disregard his contempt for these men and the diabolical system of slavery and repression they represented.

They personally had not kidnapped him and his family; they personally had not brought him and his family to the island of Miskos. The KGB had. Nevertheless, Shchors, Marchenko, Szamuely, and the rest of the Russians at the complex were not only a part of the system, they supported it and were gladly a part of it. If they had sincerely believed in the Soviet form of communism, they could have been excused for their ignorance and complete stupidity, the way a religious person who truly believed in "miracles" could be excused. But none of the Russians inside Mount Posso was a convert to communism, in spite of all the propaganda they all had been subjected to.

They supported the system for only one reason: because they were hypocrites, because they were selfish, because they were members of the *Nomenklatura*, the ruling class, and didn't want to lose their precious privileges.

Nothing in nature amazed Stefanos Paspyrou. He knew there were not any true miracles or true mysteries. There were only unanswered questions, riddles that Man still had to solve. The true riddle was Man himself, Man and his incomprehensible nature. These Russian scientists were a prime example. They were not consciously evil men. They loved their wives and children. They had their sentimental side. Motion pictures were shown three times a week at the complex inside the mountain, and Paspyrou knew that sad scenes could bring tears to Dr. Marchenko's eyes. And then there was Major Sergei Diamov, the chief of the KGB on the island, a truly cruel man who regarded all non-Russians as prey. Yet even that monster was forever showing photographs of his children.

To Paspyrou, the truly moral paradox was that these very same men were calmly planning to change the weather of the world and by so doing starve hundreds of millions of people to death. Practically all of Mexico and Central America would be turned into a semidesert. Australia would become the biggest sand dune in the world. India, China, and Southeast Asia would grow warmer, with increased monsoons.

None of this troubled the Soviet scientists, who had easily rationalized that they were only "serving" their Motherland, their precious Russia, and even "defending" the Soviet Union against the "forces of imperialism."

Another paradox was that Paspyrou enjoyed the company of General Gregor Shchors, who was a first-rate physicist with numerous scientific papers to his credit. He liked the man. Shchors was an extremely intelligent and sensitive individual who enjoyed nothing better than puttering around in his garden at his *dacha* outside of Leningrad; and he was puritanical in his morals, forever condemning young men and women who fornicated and had little respect for their elders. Worse was Gregor's denunciation of women who did not want to have children: "Selfish, without respect for themselves or their husbands!"

At the same time, the grandfatherly-looking Shchors was not the least bit concerned about the millions of children who, because of his work as a scientist, would die with bloated bellies, emaciated faces, and arms and legs no thicker than a broomhandle. Nor would the pitiful little victims bring tears to the eyes of Lazar Marchenko, whose only concern was that he might run out of cigarettes. A chain smoker, he smoked four packs a day—American NOWs.

General Shchors had assured the Greek physicist that after the experiments had been completed, he and his family would be taken by submarine to the Soviet Union, where they would enjoy an honored status.

"We could not have perfected our weather modification techniques if you had not solved the riddle of Tesla's magnifying transmitter," Shchors had told him one afternoon. "We had no idea how to transmit power through the air and control it, and the neutron accelerator and deaccelerator were completely new to us. You solved that problem for us, Stefanos. Why, you will go down in history as one of the world's greatest scientists."

Stefanos Paspyrou could not forget those words: the world's greatest. . . . To him they meant that he was the scientist who would make it possible for the Soviet Union to starve millions of innocent human beings to death.

Or he would be *the* scientist who would be responsible for starting a nuclear holocaust—World War III.

"The Americans will do nothing," Major Sergei Diamov was fond of bragging. "They will not start a nuclear war! Why, they won't be able to prove we're responsible for the change in the weather."

Even General Shchors disagreed with that premise, but not openly, not in front of Diamov.

Paspyrou had toyed with the possibility of sabotaging the experiments. He knew that he couldn't. His every move was watched. Destroy the magnifying transmitter, which, in a few weeks, would be taken up through the shaft and assembled in the man-made crater on top of Mount Posso? How? Paspyrou knew that even if he could wreck the transmitter, the KGB would kill his family—and the Russians would promptly build another magnifying transmitter, now that they had the secret.

There was another possibility: that the experiment would never work. In Paspyrou's opinion, there hadn't been enough tests, and the Russians were leaving far too much to chance.

Paspyrou left the table area and sat down in a canvas and aluminum-frame chair. Because of weight problems, since everything had to be brought in by submarine, all furniture in the complex was made of aluminum and/or plastic.

Dr. Paspyrou said, "Gentlemen, I have never doubted that your calculations in the climatological department are correct. My concern was never the jet streams. The magnifying transmitter, in theory, can stretch them back and forth like a rubber band."

"Last night you did say you were worried," Lazar Marchenko said haughtily, "and wanted to discuss the problem this morning."

"We don't even know if we will have the power to operate the transmitter," Paspyrou said grimly. "My God! We'll need one hundred million volts to energize the stream of neutron particles—and you intend to 'broadcast' that terrific amount of energy all the way from the Soviet Union!"

"Doctor, have you forgotten that we're already receiving power from the magnet station in the Motherland?" Marchenko said derisively. "Not once in all these months have we had to turn on ordinary electric generators. Every bit of our power has come from Moscow."

"The relay station in Smolyan is functioning perfectly," Alexander Szamuely said. "And let's not hear again that nonsense about American satellites discovering the relay station in Bulgaria. The six dispersers in the station are too cleverly disguised within the radio towers. The Americans can photograph all they want. The station has been broadcasting short-wave programs for the past eight months. American intelligence can only conclude that the station is just that—a radio station."

"Dr. Szamuely, you have the annoying habit of putting words into other people's mouths," Paspyrou said indignantly. "I was not even thinking of the energy relay station in Bulgaria. The danger is in our tampering with the ozone layer."

" 'Tampering' is not the correct word," snapped an irritated Dr. Szamuely. "We will be conducting a carefully controlled experiment—not 'tampering'!"

"Dr. Szamuely, you are not using the scientific method. All you're doing is using nice-sounding phrases to cover the reality of a situation," Paspyrou said reproachfully. "All of you are doing what your nuclear engineers have done—closing your eyes to the flaws in the system. No matter how well we control the intensity of the beam, we still don't know what it will do to the ozone layer. We don't know any more than we have solid data on the effect that a hundred thermonuclear bombs would have on the world's weather."

"You're attaching too much importance to the ozone layer," Marchenko said, shrugging off Paspyrou's warning. "There's more to the troposphere than the ozone layer."

"I must agree with Lazar and Alexander," General Shchors said, leaning back in his chair, his eyes steady on Paspyrou. "I can appreciate your concern—we all can and do—but the ozone layer is not necessarily that important to any of our experiments. It has nothing to do with the reshuffling of the jet streams."

Dr. Paspyrou's response was immediate. "The three of you are completely missing my main point. As I said, I am not the least bit concerned with the manipulation of the jet streams. Forget them. But don't say the ozone layer is not important."

"Now see here!" Marchenko began angrily. "We are not—"

"Lazar! Let him finish!" ordered General Shchors.

"We can't ignore the fact that the diffuse layer of ozone screens out over ninety-nine percent of solar radiation—those wavelengths shorter than three hundred twenty nanometers," said Paspyrou. "Because ultraviolet radiation of high intensity is so harmful to all forms of life, many biologists believe that life on this planet didn't begin until after formation of the ozone layer. Yet the three of you sit there and blissfully maintain that the ozone layer is not important!"

"Stefanos, if I didn't know better, I would think that you were under the impression that the ozone layer was some kind of solid shell around the earth, a shell that could break!" Shchors retorted. "Why, all kinds of things have gone through the ozone layer—space vehicles, satellites, and even laser beams bounced to the moon and back."

"Let's not forget the millions of tiny meteorites constantly coming in and bombarding the earth—well, burning up in the atmosphere," said Szamuely.

"Exactly, so why all the concern, Doctor?" Marchenko took a long drag on his NOW and forcefully expelled smoke, as if he were giving birth to a fresh thought.

"Because we don't know what half a billion volts of positive neutron energy will do to the ozone layer," said Paspyrou, feeling helpless. "We will have all that positive energy hitting negative electrons, or negatrons, in the atoms of the molecules of the ozone layer. I repeat: It has never been done. Damn it! We don't *know* what will take place!"

Marchenko and Szamuely wisely remained silent. They weren't particle physicists.

"But we *do* know," said Shchors, who was a physicist and was visibly annoyed. "Nothing will happen. The magnifying transmitter isn't a cyclotron. Even if it were, it couldn't reorbit the neutrons and protons in the nucleus of any atom, much less knock out the electrons." On the verge of losing his temper, Shchors removed his eyeglasses, pinched the bridge of his nose, then glared at Dr. Paspyrou. "Let's not have any more of this nonsense. Your argument about the ozone layer is as ridiculous as your nonsense about the oceans and the Antarctic ice sheet."

Szamuely snorted. "We proved you didn't know what you were talking about. For years Soviet oceanographers have been monitoring currents, temperature, and salinity around the Antarctic ice sheet. We are positive that warmer weather will not cause the ice sheet to melt and flood the coastal cities of the world."

Paspyrou was tired of arguing. He was not a climatologist and, therefore, had very limited knowledge. He wasn't an oceanographer either. Nonetheless, he did have some facts. He did know that the West Antarctic ice sheet consisted of over one million cubic miles of ice that rested on underwater bedrock, the ice flow impeded by two partly floating ice shelves. Should warmer ocean water and heated air above the pole begin to melt the shelves, the ice sheet would begin to melt as well. Theoretically, this added volume of ice would cause the levels of the oceans to rise from sixteen to nineteen feet.

Paspyrou had to admit that the Soviet scientists' argument why this rise would not take place was good. According to them, the ice sheet would melt so slowly that the runoff would be inappreciable; and although floating ice would melt rapidly in warmer oceans, the water level would not rise dangerously. As evidence, glaciologists used the analogy of ice cubes in a glass filled with water. The ice cubes melt, but the fluid doesn't pour over the brim.

Soviet scientists had concluded that by the year 2100, the sea level would rise about nineteen inches.

As usual, thought Paspyrou, the Russians hadn't conducted enough research. They hadn't considered the oceans as a whole. For example, they still lacked much hard data on changes in the circulation pattern of the oceans. Any severe change in the world's weather would have to affect the Gulf Stream and other currents. These currents would be greatly weakened because circulation is driven by the thermal contrast between the poles and the equator, with the oceans functioning as a pump that redistributes solar heat. Should the earth become warmer, the poles would have to get hotter, which would reduce the thermal contrast and the strength of the "pump." The Russians had ignored the very real possibility that circulation would become less vigorous.

Frowning slightly, General Gregor Shchors studied Paspyrou. A slender, balding man in his sixties, Stefanos Paspyrou had the inquisitive face of a thinker, of a scholar . . . and the morals and the manners of a gentleman.

"Well, Stefanos! It's not like you to remain so quiet!" Shchors joked, smiling thinly. "Surely you have some new dangers and pronouncements of doom to warn us about!"

Lazar Marchenko and Alexander Szamuely laughed mockingly. Marchenko—inelegant smoker that he was—lighted a fresh cigarette from the stub of the old one, after which he snubbed out the old cigarette and brushed ashes from his lab coat.

Paspyrou made all three Russians feel vaguely uneasy by giving them a big smile. "Gentlemen, you are going to do what you feel is best. Why should we waste each other's time in useless and nonproductive discussions? Should the experiments fail, you will have only yourselves to blame. . . ."

From where Major Sergei Diamov stood in his small office in the one-story prefab KGB building, he could look out over the complex whose code name was *Veliki*—"Friend." To the west were the rows of magnatrons where power was stored, energy picked from the air on something the scientists called a neutron klystron sweep. Diamov knew little of the process and cared even less. He did know that some kind of amazing new energy was stored in the magnatrons and that by moving the power back and forth through the special magnets the strength of the energy was vastly increased.

Also to the west were the living domes and the assembly areas. To the southwest were supplies, recreation, the hospital, kitchen, general mess, and planning and headquarters.

Due south were the submarine pens. Almost half a century earlier, German engineers had built them to hold their submarines. Soviet engineers had enlarged the pens to accommodate two large Soviet OSCAR-class nuclear-powered submarines. Twice a month subs brought supplies from the Soviet Union.

In the large area between the sub pens and the row of magnatrons was a square column of metal that was twenty-five yards on all four sides. The tower rose from the solid bedrock floor to the uneven rock ceiling ninety feet above. The shaft did not stop at the ceiling, but continued upward through the rock to the bottom of the crater on top of the mountain. The installation in the crater was now being completed, and in another month the weird-looking beam device would be taken on the elevator to the top and mounted in its special frame.

"Comrade Diamov, did you hear me?" Colonel Boris Malenkova said in a loud, impatient voice. "I asked why there were not any underwater sound detectors positioned around the island."

A look of cunning flashed across Diamov's slab-sided face, a look that was gone by the time he turned from the window and looked at the Spetsnaz commander relaxed in a folding chair.

Since Malenkova and his unit had arrived at *Veliki*, there had been a silent and unspoken but acknowledged truce between the two men. Each recognized in the other a danger to his career, a dangerous obstacle that could not be removed. Why risk the other man's sending a bad report about him to Moscow? Better to play the game of cooperation.

"It's a matter of security," Major Diamov explained in an easy, affable manner. He walked to the pot of hot tea on a table. "Underwater sensors would be spotted by divers. The devices would only increase their curiosity and prompt them to make a closer inspection of the island. We wouldn't want that, now, would we, Comrade Malenkova?"

Forced to accept the reality of this logic, Malenkova nodded, a calculating glow in his gray-green eyes. He had to back Diamov into a corner and force the KGB boss to admit that he had been lax in security.

"Without any underwater sensors, divers could approach the island from any direction and come ashore and we wouldn't be aware of them," Malenkova said with pseudoseriousness. "I wouldn't call that closed security, Comrade."

"I would." Diamov finished pouring tea into a mug, glanced at Malenkova, and smiled. "Or didn't I tell you that there are ground sensors buried on the island? They ring the entire island. You see, there is absolutely no way anyone can set foot on this island without our knowing it." He repeated firmly, "No way."

Diamov sat down, crossed his legs, and smiled again at an unhappy Malenkova. "There isn't any breach of security at this base, Comrade Colonel. Naturally, if you have detected any cracks, I should be happy for you to tell me. We could then work together to remedy the situation."

Malenkova could only acquiesce with a slight nod of his head. He avoided Diamov's eyes—the bastard! It was all Malenkova could do to sit there with a calm, neutral expression, all the while knowing that Diamov was aware that he and Major Valeri Fedchenko had gone over every foot of the island looking for a flaw in Diamov's security.

Colonel Malenkova thought again of the American motion picture he had seen the previous night in the recreation building. Russian dialogue had been dubbed in. The film was known as a "western," and it was the first American motion picture Malenkova had ever seen.

Unable to bring himself to admit to Diamov that he had not found any weakness in the security system, Malenkova changed the subject. "Comrade Diamov, did you see the film last night?" he asked.

"Yes, what about it?"

"You have seen many of these 'westerns'?"

"Quite a few. I was once stationed in the United States."

"Maybe you can answer a question for me. Why is it that when everyone is in a drinking place—"

"A saloon!" Diamov corrected him with a low laugh.

"Why is it that when they are in a saloon and everyone starts to fight—why does a piano start playing?"

Chapter Twelve

It isn't true that when two people agree on everything, one of them is doing all the thinking. At the moment Richard Camellion, Joseph Pappas—and Anna Sofoulis too—had identical thoughts on their present situation, and they were in agreement.

This section of Stazoukis Avenue was a quiet middle-class residential neighborhood, the apartment houses old with rebuilt fronts, many with fresh coats of paint. In this section of Athens lived white-collar workers, junior executives, and the owners of small businesses.

Joe Pappas, who was driving the cab, used a false name when he called over his shoulder to Anna. "Maria, if he starts to wiggle around back there, knock him in the head with the butt of the pistol."

"I think he's still unconscious," Anna murmured.

Sitting next to Pappas, the Death Merchant watched the house numbers vanish behind the cab. The odd numbers were to the left, the even numbers to the right, on Camellion's side. The next block would be the seventeen-hundred block. Camellion nudged Pappas and pointed ahead. Pappas nodded.

The seventeen-hundred block was similar to the block that preceded it, except that now the fronts of the four-story apartment houses, on both sides of the street, were exactly alike, with iron fences enclosing the very tiny yards.

Pappas slowed the cab and the numbers began to roll by—1795, 1780, 1772. Black numbers painted on a white background. There was a streetlight close to number 1766, and Pappas had soon pulled over by the curb and was parking. It was 11:30 P.M. and the street was very quiet. Silence could be deceptive. For all they knew, KYP agents could be watching . . . waiting to close in on the fourth-floor apartment.

Pappas leaned close to Camellion, who was shoving the Steyr into his shoulder holster, and whispered, "Good luck, American. May God protect you and Anna." Then he turned and looked at Anna Sofoulis. *"Kali andámosí, Marie!"*

Pappas didn't watch the Death Merchant and Anna move through the gate and walk up the white concrete steps. By the time Camellion was opening the front door of the apartment house, Pappas was almost to the end of the block and getting ready to turn and go to his own secure house, wherever it might be. He had told Camellion that his safe house wouldn't be all that secure; for that reason, Pappas had asked the Death Merchant to take Anna with him: ". . . and take her out of the country with you. I know your people will have an escape route prepared. I want your word that you will get her to the United States. It has always been her dream to go to America."

"How do you know I'd keep my word?" Camellion had said.

"I know people. Some people strengthen society just by being the kind of people they are. You are one of those people."

In turn, Pappas had presented his plan for getting Camellion and Anna to 1766 Stazoukis Avenue in a hurry. Once the three of them had reached Athens in the KYP Zigarkas, Pappas had shut off the siren and the revolving red lights and had driven into an alley. Anna had hurried ahead to another street to hail a cab. If Athens had anything of merit, it was plenty of taxis, even more than New York City. Athens had more than a quarter of a million private cars and almost fifteen thousand taxis. Per ratio of population, this was six percent more taxis than were in New York.

Once Anna was inside the cab, she had reached inside her shirt, pulled one of the .45 Detonics pistols from the waistband of her jeans, and told the driver to pull over and stop for the two men who had just come out of the alley and were walking west—or she would blow his head off. The terrified driver, having no desire to go headless through life, had quickly complied.

Several blocks later Camellion had forced the driver to pull into another alley. The cabbie had been forced to lie on his stomach on the floor between the seats while Pappas tied his wrists behind his back with strips of cloth fashioned from a freshly laundered KYP shirt that had been hanging on a hanger on a side hook inside the Zigarkas. He had also used a handkerchief to gag the man. Pappas had then driven the taxi to Stazoukis Avenue. Having grown up in Athens, he knew all the shortcuts and side routes.

Beyond the front door was a short hall that led to the first-floor apartment. To the right were four large mailboxes built into the wall. To the left, the stairs to the second floor. The Death Merchant and Anna climbed the stairs quickly to the fourth floor.

Camellion glanced sideways at Anna, who couldn't conceal her nervousness. He didn't blame her for being afraid. They might very well be walking into a trap. Camellion didn't think so. His main worry was how the Soviet KGB had learned about him. In all likelihood, the KGB and the KYP knew the whole nine yards. The enemy had known enough to close in on Pappas's warehouse, and it was almost a certainty that they knew about Arnold Cahill and Rene Beaufault. *Uh-huh . . . and maybe even about Arzey Holcomb.* But did the KGB and the KYP know about the safe house?

The Soviet Union couldn't manufacture a decent roll of toilet paper, but the pig farmers did have a first-rate intelligence service. If the KGB knew about the safe house, the Greek KYP also knew. If so, the intelligent thing for the KYP to do would be to wait and see who came to 1766 Stazoukis Avenue. The Death Merchant's logic was that since the Russians and the Greeks wanted him badly and since he was now in the building, he'd soon know if his theory was correct . . . sooner or later, no doubt sooner.

Ahead was a short hall, at its end the door to the fourth-floor apartment. The name on the card above the doorbell button was printed in Greek, looking like carefully scratched turkey marks to Camellion.

"The name is Vyron Rozakis," Anna whispered. "What do we do, Mr. Camellion?"

"The only thing we can do," he said, and pressed the button.

The five- by ten-inch inspector door opened, and Camellion could see a dark-complexioned man with a crooked nose peering suspiciously at him and Anna. He assumed the man was Vyron Rozakis.

The man said something in Greek in a low voice.

Anna interpreted. "He wants to know who we are and what we want."

The Death Merchant looked at the man and gave the first Latin sentence of the recognition code—

"Dives agris, dives positis in foenore nummis" ("Rich in lands, rich in money laid out in interest").

"Let them in," Camellion and Anna heard another voice say in English. Evidently a second man had been standing just inside the door.

Camellion and Anna heard the Greek removing a chain. He then pulled back bolts at the top and the bottom, opened the door, and motioned them inside, then quickly replaced the chain and shoved the bolts back into place.

Arzey Holcomb had been standing next to Vyron Rozakis; the Death Merchant recognized the ONI agent from photographs he had viewed in the States.

Wearing a leather Safariland upside-down shoulder holster filled with a 9-mm Llama Omni autoloader, Holcomb was a thin-boned man in his early forties, his sparse light-brown hair topping a high forehead and a weather-lined face. However, his gray eyes were quick and alert as he stepped forward, lowered the Uzi submachine gun in his left hand, and held out his right hand to the Death Merchant, saying "I'm Arzey Holcomb. You must be Richard Camellion." His eyes moved questioningly to Anna Sofoulis. "Who is she?"

The Death Merchant had also noticed that Rene Beaufault was in the front room, sitting on the arm of a couch, an Uzi SMG in his hands.

Camellion shook Holcomb's hand, said, "Yes, I'm Camellion," then turned to the tall French intelligence agent. "I'm glad you made it here safely, Rene. Any word from Arnie?"

"Cahill is dead," Beaufault said, his voice as sad as his phlegmatic-looking eyes. "I passed his place on my way here. KYP and *Asfaleia* cars were parked in front of his apartment house and on the other side of the street. I parked in the next block, walked back, and asked people looking on what had happened.

They said the security police had shot it out with a foreign terrorist and had killed him. From where I stood, I could see a body being carried from the apartment house." He continued pensively. "The KYP also raided the apartment on Ridakino Avenue within an hour and a half after I received your phone call."

"There can be no mistake about it?" Camellion demanded harshly.

"I'm positive," Beaufault said, this time in a louder, more firm voice. "Vyron Rozakis, the man with Holcomb, was there. He saw it."

In response to Camellion's turning to him, Rozakis lumbered forward. A very stocky man who appeared to lack a neck—his head rested solidly on top of his broad torso—he had dark bushy hair, a thick mustache, and a deep voice that fit his hard-rock appearance.

"Two others—I no tell their names—and me, we see the uniformed KYP they go into the building," he growled in broken English, facing the Death Merchant. "They come out an hour later, get into cars and they go way."

Holcomb, an unlit cigarette in his mouth, said hastily, "What about Ridakino Avenue? What does it mean, Camellion?"

"It means that Melina Arnaoutis—your courier and the gal whose apartment I was sharing—is working for either the KGB or the KYP," Camellion said. Smiling ironically, he eased his body into an armchair. "I told her I was going to an apartment on Ridakino Avenue. She's the only one who could have tipped off the KGB—or the KYP. I never did fully trust her, but I didn't really suspect her until this afternoon. The KGB—I think it was the KGB—tried to ambush me."

With a loud sigh of disgust, Holcomb sat down and

put the Uzi on the rug. "She was my courier for almost three years," he said. "My God!" His eyes were pure panic as he stared at the Death Merchant. "You didn't tell that bitch about—"

"About Operation Zeus?" Camellion finished. "No, I didn't. She knew only about you—and me. The KGB or the KYP trailed you to Cahill and Beaufault. They played with us and we made fools of ourselves. You're the one that sent the microdot to me, so I assume you've already given ONI Center in the States the location of the Soviet base?"

"Early this morning. I used the shortwave at my store." Holcomb stole an oblique look at Anna Sofoulis, who had sat down on the couch. "I don't know why I was supposed to send the information to you in an m-dot. I had already given them the name of the island; yet my orders were to get the same information about Miskos to you. Frankly, it doesn't make any sense."

Camellion first explained who Anna was and why she was with him. He then said, thinking of Nicholas Notaras, "There's a lot about this mission that doesn't make sense . . . too many loose ends, too many unanswered questions."

"The whole damn network has fallen apart!" protested Holcomb. "All the Greek street men are underground, and we're sitting on tissue paper over quicksand. And to think that those idiots in the States expected us to actually rescue Dr. Paspyrou!"

"In my opinion, we were never intended to rescue the good professor," Camellion said. "It was all hype!"

Holcomb thought for a moment, the deep worry etched in his face changing to anger. He stared at the Death Merchant. "You think we were lied to deliberately?" he asked sharply.

"Not lied to as much as we were used as bait,"

Camellion amended gently. "Your wife—she's with you?"

"She's in a hospital, recovering from a gall bladder operation," Holcomb said, looking dismayed. "She was operated on only three days ago. She'll be arrested for espionage, but there isn't any way we can help her."

The Death Merchant brushed aside the gravy and went straight to the meat of the matter. "If the KYP know about this place and were watching, they saw Anna and me come in. The quicker we leave, the longer we'll live. I was told you have the details of the underground escape route."

"Correct." Another worried look skidded across Holcomb's lined face. "We were supposed to hole up here for a week. In the meantime, others would arrange for us to go by cabin cruiser or fishing boat out onto the Ionian Sea. There we were to rendezvous with a British sub."

It was all coming together for Camellion, who now knew why Grojean had given him the telephone number.

"We still can meet the sub," he said. "I have a place. We'll get to that later. Right now let's get the hell out of here. We still have to go down those steps and get to cars. You had better have transportation!"

"We have, but we're not going down any stairs." Holcomb looked across at Vyron Rozakis and spoke in Greek. Rozakis nodded and hurried from the room.

Getting to his feet, Holcomb explained to the Death Merchant that all the apartments on the north side of that block of Stazoukis Avenue were actually in one long building. "To the west there is only one complex that isn't connected to this building—the last four apartments, on the corner of Stazoukis and Epidrotou Street. Five years ago the socialist govern-

ment decided it would be cheaper to remodel than
tear down all these old buildings and start from
scratch."

"Get to the point," urged Camellion, watching
Rene Beaufault leave the room.

The point was that there was one long attic that
stretched across all the apartments on the fourth
floor—not a true attic but a ventilation space, to permit air to circulate, acting as a buffer against heat in
summer and cold in winter.

The pièce de résistance was that Vyron Rozakis
had rented another apartment years earlier under an
assumed name. This fourth-floor apartment was to
the west, next to the building on the corner of
Stazoukis and Epidrotou.

"Camellion, have you noticed the ceiling in here?"
Holcomb said. He smiled for the first time. "See how
it is paneled? The ceilings in all four of the rooms are
like that. What we'll do is go through one of the
ceiling panels in the bedroom, move west through
the dead space, and come down in the last apartment. From there to the garage where we have a
medical service van. Now, about the place you mentioned?"

"First I have to phone," Camellion said. "Not from
here, after we leave. How far can you trust Rozakis?"

"All the way," replied Holcomb. "I can assure you
that no one knows about the apartment at the end of
the block but him and me."

Rene Beaufault, who had returned to the living
room with a leather satchel in his hands, glanced up
at the Death Merchant as he placed the satchel on
the floor and opened it.

"I didn't know about the apartment down the
block until I arrived this afternoon," he said, and
began taking out flat packages wrapped in oily
brown paper.

"What are you going to do with the explosives?" Camellion demanded. He walked over to Beaufault and picked up one of the packages of Vertung-Y, a West German plastic explosive, which, with a base, was mostly TNT. "There's enough there to blow up this place, the apartment below, and the ones on each side."

Rene Beaufault sighed and stood up. "It's his idea." He looked across at Arzey Holcomb. "We get into the crawl space and the V-Y explodes ten minutes after we depart."

"It's an urban cellular warfare trick," Holcomb said, feeling annoyed and uncomfortable at the way the Death Merchant was glaring at him.

"You're mixed up," Camellion said coldly. "In urban cellular warfare, the terrorists hide in an apartment house full of innocent people. If they're discovered, they threaten to blow up the building and the occupants. But we're not terrorists."

"Wait a minute!" Holcomb protested angrily. "The explosion will create confusion and—"

"And kill scores of innocent people!" Camellion lashed out. "Think of your wife, Arzey. If we blow up half this block, what do you think the Greek authorities will do to her?"

"Monsieur Camellion is right," Beaufault said with a look of cool triumph. "There are several Russian stick grenades in the satchel. We could hook them up to explode when the front door is opened. The explosions would wreck this room but not injure anyone in the other apartments."

The Death Merchant made the decision without giving Holcomb a chance to speak. "Forget the Vertung-Y. We'll take it with us. We'll use the grenades. But first Arzey and I will check the fourth-floor stairs. Anna, stay with Beaufault."

Beaufault removed the two Russian RGD-33 grenades from the satchel, each of which was a tin container filled with seven ounces of TNT, fastened to a metal handle. "I'll pull the pins and hold the fuses down with rulers. I'll place one end of a ruler underneath the bottom of the door and the other end on top of the fuse release. Simple! The door opens, the grenades explode."

"Why bother looking down the stairs?" Holcomb asked with as much vigor as he could muster after Camellion had canceled his order. "By now Vyron has the panel down from the ceiling. All we have to do is leave."

"We can't, not yet," Camellion said, taking the Uzi SMG that Beaufault had been holding. "Use your head. If the KYP is going to raid this place, they were watching and saw me and Anna come in. They could be placing men in the front and back right now. If we can hold them off for a few minutes on the stairs, they'll proceed with greater caution, which will give us extra time in getting away. Otherwise they'll break down the door and soon discover the route we've taken. They'll find out anyway. They'll know we just didn't vanish!"

"It makes sense," Holcomb was forced to admit. He picked up the Uzi from the rug and glanced disdainfully at Camellion. "All right. Let's get out there."

"Rene, keep the door open so that you can keep an eye on us," Camellion said. He paused and smiled. "Once the door is shut, you don't want to open it to just anyone."

Vyron Rozakis came from one of the bedrooms into the living room, a .380 Turkish MKE pistol in his hand. He looked from Holcomb and Camellion to Beaufault, who had a stick grenade sticking out of each back pocket and was removing the chain from the door.

"Why you wait? Panel from ceiling is down," Rozakis said, clearly puzzled.

Holcomb, speaking Greek, gave him the facts of life.

"Malista! I go with you," Rozakis said, his expression showing that he thought waiting at the top of the stairs was a good idea. "We kill some KYP and make other KYP creep like snails!"

Beaufault opened the door, and Camellion and the other two men moved out into the hall. They were soon at the end of the hall, in the corner where they could look down the steps and, if necessary, jerk back to the wall. Camellion looked carefully around the edge and down the steps. The steps from the third to the fourth floor were empty.

"This is a waste of time," whispered Holcomb. "Why don't we—"

"Listen!" Camellion motioned for silence. "I thought I heard something."

He turned and looked at the half-open door. Rene Beaufault was on a knee, a French MAB pistol in his hand. Because the hall was ten feet long, Rene could see only the very top step.

Ten seconds passed. This time all three heard subdued voices at the bottom of the stairs. "Hold your fire," Camellion whispered. "Give them time to move up six or seven steps."

He slowly began to count. Reaching ten, he said *"Now!"* stepped out from the corner, pointed the Uzi down, and fired. The submachine gun chattered, spitting slugs from the barrel and tossing brass cartridge cases from the open receiver of the weapon.

The two gray-uniformed KYP troopers, halfway up the steps, were struck in the chest, the hot metal tearing off pieces of their shirts, which fluttered to the stairs as the two corpses fell back toward two more troopers who were six feet behind them. These two men died seconds later, Camellion's Uzi projectiles exploding their skulls before knocking them to the bottom of the steps, just ahead of the first two corpses.

A fifth man, still at the bottom of the stairs, tried frantically to bring up his Beretta submachine gun while other troopers in the hall and on the third-floor stairs either dropped or snuggled against the wall. The fifth man never got off one round. A 9-mm Uzi parabellum bullet caught him in the forehead and snapped his head back. A second slug tore off his chin. A third struck him in the chest. It cut through a cross strap, his shirt and his flesh, and went through his breast bone. He let the Beretta slip from his hands and, dripping blood, dropped.

"Get back to the apartment," the Death Merchant said. "The KYP will not use concentrated firepower, and we could be trapped too easily here."

He turned and sprinted to the half-open door, Holcomb and Rozakis racing after him. Rozakis, the last man, was going through the doorway when there was a *plop* in the hall behind him. From the bottom of the fourth-floor stairs, other KYP troopers had tossed up a canister, which had exploded and was spewing out a white cloud of tear gas. *Plop!* Another canister burst.

Rene Beaufault slammed the door, put on the chain, pushed the bolts into place, and pulled the two Russian RGD-33 grenades from his rear pockets.

"You two and Anna go ahead," Camellion said to Holcomb and Rozakis. "I'll help Rene. We'll be there in a moment."

"Make it snappy," Holcomb warned. "The KYP will storm in pretty fast." He turned toward an ashen-faced Anna Sofoulis standing against a wall. "Come along, young lady."

Beaufault had slipped two twelve-inch metal rulers underneath the bottom of the door and was bending one upward. "Pull the pin and slip the grenade under the end of the ruler," he told Camellion. "Be sure the fuse release is centered underneath the ruler. I'm sure there'll be enough pressure to hold the release down—ever do this before?"

If you only knew! "Oh, a few times," said Camellion, pulling the pin of the first grenade.

It took only a few minutes for Camellion and Beaufault to set the two booby traps. Then, after Rene picked up the satchel full of Vertung-Y, they hurried into the bedroom from which they would crawl into the ventilation space. The ceiling panel over the dresser had been removed, and Arzey Holcomb's head was sticking out of the small opening.

"Get on the dresser and we'll pull you up by the arms," Holcomb said. "Be careful. Don't break anything on the dresser or disturb it in any way. It would be an instant tipoff to the KYP."

The transfer from dresser to dead space went quickly, and soon Vyron Rozakis, using a long rachet-type screwdriver, was fastening the plywood panel in place, working by the light of two flashlights held by Holcomb and Anna Sofoulis.

After Rozakis had completed the job, Holcomb shone the beam all around the area, so that they could see they were on a wooden four-foot-wide catwalk that stretched off in the darkness to the west.

"Whatever any of you do, don't step off the catwalk," Holcomb whispered. "If you do, you'll be stepping on the panel of the ceiling of another apartment. Your weight could take you through it. I'll go first with one light. Camellion, you go last with the other flash. You can light the way for yourself and the others. Let's go—and *don't* drop any of the weapons."

The slanted roof was not even six feet above them, and they had to walk slightly bent over. Soon they began to move at a brisk, settled pace—straight west —able to do so because there was nothing, no barrier, to impede their progress.

They were three-fourths of the way to their goal when they heard the two Soviet grenades explode far behind them, muffled booms that told them the KYP were entering the apartment.

Even the Death Merchant, with his cast-iron nervous system, was relieved when Holcomb announced that they were over the target apartment. As proof, he pointed to a large white *X* painted on a panel to the left of the catwalk. Once again Vyron Rozakis went to work with the rachet screwdriver, freeing the panel, which he lifted and placed across the tops of several joists.

Holcomb flashed the beam of his light through the opening. Below the opening was a table.

"Who wants to go first?" Holcomb asked with a nervous little laugh.

The Uzi submachine guns were not a problem. When the Death Merchant pointed out that they could meet occupants of the building on the way to the garages in the rear, Holcomb replied that they would leave the SMGs in the apartment. "We won't need them. There are automatic weapons in the van."

The five hurried through the darkened apartment to the front door, which Holcomb carefully locked once they were in the hall. They hurried down the four flights of steps. On the ground floor they turned into the side hall to reach a door that opened to the outside rear and the four private side-by-side garages.

Time: 12:41 A.M. The night air was cool. The moon

was out, and there was only stillness, and fear and uncertainty. While Camellion held the flashlight, Arzey Holcomb opened the combination lock on the rear door of the second garage. He then removed the lock, opened the door, and they went inside the garage.

Camellion was slightly surprised when he saw that the blue van, with a wide horizontal white stripe down the center—the national colors of *Vasileion tis Ellados* (Greece)—was almost an identical replica of a National Health Service medical vehicle. There were even blue strobe lights on top and the words "National Health Emergency Service" in Greek on both sides of the van.

Holcomb opened the door on the driver's side, took out two white coats, handed one to Vyron Rozakis, and looked at Camellion, who was holding the beam of the flash downward.

"The place you mentioned. It is a safe house?" Holcomb asked as he put on the white coat.

"I don't even know its location," Camellion said. "All I have is a phone number. I was told I could use it anytime day or night, but for emergencies only. I'd say we're facing an emergency."

Rene Beaufault sounded not only serious but worried. "The KYP will have men stationed in the alley up the block. They'll see us leave in the van."

"The odds are that they won't even notice us," Camellion said. "For all they know, we could be night workers. We could be a lot of things, but it's unlikely that the KYP will link a van here with terrorists who vanished almost a block away. By the time they discover the way we left, we'll be gone. Searching for booby traps will slow them considerably."

"Right or wrong, we have to risk it," Holcomb ventured. "We have nowhere else to go, and I've never found a way to intimidate death." His attention went to the Death Merchant, Rene Beaufault, and Anna Sofoulis. "The three of you get in back and stay down. There are submachine guns in a bandage case. If we're unlucky, we might as well shoot it out with the bastards and die quickly rather than slowly in some KYP interrogation room."

"Arzey, tell Rozakis to lock the other door once the other two doors are open," Camellion said.

"A good idea," Holcomb said amiably. "There's not much point in making it easy for the KYP, is there?"

"We'll gain another ten minutes or so when they reach the apartment," Camellion said. "Maybe even an hour if the damn fools think we're still in the building."

Holcomb spoke in Greek to Vyron Rozakis, who nodded. Holcomb then said to Camellion, "The nice part is that no one knows what kind of vehicle we have. Even after they wise up and find this empty garage, they won't know what kind of car description to put out."

Rozakis took the long iron bar from across the two garage doors, pushed them open, and hurried outside to lock the other door. The Death Merchant, Beaufault, and Anna got into the rear of the van. Holcomb drove out into the alley and turned west, slowing down only long enough to pick up Rozakis. From the rear windows, Camellion and his two companions could look east and see red lights revolving on KYP patrol cars. There were also several portable spotlights trained on the rear of the building.

Holcomb reached Epidrotou Street, made a right turn, increased speed, and turned on the blue strobe lights but let the siren remain inactive. In the rear, the Death Merchant opened the bandage case and took out two Star Z70 submachine guns and two clips of 9-mm cartucho Largo ammunition. He handed one of the chatterboxes and a magazine to Rene Beaufault, shoved the magazine into the Star he kept, and made the weapon ready to fire on three-round bursts.

"Is this all the ammunition we have?" asked Beaufault, a long click coming from the Star as he pulled back the cocking knob.

"What you see is what we have," Camellion said, a mental picture of Courtland Grojean flashing in his mind: *I wish he were twenty years younger!*

Beaufault meant his half laugh, half chuckle to sound ironic. "If they come after us, it will be a short battle."

"Anna, I want you to keep watching through the rear windows. Sing out if you see red lights flashing and coming our way."

" 'Sing out!' " she parroted.

"Tell me."

Keeping his head low, Camellion went to the front of the van and eased up behind the driver's seat.

"How far are you going to drive?" he asked Holcomb. "I'd suggest a few kilometers before we stop and I make the phone call."

"I think you're right." He paused and added, his voice very determined, "By the way, Vyron is leaving the country with us."

"Why not? He's welcome," said Camellion, who sensed that Rozakis was highly suspicious of everyone except Holcomb.

Why shouldn't he be, considering how the network fell apart? I don't like mysteries either. . . .

The Death Merchant renewed his determination to get to the real truth, the real reason why he had been sent to Greece.

Provided I'm not buried in Greece!

Book Two

Chapter Thirteen

1000 hours
London, England

It is not likely that when Sir William Bond created Old Bond Street from a muddy country lane in 1686, he envisioned the city that would be London 301 years later. Today, in 1987, there is still an Old Bond Street, which leads out of Piccadilly to join *New* Bond Street (built in 1700). Both are in London's West End, a section that contains Piccadilly Circus—the hub of the universe, the "Times Square" of London, to the British.

It is also extremely doubtful that Sir William Bond would have even considered the possibility that a secret station of the future British Secret Intelligence Service would be located in one of the fine old country houses on Old Bond Street.

The same night that the HMS *Trafalgar* docked at Sheerness—not far from London—Richard Camellion and the other four members of his party were driven in an enclosed bus to the CIA safe house in Chelsea. However, one of the three men who had accompanied them—presumably CIA personnel— had politely ordered Camellion to remain in the bus.

They had driven him to a large Tudor-style house on Old Bond Street. A polite young man and a middle-aged, frosty-faced woman had escorted him to a large room on the third floor, the woman telling him that he would find clothes—"Your exact size," she had said—in the closet.

She had added, "After you bathe and shave, call on the phone and order anything you want. Please do not try to leave this room. The door will be locked for security purposes."

Just to shake up her morals, Camellion said, "Anything I want? How about a woman—a brunette with long legs?"

"I was referring to food and drink," the woman snapped, glaring at Camellion. "This is not a house of assignation."

The man, who followed the woman out of the room, turned and winked at the Death Merchant before he walked out and closed and locked the door.

The same young man had awakened Camellion the next morning at eight-thirty, informing him that he had an hour and a half to wash, dress, and have breakfast. "At ten o'clock you are scheduled to meet someone in the library. By the way, my name is Adam."

"Don't tell me the stone-faced woman with you last night is named Eve!" Camellion said sleepily, sitting up in bed.

"Hardly," replied Adam. "She's in charge of this station and runs it like Hitler."

"Whom am I scheduled to meet?"

"I don't know. I couldn't tell you if I did. What do you want for breakfast?"

Feeling relaxed and comfortable in a lightweight tan suit and with a stomach full of ham and eggs and fried potatoes, the Death Merchant entered the library at nine fifty-eight, fully expecting to meet CIA and ONI debriefing officers. What he found was Courtland Maddock Grojean sitting at a massive antique desk, drinking cocoa.

Grojean pulled back his lips in a version of a smile but didn't stand and offer his right hand. That was not his style. Even if it had been Grojean's way, he would not have gotten up. He was sure that his best on-contract free-lance operator had a lot of unpleasant questions for which he was going to demand answers.

"I'm happy to see you, Camellion," Grojean said gregariously. "Surprised to see me in the UK?" He leaned back in the black leather swivel chair, which, with its sides half enclosing the spy chief, was as large as a throne. "We knew you'd be able to escape, if you had to flee Greece. Sit down and give me a full report."

With a thin-lipped smile, the Death Merchant dropped to a leather chair that matched the one in which Grojean was sitting.

"There isn't any report to give, and you know it," Camellion said, crossing his legs. "Holcomb radioed the location of the Soviet weather base. Dr. Paspyrou has to be on the island. I daresay he's a lot safer with the KGB than I was with the Greeks. You know that too. You knew it before you sent me to Greece with Nicholas Notaras, who's no more of a physicist than I'm a gynecologist! What's his real name?"

A deep furrow marred Grojean's smooth brow. "Nicholas Notaras is his baptismal name. I told Skarett that you'd see through Notaras rather quickly." He leaned forward, placed his hands on the desk, folded them, and for four seconds studied Camellion. "I know I owe you an explanation."

"Plus a bonus," Camellion said promptly. "For setting me up."

"Oh, come now, Camellion! It couldn't have been all that bad," Grojean said urbanely. "With your know-how and experience, we were confident you would obtain the information and—"

"But I didn't!" Camellion interrupted with savage pleasure. "It was Holcomb, Cahill, and Beaufault who learned that the Russian base is on Miskos. Come off it, Court! You know it was Arzey Holcomb who sent the name of the island to me on an m-dot. Earlier he had contacted ONI Center by shortwave. He was instructed to send the microdot to me for only one reason: to make me feel I was accomplishing something."

"We were counting on you," Grojean said evenly, with a straight face. "Why, we had as much to lose as you."

"No, you didn't," Camellion retorted acidly. "I had my life to lose. The Agency could only chalk up the flop of an operation. And what do you mean by 'we were counting on you'? You had the name of the island before I did. I could have been grabbed by critters out of a pink flying saucer and whisked off to another galaxy, and it wouldn't have made any difference. You already had the location." Camellion regarded Grojean with the victorious gaze of a hunter who knows he has his quarry trapped. "Let's stop this nonsense. I suspect it was never intended for me to find Dr. Paspyrou. Suppose you tell me why I really went to Greece—with a phoney physicist?"

Grojean's voice dropped several octaves and his expression became worried. "For quite some time, we in CIA have known there's a hole in the dike of the French SDECE. We've known it, and the British know it. We also suspect—CIA and SIS—that the leak in Paris is very high up."

"Then why did we ask the French to join Operation Zeus?" By now the Death Merchant's curiosity was more than slightly aroused.

"Pure politics. It's my feeling that the powers that be in Washington wanted the French to refuse. They could then accuse the French government of not cooperating. But the French government agreed to help, and by so doing vindicated itself for refusing to let us fly over France when we bombed Libya."

"Bringing in the French created another problem for the Company."

"And for SIS," admitted Grojean. "We couldn't refuse SDECE help without tipping off the mole we suspected. To compound the problem, there was the French network in Greece. We were certain that anything of value that you or anyone else learned would be reported back to France as a matter of routine."

"I'm sure that Rene Beaufault played it on the level," Camellion said. "He and some of his Greek street boys helped me to prove that Melina Arnaoutis is working for either KGB or KYP."

"I said, as a matter of routine," Grojean said in a businesslike tone. "Let me finish."

The Death Merchant folded his arms and remained silent.

"Furthermore, we couldn't be certain that there wasn't a traitor in the Delphi Circle. Don't ask for all the little details; it's NTK, all of it. We and SIS were stuck. We had to work with the French and with the Delphi Circle. We realized that if we were right about a leak in French Intelligence, once we found out where Paspyrou was hidden, the KGB would find out that we knew."

"The SDECE has to know the name of the island," Camellion said quietly. "Beaufault had to report it— as a matter of routine."

"We'll pick up on that later," Grojean said impatiently. "At the time we also realized that if a traitor existed in the Delphi Circle, he or she would report your progress to the KYP. The upshot was that we came to the conclusion that what we needed was bait, a tantalizing lure that could possibly force the traitors and enemy agents to surface."

"Enter Richard Camellion and Nicholas Notaras!" the Death Merchant said with a reminiscent chuckle, enjoying the ungracious look in Grojean's eyes.

"You got it, sport! We assumed that if the KGB and the KYP learned that a high-powered agent and a physicist were in Greece on the trail of Professor Paspyrou, they wouldn't be able to resist temptation. They would either try to black bag you—both of you —or kill you."

"They did try executive action against me," Camellion said dryly. "All it got them was permanent residence in the Far Country."

"They tried and failed. You succeeded. I also knew the odds were in your favor. Do some brain work and you'll know why I gave you that special phone number. I didn't dare give it to ONI. Holcomb didn't realize what was going on. He would have given it to Cahill and Beaufault—and need I remind you what happened at the safe house on Stazoukis Avenue?"

"We know Holcomb was on our side," Camellion said rapidly. "Cahill was killed, and I don't think Joe Pappas—"

"Pappas is dead." Grojean was matter-of-fact. "I learned about it this morning, before I came over here. He was trapped by the KYP and blew out his brains when they closed in on him. It was Joseph Pappas. The report stated that he was positively identified by the KYP."

"The only suspect left is French Intelligence." The Death Merchant looked and sounded contemplative. "Poor Rene made his report, never suspecting that a

KGB mole—no doubt an agent in place—would see it. By the way, did you also suspect Pappas?"

"We weren't sure of him. We knew we'd find out though, one way or another, after Notaras told him he was a physicist."

"What's the real story on Notaras? Or is it on NTK?"

Grojean stood up and unbuttoned his textured natural silk sport coat, a smug expression on his face. It was said of Grojean (behind his back) that if he ever went to a hospital, he'd take tailored pajamas with him—and if he died, he'd be the best-dressed resident in Hell.

"Notaras was a physicist," the spy boss said, "but he didn't have the expertise to 'read' Dr. Paspyrou's notes. It would take an Einstein to do that." He walked around the desk, went to the back of a black leather chair, picked it up, and started to move it toward the Death Merchant. "He taught physics in a junior college in Maryland. How we found him is not important."

The Death Merchant watched Grojean place the chair in front of him and sit down, first pulling up on his pant legs. "If Notaras has a Ph.D., in his case it can only mean 'pile it high and deep,' or your people wouldn't have been able to talk him into sticking his head next to a buzz saw—and what kind of medicine was he taking?"

"He volunteered. We didn't talk him into going." Noting Camellion's taken-aback look, Grojean permitted himself an indulgent smile. "I think Notaras hoped he would stop a bullet in Greece. He has cancer of the liver. If he's alive six months from now, he'll be wishing he could die and get it over with."

The Death Merchant nodded quickly. "The pills were to kill the pain. But why did you call him back to the States?"

Grojean seemed surprised. "I thought you would have guessed by now. It's really very simple. When the KGB and the KYP didn't make a move toward either of you—"

"Until after Notaras had left Greece!"

"—we assumed we had drawn a no-win lottery ticket. It was best to get him out of Greece; his job was done. We knew Notaras would be a dead weight if you had to do an E and E."

"We still did a pretty good job with evasion and escape," the Death Merchant said with a lopsided smile. "Of course, the people with me were trained. Even Anna Sofoulis knew how to shoot. You're aware of her?"

Grojean looked intently at Camellion. "You're a realist, Camellion. You know that the bottom line is the end result or, to use the old cliché, 'Nothing succeeds like success.' You made it out in one piece. Why complain?"

"I'll buy that," Camellion said, sounding unconcerned. "The rest of it is your problem. A big problem it is. Holcomb, Cahill, *and* Rene Beaufault had the location of the Soviet base in the Aegean Sea. French Intelligence got the same information. *Ipso facto,* the KGB knows that we know."

Grojean's silence indicated he was in agreement.

"I have another puzzle for you. After the KGB learned about the blackmail scheme against Petros Makarezos, why didn't the pig farmers take steps to stop it? As a matter of routine, Rene must have reported the plan to SDECE Center in Paris."

"He didn't." The words jumped from Grojean's mouth. "Apparently Holcomb and the others didn't tell you. For security the combined network in Greece never reported any operation until it had been completed, whether it succeeded or failed. Beaufault didn't report to Paris until after he and

Holcomb and Cahill had obtained the name of the island from Makarezos. The proof is that the KGB didn't try to prevent the blackmail operation."

Camellion's eyes remained steady on Grojean. "None of which solves your problem regarding the Soviet base on Miskos. I can't imagine the U.S. navy going in on an armed assault—storming across the beaches and all that gung-ho nonsense! And our Uncle Sam can't tell the world what the Soviets are doing, not without positive proof."

From the self-satisfied expression that bloomed on Grojean's face, the Death Merchant sensed that a plan had already been developed.

"A covert assault!" Camellion said. "The U.S. and Great Britain are going to attack. And the French? Another thing, old buddy! Where is your proof that the Russians are on Miskos? Maybe the KGB did interfere—ever consider that possibility? It would be a master stroke if the KGB had Makarezos give a false location. The Soviets would gain all the time they needed, and the U.S. and Great Britain would be left with egg in their faces."

Grojean almost beamed. "We have already done a lot of checking on Miskos. The Nazis used Miskos as a sub base in WW II. They built numerous giant bunkers inside the base of Mount Posso, a mountain on the west side of the island. We have to tell the French, giving a false date for the attack. In the meantime, while we're supposedly working out the C-of-F with the French, we'll attack, the same kind of attack that the British wanted us—and them—to use against Libya. Afterward, it will be up to our people in State to give some excuse to the French. The same applies to the British Foreign Office."

Grojean frowned and his mouth tightened. "Why the glum look? Within a week, our SEALs and British marine specialists will make an underwater survey of

Miskos. Or maybe you think the Russians will pack up and go home and not be there! They can't! They haven't the time. I could tell you a lot more we're doing, but I'm not going to at this stage of the game."

"I was thinking of the British," Camellion explained. "They have a strange attitude about covert operations. They shy away from assassinations and black-bag jobs and always confuse necessity with murder. Unrealistically, they prefer to believe the myth that killing is 'honorable' only when it's done for Queen and country."

Grojean noisily cleared his throat. "I can assure you that we've convinced London that its help is a vital necessity. Should the Russians succeed, the British weather will be in danger as well as ours. They'll do their share—you'll see. . . ."

"Not I. I won't be there," Camellion said pleasantly. "My part in this mess is over and done with. I'm going back to Texas."

"I'm afraid your part has just begun," Grojean said after some hesitation. "We want you and a dozen handpicked men to go in with our Special Forces and the British."

Grojean leaned back and waited for the verbal explosion he was sure would come. What made it so damned annoying was that Camellion's expression didn't betray his thoughts.

The Death Merchant said calmly, "I gather you want me to grab Professor Paspyrou before the Russians could kill him, or maybe use some secret escape route."

"That as well as protect his papers and photograph the magnifying transmitter before they can destroy it."

"Very well, we have a deal. It will cost my generous Uncle another hundred thousand dollars."

"Impossible." Grojean was firm. "We don't have an extra hundred thousand in the budget."

"Then forget it," Camellion said.

"Then you can forget Anna Sofoulis's going to the United States," Grojean said. "We'll ship her tail back to Greece."

"Turkey turds! You'd drop the AIDS virus on the Russians if you could, but you wouldn't send an innocent girl to her death!"

Grojean was too intelligent to keep up the pretense. "Maybe not, but she still will not set foot in the United States. She'll remain in Britain—and you wouldn't be keeping your word to Joe Pappas. She was debriefed. I received a full report."

"I'm thinking of corals, hydras, jellyfish, and other Cnidaria, sometimes called coelenterata," Camellion said, sucking in his lower lip.

"I'm listening." Grojean forced himself to be patient. He had always considered the Death Merchant to be the Patron Saint of the Perpetually Strange and was never too surprised at anything he might say.

"Corals, hydras, jellyfish, and other coelenterata are asexual. No sex organs! No fun! In contrast, hermaphrodite or bisexual animals, such a worms, bryozoans, snails, slugs, and what-have-you, have sex organs of both sexes."

"So!" Grojean uncomfortably shifted his weight in the chair.

Camellion smiled. "If you were a worm, I could tell you to go have sexual intercourse with yourself. That should give you some idea of the odds against my going to Miskos without being paid to do so."

"Seems fair," Grojean said mildly. "You could still tell me to go screw myself. But remember this: While I'm trying to perform that physical impossibility, Miss Sofoulis will still be in England."

He has me up against the wall and knows it! He's not going to back down!

"It seems I'm going to the island of Miskos," the Death Merchant said, admitting defeat. "But your damned budget had better provide citizenship for Anna. What do you intend to do for her?"

Relaxing, Grojean said, "We have a lot of friends in Greek communities in New York and other cities. We'll get Anna a job and settle her in one of them. I'll personally see that Immigration and Naturalization starts a file on her. She'll get her first citizenship papers on the same basis as any other immigrant. Fair enough?"

The Death Merchant smiled briefly. "It will be weeks before we attack the island," he said lazily. "What am I supposed to do in the meantime, sit around here and stare at Adam and the virginal housemother who runs this safe house?"

"Not quite." Grojean didn't mean to sound semi-apologetic, but he did. "I was thinking of your taking a short vacation in Bulgaria or perhaps to Riga, in the Soviet Union."

"You're lucky you're not twenty years younger, Court," Camellion said, knowing full well that Grojean was hedging.

Grojean's questioning eyes asked him why.

"If you were, I'd beat the hell out of you. Now stop playing games. Give me the whole cake without the frosting."

Grojean did. The story he told did not exactly fill the Death Merchant with joy. During the past month, one of the National Security Agency's DSP-647 satellites had photographed a shortwave radio broadcasting facility in the foothills of the Rhodope Mountains, near the city of Smolyan, Bulgaria.

For many months NSA had been conducting EL-SUR on the radio station, the electromagnetic surveillance sparked by the first photographs, which revealed that the "Bulgarian Voice of Socialist Freedom" had *six* towers, each 240 feet tall. The most powerful shortwave transmitter in the world would not require *six* towers of that height. NSA decided on continued ELSUR and began the precise business of building an electromagnetic profile of the station.

Grojean spoke rapidly. "I suppose you know that NSA has satellite cameras that can photograph an object as small as a package of cigarettes on the ground! The last satellite that went over Bulgaria—"

The last satellite found that something new had been added to the six towers. Square rods had been fastened on the outside of each tower section, four rods to a tower, twenty-four rods in all. The tip of each rod extended an estimated four and a half feet above each tower.

Lightning rods? Not likely. Lightning rods wouldn't be on all four sides of each tower and end six feet above the ground. Lightning rods wouldn't have thick insulated cables leading from the ends, the cables moving to a central building in the center of the six towers, next to the transmitter.

NSA had been apprised of Operation Zeus. It had been NSA that had made thousands of photographs of Greece in an effort to find any odd and unusual complex. NSA had immediately contacted the CIA and ONI. These two agencies had then consulted with scientists familiar with Tesla's work. The physicists had concluded that the six towers could be a relay station for transmitting an enormous amount of power from another source—*through the air and without wires!*

"It made sense," Grojean told the Death Merchant. "We already knew that the magnifying transmitter would require hundreds of millions of volts, but not of conventional electricity, not the way we ordinarily think of it. For this amount of power special magnets would be needed, weighing hundreds of tons. Those magnets had to be—*have* to be—in the Soviet Union."

"Let me get this straight," Camellion said, intrigued. "The CIA believes that this energy is broadcast from the Soviet Union to Bulgaria, and from Bulgaria to Greece—to Miskos?"

"Yes—that's what we believe."

The Death Merchant shook his head in disgust. "What do you think I could do in Bulgaria? Run in there and pull down the six towers with my bare hands? The Bulgarian DS will have more guards around that station than a sleeping coon dog has fleas." Camellion paused and looked straight at the Fox. "Seriously, Court—it can't be done. Not for a million dollars and ten Annas!"

"I didn't think it could be," Grojean said. "I did, however, want your opinion."

Camellion moved a hand wearily. "What's the sit-rep on Riga?"

"The situation is still too fluid for there to be a situation report." Grojean continued to talk for five minutes, ending with "I think you will agree that Michael Kartemesk's information could be of immense help."

The Death Merchant was not convinced. "Why couldn't Kartemesk have sent the diagram and the other information out of the Soviet Union with his friend? And how do you know that Hork Zevv isn't a KGB destabilization agent?"

Grojean laughed. "You don't miss a trick, do you? We know from other sources that Kartemesk and Zevv have been friends since boyhood. As to your first question, suppose Zevv had been trapped on the vessel going to Sweden. Suppose the KGB had found the diagram of the magnifying transmitter on him. The route would have led straight back to Kartemesk."

"Yes . . . the KGB would have forced the truth out of Zevv."

"As it was, the KGB questioned Kartemesk for an entire day after Hork Zevv was reported missing." Grojean looked at his wristwatch. "Kartemesk came up with the idea of giving Zevv a photograph of his great-great grandfather. The agent who goes into the Soviet Union and makes contact with Kartemesk will use the photograph as a recognition sign. That is where you come in."

"It won't be all that difficult." There was an impish lilt to Camellion's voice. "All I have to do is hop over to what used to be Latvia, make contact with Michael Kartemesk, get the diagram, and skip back to Sweden."

Grojean concealed his concern. At the moment, the most salient part of this interview was the Death Merchant's lack of concern for the great danger involved. This was unusual. Grojean knew that while Camellion often gave the impression of devil-may-care, he was actually an extremely cautious individual. That was the main reason he had survived so many years.

"Riga is on the Soviet mainland," Grojean said prosaically. "I should think that it would pose an even greater threat to success than Bulgaria."

"I wouldn't have had one chance in Bulgaria," Camellion said laconically. "I'd have been in a very closed society without any help whatsoever, in a country whose masters are even more paranoid than the Russians." In the same breath he added, "Latvia is different. It has a small but very effective underground that's willing to lend all the aid it can. The Spear of Vengeance has been driving the KGB crazy for the past seven years, even if Moscow does like to pretend it doesn't exist."

"And what does your encyclopedia of useless facts tell you about Riga?" asked Grojean, feeling Camellion had something in mind that could be of use.

"In a few weeks the Latvians will be celebrating Ligo, the Holiday of Song Festivities," Camellion said, proving the Fox correct. "Thousands of Swedes, Danes, and Norwegians will be pouring into Riga for a three- or four-day stay. The government loves to see them bring in money to pump up the sagging Soviet economy."

Grojean's chuckle sounded positively diabolical, and for a moment Camellion thought the spy chief might even rub his hands together. "The KGB can't keep track of all those thousands of foreigners, now, can they?"

"The KGB does a good job, but they still can't watch everyone, not all the time. It's not like trying to make contact with a Russian in Moscow. It will be a lot easier than in Siberia."* Camellion tilted his head and looked up at the cream-color ceiling. "I'll need a partner, a 'wife.' A man going in alone would be an instant suspect. She and I will leave Stockholm under a Swedish cover. Whoever you get, she'll have to be well trained and experienced at this sort of thing."

Grojean again looked at his watch, then he got to his feet and carefully straightened his coat and made sure the creases in his gray trousers were straight. "It's almost time for Sir Clifford Blassingame and Russell Wirbeck to arrive. Blassingame is an official with SIS, and Wirbeck is ONI's liaison here in London."

"A gentle hint for me to leave." Camellion eased himself to his feet. "I want to move rapidly in this

---

* See Death Merchant #67, *Escape From Gulag Taria*, also published by Dell.

operation. One more thing: Either have the door to my room unlocked, or you'll have to replace a door. Being confined by the people I'm working for is repugnant to me. I mean it."

Grojean knew the Death Merchant never made empty threats. It would be typical of him to smash down the door and come storming into the library while Grojean was meeting with Wirbeck and Blassingame.

"I'll give orders to leave the door unlocked," Grojean said. "But don't wander about the premises."

"I'm not interested in the house. I just don't like being locked up."

"I'll be back here tonight after dinner." Grojean sounded calm and relaxed. He carefully scrutinized Camellion for a reaction as he followed with "I'll bring your 'wife' with me, and the three of us will have an in-depth discussion on the Riga mission. Tomorrow I'll arrange for you both to meet with Hork Zevv."

The Death Merchant's blue eyes sharpened, and for a moment Grojean had the ridiculous idea that his mind was being probed and each thought dissected.

"Why the fast work with the woman?" Camellion's tone was soft. "How do you know she's right for the job?"

"She's very experienced." That sly I-have-a-secret look rose again in Grojean's eyes. "In a manner of speaking, she was in Operation Zeus before you were. You've never met her, though I'm sure you have heard her name mentioned—her cover name. . . ."

"The suspense is sticking icepicks under my toenails and setting off grenades behind my eyeballs," Camellion said in a bored tone.

"Have you ever heard the name Karen Spreitler?"

Chapter Fourteen

In the bus that was going into Riga from the airport, Richard Camellion and Karen Spreitler saw the bristling examples of Latvia's famous pines and meadows full of brown dairy cows. The setting sun, painting the trees with splashes of red, yellow, and orange, made the scene especially beautiful.

"Mr. Knud Haekkeruo" and "Margrethe Haekkeruo," his "wife," were Danish citizens and had properly stamped passports, which proved they had flown from Copenhagen to Great Britain, had spent two weeks in London, and had then flown to Stockholm, Sweden, where they had spent a week. Now they were in Latvia, in the Soviet Union, to spend a week in Riga enjoying Ligo, the Holiday of Song Festivities.

Karen, sitting next to the window, turned and flashed a smile at Camellion. "It looks very peaceful and pretty, doesn't it, dear?"

She spoke English perfectly, but deliberately used a strong accent to give the impression, to other passengers, that she was not that familiar with English. Speaking English, even excellent English, would not cause anyone to be suspicious. Most Europeans who traveled did. In fact, English was a second language to Europeans, and even to Russians in the Asian sections of the Soviet Union.

In replying, Camellion also affected an accent, as well as inserting the Danish word for "yes." *"Ja,* very nice." *Even if it is in pig-farmer land.*

He was very pleased with Karen Spreitler. She was trained and was very experienced. The Fox had not exaggerated. In 1975 the Central Intelligence Agency had smuggled Max and Karen Spreitler out of East Germany. Max had been a computer expert at the Institute of Applied Cybernetics at Dresden, and had special talents the CIA felt it could use. From Grojean's explanation, the Death Merchant felt there was far more to the story than Max Spreitler's being a computer whiz. It was on a NTK basis, or Grojean would have given the details.

The escape had both failed and succeeded. Max had been wounded by a bullet during the escape and had died two days later in a West Berlin hospital. In gratitude to the CIA for helping her and her husband, Karen Spreitler had agreed to work for the Agency, which helped her obtain employment with the West German Archeology School of Applied Techniques. This institute specialized in improving techniques by which archeologists and paleontologists remove relics from the earth without destroying them in the process.

In 1983 Karen had been sent to Athens to work in the school's Greek office. The CIA had then ordered her to try to become acquainted with a high member of the Greek Socialist government. This was part of the CIA's probe to find out how well the Soviet Union was entrenched (behind the scenes).

By the time Operation Zeus was started, Karen was the mistress of Petros Makarezos, the Greek Minister of Foreign Affairs. The CIA had then given her name to and had conferred with the U.S. Office of

Naval Intelligence. In turn, ONI had informed Arzey Holcomb, its major agent in Athens. ONI had also given firm orders to Holcomb: Under no circumstance was he to give her name to Arnold Cahill and Rene Beaufault. ONI did not tell Holcomb that the CIA suspected there was an agent in place within the high offices of the French SDECE and that if Beaufault sent in a routine report, Karen would probably have a fatal accident. Since short-term operations were reported to the CIA, the SIS, and the SDECE only after the fact, the CIA and the British knew that French Intelligence would not know of Karen Spreitler's existence until the blackmail attempt had either succeeded or failed.

Karen had been responsible for the blackmail attempt, Grojean had explained to the Death Merchant. When she had reported to the CIA, via her own contact, that Makarezos was a likely candidate for extortion, the CIA had again held a conference with ONI. The two American Intelligence agencies had let British SIS into the scheme. Two things had followed. ONI had ordered Holcomb to let Karen's existence be known to Arnold Cahill and Rene Beaufault and to inform them that she would be used in an attempt to blackmail Makarezos. At the same time, SIS had radioed Cahill that Karen Spreitler had been working for British Intelligence for several years. As part of a cover for Karen, SIS added the lie that she was a double agent and that she had sold bits and parts of information to the *Service de Documentation Extérieure et de Contre-Espionnage*—SDECE. However, Karen could be trusted for the operation because the Americans were paying her a large sum of money for her part. Holcomb, Cahill, and Beaufault would act as her controls.

The CIA realized that it was still risking Karen's life. There was that slim chance that Rene Beaufault might innocently, in one of his weekly reports, mention her name before the blackmail operation was complete. It wasn't likely, however, that he would, or could. He could hardly mention her name without getting into generalities about the operation. Or he might wonder why SDECE Center in Paris hadn't mentioned her in any of its communications. What it amounted to was that the CIA, ONI, and SIS were counting on Beaufault's being the kind who would follow orders to the letter and not mention the operation until it had been completed.

To protect Karen, ONI had sent Holcomb $15,000. He was to give it to Karen and put her on a plane for Paris the instant Makarezos knew she was part of the plot. Three CIA agents had met her plane in Paris and had brought her to London.

The Death Merchant liked Karen for another reason. Ten minutes after he had met her in the safe station in London, he knew she was as sexually oriented as Melina Arnaoutis. She was also as pretty as Melina, only in a different way. Karen's beauty was more classic.

Truly intelligent people, realizing that money is only a tool, do not make wealth the center of their lives. At the same time, they are quick to stoop and pick up a ten-dollar bill they might find on the sidewalk.

Richard Camellion was that way with sex. It wasn't that important in his life, but he wasn't going to ignore it when it was there in front of him. He was going to take advantage of it and enjoy himself.

Karen was older than Melina. Karen might have been thirty-one or thirty-two—to look at her. In reality she was forty-one. Slim, she had the kind of breasts that always rode high on her chest, her waist almost tiny, her hips in perfect proportion to the rest of her. Short blond hair, worn midi-style, framed a small face.

It was Karen's hazel eyes that intrigued Camellion, intelligent, sensitive eyes quick to focus and in whose depths lurked strange enigmatic shadows. The main difference between Karen and Melina was that while Melina was open, Karen was more subtle and reserved. Melina was frankly sensual. Karen tempted you with what she had to offer.

Karen was not reserved that night. By the time the Intourist bus reached the hotel in Riga and Mr. and Mrs. Haekkeruo had their papers checked and were shown to their room, it was too late to do anything but have dinner, unpack, and go to bed.

Neither Camellion nor Karen had discussed sleeping arrangements. Looking at the large double bed, Karen said only, "It looks comfortable. We'll have a good night's sleep."

Whether she was telling him he could do more than merely sleep next to her in the same bed was a moot point. The Death Merchant's accomplishments did not include mind reading. He made his move a few minutes later, after he had removed his shirt and shoes and socks.

The room did have a full-length mirror, in front of which Karen was brushing her blond hair. Camellion walked over to her and unzipped the back of her dress. At once, Karen put down the brush, turned, put her arms around his neck, and offered her lips. As they kissed, he slid his hands through the open slit of her dress, unsnapped her bra, and began to caress the gentle curve of her back and the velvet softness of her shoulders. Soon, he was pulling down the dress, and with it her panties. Time did not exist. They were nude and on the bed and Camellion was massaging her breasts and brushing his lips over her hard nipples. Stirred by her increasing moans of pleasure, Camellion moved his right hand down across her smooth belly and found that part of her that made her Woman. She grasped his hardness and whispered softly, "I told you the bed would be very comfortable. . . ."

Do not act conspicuous! Act like tourists! The next day, after breakfast, Camellion and Karen spent an hour watching a parade of Young Pioneers, the Soviet Union's version of boy and girl scouts. There were bands, precision marching, and numerous flags. To the Death Merchant, it was a far worse obscenity than hard-core pornography. It wasn't the parade itself, nor the red flags with their hammers and sickles. It wasn't the boys and girls singing the battle song of the Young Pioneers—*We will win the future, where Dawn blazes bright.* It was the way the communists had perverted young minds, had brainwashed the innocent young into believing that the Soviet system was the best. It was the sheer Mephistophelean evil of the method that made Camellion despise not the Russian people but the gangster government that controlled them.

With other tourists, Richard and Karen went to view Riga from St. Peter and Paul's church tower, a steel copy of an antique wooden spire that burned during World War II. From its nearly four-hundred-foot height, they could see the flat city on the Baltic, the port city that, coexisting with its past, was a fascinating jumble of architectural styles.

Riga and the rest of Latvia were unusual in another respect. Moscow didn't treat the Latvians (and the Estonians and Lithuanians) with the same harshness it applied to even ethnic Russians. It was not because of any kindness. For one thing, the proximity of the Latvians to the West meant that news could filter out very quickly. Swedes, Danes, and Norwegians visited

Riga every week. Moreover, the people of Riga couldn't be fooled by Soviet propaganda into believing that the United States was a land of millions of starving people and homeless out of work. The people in Riga knew better. They watched television from Norway and Sweden, and this included many American programs, with American advertising.

Another sharp thorn in the tender side of the Soviet Politburo was religion. One-third of the Latvians were Roman Catholic; two-thirds were Lutheran. Even young adults went to mass and to Protestant church services—and not just on Easter and Christmas either. There wasn't anything the KGB and the *Napravleniye*, the KGB border guards, could do about it. The Russians knew if they tried to interfere with religion, if they attempted to close the churches, the result would be an open rebellion. How would an uprising look to the West? Far worse, it would give dangerous ideas to the satellite nations in Eastern Europe. And to those fanatical Ukrainians! The KGB realized that there was a well-organized resistance movement in Latvia, the Spear of Vengeance. But Free Ukraine was ten times larger, and since the terrible nuclear disaster at Chernobyl, only eighty miles from Kiev, the Soviet Union's third largest city, Free Ukraine was gaining even more converts.

Moscow was also keenly aware of Latvian productivity. Riga was a major manufacturing center, especially in electronics. Not one Russian in ten thousand knew that the giant VEF electronics plant in Riga manufactured half the telephones and a fourth of the radios in the Soviet Union. Other factories produced electric light bulbs, stoves, medical instruments, bicycles, and motorcycles. Olaine, another city, manufactured chemicals, plastics, paints, and enamels. Latvia didn't have any ores, but it did possess sixty percent of the world's amber. Latvian artisans in amber were among the best in the world.

Hard-working, formal in manner, and very close to the land—these were the Latvians. And creative, compulsive, and always spotlessly clean (unlike the Russians, they never had any underarm odor).

A pert woman taxicab driver (she explained that she was a teacher who drove a taxicab for the extra income) who drove Camellion and Karen to Kovissin Castle, two miles from Riga, said that her people had two chief attributes: hard work combined with tenacity.

"It is because we have always been oppressed by other nations," she said cheerfully. "Even the German knights once held this land. Now it is the ignorant Russians, who think they will someday rule the world." She went on to remark that the Russians were "idiots" who took well to collectiveness. "We Latvians don't. We are individualists."

The Latvian language, perhaps the oldest in Europe, was related to Sanskrit, so much so that Hindi-speaking Indians could understand many Latvian words. For example, the word God—in Sanskrit *Devah*, in Latin *Deus*, and in Latvian *Dievas*. Or tooth—Sanskrit *dan*, Latin *dens*, Latvian *dantis*.

Another thing that made the Russians grit their teeth was the Latvian refusal to learn and speak Russian. Few people that Camellion and Karen met spoke the language. In a restaurant, when Camellion ordered salad in Russian, he got smoked fish. Tactfully, he switched to the Latvian *palun* and *tana* for "please" and "thanks," and traded his Russian for English mixed with German.

That night they went to church, to the center of Vilnius Square, where a new opera house shared the atmosphere with the seventeenth-century Church of St. John, whose inside was a cavern of white baroque composition-marble sculptures: angels, saints, martyrs, apostles—three thousand in all. A mass was in progress, and Camellion and Karen could easily understand why the Soviet atheists were worried about the Latvians. Entire families were there: mothers and fathers with wide-eyed youngsters looking and wondering at the wealth of sculptures; teenagers and young men and women in their twenties; grandmothers softly clicking rosary beads and whispering fervent prayers. The Death Merchant did enjoy the singing, although the rest of it bored him.

Although Camellion and Karen appeared to have all the time in the world, they were on a precise schedule. There was an exact time for them to make themselves known to the contact. It was annoying that they couldn't discuss the possibles and the probables except when they were out of their room. The KGB was not so paranoid that it attempted to bug the room of every tourist who might come to Riga. Just the same, the hotel was Intourist, the Soviet travel bureau. It was possible that every room in the place was bugged. In the Soviet Union the KGB used this system not only in Intourist hotels but also in such hotels as the Metropole and others favored by foreign visitors.

During the morning of the fourth day, Camellion and Karen discussed meeting the contact that night. They were in the older section of Riga where narrow old streets neighbored modern boulevards. Stuccoed walls, arched entranceways, and cobblestone courtyards characterized the Riga of bygone days.

"I'm curious how we're going to meet Michael Kartemesk," Karen said. "If the KGB is still keeping him under surveillance because it feels he helped Hork Zevv escape, I don't see how we can see him."

The Death Merchant, still mulling over how

Courtland Grojean had held Anna Sofoulis over his head, didn't reply.

"Richard, I said—"

"I heard you." Camellion gave her a quick glance to prove he was being attentive. "We have to assume that members of Kartemesk's cell have made some kind of arrangement. All we can do is go to the Scheherazade Café and follow the procedure as Zevv instructed us to do."

Karen stopped in front of a bakery and admired the numerous cakes and pastries in the window. Dressed in a two-piece heather-gray suit—skirt, coat, and white blouse—she had a sexiness about her that would stir any normal male.

The pause gave her and Camellion a chance to watch passersby in the reflection of the plate-glass mirror. Anyone following would have to stop, go across the street, or walk on by.

Karen said, "We'll have to keep the drawings of the device with us at all times. We can't risk anyone searching our room. I still think we should have brought a special suitcase with a secret compartment. After all, how much space is required for two or three sheets of paper?"

"The CIA decided it would be too dangerous," Camellion replied. "There are only so many hiding places in a suitcase and the KGB knows them all. If the KGB searched our room and found even an empty compartment, they'd be suspicious."

"We'd better start back," Karen said. "It's almost five o'clock."

The problem was to get to the Scheherazade Café without arousing anyone's suspicions. The café, not a tourist attraction, was a small, out-of-the-way establishment on Ozhog Street.

"It has only one counter and ten tables and specializes in Ukrainian wines," Hork Zevv had said during the briefing in London. "Tourists have never heard of the place, but any cab driver will be able to take you there."

Richard and Karen left the hotel at six o'clock, walked a few blocks, hailed a cab, and told the grim-faced driver to take them to "the Scheherazade Café. It's on Ozhog Street. I'm sorry that we don't have the exact address. Friends of ours in Denmark said they happened to stop by there last summer when they were here in Riga on vacation. They told us the café has excellent wines."

The round-faced, middle-aged driver squinted at them and then smiled. "I know where the café is. I want to apologize for not getting out and opening the door. I am sorry, but I thought you were Russians. But you're from Denmark. I like the Danes. I like the Swedes. I don't like the Norwegians. They are too sad. Okay, we go to the Scheherazade Café."

An annoyingly loquacious man, the cabbie talked all the way along the route—one long stream of condemnation against the Soviet Union. Yet what he said was the truth: that the Soviet Union was one of the most backward nations in the world, that if it weren't for the Soviet military machine, the USSR would be one giant joke.

"Why, those Russians can't even make up a decent pop-up toaster! The Soviet Union is actually a nation of farmers, and they can't even do that very well."

Camellion and Karen felt it was rather paradoxical that the Scheherazade Café was in the same section of Riga they had visited that morning, an area that was a maze of narrow, twisting streets, and cobble-stone roads. Ozhog Street was only several blocks long, and made Richard and Karen feel they had stepped backward in time a hundred years.

The driver pulled up in front of the café. Camellion paid the driver (including a generous tip), and he and Karen got out and looked at the front of the establishment. Two iron posts in front of the doorway, a caryatid on each post. To the right a spotlessly clean window in the center of which was painted a fanciful troika, a three-horse team and sleigh, and candlelight beyond the window.

"I guess it's about time we officially go to work," Karen said as Camellion took her by the arm and began escorting her inside.

"Yeah, let's earn our daily CIA bread. It does beat writing bumper stickers for a living. . . ."

Chapter Fifteen

"Stin iyia sas"—"To your health, General Cyatorus," said Major Kostyan Muzychenko, raising his
glass of retsina, Greece's unique resin-flavored wine.
He added cleverly for the benefit of Cyatorus's mammoth ego, "And no doubt to the health of this nation's next ruler."

Pleased, Cyatorus smiled and clinked his glass with
Muzychenko's. Both men then downed their wine in
one gulp.

Tall, well muscled, though not bulky, Nikos Philip
Cyatorus gave the impression of steel strength and
perfect confidence. A good-looking man with a large
head, angular features, and intense dark eyes, his
thick black hair was always neatly combed and his
long but thick mustache trimmed to the last hair. He
wore an expensive Italian silk suit and smelled of
after-shave that came in small bottles and could be
purchased only in the most expensive men's stores.

"I gather all the arrangements have been made?"
Cyatorus said, putting the empty wineglass on the
silver tray on the cocktail table and sitting down
comfortably on one of the carved antique chairs.

Major Muzychenko glanced out the window of the
twelfth-story luxury apartment that the KGB in Ath-

ens maintained for meetings with special people. As usual, the air in the distance was yellow with smog. He could, however, still see the whitewashed nineteenth-century chapel of St. George gleaming on the summit of Mount Lycabettus.

Muzychenko strode over to the silver tray and smiled as he put his glass down. "My people are making arrangements for you to come to the island and witness the experiments," he said with a completely false friendliness. "There is plenty of time, General. It will be weeks yet before the experiments take place."

A look of puzzlement and disappointment fell over Cyatorus's face. "Why did you ask for this meeting?" he asked. "Anything minor could have been sent by the usual route."

Muzychenko took his time sitting down on a twocushion divan. He wouldn't have liked Cyatorus even if the man had not been a traitor to his own people. One could respect, even admire, intelligence officers of the opposing side. They were only doing their job, following the orders of their governments. Men like Cyatorus were of a different breed. Such scum were loyal only to their own selfish desires. Eventually they would betray even the people who had paid them to deceive their own nation.

"It was on direct orders from Moscow that I arranged this meeting," Muzychenko said. "My superiors are not satisfied with your report explaining the recent failures of the KYP at the Pappas warehouse and the CIA safehouse on Stazoukis Avenue."

The disappointment on Cyatorus's face was replaced by caution.

"I explained in detail," he said. "What could my men do? The terrorists blew up the warehouse. Captain Frangopoulos and his group didn't even know the escape tunnel existed. That's how Camellion and the others were able to ambush the guards and escape."

"In a KYP vehicle!" Major Muzychenko said coolly, his gaze steady on the other man. He wasn't trying to unnerve General Cyatorus; such a tactic wouldn't have served any useful purpose; nor would it have been easy to do. The Greek general was not a man who frightened easily.

Cyatorus let the remark pass. "The terrorists also had an escape route planned in the apartment on Stazoukis Avenue. I gave you the details; I gave the same details to Moscow. There isn't anything I can add. In my opinion, Moscow has a very short memory."

Major Muzychenko's eyes asked for an explanation.

"Moscow seems to have conveniently forgotten that we did trap and kill Arnold Cahill, the Englishman. We also killed Joseph Pappas. Neither are a problem any longer."

"The trouble with that is both died before they could be questioned," said Muzychenko. "Richard Camellion, Arzey Holcomb, and several others escaped. By now they are out of the country. And Holcomb's wife is dead."

"Don't be facetious, Major. She died in the hospital of natural causes. Her heart gave out due to the operation. As for Pappas and Cahill, we did get them. That's more than we can say for the five KGB specialists who made fools of themselves trying to kill Richard Camellion—and in an ambush at that! He killed all five of them." Cyatorus smiled, and his voice dripped derision. "How does Moscow feel about their failure?"

"General, I asked you to come here because I wanted to inform you that the Americans know about the experiments we will conduct." Kostyan

Muzychenko delighted in seeing the look of genuine fear that crossed Cyatorus's face. He couldn't have been more pleased. Good. Let the son of a bitch worry!

Before Cyatorus could speak, Muzychenko cut him off. "I have more bad news. There is a traitor high in your government. It was he who divulged the location of our weather experiment base to the CIA."

For once, Cyatorus could not react fast enough to cover his shock. He stared at the Soviet KGB officer. When he was able to speak, his voice was tight in the grip of nervousness.

"Who—who is the traitor?"

"The assistant head of the Greek Ministry of Foreign Affairs—Petros Makarezos," Muzychenko said in an accusing tone. "Makarezos was fucking a woman named Karen Spreitler. The CIA took numerous photographs and tape recordings and used them to blackmail him. In return for the CIA's keeping quiet, he told them about Miskos."

General Cyatorus got to his feet, his face almost purple with rage, frustration, and embarrassment. "That's impossible!" he raged. "No one in the office of Foreign Affairs has any information about the island!"

Stretching his right arm out over the top rear of the couch, Muzychenko taunted Cyatorus with a slight smile. "In that case, we have a miracle, General! It did happen! Petros Makarezos did reveal the island to the Americans. We of the KGB know that for an absolute fact, and since American Intelligence knows about the weather experiments and where they will be conducted, the Americans also know your part in the matter."

Major Muzychenko didn't add that British and French Intelligence also had the same information. It would have been poor strategy to reveal too much to the Greek general. It would also have been unwise to inform him that the KGB hadn't known about Makarezos and Karen Spreitler until after the blackmail had been successful.

"Don't ask me how we came by this information," Muzychenko said. "I am not at liberty to tell you. Your only concern should be the leak in your own department." He could tell Cyatorus was searching for words and running his mind in high gear in an effort to solve the puzzle of how Petros Makarezos could have obtained the name of the island where the Soviet station was hidden.

General Cyatorus sat back down once more. "Where is this Karen Spreitler now? Is she still in Athens?" he inquired in a subdued voice.

Major Muzychenko said vehemently, "She was the director of the Athens office of the Archeology School of Applied Techniques, an organization that is headquartered in Cologne, West Germany. It is not a cover-flap for either the CIA or the West German BND. Spreitler resigned abruptly. She left her apartment. We can only conclude that the CIA got her safely out of Greece. Forget about her. She is not important."

"There are only thirty-one people in the KYP who know about the base," Cyatorus said defensively. "I am positive that none of them could have given the information to that traitor Petros Makarezos. But I can assure you, I'll soon find out who did! By the time I'm done with Makarezos, that melon-bellied whoremaster will beg to tell me how he obtained the information and who gave it to him."

"Do nothing!" Muzychenko's voice was sharp. "Should you arrest him—" He continued angrily, "But you're thinking of having him disappear!"

"Exactly!" snapped Cyatorus. "By the time he feels

the flame of a blowtorch on his bare ass, he'll be happy to tell me anything I want to know."

"Brilliant! Brilliant!" Muzychenko sneered, screwing up his face. "Have you thought of the stink his disappearance will generate? Have you considered how the press will treat the matter? It will spread the story all over the world, and attention could begin to focus on you. Face facts: You are the head of the KYP. With the experiments only a short time away, we do not want investigations of any kind. You will not do anything about Petros Makarezos. That is a direct order, and I speak for Moscow."

"What do we do about the Americans?" Cyatorus asked through clenched teeth.

"We don't have to do anything about them." Muzychenko presented Cyatorus with a huge smile. "There isn't anything the Americans can do. They can't attack us—and don't bring up Libya. Bombing the airfield of a known terrorist dictator is one thing. Bombing a peaceful nation like Greece is another matter. The Americans won't even look hard in the direction of Greece—the U.S. is too concerned about NATO bases here."

"I would not underestimate the Americans," Cyatorus said quickly. "They are a very powerful nation."

"They were once a powerful nation," Muzychenko corrected him. "Every day the Americans grow weaker."

"When will the experiments take place?" Cyatorus asked.

"In five weeks," said Muzychenko. "We'll let you know in time for you to make an inspection of many of the islands in the area."

Chapter Sixteen

I

Unlike religious people who insist on simple, uncomplicated answers, Richard Camellion had known for most of his existence that life is actually the fine art of drawing sufficient conclusions from insufficient premises. It was too early to draw an operational judgment based on the interior of the Scheherazade Café. There was a short counter on which were piled sandwiches; next to the counter, a bar. Behind the bar, an opening to a room beyond. At one end of the large area, to one side of the lunch counter, was a curtained archway with a sign over it. Presumably it said "Restrooms" in Latvian.

The outstanding feature of the furnishings was age. The slightly vaulted ceiling was gray with age; the linoleum on the floor was worn with age. The eleven metal tables, covered with red-and-white oilcloth, and their curved wire legs, and the chairs around the tables, and their curved wire legs, were sorely in need of several coats of paint. In the far corner was a green parrot in a cage.

Most of the patrons looked as if they had been there for weeks. There were seven men at the bar,

some smoking cheap Latvian cigarettes, others
pipes, all in working clothes. There were two elderly
couples at two separate tables. At another table were
two men and two women, all four in their thirties.
They merely glanced at the Death Merchant and
Karen Spreitler as the two sat down at a table toward
a corner where they could watch everyone.

"I'm not thirsty at all," Karen said. She opened her
handbag and took out her cigarettes and lighter.

"I'll order some kind of weird wine for both of us,"
Camellion said, "for the looks of it." He idly speculated about her real name. Courtland Grojean had
told him that "Karen Spreitler" was her cover name.
Grojean had also made it clear that "Max Spreitler"
was also convenient fiction for the purpose of his
explaining "Karen's" story.

Camellion thought he saw the bartender, a grandfatherly-looking man, lean down and apparently
press a button underneath the bar. He was sure that
he had seen the bartender look over at them.

The waiter will be a man in his late sixties, Hork
Zevv had said, of medium height and slightly
overweight. He will have a long scar from the
end of his nose, on the right side of his face. The
scar will go down across his mouth to the end of
his chin. He was a partisan during the Great
War and got the scar from the tip of a German
bayonet that raked across his face. His name is
John Divak. When he serves you, you will have
the photograph of Michael Kartemesk's great-
great grandfather toward him on the table, and
you will say in English, "I'll bet your name is
John. It is a common first name with Latvian
men." He will then tell you what to do. Follow
his orders to the letter.

A fortyish man came out of the back room, walked around the bar, and started toward Camellion and Karen's table. A white serving apron around his waist, the waiter was of average height, but he wasn't even slightly overweight. If anything, he was on the thin side, and when he reached their table, they saw that he didn't have a scar on the right side of his face.

He was neither friendly nor unfriendly as he said something in the Latvian tongue.

"I'm sorry," Camellion said politely. "We do not speak your language."

"I speak English," the waiter said. "What would you like?"

"A friend told us this café has excellent wine from the Ukraine," the Death Merchant said.

"Yes, that is true."

"Bring us several glasses of Kevrorissi. We understand it is a sweet plum wine, but not too sweet?"

"Yes. It is bittersweet as you will see."

Karen watched the waiter walk toward the bar, then turned toward the Death Merchant, who had taken his wallet from his plaid sport coat and was gently pulling the small, tattered photograph from one of the compartments.

"He's not John Divak," Karen said, exhaling cigarette smoke. "He could be a KGB plant. Do we play it out and see what happens?"

"If he were KGB, I'd be feeling the hairs on the back of my neck standing up," joked Camellion. He took a 500-ruble note from his billfold and placed it on the table next to the photograph, which was turned so that the waiter could clearly see the face when he put Camellion's glass on the table.

The waiter returned with the Kevrorissi in two tall wineglasses that looked more like goblets. He put the glasses on the table, Camellion watching his eyes. He knew the man had to see the photograph. When the man picked up the 500-ruble bill, Camellion said in a low voice, "I'll bet your name is John. It is a common first name with Latvian men."

The waiter's lips barely moved. At the same time, he pulled a small towel from the side of his apron and began to wipe up nonexistant wine from the red-and-white oilcloth.

"Take no longer than ten minutes to drink the wine. Leave and walk two blocks east. A taxicab will be parked at the curb on the right side of the street. The license number is ZL 297-49-Y. Get into the cab and tell the driver you came straight from this place. He will take you to your destination."

"We were supposed to meet John Divak," Camellion said.

"He had a wreck on his motorcycle and broke his hip." The man turned, went back to the bar, and handed the bill to the bartender. Sipping the plum wine, Camellion and Karen watched him return and place the change on the table, all the while acting as if they didn't exist.

"The wine does have an unusual tang to it," Karen said, glancing at her wristwatch. "It could be because I'm drinking it through smoke. Did you ever smoke, Richard?"

"I think it's illogical to inhale smoke from a weed wrapped in paper, and pay money to do it. We have seven minutes left."

Soon they left the café and began to walk east on the cobblestones—leisurely, as if they were sightseeing and didn't have any definite destination. In this old section of the city, there weren't any sidewalks. There was only the cobbled pavement that stretched from the front of buildings on both sides of the street. Now and then a man or woman went by on a bicycle or a motor scooter. Occasionally a car passed. By now it was dark, and while the blocks were long, there was ample light. Streetlights were not only at the ends of each block, they were also in the middle.

A short distance from the rear of the taxicab, Karen whispered, "You could be wrong, Richard. Writing bumper stickers might be a better way to make a living, certainly much safer."

"But far less exciting." Camellion stepped over the small curb that separated the sidewalk section from the cobblestones of the road, his eyes going to the taxicab's license plate—ZL 297-49-Y.

And all of this without even a slingshot for protection!

Camellion opened the right rear door and followed Karen into the cab. Once inside, he leaned forward and told the curly-haired driver, "We have just come from the Scheherazade Café."

"Yes," the driver said, his voice low and mechanical. "I know where you are going and whom you want to see."

For the next half hour, the man drove all over Riga, but he always avoided the main downtown sections. They knew what he was doing: attempting to foil anyone who might be following. Camellion and Karen could see his eyes dart up to the rearview mirror every now and then, but they were pros and knew that aimless driving alone would not shake a tail. All of it fit in with another concern they had— dealing with nonprofessionals, with butchers and bakers and candlestick dippers—with clerks, cab drivers, waiters, dock workers, and only God knew what else, people who were dedicated but untrained.

"You'll never shake any tail this way," Camellion told the driver at one point. The man did not answer.

After forty-eight minutes—Camellion timed it on his watch—the man swung the Russian Volga into an alley on the west side of the city and said, "Be prepared to get out fast on the left-hand side."

Halfway down the alley, the driver brought the car to a full stop without burning rubber on the pavement. "Out!" he ordered. Karen's left hand pushed down on the handle of the door.

No sooner had she and Camellion left the cab than another couple stepped out of the darkness, climbed into the rear of the Volga, and closed the door quietly. Immediately the driver pulled away, and the vehicle soon became only two red lights in the distance.

"Quickly, this way!" a man's voice called out softly behind Camellion and Karen, and they saw the tiny beam of a penlight close to the ground. They moved toward the man, found him in the darkness, and heard him whisper, "Follow me. Don't make any noise." They followed him a dozen feet, made a sharp turn, and saw him open a door.

Once the three of them were inside, the man closed and locked the door. "Turn on the light," he said.

Instantly, an overhead bulb in a round metal shade went on. They were in a grocery store. Loaves of bread were stacked fragrant and unwrapped on a wooden rack. There were cases of canned fruits and vegetables. To one side was a huge butcher block, a cleaver and long-bladed knives attached to its side. On another long table were heads of cabbage and other fresh produce waiting to be washed.

Camellion and Karen's attention was not focused on food. They found themselves facing six suspicious people, four men and two women. Two of the men had pistols trained on them, the hand of one man steady around the butt of a German PO8 Luger, the other man holding an older model of a Soviet 7.62-mm Tul'skiy Tokarev.

"This is hardly the warm welcome we expected," Camellion said quietly. He and Karen recognized the women and two of the men. The four had been at a table in the Scheherazade Café.

"We must be sure of you," the big man with the Tokarev said in a voice that was not unfriendly. Their escort into the building, he was bearded and looked fast on his feet. "Simon, Tamara. Search them."

A man and one of the women stepped forward. They moved over to Karen and Camellion and began to pat them down. The man was not more than twenty-five, sharp-faced and strong. The woman, perhaps thirty, had the high cheekbones, deepset eyes, and finely pointed nose of most Latvian women. So did the other girl.

After patting Camellion's chest and back and moving his hands along the Death Merchant's legs, Simon Tedre went through Camellion's pockets. He finally handed Camellion's billfold to Zvezdny Gorodik, the well-built man with the Russian Tokarev and the manager of the state-owned grocery store.

For a full minute, Gorodik looked at the photograph, then put it into the billfold, which he handed back to Camellion.

Tamara Tholberg had gone through Karen's handbag, and now she said, "She has only ordinary items, cigarettes, makeup, and the like."

Gorodik and Serms Saku—the man with the Luger —put away their weapons. The caution faded from the eyes of the other Latvians and they relaxed.

Gorodik motioned for Camellion and Karen to sit down on two empty wooden boxes. "Wait," he said anxiously. "Let me put some clean towels on the top. I don't want you to dirty your clothes."

As soon as they were seated, Gorodik introduced himself and the others. Camellion and Karen were amazed when Gorodik indicated a loose-limbed man with a weathered face, graying hair, and horn-rimmed glasses. "This is Father Ulo Melbardis. He is a Catholic priest."

Father Melbardis, seeing the surprise in their eyes, said solemnly, "There is more to being a priest than saying mass. In these trying times, a man of God has to sometimes fight physically for God. He has not a choice. He must fight for his flock, not only his own people but for the godless. No one suffers more, no one sheds more tears in life than those deprived of God. One cannot rear children without Christ."

"Where is Michael Kartemesk?" Camellion asked. "Don't tell us he's been arrested by the KGB."

"He felt he was going to be arrested," Luule Allokak, the other woman said. Tall and dark-haired, she was very attractive. "The KGB is convinced that he helped Hork Zevv to escape to freedom. He didn't, but that is beside the point."

"We will take you to Michael now," Father Melbardis said. Dressed in the clothes of a working man, he in no way resembled a priest. "We will use the store's produce truck. No one will see us in the back. It is covered with canvas."

"We go now," Gorodik said. "I drive the truck. It is in a garage in the rear."

II

The Russian GRD truck—it resembled a small American MAC of the 1940s—rattled along. Tamara Tholberg explained that they were on the same highway that connected Sherpty Airport with Riga and that their destination was the home and workplace of Feliksas Imkant, one of Riga's best designers of amber jewelry.

"I am very familiar with Sherpty Airport," said Simon Tedre wistfully. "I was a pilot and flew often to Sweden and Norway. They—the officials—decided I was politically unreliable when someone reported that I had said that the Soviet Union could learn much from the West. I am now working at a state farm where scientists are using the water of the Baltic for agriculture. We use seaweed to make chocolate and vitamins."

Father Melbardis told Camellion and Karen that Michael Kartemesk was hiding out with Imkant and his wife, Elizerbet, because there wasn't any social or professional connection between them.

Luule Allokak gave a small laugh. "Kartemesk could not be in a safer place. Feliksas and Elizerbet are 'good' members of the Party. The KGB would never suspect them of hiding a dangerous traitor with counterrevolutionary ideas."

Zvezdny Gorodik turned into the driveway that led to the Imkants' house and parked behind the house. Getting out, the Death Merchant and Karen saw that they were several hundred feet from the highway. The house, nestled among birch and pine trees, was a seven- or eight-room affair made of stone, built on a flat slab close to the ground.

It was 10:30 P.M. There was a half moon in the cloudless sky and a cool breeze blowing in from the Baltic. To the northwest was the glow of lights that was Sherpty Airport.

The group hurried to the back door, and a man— tall, half bald, and carrying a Soviet AKR assault rifle with the stock folded—let them in and ushered them into Imkant's studio in the front of the house. It was very large, with a large picture window composed of scores of small panes facing the front lawn.

"These are the two agents," Gorodik said to Feliksas Imkant, who was sitting in a wicker rocker next to his wife. Both were middle-aged, rosy-cheeked, and healthy-looking.

The Imkants scrutinized Camellion and Karen closely, then Feliksas said to the man with the AKR, "Tell Michael they are here."

"Feliksas, I will get coffee and wine and sausages for our guests," Elizerbet said, and got to her feet.

"We will help you," offered Tamara. She and Luule followed Elizerbet into the kitchen.

Michael Kartemesk was thin and stooped and in his late sixties, his hair bristly gray, his face unusually free of wrinkles, and his manner one of exhaustion. With him he had brought a leather briefcase that bulged—with hundreds of photographs of the magnifying transmitter, he said!

"Hork Zevv did not tell us how you, a janitor, could obtain photographs of the magnifying transmitter," said Camellion, who was sitting across from Kartemesk. He looked down at the large photograph in his hand. The transmitter looked like some "death-ray" device from a science fiction movie. Camellion glanced over at Kartemesk. "He didn't even mention all these photographs."

"Zevv said you had only a diagram, a drawing, of the transmitter," Karen said, taking out her cigarettes and offering one to Tamara, who was sitting next to her.

"Hork did not tell you about the photographs because he did not know about them," Kartemesk said in a weary voice. "I did not tell him. He could have been caught by the *Napravleniye*. He could not reveal under torture what he did not know."

"Then you were a janitor at the installation where the Russian scientists conducted actual weather experiments with the magnifying transmitter?" Camellion leaned forward, put his hands on his knees, and peered closely at Kartemesk. The man looked as if his entire life had been filled with mental and emotional suffering.

"Yes, I was one of the janitors at the installation," Kartemesk said emotionlessly. "It was a large building twenty-four miles south of Riga. I am not sure, but I think there were over fifty Soviet scientists there. I was able to acquire the photographs because Russian scientists are not as security-conscious as the KGB.

"The scientists took numerous photographs as the device was being assembled under the direction of a scientist named Vladimir Dostrimolesky. Another one of the scientists was named Lazar Marchenko. But the main scientist and the director was Gregor Shchors. These men threw away many of the photographs, assuming they would be burnt with other trash. We did burn most of them. I took the two hundred photographs over a four-year period. I put them under my clothes in order to get them out of the plant. We knew that eventually we would make contact with the CIA. We wanted the Americans to know what the Russians were trying to do with the weather."

"Zevv told us you had a comprehensive diagram of the transmitter as well." The Death Merchant knew it would be impossible to get the photographs out of Latvia. A moment later Karen Spreitler, crushing out her cigarette, said so.

"The photographs are useless," she said. "We have to open our bags for Soviet custom inspectors before we board the plane. We can leave with the diagram. I can tape it to my body, or Camellion to his, depending on its size."

Feliksas Imkant, who had been listening with a great deal of interest, looked at the Death Merchant. "I made the diagram from the photographs—to scale. There are fifty drawings on one large sheet of binding paper."

"See for yourself." Kartemesk had reached into the briefcase and pulled out the diagram, which he handed to the Death Merchant.

The diagram was the size of a road map. Each drawing had been executed to scale in various colored inks and revealed the magnifying transmitter during various stages of its assembly. Camellion was not interested. He wasn't a scientist and didn't know one part from another. He refolded the diagram carefully and slipped it in his inner coat pocket without further comment.

"Were you at the Soviet complex in Riga when it closed?" he inquired of Kartemesk. "Do you know why the Soviets closed the place?"

Kartemesk took a sip of wine before speaking. "I can only give you my opinion and what I believe to be the truth, based on what I overheard the Russians talking about, and I do not understand the Russian language all that well."

"Tell us what you think," Camellion said patiently.

"In my opinion, there were two reasons why the Russians closed the station. I feel they were building a much larger base somewhere else, but I think the main reason was that one of the experiments had adverse effects and affected the weather over the Soviet Union, over Russia itself. I am positive the Kremlin was not pleased. There is one more thing of importance that you should tell your superiors. The Russians never fully completed Tesla's magnifying transmitter. It never worked the way it should, either properly or at full capacity. There was some element or part that the Russian scientists could not find. God help us all if they ever do find what the magnifying transmitter was lacking!"

Then God had better start with His help. The Rus-

sians now have the complete magnifying transmitter in Greece!

"I'll make certain our superiors get the diagram and all the facts," the Death Merchant said. He looked at his watch. "It's almost midnight. I think"— he turned and glanced at Zvezdny Gorodik—"we should return to Riga. We don't know if the KGB is keeping track of tourists. Should we return to the hotel too late, it could appear suspicious."

Gorodik was prevented from replying by Basil Parshlu, the man with the Soviet AKR assault rifle. He rushed into the studio from the rear of the house, a look of near panic on his boyish face that was marred only by a beard that was ridiculously narrow. The AKR was slung over his left shoulder. In his left hand he held a Red Army infrared night-vision scope.

"There's a *Napravleniye* column coming this way," he cried, looking around the room at everyone. "Four patrol cars, a troop truck, and a BTR armored car in the lead."

Zvezdny Gorodik rushed to the picture window. He pulled back one end of the drapes ever so slightly and looked toward the highway. "I see them," he said, anxiety making his voice skid up and down the tonal scale. "The BTR is slowing down and—my God! It's turning slowly into the drive!"

Feliksas Imkant had gotten up and switched off the lights. Now, a flashlight in his hand, he said in a voice that was hollow and resigned, "Get out the weapons. We'll fight to the end. It's all we can do." He turned to Richard Camellion and Karen Spreitler. "I'm sorry that the two of you are trapped here. The KGB must have trailed you in the truck. Anyhow, they're here."

"What's to the rear of the house?" Camellion was coldly professional. "Can we run for it?"

"Nothing but open fields." Imkant hurried toward

a massive table that Father Melbardis and Serms Saku had pushed to one side. "They would cut us down before we got thirty meters."

A large throw rug had been underneath the table. Tamara and Luule pulled it to one side. The Death Merchant and Karen saw that the rug had concealed a trapdoor that, when Saku pulled it up and pushed it back, revealed a compartment filled with weapons.

"Richard"—Karen turned to Camellion, naked fear in her eyes, her shadowed face tight with expectancy. Her heart pounding against the inside of her chest, she stopped when she realized he would not be able to give her any magic answer that would guarantee life.

"We play it by ear," Camellion said. He didn't know what else to tell her. He could have said, *We're trapped. We'll be surrounded and there isn't anything we can do about it. We'll fight until our ammo runs out or until they kill us. Or I could tell her it's possible that the KGB intends to kill us. It's almost a Soviet state secret that there is armed resistance in Russia. They might feel that the less said about rebels the better—kill 'em and be done with it. Or, if the KGB knows about me and Karen, they might want us alive for a show trial and propaganda against the West.*

The Death Merchant told himself that he hadn't gone all the way to Riga to be killed by some KGB pig-farmer border guard and be dumped unceremoniously into some nameless grave. But he knew his reasoning was flawed. He was permitting hope for life to brush aside the fact that escape was impossible. Now.

In reality, being "dead" wasn't all that terrible. Most people went through life shoving the thought of dying and death to one side, never really coming to grips with their own mortality and living as if they were immortal. Death was always in the "future," even if they were eighty-five years old! Camellion was not that impractical; he lived with the realization that the Cosmic Lord of Death always was present. He walked with everyone, even children, constantly. He could strike anytime, and often did, very unexpectedly.

Fudge! Who says I can't stop a slug and within the next hour become a new resident of that far land of Pale People ruled by that Mute Priest! Mors ultima linea rerum est!

"They're deploying out in front," Gorodik called from the window. "They're taking positions on the slope, and I can see men running east and west. They'll be coming in behind us as well."

"Get over here and arm yourself," Feliksas Imkant said. "I'll watch the window until the others are in position."

The compartment in the floor was a treasure chest of firepower. There were Russian army gas masks, four dozen RGD-5 grenades and a dozen RKG-3M grenades with HEAT charges that could penetrate 165 millimeters of armor; plus AKR assault rifles—really submachine guns—Vitmorkin machine pistols, and enough ammo for the weapons to hold off a small army for . . . ten minutes. In only a few minutes everyone was armed, including Karen, who had never fired a submachine gun. The Death Merchant quickly showed her what to do—press this and shove in the magazine. Pull back on this—see it? Right here!—and press down on this small lever. It's the safety. This is the rate of fire lever. Keep it here, on bursts. On full auto, you'll exhaust your thirty-five rounds in seconds. The cyclic rate of fire on full auto is six hundred rounds p.m. Aim, squeeze the trigger, then pull back.

From the way the Latvians mulled around, it was

apparent to the Death Merchant that none of them had ever been in a fire-fight and were confused about deployment.

"All of you, listen," he said. "I've had a lot of experience in this sort of thing. Spread out all over the house by the windows. Pick where you want to go, but do it fast. Tedre, you and the girl stay with me in the studio."

"I'll remain here also," Zvezdny Gorodik said. He didn't know why, but for some reason he felt safer with Camellion.

No one spoke, although many glances were exchanged from underneath the glass of the gas masks each person wore. Feliksas Imkant thought of telling "Knud Haekkeruo" that this was his house and his studio and that he would go where he damned well pleased. Imkant could see from the way the agent from the West handled an AKR that he was very familiar with such weapons, and common sense told Imkant that Camellion knew what he was talking about. Why argue? In an hour or so they would all stand before God. . . .

"Elizerbet, we'll defend the windows on the east side," Imkant said, and started for the doorway at the end of the studio. Tears coursing down her cheeks, his wife followed.

Now that Imkant had responded to the Death Merchant's order, the rest of the Latvians followed suit. Some moved toward the rear of the stone house. Others went east to defend the front windows in the remaining three rooms facing the south.

Simon Tedre's sharp features screwed up in perplexity. "Knud Haekkeruo, why did you want me to remain here in the studio? I don't understand." His voice did not sound muffled; the gas masks had voicemitters.

The Death Merchant, a Vitmorkin machine pistol

in his belt and an AKR in his hand, went over to Zvezdny Gorodik, who had moved again to the east end of the large picture window. He did have a plan germinating in his mind, but why give what could be a false hope to Tedre? So very much of the plan depended on what the Russians would do. Camellion was hoping that the *Napravleniye* commander would not want prolonged battle. The longer the battle lasted, the greater the chance that the news would reach all of Riga and spread to the rest of the Soviet Union; and as every good citizen knew, there was no armed resistance in the "Workers' Paradise."

Camellion was positive that the Russians outside wouldn't use the troop truck—it was too large.

"What did you mean by 'slope'?" Camellion asked Gorodik.

The man looked at him for a moment. "Say, that's right. You were in the rear and didn't see the front. The front yard is about a meter higher than the highway. From the highway to the top of the lawn there is a long slant. I'd say it's six meters long. See for yourself." He moved from the side of the window, making room for the Death Merchant, who looked out.

The four patrol cars and the troop transport truck were parked off the highway. The BTR armored car was thirty feet inside the drive, its SGMB light machine gun sticking out of the turret, pointed toward the front of the house. Toward the south, thirty feet from the highway, were dark-green helmeted heads on the top of the rise.

It was the BTR-40 armored car that held Camellion's interest. A BTR standard recon vehicle is small but tough, its combat weight 5.2 tons. It also has plenty of escape hatches in case of fire—one to the rear, one on top the turret, and a large one in front of the two drivers.

Camellion had a good feeling when he saw that the

two half-round sections of the turret hatch were open. Even in a cool breeze, a chunk of metal like a BTR-40 gets hot inside. The gunner had opened the turret hatch to keep cool.

"Let's fire a few rounds and get a response out of them," suggested Gorodik. "The bastards can't do any more than return our fire. They'll be shooting soon enough anyhow."

"Wait," Camellion ordered. "I see one of them with a bullhorn. He's moving toward the rear of the armored car."

Everyone in the house soon heard the Russian border guard officer call out, "We demand your immediate surrender. We know that the spies Knud Haekkeruo and Margrethe Haekkeruo are inside. Come out with your hands in the air and your lives will be spared. We will wait five minutes."

"Damn them and their five minutes," Zvezdny Gorodik spit out, starting to raise his AKR.

Camellion's left hand shot out. "I said *wait!*"

"For what?" Gorodik demanded angrily. "We're as good as dead. Let's die on our feet, not on our knees."

If I don't tell them now, I won't have time later. They won't know what I want them to do.

"I have a plan," Camellion said evenly. "Karen, Tedre, come over here." As soon as they were close to Camellion and Gorodik, the Death Merchant told them what he thought might happen, and if it did: "Here is what we'll do." He glanced at Gorodik. "You're fast on your feet and shoot well, right?"

Gorodik nodded.

"Here's what I want you to do. . . ."

Camellion talked rapidly, finishing with "If there's one slip, we'll all end up dead."

"It's still a very slim chance," Tedre said skeptically.

"A hairline chance is still better than none at all."

Camellion glanced at Karen, who was picking up the briefcase with the photographs of the magnifying transmitter. She had conquered her initial fear and her hands were steady.

"Don't forget to drop the instant the firing begins," Camellion reminded them. "The picture window will be going in a second." He nodded at Gorodik. "All right, my trigger-happy friend. Now you can answer."

"It's about time!"

The Russian *Napravleniye* officer was just starting to give a warning—"This is your last"—when Gorodik stepped back and fired off a short burst through the heavy brown drapes. The roaring of the AKR had not even set up an echo by the time he moved to one side and dropped to the floor. Camellion, Tedre, and Karen were already on the smooth hardwood.

The Russian reply was instantaneous. The SGMB light machine gun in the turret of the BTR began roaring, the gunner raking the front of the house with streams of solid-steel-core 7.62-mm projectiles. Many of them hit the stones and glanced off; the rest dissolved the windows of the three rooms to the south as well as the picture window in front.

The drapes jerked violently as slugs, blowing out most of the individual windowpanes, tore through the material and buried themselves in the opposite wall. Feliksas Imkant's drawing board was ripped apart. Amber jewelry on shelves exploded. A few chairs were knocked over by the impact. Pictures on the wall were destroyed. In only seconds the studio was turned into a trash dump.

The SGMB light machine gun stopped firing, but there was no longer a heavy silence. AKRs and Soviet PPS submachine guns roared from the outside, to the rear of the house. Simultaneously, Father Melbardis, in the kitchen, and Serms Saku, in one of the bedrooms, answered with bursts from their AKR assault rifles.

Prone on the floor, the Death Merchant said, "Hold your fire. I want them to wonder what's happened at this end of the house."

This time the Soviet border guards did not use the machine gun in the BTR armored car. Instead, a dozen of them lying on the slope raked the front of the house with horizontal fire from their AKRs, scores of 5.45 by 39-mm projectiles striking the house, ninety percent of the slugs going through the shotout windows.

Luule Allokak let out a short scream, then an even shorter gurgle. She fell back to the floor and lay there, her left leg twisted under her. A single 5.45-mm bullet had bored into her left breast and had gone all the way through her body.

Above the snarling of the AKRs and the loud notes of the Soviet PPS chatterboxes, the Death Merchant detected another sound, the deeper sound of an engine. It was a sound that he had heard before in different parts of the world. The driver of the BTR-40 had started the engine.

"That noise!" Tedre exclaimed excitedly. "It's an engine! Is it the armored car?"

"Yes," replied the Death Merchant. "Gorodik, get ready. Karen, did you get the rest of those RKG grenades—the stick grenades?"

Karen muttered, "Uh-huh." She was crouched in the southwest corner, sitting on her heels, her AKR pointed at the single window on the west side of the studio.

"Suppose the driver doesn't do what you think he will?" asked Gorodik. He had pulled a Vitmorkin from his belt and was checking to make sure the machine pistol had a full magazine and one round in the firing chamber.

"In that case, we'll not be any worse off than we are now," Camellion drawled. He rolled over, got to his feet, went to the east end of the picture window, making sure the second machine pistol he had taken from the compartment was snug in his belt. Then he pushed the tattered drapes six inches to one side and looked out. Across from him, Zvezdny Gorodik was next to Karen, flat against the south wall. Simon Tedre was in the southeast corner of the studio, a Vitmorkin in each hand.

Camellion saw that the BTR-40's driver had driven the vehicle west and had turned to face the front of the house. Furthermore, the front of the vehicle was centered on the picture window.

A lot of factors were involved. Normally, a BTR carried a crew of three: driver, relief-driver/radio-man, and gunner. Camellion doubted if this one carried more than a driver and the gunner. On a short operation like this, a relief/radio-M would be super-fluous.

There were other dangers. The pig-farmer gunner might close the hatch above him. Or the driver might have his side window closed. It was almost a certainty that the driver would drop the plates over the driving rectangular slots just before the vehicle hit. But the side had to be open.

Camellion patted his left coat pocket to make sure the small flashlight was available. He pulled one of the Russian machine pistols from his belt, switched off the safety, and waited. The armored car had to move forward. It didn't have to—*But it had better!*

The BTR did!

The car had not moved ten feet when the gunner once more opened fire with the SGMB machine gun. This time, however, he didn't hose down the house.

He directed all his 7.62-mm projectiles at the picture window, wanting to make sure that the entire framework of individual frames was shot away—or as much as possible.

"Here it comes—straight at us!" Camellion shouted to make himself heard above the roaring of the SGMB.

The firing increased, but not from the armored car. It came from the rear of the house, both from inside and outside, and from the border guards on the rise. They were firing at the windows of the three rooms to the east of the studio, wanting to divert attention from the armored car.

The Death Merchant didn't move from the side of the window, although several 7.62-mm pieces of metal made the drapes jump a few inches from the right side of his head. The hell with it. It was relative. Whether he stopped a bullet by the window or a minute—or ten minutes—later was irrelevant. One could not be "more dead."

At twenty miles per hour, the BTR-40 headed toward the giant gap that was the picture window, a maw except for pieces of frame molding.

The Death Merchant just knew that the stinking piece of Russian trash would have to do it—and he was ready for the gunner's move.

The bulky little fortress on four big wheels was only twenty feet from its target when, apparently, Mikhail Kolesov, the gunner, remembered the open hatch above his head and, with his left hand, reached for the pull-down bar.

Your father set a good example, pig farmer! He never married!

The Death Merchant gently squeezed the trigger of the Vitmorkin. On full automatic, the machine pistol went *BRRRRRRRR* and spit out eighteen 9-mm flat-nosed slugs. Two hit Kolesov's hand and left it almost nonexistent. Three more severed the hand at the wrist. Kolesov screamed and dropped to the bottom of the turret platform, the stub of his wrist spurting blood from ripped-open digital arteries and metacarpal veins. Just before he passed out from shock and loss of blood, Kolesov looked up and, in horror, saw that several fingers of his hand were still wrapped around the pull-down bar.

Sergeant Gavriil Ivolginsk, the driver, heard Kolesov howl, but he was too close to the house to turn around and see what had happened. All he could do now was peer through the driver's slot, take the BTR through the window, and drop the plate over the slot the instant the vehicle slammed into the room. Then he could put the BTR in reverse and move back.

Clang! The armor plate dropped over the slot. *Bang!* The BTR crashed through the individual window frames of the window, the front end smashing into the table that had been over the trapdoor in the floor.

Ivolginsk was putting on the brakes as Camellion charged in from one side and Zvezdny Gorodik from the other side. By the time the Death Merchant reached the right side of the BTR and his foot was on the rung that would enable him to get to the top of the turret, Gorodik was shoving the long barrel of a Vitmorkin through the ten- by four-inch driver's slot on the left side and pulling the trigger. *BRRRRRRR!* Ivolginsk's head exploded from the impact of the flat-nosed projectiles. His green cap, with the red star on the front, flew upward while parts and pieces of his skull and brain splattered over the roof, back toward the dead Kolesov, against the inner left side of the driver's compartment, and over the left side dash. Headless, he slumped to the right, a thick river of red running from the stump of his neck.

The BTR sat there, its engine idling.

By then the Death Merchant had reached the top of the open turret and was firing three rounds downward with the other Vitmorkin, just in case. Without waiting to see what effect his slugs might have had—all three had hit Kolesov's dead body—Camellion took the flashlight from his coat pocket, yelled, "All of you get ready!" and lowered himself into the BTR. The first thing the beam picked up was the face of Mikhail Kolesov, fixed in horror, the dead eyes wide and staring. Almost slipping on the blood on the floor, Camellion got down and shone the light into the driver's compartment. It resembled a slaughterhouse. The floor was thick with blood; there was blood on the dash and on the seats.

Damn it, there was no other way. There wasn't time to haul the two dead dummies out through the turret.

He squeezed past the driver's bloody corpse and, kneeling in blood, forced his way between the two dashboards into the cubbyhole underneath the forward escape hatch. He found the release, pushed upward on the plate, and threw the hatch open. Then he turned around, went back four feet and grabbed the dead Ivolginsk by his boots, pulled the corpse from the seat, and tugged the dead man into the cubbyhole. With his bloody hands on top of the man's boots, Camellion half raised himself out of the forward hatch and pushed the feet and lower legs of the corpse through the opening. He found Gorodik, Tedre, and Karen staring at him in shock and revulsion at all the blood on his clothes.

Camellion looked at Tedre, who was closest. "Grab his legs and hang on to him while I get out."

He pulled himself all the way out of the hatch, then helped Tedre pull the corpse from the BTR.

"What about the gunner?" asked Simon Tedre,

who was becoming more nervous by the second. "Hear that firing from the rear and the front? Some of them must be dead by now."

"We haven't time to get the other pig farmer out," Camellion said. "Karen and I will stand on him. It will be a damn tight squeeze, but it will have to do. Gorodik, you drive. Tedre, ride in front with him. Both of you can go in through the hatch. Be sure to secure it after you're in."

Tedre and Gorodik stared at him, both wondering why he sounded so calm and unconcerned.

"I hope you know what you're doing," Gorodik muttered. "If—"

"If you don't think I do, stay here and die."

Gorodik sighed and put a leg into the hatch.

The Death Merchant crawled up the left side of the armored car and was soon looking down from the turret. Karen first handed him two AKRs, then the briefcase full of photographs. Last of all, she pushed up to him seven stick RKG-3M grenades tied in a large towel. She was last. She crawled up the two rungs on the side, and the Death Merchant helped her climb down into the turret.

"M-my God!" she muttered. "One of my feet is on his chest!"

"You're going to have to get down and give me room to fire. Two can't stand in the turret." He put the box of ammo on the side of the SGMB LMG and pushed down on the holding lever.

"Get down? Where?" She sounded almost angry. "A grave has more room than this!"

"Sit on the dead russkie's chest," Camellion said. "He won't mind. Stretch your legs toward the driver's compartment."

Karen began to scoot down into the turret compartment. "I could sure use a drink—a whole damn bottle!" she said in disgust. "God, it stinks in here."

The interior of the armored car did have a new smell that mixed with the odor of gas and oil, metal and rubber, a sweet smell, the stink of Death.

Camellion made sure the end of the belt was in the receiver. He pulled back on the handle and sent the first cartridge into the SGMB's firing chamber.

"Where do you want to drive to?" Gorodik called up.

"Back it up, turn around, and go down the driveway," Camellion said. "We'll first kill the ivans by the road."

Gorodik stepped on the gas and the BTR-40 moved backward out of the studio.

The Russians to the rear of the house and to the east began to close in, the roaring of dozens of AKRs and PPS submachine guns sending a wall of sound against the cloudless sky.

Father Ulo Melbardis didn't pull back in time. Half out a window, he stopped two 7.62-mm projectiles, one in the forehead and one high in the chest. Without even time to say an Act of Contrition, he was dead and in the Ultimate Elsewhere. Tamara Tholberg was already dead, but Basil Parshlu was still firing from the first room east of the studio. His time was running out. He had only two magazines of ammo left.

Serms Saku and Elizerbet Imkant were cut down within seconds of each other. Saku caught slugs in his right arm and in the right side of his chest. Elizerbet was hit by several bullets that went straight through her forehead into her brain.

Feliksas Imkant could hear the Russians on the outside shouting as they moved closer. For a long moment he looked down at his dead wife. She hadn't suffered. She had died instantly.

Feliksas thought of surrendering. Impossible. Life

in a Soviet prison would not be living. It would be
Hell. He shoved the barrel of a Vitmorkin into his
mouth, pressed the muzzle against the roof of his
mouth, and pulled the trigger.

Zvezdny Gorodik drove the BTR-40 south on the
driveway at 20 mph, he and Simon Tedre watching
the unsuspecting Russians ahead through the two
front driver's slots—until Richard Camellion called
down from the turret and said, "Simon, if you opened
the plate over your front see-through, close it. We
need you to fly. Should some Russian see two men in
the driver's compartment, he might get wise to what
we're going to do. Stop seven meters from the highway, then I'll go to work."

Far behind the armored car, two grenades exploded in one of the rooms east of the studio. One of
the Russians had crawled along the front of the house
and tossed two RGD-5 grenades through the window
of the room in which Basil Parshlu was firing. The
first explosion tore off Parshlu's left arm and blew his
body halfway to the ceiling. He was dead by the time
his body came down and the second explosion decap-
itated him.

Captain Vladimir Gluzez and the rest of the Russians by the highway did not suspect that Death was
moving slowly toward them. Neither did the seventeen border guards behind the house and to the east.

The Death Merchant waited behind the SGMB
machine gun, his gaze steady as he looked through
the firing slots above and on either side of the armored shield curving around the weapon in the turret.

Gorodik stopped the BTR-40's forward movement, and Camellion saw that he had guessed correctly. He had a clear, unobstructed view not only of

the border guards on the slope but also of the others scattered around the vehicles.

A turkey shoot—in this case, a pig-farmer shoot! The cyclic rate of an SGMB light machine gun is 600 rpm, or ten 7.62-mm projectiles a second. Of course, any machine gun is fired in bursts. You don't hold down the trigger and fire off the entire box. The Russian *Napravleniye* troops weren't lined up like glass bottles, but twenty-five of them might as well have been. They had been lying on the slope and were getting to their feet when the Death Merchant opened fire, killing all twenty-five within ten seconds, so quickly that the Russians never knew what was happening. For that matter, neither did Captain Gluzez and the rest of the border guards.

Gluzez couldn't believe what was happening. He suddenly guessed that, by some strange twist of fate, some of the enemy had gotten inside the BTR-40. It was a catastrophe, but he didn't know what to do about it. He also didn't know that the Death Merchant had spotted him and knew that he was an officer because of his red shoulder tabs and the wide band of red around his peaked uniform cap.

BBBBBEEEEEERRRRRRRRRRRRRRR.   The SGMB snarled and Captain Gluzez's legs were amputated, cut out from under him just above the knees. The Death Merchant had deliberately fired low. He wanted the officer's coat and hat, and didn't want them soaked in blood.

Another Russian, ten feet in front of the first Rill patrol car, was next to die, five 7.62-mm projectiles blowing open his chest. The impact picked him up and, while shot-off bits and pieces of his shirt fluttered to the ground, slammed him back six feet before he sagged to the ground in a spray of blood.

A single Russian on the highway had been flagging traffic by. In desperation, he tried to reach the opposite side of the highway and dive into the weeds. He reached the other side but didn't get to throw himself down. Half a dozen projectiles stabbed his back, blew out his chest, and knocked him to his face.

Three more border guards, trying to crawl underneath two of the patrol cars, were slammed against the left side of the Rill. There were loud *bzzub-bzzub-bzzub-bzzub*s as the slugs, tearing all the way through their bodies, stabbed into the metal of the vehicles. The three corpses dropped, dripping blood, chipped red ribs showing in the front and the back, through shot-apart clothing, of the dead men.

Two men had been in the cab of the troop truck. The man on the left side managed to open the door, throw himself out, and drop flat to the ground before a rain of slugs chopped into the cab and wrecked the motor, dissolved the windshield, and sent the driver's head flying. Another long burst and three short ones from the SGMB and the three patrol cars were effectively wrecked. The last burst blew away the man who had gotten out of the cab. He had stupidly tried to crawl into the rear seat of the patrol car parked in front of the truck. Some of the projectiles that had plowed through the left and the right sides of the Rill caught him in the chest and knocked him to the ground, dead.

The unhappiest occupant of the armored car was Karen Spreitler. Not only was she sitting on the chest of the dead gunner, she was forced to inhale the sharp, pungent fumes from the exploded cartridges and to keep her hands over her head to keep from being hit by the torrent of empty brass cases raining down on her from the machine gun's extractor.

In the driving compartment, Tedre and Zvezdny weren't exactly in ecstasy. For one thing, their feet were almost pasted to the metal floor in drying blood. For another, when they speculated about what would happen—one way or another—after they left the area, they both wondered if they would live to see the dawn.

When he was working, the Death Merchant was neither happy nor sad. At the moment he was busy attaching another full box of ammo to the light machine gun. Once the SGMB was loaded, he stepped on the turret pedal and swung the turret around to face the house to the north. He was just in time to hear a dozen 5.45-mm AKR ricochet off the turret. The seventeen border guards around the house had finally realized that something had gone wrong and that whoever was inside the BTR-40 was an enemy.

Camellion swung the machine gun from left to right and up and down on its mount, the SGMB roaring. Some of the projectiles wasted five of the border guards, two fifty feet west of the house and two by the northeast corner. The other dropped flat and stayed down.

Camellion dropped down into the turret well and yelled at Tedre and Gorodik, "Go out through the front hatch and wait for the girl. Let us know when you're out of the car." Then he said to Karen, "Go to the front and wait in the compartment in front of the driver's seat. Take the AKRs and the briefcase with you."

"Why don't you ask me to do your washing while you're at it!" Karen snapped. "I'm not an octopus."

"Take the two AKRs. I'll bring the grenades and the briefcase."

Camellion stood up in the turret and looked through the slots. He slowly moved the turret in a half circle and every now and then triggered off short bursts. The remaining border guards presented only a slight danger. Only men with an intense death wish would charge a BTR-40 with a light machine gun spitting 7.62-mm slugs at them.

Soon he and Karen heard Simon Tedre's voice. "We're out and waiting in front."

Holding the two AKR assault rifles several inches off the floor, Karen started to squirm through the round opening from the turret well into the driver's compartment, almost gagging when she saw the blood splattered over the dash and on the floor, its color an odd shade in the green light from the three tiny bulbs in the slanted roof.

At length she reached the cubbyhole and smelled fresh air rushing in at her through the open hatch. She moved faster, anxious to be free of the stinking mess of steel, and had soon pushed herself up through the opening, using the two AKRs as "crutches."

She handed the two assault rifles to Zvezdny Gorodik and Simon Tedre, then got back down and called out to the Death Merchant, "Okay, I'm up here. What now?"

"Wait, I'll be there shortly," Camellion yelled. He finished firing the rest of the ammo, raking the entire forward area with slugs. Then he got down and, pushing the towel full of grenades and the briefcase full of photographs ahead of him, began to crawl forward. He moved through the now jellylike blood on the floor, came to the forward compartment, and told Karen to get out and stand between Gorodik and Tedre.

"Here, take these," Camellion said.

Karen made a face when she saw that the bottom of the towel and of the briefcase were covered with blood. Again she fought to keep from vomiting.

The Death Merchant hoisted himself from the compartment and took the AKR from Tedre.

"Tedre, you and Karen run to the road," he said. "Move in a straight line so that the BTR will be between you and the border guards around the house. Once you reach the road, go to the first car and wait."

"I'll carry the grenades; you take the briefcase," Tedre said. He untied the towel, removed two stick grenades, and placed them on the ground.

"Get moving. We'll cover you." The Death Merchant leaned around the left side of the BTR-40 and triggered off a short burst. Gorodik fired off another blast from the right side. When Camellion saw that Karen and Tedre had reached the patrol cars, he turned to Gorodik, who was securing a spare AKR magazine in his belt; he had two more in his back pockets. "Get going! I'll cover you."

"Why don't we go together?" Gorodik was confused. "There can't be many of them left. I don't think they're going to give us trouble."

The Death Merchant stabbed a finger at the *Napravleniye* officer whose legs he had just-about amputated with machine-gun slugs. "I want his coat and hat," Camellion said. "I've got to drag him to the cars."

"His coat and hat! Why?"

"I'll tell you later. Make it snappy. We have to get out of here. Should more border guards pass on the highway and see this mess, we'll be finished."

Gorodik made the run. The Death Merchant stepped five feet in front of the BTR, pulled the pin of the first RKG-3M grenade, and flipped it just right. It landed at the bottom of the turret well. Right behind it came the second grenade through the turret.

The instant the second grenade left Camellion's right hand, he turned and sprinted the forty feet to Vladimir Gluzez's corpse. There he dropped flat and put his face to the ground, the AKR, on his shoulder, hitting his back.

BLAMMMM-BLAMMMMMMM! The two RKG-3M stick grenades, each having a HEAT charge, exploded with muffled but clanging roars, the twin blasts blowing out the sides and the bottom of the BTR-40 and setting the wreckage on fire.

Camellion reached out to his left, picked up the green uniform cap, and put it on. It was only slightly too small. He got up, grabbed Captain Gluzez's wrists, and began to drag the corpse to the patrol cars, the thick, oily smoke of the burning BTR-40 a moving wall of black between him and the house. He pulled the dead officer to the right side of the second Rill, mentally reviewing all the ways the KGB could have known about him and Karen. Time for that later. *If we get out alive.*

Gorodik watched over the hood of the patrol car, his eyes fixed to the north. Camellion unbuckled and removed the Sam Browne belt and holstered pistol from the corpse. Next came the green coat with the red shoulderboards. As Camellion undressed the dead man, a Soviet Volga and a Zhigulis passed, headed toward Riga. Both drivers put on speed when they realized that a shootout was taking or had taken place. No citizen wanted to be involved with the dreaded *Napravleniye.*

They got into the first patrol car, Gorodik driving, the Death Merchant in the rear seat on the left. Next to him sat Karen. As Gorodik pulled onto the road and headed east, Camellion took off his coat, removed his billfold and the diagram of the magnifying transmitter, and handed them to Karen. "Put them in the briefcase," he said, dropping the coat on the floor. He put on the green uniform coat and buttoned it all the way to the collar. Then he slipped into the Sam Browne belt. He buckled it over the coat and pulled the leather cross strap underneath the right shoulderboard, down sideways across his chest, and fastened it on the left side of the belt.

Simon Tedre, next to Zvezdny Gorodik, turned

and stared at the Death Merchant, his young face a mask of deep concern.

"Listen, it's been eight months since I flew with Aeroflot," he said nervously to the Death Merchant, who had pulled out a blue identification case and was looking at the ID card and the photograph of Captain Vladimir Gluzez. He resembled the pig farmer as much as a midget resembles a sumo wrestler. It wasn't all that bad. The ordinary border guards at Sherpty Airport wouldn't want to insult a *Napravlen-iye* officer by asking that he hold the card out of the window of the car, close enough for them to actually see the small photograph and compare it with the owner's face. In the Soviet Union everyone was equal with everyone else, but officers were one thousand times more "equal" than the rank and file.

"You haven't lost your ability to fly," replied the Death Merchant. "Flying is like swimming or riding a bicycle. Once you know how, you never forget."

"I'm not concerned about my ability to fly," Tedre said, insulted. "I'm good, very good. I was the youngest pilot ever to fly the Leningrad route. I mean that in eight months, the one-forty-five flight over Estonia could have been rescheduled. The plane might not be warming up on the field! And what do we do when the fighter jets from Rezloyre catch up with us? One missile and we're out of the sky!"

Zvezdny Gorodik snapped angrily, "We've come this far, and by the grace of God, we'll go all the way to Sweden!"

Camellion put the ID book in the left breast pocket of the uniform coat and pulled the pistol from the holster on his belt. He looked at Tedre before studying the weapon.

"Am I to deduce from your brand of logic that we could be 'more dead' if we got killed in the air than if we'd been gunned down at Imkant's house?"

"Don't talk nonsense!" Tedre was openly angry. "I didn't say we should pull over to the side of the road and wring our hands. I was only pointing out the possibilities. Should Flight 141 have been rescheduled, I'm sure we'll find some kind of plane on the field. A lot of flights to White Russia and the Ukraine originate at Sherpty."

"We'll play it like we see it and use the hand Fate deals us," Camellion said. He looked at the pistol that had been in Captain Gluzez's holster. He had heard of the new Soviet *Pistolet Samozaryadniy Malogabaritniy,* but he had never seen one until now. The PSM was a small weapon and held a magazine of eight 5.45-mm cartridges. Camellion didn't think much of the weapon. It didn't have enough power.

He shoved the pistol into the holster and secured the flap. In contrast, the 9-mm Vitmorkin machine pistol in his lap was a first-rate weapon.

"How far are we from the airport?" Camellion asked Gorodik.

"I'm not sure. About eleven kilometers, I think."

There was more than an airport waiting seven miles away. There was also Life or Death.

It had to be one or the other. . . .

Chapter Seventeen

Traveling by air in the Soviet Union is far different from flying in the free world. You don't sit in a lounge and walk through a moveable corridor onto the plane, without having to take a single step. In the Soviet Union, you walk out onto the field (even in Moscow)—rain or sunshine, through snow and sleet—and climb wheeled stairs to board the airplane.

There are other paradoxical facts about air travel in Mother Russia. There are no competing airlines. There is only the government controlled *Grazhdanskaya Vozduzhnaya Flot,* the Civil Air Fleet—Aeroflot. Impossible to compare with any Western airline, Aeroflot has thousands of aircraft of all sizes. Yet there has never been a single accident, never a single passenger hurt or killed, never a single crash. There never has been because the "press" in the Soviet Union is forbidden to report any such incident.

Aeroflot has thirty-one directories. Sherpty Airport, outside of Riga, is in the Far East Directorate.

"There it is. The airport is less than half a kilometer away," Zvezdny Gorodik announced to the Death Merchant. "Simon brought up some good points, but he forgot to ask you what you'll do if the guards start asking questions in Russian."

"I'll answer them in Russian," Camellion replied. "I speak and write Russian idiomatically." He smiled slightly to himself, knowing the thoughts that were tumbling about in Gorodik's mind—and in Tedre's too. "If we hadn't gone through the shootout back there and you didn't know I was on your side, you'd think I was a KGB spy, wouldn't you?"

"Yes, we would," Gorodik admitted frankly. "The KGB is very clever, but so far we have outsmarted them. I must tell you that I and most of the others were against meeting with you and the woman. We didn't want to risk the two of you being KGB plants. Feliksas had the final say. He was the leader of our cell."

"We were afraid and confused," Simon Tedre added. "I'm sure the two of you understand."

Karen Spreitler was even more confounded—by the many-sided Richard Camellion. He didn't seem to be a sexual man, but as a lover, he was almost perfect. He knew what to do and how to do it. One reason she enjoyed going to bed with Camellion was that he never hurried and, unlike most men, waited until the woman was so erotically aroused that she was about to scream for him to fuck her.

Not only was Sherpty Airport different from Western airports, one feature made it unusual among most airports in the Soviet Union. Because Riga was on the front doorstep of the Capitalistic and Immoral West, there were four fighter craft at Sherpty, ready to take off and chase any "terrorist" who might try to hijack a plane.

"Tedre, tell me again about the fighter planes at the airport," Camellion said.

"I can't add anything to what I have already said."

Tedre sighed. Staring ahead, he saw that the gate was only one hundred meters ahead, to the left. "When I was still with Aeroflot, the jets at Sherpty were MiG-17s. Each one carries four missiles and can reach eleven hundred ninety kilometers per hour. If we don't wreck them, they'll come after us. They are old-style fighters, but they can hit the blue in ten minutes. They're always fueled and ready to go."

Hmmm . . . 1190 klicks per hour. That's 750 mph. Slow by today's standards, but fast enough to catch us in five minutes.

"I'll be turning by the time you can blow your nose," Gorodik said. "Any last-minute orders?"

"Make sure the AKRs up there can't be seen," Camellion said, "and let me do the talking. Tedre, Karen, make sure your machine pistols are ready to fire. Anything can happen!"

The Death Merchant scooted over close to the left rear door and shoved the Vitmorkin machine pistol between his left hip and the inside of the Rill. At his feet were five RKG grenades and the other AKR assault rifle.

"Here we go." Gorodik sighed. "Let's try to look like Russian scum."

He swung the patrol car easily to the left, turned and drove through the open cyclone steel gates, on either side of which were four *Napravleniye* border guards, one, to the right, with a shouldered AKR rifle. The other three carried PSM pistols. Beyond were the brightly lighted administration building, the large lounge, and the hangars and the repair section of the airport. In front, the wide and long field.

With his left hand, Camellion pulled the blue ID case from his left breast pocket, flipped it open, and, with his best annoyed look, thrust it toward the open window of the left rear door at one of the guards, who, seeing Camellion's officer's cap, was walking toward the left rear of the patrol car.

Before the man could get a good look at the identification card and its photograph, Camellion closed the ID case and returned it to his coat pocket.

"I am sorry, sir. Regulations have been tightened," the guard said, leaning down close to the window. "I must see your identification card."

"Certainly," Camellion replied in Russian. "We must follow regulations." *He might as well have asked me to take a bath on top of a flagpole! One look at the card, then at me, and he'll know I'm not Captain Gluzez. Ahhhh, sweet mystery of life. . . .*

Pretending to reach for the ID case with his left hand, he pulled the Vitmorkin MP with his right hand and shot the guard in the face at point-blank range. The Russian's head jerked violently as a bullethole appeared an inch and a half above the bridge of his nose. The three other border guards didn't have any more of a chance for life. They were just beginning to realize they were face to face with death when Camellion blew up the other guard on his side of the car and Simon Tedre killed the two on the right side of the vehicle, his Vitmorkin roaring on single-fire. One man crumpled with a 9-mm bullet in his chest. His partner went down with a tunnel bored through his throat and his life's blood spurting out, the gush weaker as the heart began to slow.

"Drive!" Camellion ordered. "Tedre, direct him."

Karen Spreitler reached behind her and pulled out her machine pistol. Camellion leaned over and picked up the AKR assault rifle and three of the Soviet stick grenades. Zvezdny Gorodik, looking fierce, shot the Rill patrol car forward.

"Turn to the left of the big building ahead," Tedre said. "That's the ticket office and lounge. We'll go between the parking lot and the rear of the office and the hangars."

"Why not drive straight to the MiG-17s?" asked Gorodik, increasing speed. He turned on the siren and the flashing red lights. "Didn't you say they were lined up by the control tower?"

"We can move faster by going behind the hangars, and we won't run the risk of colliding with some incoming aircraft." Tedre swung around and looked at the Death Merchant. "I'll be able to tell you if the Ilyushin is there as soon as we're past the control tower and the MiGs."

The ticket and lounge building loomed close. Gorodik turned to the left so sharply and with such speed that the vehicle rocked on its springs and the rubber of the tires screamed loudly in protest. In another five seconds he had turned to the right and was taking the patrol car at 65 mph through the wide area in back of the hangars and in front of the parking lot, which contained not even a hundred cars. This wasn't the parking lot of an airport in the U.S. of A. Most passengers came to Sherpty Airport by bus.

They had only a very brief look-see at the hangars and the parking lot as the Rill charged southwest, its siren wailing *AH-OU-GA, AH-OU-GA*, its flashing lights tossing out quick whips of red that were soon lost in the lights in the rear of the buildings and in the deep shadows beyond the cyclone fence with its five strands of barbed wire that, at the top, slanted inward and upward. Another common feature of airports in the Soviet Union were the fences, similar to those in U.S. minimum security prisons—perfectly normal in a nation that needed 360,000 internal border guards to keep its citizens from fleeing to other nations.

"Turn off the lights and the siren," the Death Merchant ordered. "Let's not advertise where we are."

"Turn right at the end of the last building, the small one," Tedre told Gorodik. "It's the pilots' lounge and the hotel where they live between flights. Then drive northwest. You'll see the control tower and the MiGs."

Gorodik began making the turn to the right, and Camellion, his body swaying to the right, shouted, "Stay south of the tower and far enough away from it so that Simon can see the top and rake the control center with slugs."

"You're the boss," Gorodik said, who had begun to admire intensely the man who called himself Knud Haekkeruo. Zvezdny knew the name was fiction. He had heard the woman call him "Richard."

"Why bother with the tower?" protested Tedre. "We have only eight AKR magazines left."

"Splatter the top of that tower," Camellion ordered, heavy-voiced. "I want to interfere with their communications. We'll still have seven mags left. What do you think we're going to do once we're airborne, shoot birds?"

Kneeling on the rear seat, Karen had been watching through the back window. Camellion, seeing the expression of dread on her pretty face, knew that something was wrong before she had a chance to tell him that a Russian ZIL jeep was coming up fast behind them and moving in to their right.

"Move over and get down," Camellion told her. Gorodik had spotted the jeep in the rearview mirror and was taking the patrol car at a steep angle to the southwest.

"Keep the vehicle straight," Camellion told him. "I have an idea."

After Karen had moved to the left, Camellion got down on both knees on the right, between the seats, and put the barrel of the AKR out the window of the right rear door. Leaning forward, he saw that the driver of the jeep was about to turn to his left and come straight alongside the patrol car. Camellion knew there would be a single second, a single .001, when the ZIL jeep would be in a perfectly straight line with the AKR, a perfectly straight trajectory, unless Gorodik had to swerve. Gorodik didn't but the driver of the ZIL did—he moved where the Death Merchant had calculated he would take the ZIL.

Poor pig farmer. You overrate yourself. You think you're an idiot!

Camellion squeezed the trigger and the AKR roared, vomiting a stream of 5.45 by 39-mm projectiles. Faster than God can think a new galaxy into existence, the driver's head exploded into a brief, bloody cloud of flesh and bone, blood, and brain. So did the head of the border guard in back of him.

Out of control and moving at 50 mph, the jeep flipped over to its left. It bounced, came up on its four tires, and rolled over again, this time remaining upside down, wheels spinning. Of the two men who hadn't been hit by Camellion's blast of metal, one was dead. The jeep had fallen on him and mashed him to a pulp. The other man and the two headless corpses had been thrown clear. The man whose heart was still beating was lucky. He only had a fractured right arm and a broken left hip.

Three of the seven air controllers in the control tower were not as fortunate. Zvezdny Gorodik slowed to a mere 25 mph and Simon Tedre fired upward at a distance of 214 feet. Projectiles shattered the large window and killed almost instantly three of the controllers who had been wondering what all the shooting was about. More slugs from Tedre's AKR wrecked radar screens and other equipment. It would take a week to get the tower into operation.

Three hundred feet northwest of the control tower

were three MiG-17s and one Sukhoi-15. Gorodik got the patrol car up to 40 mph but slowed as he approached the four Soviet fighter planes. By the time he had driven the patrol car ten feet to the rear of the large stabilizer of the first fighter, the Rill was moving at only 20 mph.

Karen had placed the five grenades on the seat. The Death Merchant flipped the first RKG between the SU-15 and the first MiG-17. He was pulling the fuse pin of the second grenade and the Rill had gained another twenty-five feet as the first grenade exploded into full life. Then the second RKG exploded with a terrific roar. Camellion pulled the pin of the third shaped-charge grenade and tossed it to the left of the last MiG. Seven seconds later it exploded into a ball of red and orange and ripped out the cockpit of the craft. One of the grenades had almost ripped one MiG in two and it was burning, the fire eating hungrily into the wrecked MiG next to it, a large column of thick black smoke climbing skyward.

Gorodik had turned northeast. The patrol car was 130 feet from the demolished fighters when the first fuel tank of one of the wrecks exploded and briefly lighted up the area, also throwing flaming debris in all directions.

The entire field, the fronts of the hangars, and all the buildings now lay before the Death Merchant and his people, all of it clear in the large lights that illuminated the field and the nine runways. A fire truck pulled out of the middle hangar and started southwest, heading toward the burning fighters.

On runway 6, a four-engine turbojet Tupolev-114, carrying 160 passengers, was lifting off. On runway 4, a KA two-engine turboprop had landed and was taxiing southeast to the front of the runway, several hundred feet from the administration building. Several other aircraft were overhead, the pilots preparing to come in for a landing.

"I see the plane for Flight 141," Tedre said excitedly. "The two-engine Antonov 24V. As you can see—"

BERRRRRUUUUUMMMMM! The explosion came southwest of the patrol car. The First SB-2 Guriv "Shark" missile had exploded, both the propellant and the warhead. If only the propellant had ignited, the Shark warhead would have shot in the direction in which it had been pointed. The grenades had twisted the wings, and the missiles in their pods were pointed to all points of the compass.

BERRRRRRUUUUUMMMMM! Another Shark exploded, this time only the solid fuel propellant igniting. With a *whoossshhhhhh* the warhead streaked toward the front of the control tower. It struck ten feet to the left of the entrance. There was an ear-shattering BLAMMMMMM, and when the fire and smoke cleared, there was a ten-foot hole in the concrete, the inside of the jagged, circular rent ringed with the ends of twisted and smoking steel rods that had been part of the reinforcing.

Gorodik's foot jammed down on the gas pedal, and his eyes darted from left to right, then back to the left. He didn't want to drive straight into the flight path of a plane that had just landed. At the same time, he knew it was only common sense to reach the Antonov 24V as soon as possible. At 75 mph, the Rill shot northeast across the concrete runway and headed straight toward the AN-24V, which was taking on frightened passengers.

Rodion Voroshilov didn't know what was going on, and the Soviet pilot didn't want to find out; neither did John Lisbomed, the Latvian copilot. All they wanted to do was taxi northwest and take off, even if they had lost contact with the control tower.

A small craft, the AN-24V carried a crew of three: pilot, copilot, and one stewardess, who serviced fifty passengers. Powered by two 15,000 shp Kuznetsov NK-12M turboprops, the craft's top speed was 460 mph, far too slow to outrun modern Soviet fighters.

The aircraft did not sit high off the ground on its tricycle landing gear; the bottom fuselage was only five feet above the ground. The forward wheel was under the control compartment; the other two were in recessed wells underneath the two engines.

"Tedre, if we park to the rear, will it interfere with the craft's taking off?" the Death Merchant asked, shoving a full magazine in the AKR and sending a cartridge into the firing chamber.

"Not at all," Tedre said enthusiastically. "I'll taxi forward, turn, then head northwest down the runway and take off—if we ever get on board."

"Park behind the tail? Is that the way we do it?" Gorodik asked the Death Merchant.

"Yes—and angle us away from the craft. We don't want the pilot and copilot to see us and have them or the stewardess lock the port side door. We'll sneak up on them and"—Camellion let out a small laugh of victory—"be on board before they can do anything about it. How many passengers does that baby hold?"

"Fifty—why?"

"It won't take long to chase them off, that's why. Less weight, more speed."

By now the entire airport was in an uproar. The four guards at the gate had been found only a minute after they had been killed. At the time, the patrol car was headed toward the back of the hangars. It was Gorodik's turning on the flashing lights and the siren that had tipped off the rest of the border guards at the airport. They had correctly deduced that the vehicle had been commandeered by counterrevolutionary terrorists.

The Shark missiles continued to explode. One shot southeast and narrowly missed the lounge and ticket office building. Another came close to hitting the control tower. Several more had shot out north across the landing strips.

In the pilots' lounge and hotel building, Captain Anastas Benediktov was on the phone, frantically requesting reinforcements from *Napravleniye* district headquarters in Riga, plus additional fire-fighting equipment.

Benediktov then learned of the massacre of other border guard officers and was told that the terrorists were probably the same ones who had slaughtered the comrades at the home of the traitor Feliksas Imkant. Headquarters believed that two Western intelligence agents were with the revolutionary group, agents of either the American CIA or British SIS.

Gorodik parked the patrol car ten feet behind the tail of the AN-24V. Before he could turn off the engine, the Death Merchant was climbing out. He saw that the steps from the ground to the port door of the aircraft were only eight feet long and that passengers were getting on board. Behind him Tedre, Gorodik, and Karen got out of the Rill, an AKR, machine pistols, and a single Tul'skiy Tokarev in their hands—plus a briefcase full of photographs and a diagram of the magnifying transmitter.

The passengers waiting in line to board and those going up the steps didn't have half enough time to put together what was happening before the Death Merchant was upon them, a terrible look on his lean face, a Vitmorkin machine pistol in each hand.

"Down on the ground or we'll kill you!" he snarled in his best threatening voice. "We're taking over this aircraft."

A woman on the steps uttered a sharp cry and

dropped her handbag. Afraid that Camellion would kill her, her husband pushed her sideways from the steps, then jumped after her. Two other men, at the top of the steps, acted as if they might try to jump Camellion. Their initial looks of anger changed to fear when they saw Camellion's three helpers pointing weapons at them and the rest of the passengers. The people in line didn't argue. They promptly dropped to the ground.

Just inside the plane's doorway stood Venya Giskin, the stewardess, and John Lisbomed, the copilot. Lisbomed reached for the lever, which was partially outside the plane, by which the curved, outside-opening portside door could be closed. He had reacted automatically, otherwise he would have realized he was committing suicide.

BRRRRRR! The Vitmorkin machine pistol roared and sent three 9-mm projectiles into Lisbomed's lower chest. With a choked, short *UH!* he fell back and collapsed in the aisle.

Venya Giskin screamed, put her hands to her mouth, stumbled back, and stood by the end of a seat, a frozen, horrified look on her face.

The Death Merchant tore up the steps, two at a time. Knowing that the other three were close behind him, he called over his shoulder, "One of you watch the people on the ground. If they move, kill them."

Camellion moved inside the plane in time to see Rodion Voroshilov, the pilot, pull the cockpit door shut—*FUDGE!* Warned by the blast of bullets that had killed Lisbomed, the pilot had acted accordingly.

Right behind Camellion came Simon Tedre. Behind Tedre was Karen Spreitler, carrying the reason she and the Death Merchant had come to Latvia. Zvezdny Gorodik stood in the doorway, looking down at the terrified people lying prone on the ground, his AKR set to send streams of projectiles into their warm bodies, but only if he had to. He felt that the Death Merchant had given the kill order not because he was ruthless, but because he wanted to instill naked terror in the passengers.

Camellion glanced along the length of the interior. Eleven frightened faces—six men and five women—stared back at him.

"I'll move them out of here," Tedre said, jerking the barrel of his AKR toward the ten passengers and the stewardess.

"Not yet," Camellion said sharply. "They're our bargaining power with the pilot. He's closed and locked the door."

"Kick it in. The lock on the door isn't very strong."

"I don't want to risk the pilot's wrecking the instruments if he has a gun. I've a better way."

BLAMMMMMMM-BLAMMMMMMMM. There were several more Guriv Shark explosions. This time one of the warheads rocketed northeast across the wide field and shot only twenty feet above the AN-24V. The second warhead shot into the front of the middle hangar, hit a four-engine Ilyushin I1-28 that could carry two hundred passengers, and exploded. The warhead had struck close to a fuel line in the wing and instantly there was a loud WHOOOOSSSSSHHHHHHHH, followed by another explosion. In seconds the cloud of fire had spread, and the interior of the hangar became Hell.

The Death Merchant stepped over John Lisbomed's corpse and hurried to the door of the cockpit compartment, careful to stand to one side. Aeroflot pilots had been known to carry weapons.

"I know you can hear me in there," Camellion yelled in English.

"I speak only Russian," Voroshilov called back, the nervousness in his voice revealing his fear.

"Open the door right now or we'll kill everyone inside the plane and the ones on the ground outside. Then we'll blow up the airplane and ourselves," the Death Merchant screamed in Russian, doing his best to sound like a paranoid terrorist. "We're members of the Revolutionary Order of St. Andrew and have nothing to lose. Death is our friend. Death is our master. Death is our love." He added in a higher pitch, wanting to give the impression that he was hysterical, "NOW—or die! We'll take you with us! Look around at the airport and see what we have done!"

Rodion Voroshilov had looked and had seen! "I-I'll open the door," he called back to Camellion.

"Come out this instant with your hands on your head," screamed Camellion, "or we all die."

There was a *click*. The door opened, and Voroshilov, hands on top of his head, stepped out, his mournful eyes dark pools of deep dread. He was convinced that he and the aircraft had been taken over by complete crazies.

Camellion had shoved one of the machine pistols in his belt, and now he grabbed the pilot by the shoulder, poked him in the head with the muzzle of the other Vitmorkin, and pushed him face forward against the wall. "You stay there until we've checked the controls!" Then he yelled at Tedre, Karen, and Gorodik. "Get them out of the plane. Make them lie on the ground with the other slaves of the Kremlin."

Camellion caught Simon Tedre's eye; he first winked, then said in a half-screaming, fanatical voice, "Check the instruments and the controls. If the pilot has wrecked anything, we'll kill the son of a bitch and all the people out there on the ground."

Simon Tedre practically ran to the cockpit. By the time the last of the ten passengers and the stewardess were going down the steps to join the others on the ground, he called through the open door. "Everything is all right. Let's get out of here. Remember those jets based at Rezloyre!"

"You!" Camellion screamed at Rodion Voroshilov in Russian. "Get out of here and move those steps clear of the aircraft—MOVE! Move or I'll kill you! *WAIT!* I want to ask you something."

Voroshilov stopped dead in his tracks and stared at Camellion.

"Do you realize that the human race is made up of only passionate vegetables?" Camellion said, twisting his mouth into a maniacal grin and opening his eyes as wide as possible. "Do you realize that if you placed a dozen tomatoes or a dozen cucumbers in a sack and shook them, they would have as much passion as we have—*DO YOU? ANSWER ME!*"

"Yes y-yes! That's true. You're r-right!" Voroshilov quickly agreed. At the moment, he would have agreed that an ant could stack a ton of hay in half a minute.

"Get out, you mental defective!" Camellion pointed the Vitmorkin machine pistol at Voroshilov, who was only too happy to leave the company of a man whom he considered a dangerous maniac.

The pilot rushed out the door and ran down the steps. With Gorodik and Camellion telling him to hurry up or die, Voroshilov went to the highest part of the steps and began to push them away from the plane, moving them back on their six small rubber wheels.

"Get us out of here, Tedre," Camellion yelled at Tedre, who had already started the two Kuznetsov NK-12m turboprops and was revving them up with more power, and setting the flaps in the wings and on the elevators.

Karen said in a small voice, "I don't know what you

said to that pilot, but you sure made a believer of him."

"Other than making him think we were stark raving mad, I told him we were members of the Revolutionary Order of St. Andrew." Camellion laughed. "He'll faithfully report it to the KGB. It should drive them nuts!" Then all in the same breath: "I'm going to the cockpit to watch Tedre take off."

At no time did Camellion reveal his concern over the time factor. The fighter jets at Rezloyre could be in the general vicinity very fast. However, the Death Merchant was counting on the strict chain of Soviet command to delay the planes getting off the ground at Rezloyre. No matter what the Russians said about the efficiency of their armed forces, the entire system lacked flexibility. If a superior officer was not available, the officer under him would not dream of taking over and doing what had to be done. Stories were still told about the "brave" Russians in World War II, and how they refused to retreat before the Germans and fought to the last man. The truth had nothing to do with "bravery" and an overzealous love of Mother Russia. It had to do with orders bound in iron and sealed with blood. The dumbbell ivans fought to the last man because they had been ordered to.

Adolf Hitler had given the same order to his troops. The Germans, however, had more sense than their Russian counterparts. They ignored the order and retreated when they had no other choice.

The Soviet armed forces still have the most rigid command structure in the world. The truth is that the Russian army is the last imperialist army on the planet. In the Soviet army, the equivalent of a corporal has the authority of a master sergeant in the American army and is ten times more feared. Officers in the Soviet armed forces are regarded by the rank and file as evil "gods."

Orders would have to go through the proper channels before the fighter planes at Rezloyre could take off and come after the AN-24V airliner. First, the lower-rank ivans would have to contact the middle echelon. In turn, the middle-of-the-road officers would have to contact their superiors and give them a detailed appraisal of the situation. Such and such a member of the Soviet General Staff in Moscow would have to be awakened. He might even have to disturb a ranking member of the Politburo.

The Death Merchant calculated that it would take an hour and a half—at minimum—for the order to be given. More likely two hours before the fighter planes got off the ground at Rezloyre. *With luck Tedre should be landing by then—in Sweden!*

Simon Tedre, an anxious look on his young face, moved the aircraft southwest, toward the hangars and the other buildings, in preparation for the turn and the takeoff down the long runway—without instructions from the control tower, which no longer existed.

The Death Merchant, settling in the copilot's seat, and Gorodik and Karen, standing just inside the cockpit and staring out the windshield and side windows, could see that two of the hangars were burning fiercely. The fire looked out of control, the flames, leaping fifty feet in the air, were about to engulf the third hangar and the administration building. Personnel and mechanics were running around helplessly, their efforts to put out the raging inferno useless.

Tedre turned the airplane and fed fuel to the two turboprops. The four-bladed props spun faster. The craft raced northwest, its two Kuznetsov engines roaring, the three wheels of the landing gear racing over the concrete.

Tedre was good. Not once did he waste time or

motion. He glanced at the airspeed indicator, pulled back on the control pedal, pressed down on the left rudder pedal slightly, and lifted the big bird from the concrete. He had turned on all the flight lights outside the airplane, and now he switched on all the lights over the seats in the passenger section, explaining, "Until we're away from this area, it's best to have the entire plane lighted. There must be five or six planes flying around up there in their own holding patterns. We'll switch off all the lights at six thousand meters. I think that's about twenty thousand English feet. I'm not sure."

"To be precise, six thousand ninety-six meters is twenty thousand English feet—not that it matters," Camellion said mechanically. "Do you know the air route to Sweden?"

Zvezdny Gorodik spoke in an attempt to inject some levity into a situation that could be likened to riding a tidal wave in an open coffin. "All we need is to make a mistake and come down somewhere in the Soviet Union."

"If we're not scattered all over the sky by a missile from one of the Soviet fighter planes," Karen said quietly. Her hair was dirty. Her face was smudged from fumes and smoke, and her clothes looked as though they had come unwashed from some Goodwill store.

"I've never flown the route to Sweden," Tedre muttered to Camellion. He raised the landing gear and looked at the altimeter. "Leningrad is northeast of Riga, Stockholm northwest. We could take a heading of west by northwest and we'd come to Sweden, but we could miss Stockholm by fifty or sixty kilometers." He indicated the pilot's case between the seats with a nod of his head. "Get out the flight maps and we'll calculate a heading that will take us straight to

Stockholm. It's roughly four hundred eighty-five kilo-meters from Riga."

Two hundred eighty-five miles! Not quite an hour's flying time!

They had been in the air 31.6 minutes and were over the Baltic Sea, flying northwest and at only three hundred feet above the black, uncaring water. The Death Merchant had ordered Tedre to fly very low to make it more difficult for Soviet jets to detect them.

Karen Spreitler said, "Maybe we should have made all the passengers get on board. The fighter pilots wouldn't deliberately destroy a planeload of innocent people."

Camellion turned in his seat and stared at her in dismay. "What have you been, doll, during the past three years—living at the bottom of a mine shaft? Do you recall the Korean KAL flight that strayed over Soviet territory some years ago? A Russian pilot knocked it out of the sky with a missile. But it took the savages in Moscow two hours to make up their minds."

"Are you intimating that it will take that long for them to decide what to do about us?" said Tedre, who was fast at drawing conclusions. "The difference between the KAL flight and us is that we are in a Soviet aircraft. This plane belongs to the Soviet govern-ment. They can blow us out of the sky if they want, until we're over Swedish territory."

It was only four minutes later that the Death Mer-chant detected approaching aircraft in the radar screen—seven aircraft coming in very fast from the southeast, at an estimated 25,000 feet.

"We have company," he said. "From the southeast, at an altitude of maybe seventy-six hundred meters."

"It has to be the fighters coming after us," Tedre

said despondently. "And we're so close to Sweden too. Only minutes away."

The Death Merchant jerked his head to the left. His eyes widened and his stare began to poke holes in Tedre.

"Minutes away! Impossible!" he said, his tone dry ice. "We're still a hundred miles—one hundred sixty klicks—from Stockholm!"

"Stockholm? Who said anything about Stockholm! I meant the island of Gotland." It was now Tedre's turn to turn and look at Camellion. "We're only sixty-four kilometers east of the east coast of Gotland!"

Gotland! Why didn't I think of Gotland? I must need a brain recharge!

Gotland was in the Baltic Sea, 50 miles east of the east *skärgård*, or coast, of Sweden, and 105 miles from the west coast of Latvia. *Yes, that historic island with its capital, Visby—the City of Ruins and Roses —is a vacation paradise par excellence. It's the middle of summer. All around the island will be sailboats, cabin cruisers, and other kinds of seacraft. Perfect!*

"Tedre, change course," Camellion said, smiling. "Head straight for Gotland, and drop to an altitude of one hundred fifty feet."

Even Karen and Gorodik smiled, a brand-new expression of hope glowing on their faces.

Pleased, Tedre turned the control wheel, all the while watching the compass. The Death Merchant kept his eyes glued to the radar screen.

Only thirty-five to sixty-three miles away and we're moving at 452 miles an hour. We might make it. I doubt it. Not this way. Those jets are coming in too fast.

Camellion said thoughtfully, "We're not going to be able to get over the island; the fighters are coming in too fast . . . far too fast."

"The hell with them," Tedre said confidently. "In a few more minutes we'll be over Sweden's territorial waters." He took a long look at the compass and at the airspeed indicator.

"Don't kid yourself, my friend. What we did to the airport in Latvia has made the Soviet high command so furious that those fighters would knock us out of the sky even if we were over President Reagan's ranch in California. Belly-land her in the water when you're three klicks offshore. There should be plenty of sailing craft about. Can you do it?"

"My God!" Karen put the side of a fist to her mouth.

"Do I have a choice?"

"No."

Gorodik was more practical than Karen. "How long will the plane float after it's on the water?"

"An Antonov is a well-built airplane," Tedre said. "We'll float for three or four minutes, time enough for us to get into the water."

He moved the control column forward slightly. "I'm going to take her as close to the surface of the water as I can. All of you clear out and get toward the middle of the plane." He glanced at the Death Merchant. "You too. Don't argue. I am the pilot and in charge of this plane."

"Who's arguing?" Camellion eased himself out of the copilot's seat. "How low are you going to drop? I suppose you know that some of the boats down there have high masts?"

"I'm going down over the water between thirteen and fifteen meters," Tedre said. "All masts have blinking lights. I can't miss them. Look out now; you can see them for yourself."

With Camellion, Gorodik, and Karen sitting toward the middle of the passenger section, Tedre flew the AN-24V with all the precision of Minnesota Fats putting a nine ball into a side pocket. At times he took the plane so low that its underbelly was only ten feet above the surface of the waves. Looking out the windows, the Death Merchant and his two companions didn't feel exactly as if they were looking forward to a long life. Only a short distance below was the waiting water shimmering in the moonlight and slightly phosphorescent from trillions of microscopic marine animals. Camellion and the others felt that the airplane was suspended on invisible wires and that it was the water and the ships that were moving at a fantastic rate of speed. They didn't feel any more relaxed when, at a speed of 294 mph, Tedre flew the plane between two large yachts that were practically on the same level as they; their tall masts were actually *above* the plane.

Tedre cut speed rapidly. Another three-fourths of a kilometer and the airplane had slowed so much that it had to land. The sweat of tension running down his face, Tedre measured the distance to the water, his hands steady on the controls, his feet firm on the rudder pedals. Even at 60 mph—slow for the AN-24V—landing on water would be the same as landing on concrete. The nose had to be up just right, or the craft would flip over and the tail would end up where the nose had been. Everyone would then be trapped underwater and quickly drown. Too fast and the bottom of the big craft would cave in and kill them.

The pilots of the seven Sukhoi-15 interceptors had cut their airspeed to 700 mph when they had been far to the east of the AN-24V. Now, as Tedre was taking the craft in for a belly landing on the relatively calm water of the Baltic, four of the jets roared over at an altitude of 692 feet. Five miles behind them came the other three SU-15s, the combined roaring of the seven Soviet warplanes so loud they awakened everyone for miles.

Major Pytor Matryona Shcherbatov, the flight leader, had been given his orders: destroy the AN-24V. Suppose, he had asked, he and his flight made an intercept over Swedish territory, then what? General Josef Malervisshenko of the *STAVKA*, the main military council, had thought for a moment. The Soviet Union did not want an international incident. Ever since the Chernobyl nuclear reactor incident, the Soviet Union had been on the defensive. More and more, the Americans and the Western Europeans were viewing the Soviet Union as a barbaric nation that could not be trusted to say even "Good morning" without lying about it. The Eastern European satellites were becoming more restless and leading the battle for more consumer goods, more friendly ties with the West, especially with the *Amerikanska*, and less emphasis on military buildup. Any incident at this time and the *Nachal-stvo* in Moscow would go berserk. The bosses in Moscow would blame him, and he would end up demoted and posted to some insignificant command in—no doubt Siberia. . . .

General Malervisshenko had said, "Should the terrorist airplane be over Swedish soil—and that includes Swedish waters—do not fire. See where the plane lands, then return to your base at Rezloyre. In either case, report to me the moment your flight returns."

Major Shcherbatov and his wing executed a sharp turn and roared back, this time a third of a klick north of the AN-24V passenger plane. Just as the SU-15s screamed by, Major Shcherbatov saw the plane touch water. The AN-24V bounced slightly, came down again on the water, and this time stayed down. *Da!* The pilot was good, very good. The pilot cut power and the plane became dead in the water, drifting at the mercy of the Baltic.

Major Shcherbatov turned on the radio and gave the order: "Let's go home, men."

Gorodik and Karen had already jumped into the water through the portside door as Camellion rushed toward the cockpit, his feet pounding the rug already wet with Baltic water. He didn't intend to leave Simon Tedre. He didn't have to. He was halfway to the cockpit when the pilot came out the narrow door and started toward him.

"Congratulations, you pulled it off," Camellion said. "Now let's take a swim before we go down with this plane into the deep of an octopus garden."

The two men were soon in the water, which was cold but not unbearably so, then they were swimming from the dying aircraft. A short distance ahead were the other two. Gorodik had run his belt through the handles of the briefcase and was hauling it after him. In the distance, half a dozen cabin cruisers were coming toward them.

At the moment, the Death Merchant had a lot of unanswered questions jumping around in his mind, one of which was how the KGB had known that he and Karen were intelligence agents. The more he thought about it, the more it bothered him.

Behind Camellion and his three people, the AN-24V started its dive to its final resting place. First the nose and the cockpit went under. The tail rose fifteen feet above the water and, for some moments, hung there. Then the airplane slid slowly under the dark water and was gone.

Chapter Eighteen

Great Britain
Three days after the escape from Latvia
The Safe House on Old Bond Street

Mrs. Rosalind Peece—"Frost-Face"—was actually friendly as she let Camellion and the two CIA agents escorting him into the house. After the other two men took their leave, she even added in a pleasant voice, "We're glad you returned safely from your mission, you and the woman." It was a tipoff that she had already talked to Courtland Grojean.

They went through the same procedure as before, with Mrs. Peece taking him up the long stairs to the same room. She said pleasantly, "Mr. Grojean will be here this afternoon at three. After you have showered and dressed, just pick up the phone and tell Cook what you would like for lunch." She added with a large smile, "Your door will not be locked."

Oh, how the worm has turned—and I don't like it!

The first thing Camellion mentioned to Grojean was Mrs. Peece's friendliness, concluding with "I don't like low-level employees knowing about any operation I'm in. It's poor security."

All decked out in a white silk shirt and off-white

pants, with lace huarache half-sandals, Grojean relaxed on an upholstered wing chair and placed his feet on the matching ottoman.

"All I told her was that you and Karen Spreitler had returned," the Fox said tersely. Then he jumped right into the business end of the meeting. "You did a good job, Camellion. The water didn't hurt the photographs, but the drawing was ruined. The water made the ink run. But we don't need it. The photographs were much better. Our scientists in the States are studying them by now."

"The KGB knew about Karen and me," Camellion said aggressively. "When the *Napravleniye* surrounded us in Feliksas Imkant's house, they called out to us, using our Danish cover names. I know that French Intelligence didn't know about the Latvian operation, but how about SIS?"

"Only our top people in D.C. knew about Latvia." Grojean didn't seem concerned. "I said 'knew.' The whole world now knows, except your identity and Spreitler's. Your landing in the Baltic Sea made headlines in the world's papers. We had a devil of a time talking the Swedes into releasing the four of you. One might say we even had to use some behind-the-scenes threats, although we prefer to call it diplomacy."

"Answer my question," insisted the Death Merchant, settling back in the club chair.

"We have told SIS and the French SDECE," Grojean answered. "It doesn't matter now. You're out, and you brought the photographs. What the mole in the SDECE might report to his KGB control doesn't matter. The Soviet Union is aware that we know about its base on the island of Miskos."

The Death Merchant would not let go. "None of that answers my question, Court."

"The leak didn't come from this end, Richard.

Take it from me—I'm certain. My explanation is that the KGB got lucky. Either the KGB picked you and Karen in one of its random checks of tourists, or there's an informer in the Latvian Spear of Vengeance. I doubt it, or the KGB would have smashed the organization by now. Forget about Latvia. It's over and done with."

The Death Merchant did not press the issue. First, the Fox was correct. Camellion and the others had escaped and were safe. He and Karen had completed the mission with double success because of the numerous photographs. Second, it was always possible that Grojean was withholding information that proved there hadn't been a hole in the dam in the West.

Camellion heard Grojean say, "We'll attack the island in seventeen days. Half the force will be our people, members of the Special Forces Operation Detachment—Delta. DELTA for short." He chuckled slightly. "I trust you shall not confuse DELTA with the Delta Project set up by our Special Forces in Vietnam in the mid-1960s."

"It's not likely that I would, Court, although Colonel Charlie Beckwith did command the Delta Project in 'Nam. Detachment B-52 was the actual name of the Vietnam DP force. But get on with it."

"The British commandos will be Royal Marines, specifically members of the Special Boat Squadron. As you know, SBS is very good. Every man is extremely well trained."

"And the French?"

"We have informed the French that we'll attack the island seven weeks from now. There is supposed to be coordinated training between DELTA, the SBS, and the French Foreign Legion's *61e Battaillon du Génie de la Légion* in several weeks. The first meeting will deal with the doctrines of force integration—whatever they may be."

"There are three types of doctrine," Camellion said easily. "The first is the employment and support of individual weapons systems, including soldiers. The second is the integration and synchronization of those systems, or command and control. This is better known to military planners as 'C-Two.' Finally, we have the governing doctrine—AirLand Battle. The only doctrine that need concern us in regard to the island is command and control."

"Yes, well, I'm not concerned with that aspect of the operation," Grojean said irritably. He always hated it when Camellion went into a monologue about tactical military matters, and he rather suspected that Camellion did it on purpose, just to annoy him. "It's rather ironic. On the day we're supposed to have the meeting with the French—we and the British—we and the British will attack Miskos. You do have questions."

Like . . . how did the Universe really begin? "Yes—thousands! My first concern is preserving my true identity. What did you have in mind for my cover with DELTA and SBS, and how do we go about acquiring the hand-picked men for my special group?"

The Death Merchant took a sip of black coffee, returned cup and saucer to the table beside the chair, and looked steadily at the Fox. "I know you have given considerable thought to those two minor problems."

"DELTA and the SBS commandos will assume you're connected with the U.S. Office of Naval Intelligence," Grojean said in a tired voice. "I've already said as much to Sir Clifford Blassingame of SIS. I didn't have to drop any hints to Russell Wirbeck. He knows you work for me. As to your second question—"

"One moment, my friend!" Camellion cut him off. "I'm speaking about out in the field. How about the commanders of SBS and DELTA? Or do we want them to think I'm only a hitchhiker with ten extra men?"

Courtland Grojean was not amused; he had too much on his mind. Operation Zeus could well be the trigger that fired off World War III. The worst possible scenario was involved: the Soviet Union pulling a fast one and the U.S. having to respond because it had no other option. It was either destroy the magnifying transmitter or permit the Soviets to control the world's weather. Once the Russians could control the weather, they would rapidly turn the United States into a desert.

Grojean said, "I'm confident that SIS will get word about you to Colonel Robyn Burrell, the commander of the Special Boat Squadron. Several days ago Wirbeck and I had a short meeting with Lieutenant Colonel Clint Ambule, the DELTA Force commander. Wirbeck mentioned that you and ten picked men would be going along on Blue Emerald. That's the code name of the operation."

"Dumb!" mused Camellion.

"What is—the name?"

"Any emerald is a variety of beryl, and it's always green. I know it doesn't make any difference, but—"

"It sure as hell doesn't!" Grojean snapped. "Who cares how the operation is coded!" He quickly regained his composure. "Wirbeck told Ambule you were ONI's special expert. That should inflate your ego!"

"It doesn't, because it doesn't mean anything—not to me," Camellion said with a smile. "Now how about the special ten-man squad?"

"I was under the impression that picking the ten men would be your department" was Grojean's enigmatic response. "I know how precise you've always been in such matters."

Precise? He really means paranoid! "Yes, as a rule," agreed Camellion. "But I don't intend to spend hours going through scores of files. I have a better way. You can get word to Ambule and Burrell and tell them what I want."

"Well, Richard, you can tell them yourself. DELTA and SBS are training as one combined force at the Amphibious School of the Royal Marines at Poole in Dorset. You'll be going there tomorrow morning. You'll remain there until the force leaves for Greece. You and the two commanders can get a lot done in the next few weeks."

"What have you found out about Miskos?"

"I was wondering when you'd ask. One of the subs attached to our task force in the Mediterranean went in close to the island, and SEALs made an underwater recon of the entire area. The SEALs didn't find warning devices of any kind, no transponders, nothing, to indicate that the Russians were inside Mount Posso."

"I hope the SEALs didn't set foot on the island," Camellion said quickly. "If they did—"

"They didn't!" Grojean said smoothly. "We didn't expect to find any underwater warning devices. We know why we didn't. Vacationing divers passing by might find them and wonder why they were there. But you can bet your two pet pigs that the Russians have warning devices *on* the island, and especially on Mount Posso."

The Death Merchant sounded very serious, and Grojean noticed an odd glint in his blue eyes. "As I understand it, there isn't one shred of evidence that the Russians are even on Miskos, much less inside Mount Posso. Or do you have information you're not revealing? When you get right down to it, all we have is the word of Petros Makarezos."

"Look, sport, we've been through that," Grojean retorted with a heavy measure of displeasure and impatience. "I admit we don't have any proof positive, but everything so far dovetails. The Germans did build submarine pens in the base of Mount Posso. We do have proof. We managed to get old Nazi charts and blueprints of the pens, and all of it without the BND knowing about it. The sub pens would be perfect for what the Soviets have in mind. Damn it! Now ask me what kind of response the Soviet Union will take."

"I'm asking."

"The DIA and our own analysts are convinced that—"

"Bunk!" Camellion saw anger flash over Grojean's face. "The Defense Intelligence Agency was a good idea at the time, but it went sour because it threatened the culture and the prerogatives of the military. The result has been a confused mismatch of tasks and personnel. You told me yourself, after I returned from Siberia*—or was it Sweden?†—no matter. You said yourself that the DIA was not capable of producing items for which it was responsible and that the service intelligence organizations inevitably began infringing on the DIA's responsibility. The DIA couldn't evaluate a Chicago street corner!"

Fighting to control his temper, the Fox stared for a moment at the Death Merchant. "Let's forget DIA," he said in a forced-calm voice. "Our own analysts have—"

Concluded that the Soviet Union was in an even worse quandary than the United States. CIA analysts envisioned two possible scenarios: The first was that

* See Death Merchant #67, *Escape From Gulag Taria*.
† See Death Merchant #66, *The Cobra Chase*. Both are published by Dell.

the Russians would feel that the United States would not take any direct military action against Miskos because Uncle Sam was helpless. CIA analysts based their opinion on intelligence received regarding Soviet military thinking about the American bombing of Libya. The Soviet military felt the U.S. should have conducted a second and even a third strike—if necessary—to knock out oilfields and the port of Tripoli. The Russian military felt the U.S. was timid and unrealistic, that the U.S. hadn't continued with a second attack because it was afraid of world opinion. On this basis, the Russians were convinced that the United States would not attack Miskos, a Greek possession in the Aegean Sea.

The second possible scenario involved the Soviet Union's inability to dismantle the magnifying transmitter and remove it from the island by submarine in time to avoid an American attack. It would require months to dismantle the base, and surely the Soviet Union knew that if the Americans did attack, it would be soon.

Grojean said evenly, "Our experts feel that the Soviet Union could believe we won't attack because we won't be able to find them, to reach them. After all, they *are* inside a damned mountain. It would take a lot of time and effort, and the more time involved, the more likelihood of the Greek navy arriving on the scene."

The Death Merchant shook his head. The overall situation was extremely serious, or Courtland Grojean himself would not be in England. In his own mind, he knew the Russians would fight.

"Court, don't sit there and try to convince me that the pig farmers are putting all their 'defenses' into their belief that Big Uncle will sit on his stars and stripes and do nothing. That's as ridiculous as saying that Joan of Arc's last request was for a match! As paranoid as the Russians are—and secrecy is a religion with them—they have to be preparing some kind of defense. After all, the Soviet Union wouldn't look so innocent either if the Greek navy and air force put in an appearance!"

"Exactly," Grojean said approvingly. "Our consensus is that the Russians on the island will fight. When they start losing, they'll blow up the mountain." He smiled contemptuously. "A nice ending to look forward to, eh, Camellion?"

"I don't know of any person who lives forever, or even to the age of one hundred eighty," Camellion said with a big grin. "No matter how fast we go in, and whether we succeed or fail, the Greek government will find out we were the ones who blew hell out of their little piece of real estate. The Aegean isn't in some out-of-the-way section of the world."

Grojean's answer was prompt and to the point. "We'll tell the Greek government and the French when President Reagan tells the world why U.S. and British forces had to attack the island." He leaned forward so far he was almost hunched over. "Furthermore, he'll be able to prove it, not only with the photographs you brought out of Latvia but also with ones of the Soviet base itself that you and your people will take once you're inside the mountain."

"If we don't get blown up!" Camellion said lightly.

Grojean pretended he hadn't heard the remark. "The reputation of the Soviet Union—what little it has left—will sink ten feet below the zero mark." Then, as an afterthought, he added, "Colonel Ambule and Colonel Burrell have come up with a TAC-plan for getting inside the base. It's based on the estimated size of the mountain."

"German figures from old records?"

"Yes—and the SEALs and the Royal Marine divers

did some quick measurements using the triangular shadow method."

Camellion changed the subject. "What's the latest on Anna Sofoulis?" he asked.

"Ambule and Burrell will give you the details of the plan when you see them at Poole. How you work out your own plan with them—you and your special force—is your business. Miss Sofoulis left for the U.S. yesterday. We're going to settle her in New York City. Any more questions?"

"Plenty, but I doubt if you could answer them."

The Death Merchant could see bright sunlight bathing the countryside of Poole. He moved his eyes from the window of the TAC room and looked at the two men sitting across from him at the large but plain wooden table—Lieutenant Colonel Clint "Ringo" Ambule and Colonel Robyn Burrell.

Both were big, well-muscled men. There was a suggestion of swift and precise movement about Burrell, who was maybe forty. He had spent his entire adult life in the military, first in the regular British army, then in SAS—and not the reserves either, which is the 21st Regiment quartered at the Duke of York barracks. Burrell had been a member of SAS F-Troop, which was—and is—composed of highly trained professionals. After six years with F-T SAS, Burrell transferred to the Royal Marines. His ruggedness was complemented by his complete confidence, a kind of self-assurance that conveyed a silent message: *If you think I can't bite a nail in two, ask me. I'll prove it to you.*

Clint Ambule was younger, on the bottom side of thirty-five. Good-looking in a rough, untrampled sort of way, with features that fit any number of races of nations. Like Burrell, he was clean-shaven and dressed in green fatigues and combat boots. Unlike

Burrell, he had a port-wine birthmark on his left
cheek. The Death Merchant, who noticed everything, felt that Ambule's most outstanding feature
was his feet, which seemed too small for the rest of
his 220-pound body.

Together, Ambule and Burrell looked like men
who could saunter into any dive and announce that
they could whip any five men in the joint, or all of
them, and then proceed to do it.

Neither man was friendly nor unfriendly. They
were neutral—all business and directly to the point,
the kind of pros Camellion liked to deal with.

Ambule ran a hand through his blond hair. "How
does the C-cubed strike you, Camellion?" he asked.
"All command, control, and communications will be
with our Blue Company, mine and Colonel Burrell's.
DELTA Major Camelback and SBS Major Eastmore
will command White Company. You and your people
will keep in communication with Blue Company.
Understand, this is not the usual kind of land incur-
sion. You and your people will be more or less on your
own once we're inside that god-damn mountain."

"The C-cube isn't bad," Camellion said. "The
method of contact you men have suggested is the
only one possible. I feel we can ignore most of the
conventional combat imperatives, since we won't
have any reserves and no combat service support, all
of which simplifies the logistics."

Colonel Burrell's smile was complimentary. "It's a
relief to know that you're experienced in these kinds
of operations," he said, his clipped British accent
making the words almost staccato. "It's my conviction that the most dangerous thing on such an operation is an armed man who doesn't know the five
functions of combat."

"Oh, I don't know. I think a newly commissioned
second lieutenant with a map, and in command, is

even more dangerous," joked the Death Merchant. "I do have some concerns, Colonel Burrell. The Royal Marines are used to fighting in sixteen-man squadrons, each squadron a unit in itself."

"And will they function as effectively in a company of fifty men?" offered Burrell, meeting Camellion's penetrating eyes. "The answer is: Yes, they will. I assure you, Yank, their fighting ability will not be impaired in any way."

"Sounds reasonable," drawled Camellion. But Burrell and Ambule could detect that he was still not satisfied.

The Death Merchant pushed back his chair, got up from the table, and walked over to a three-dimensional model of the island of Miskos and its three mountains. Not far away, on a wall, was a blackboard on which had been carefully drawn a cut-away diagram of Mount Posso, the target.

Camellion paused by the model, then turned and glanced at Burrell and Ambule, both of whom had gotten up and were coming toward him.

Camellion picked up the wooden pointer and tapped a portion of the base of Mount Posso, toward the southeast part of the model. Directions were drawn on a small piece of paper attached to one corner of the fiberboard on which the model was sitting.

"The charges will be in this area?" He looked from Burrell to Clint Ambule. "Correct me if I'm wrong."

"You're right; you have the general area," Ambule responded, pursing his lips. He moved closer to the table and moved a forefinger along the rough brown surface of the hardened thermopaste model of Mount Posso. "Just about here, the granite between the outside and the inside of the natural cave is not very thick."

"Natural cave?" Camellion frowned.

"You didn't know?" Ambule said, seeing the surprise on the Death Merchant's face. "That's what it originally was, a gigantic cavern, a kind of big bubble inside the mountain. We obtained our information from the intelligence people, who sent us a box of old German records. That's why the Germans used it for their subs. They also expanded the north and the south ends for several hundred feet. If the damn ivans further enlarged the complex on all four sides, we'll be facing a complex that could be almost a city block square."

Inserted Colonel Burrell, "If the Russians expanded on the east side, the granite there might be less than thirty meters thick."

The Death Merchant hooked a thumb onto his belt. "It's still a gamble, men. I know a bit about explosives. However, I'm not a DELTA or a Royal Marines expert. The experts are obviously in agreement over what the blasts will accomplish."

Colonel Ambule lighted a small black cigar.

Colonel Burrell, liking Camellion's frankness and honesty, scratched the end of his jaw. "Let's go over to the blackboard." He reached for the pointer in the Death Merchant's hand. "If you don't mind?"

Camellion relinquished the pointer, and the three men went to the blackboard, the Death Merchant glancing out a window on the way. In the distance he could see the English Channel.

Burrell placed the tip of the pointer on an east section of the base of Mount Posso. "Along here we'll place ten shaped charges of pentolite, each of which will weigh eighteen kilograms. They'll blast holes an estimated six meters inward—in the outside of the mountain at ground level."

"And the RDX will then be placed in the holes to blast that section of the mountain inward," Camellion said. "It's a fine idea, but you'll need over nine hundred kilograms of RDX to do the job. That's a lot of weight. But it could be done."

"Oh, yes, we think so," Burrell said. "As to the weight—by the way, we British prefer to call RDX Cyclonite."

"You British have a right to. After all, you invented Cyclonite," the Death Merchant said.

"I'll give you some numbers," Burrell said. "There will be fifty DELTA chaps and fifty of our British Marines attached to the Special Boat Squadron. Also six officers, and you, Mr. Camellion, and your ten men. That's a total of 117. Our plan is for each man to carry only eleven and a fraction kilograms of Cyclonite—a total of 1,326 kilograms. We feel, Colonel Ambule and I, that should be more than adequate."

Camellion had to agree. Cyclonite, invented by the British during World War II, was the most powerful military explosive in the world; 1,326 kilograms was almost a ton and a half.

But will it actually blow eighty to one hundred feet of solid concrete? I don't know. I'm not going to argue with them. . . .

"The Germans are very efficient," Camellion said. "Did the old records that intelligence sent down here contain a geological survey of the mountain's granite?"

Clint Ambule moved the cigar to the left side of his mouth. "As I recall, the translation from the German referred to the granite as ordinary. I had always assumed that granite was granite."

"There are different kinds," Camellion explained. "Granite consists largely of quartz and feldspar of any kind, with or without mica, hornblende, pyroxene, or other minerals. It's irrelevant. That much Cyclonite should do the job—in theory."

Both Ambule and Burrell sensed Camellion's doubt. "But you're not sure," Burrell said.

"Are you, Colonel?"

"Frankly, no," admitted Burrell. "But it's the only way we can get inside the mountain and reach the Russians. Any other way could result in the entire force doing a burton."

"A burton?" Camellion was not that familiar with British slang.

"We don't want the force to commit suicide," Burrell explained.

Colonel Ambule walked back to the table, tapped ash from his cigar, and sat back down at the table. "We've picked the ten men for you, Camellion. Five DELTAs and five SBS boys."

"And good lads too," Burrell intoned, sitting down. "Tomorrow you can talk to them; I'm sure you'll have questions to put to them."

Camellion stretched out his long legs underneath the table.

"We have yet to discuss the details of the DP and the security connected with it," he said. "The KGB and other commie services have eyes here in Great Britain."

"We'll be taken to London by buses, and there we'll 'vanish,'" explained Burrell. "Actually we'll fly to the Outer Hebrides west of Scotland and go to the British submarine base at Barvas, where the three submarines and the Whales will be waiting."

"Our boat, the *Sam Houston,* will arrive tomorrow at Barvas," Ambule interjected.

"The estimated time from Barvas to the Greek target area is six days," Burrell said. "Six days from the actual time of departure from Barvas."

Nodding, the Death Merchant renewed his conviction. Within six days he would be inside the Soviet weather base. He thought then of what Grojean had said about the possibility that the Russians might blow the base and Mount Posso sky-high.

But will any of us get out?

Chapter Nineteen

The one American and six British vessels moved south at a depth of seven hundred feet, and a strange armada it was. The USS *Hawkbill*, a nuclear submarine of the Sturgeon class, had been modified to act as a mother ship for deep-submergence rescue vessels. In this case the DSRV was a fifty-foot-long submarine carried on the afterdeck. It was designed to rescue the crew of other submarines in water too deep for the usual submarine rescue methods.

There were also two nuclear British submarines of the Gaine class: the HMS *Warspite* and the HMS *Resolution*. Each boat was small, with displacement of 2,508 tons. The power plant was a 49 MW nuclear reactor with two turbo-alternators and a single-shaft electric motor and a single diesel-generator for emergency propulsion.

The strangest vessels of all were Whales, two of which were towed underwater by the USS *Hawkbill*. The *Warspite* and *Resolution* acted as "nurses" for the other two.

Technically, each Whale was an All Purpose Underwater Vehicle for Covert Attack Against an Enemy. However, it would have been cumbersome to have designated each vessel an APUVFCAAAE, so each was simply dubbed a "Whale."

Each Whale was 97.6 feet long and 10.7 wide, and was nothing more than an underwater troop carrier. They submerged and rose in the manner of conventional submersibles—by either taking water into the tanks or blowing them out with air. A Whale was a long hollow tube with tanks to port and starboard, an airlock diving chamber that could accommodate eight men at a time, and space to carry, for a short distance, a complement of thirty troops. A British invention, a Whale had a triple pressurized hull and could submerge to a depth of 116 fathoms without blowing the hull. Otherwise, the American and the British subs could have moved at a depth of 167 fathoms, or 1,002 feet.

The trip was not boring. There was too much that could go wrong. Remaining submerged, the three submarines and their Whales moved south through the Atlantic Ocean, keeping a steady 493 miles from the west coast of France and 284 miles west of the west coast of Spain.

True speed was not possible. Every 125 miles, the three submarines had to rise to a depth of one hundred feet so that divers could go inside the four Whales and inspect the machinery. An exact amount of water had to be kept in the ballast tanks in order for them to remain submerged at seven hundred feet. Should the water somehow escape, the Whale would pop to the surface like a cork—which was unlikely, because air was needed to blow the tanks. But nothing succeeds like caution.

The task was difficult and time-consuming. The three submarines couldn't force the four Whales to a hundred-foot level. The strain would have been too great, and the cables could have snapped and/or the tow frames collapsed.

To solve the problem, tow lines from the subs to the Whales were let out to six hundred feet of cable. The three submarines would then rise and remain at a one hundred-foot level while four technicians in special deep-dive suits left the subs, swam to the Whales, and entered through the wet-wells in the undersides of the vessels. The entire process, from start to finish, took five hours.

A turn and onward east, finally through the Strait of Gibraltar. Then the open Mediterranean. At last through the Strait of Sicily—another dangerous passage. Only ninety-eight miles separated Sicily from the northeast coast of Tunisia. Yet that was very wide in comparison to the Strait of Gibraltar, which was only twenty-three miles wide.

The greatest danger was detection by Soviet submarines or even the subs of friendly nations. Or even British and American submarines whose commanders did not know about the operation. In the Mediterranean there were also Soviet electronic ships—listening vessels. But their "ears" were tuned to the air and *on* the sea. *Under* the water was the domain of Soviet nuclear submarines, and few were in the Mediterranean.

The three submarines sent up their extra-long shortwave antennas to the surface when they were 310 miles due west of the northern tip of the island of Crete, which was situated at the south end of the Aegean Sea. Via shortwave—triple scrambled, coded, and with the transmission "squirted" out— plans were finalized by the Death Merchant, Colonel Robyn Burrell, Colonel Clint Ambule, and Rear Admiral Chester G. Burrton of the U.S. Task Force in the Mediterranean.

Admiral Burrton himself reported that the two helicopters would be ready. The type chosen for the operation was the RH-53D, the minesweeping version of the Sea Stallion H-53 helicopter, selected because of its combination of range, payload, shipboard capability, and security considerations. The two big birds would leave the aircraft carrier, the USS *Idaho*, when the vessel was approximately 122 miles southwest of Miskos. The two choppers would easily be able to make the round trip. The range of a RH-53D was 340 miles.

However, the powers in Washington, D.C., did not intend to have a repeat performance of the enormous failure that had been Operation Eagle Claw, the attempt to rescue the fifty-two hostages in Iran. The two birds would refuel on the way back to the USS *Idaho*, by setting down on a cargo vessel under Brazilian registry. The *San Martine* would just "happen to be" in the area, 64.9 miles southwest of Miskos. At the proper time, the crew of the *San Martine* would erect special landing pads on the stern.

In spite of all the meticulous planning, there was a flaw in Operation Zeus. The strike force was thirteen hours behind schedule, the delay caused by the periodic checking of the Whales. The loss of time, however, was minor. Whether Miskos was blasted on Thursday or Friday made little difference.

The afternoon before the three subs would reach the stop point, the Death Merchant, Burrell, and Ambule relaxed in the large wardroom of the *Hawkbill*, amused by some of the conversations they overheard.

Carlos Minteargo, an American of Cuban extraction, a DELTA Force member and the sergeant who, under Camellion, would be in charge of the four other DELTAs in Camellion's special force, was telling several British SBS men about his views of the immigration problem in the U.S.

The Death Merchant looked at his watch. Time: 2:30 P.M. "Three more hours and we'll get the final check-down from Admiral Burrton." He gave a low, rolling kind of chuckle. "By tomorrow at this time, we'll either have succeeded or failed."

"I'm sure we've coordinated properly the attack of the two choppers with our landing on Miskos," Colonel Burrell said. "Or rather an hour after we have landed. It will take that long to set up shop and prepare the shaped charges and the Cyclonite."

Colonel Ambule lighted another one of his little black cigars whose aroma reminded Camellion of burning felt. "A lot of our success will rest with the Russians not having booby-trapped the beach or mined the water. I think they're waiting for us. They don't like it, but there isn't anything else they can do."

"We'll know in three more hours," the Death Merchant said.

5:42 P.M.—*1742 hours.* The spokesman for Admiral Burrton reported that the two RH-53D helicopters would attack Mount Posso at 0400 hours the following morning.

The Death Merchant reiterated the order he had given during his first communication with Admiral Burrton: Make sure the pilots of the RH-53D helicopters do not attack the top of Mount Posso. I repeat: *Do not attack the summit of Mount Posso.*

The latest recon of Miskos?

SEALs from *Bluefin,* an American sub, had not found anything unusual in the water leading to the south beach. There was no evidence of explosive devices that could be detonated either by direct pressure or by undue wave motion.

2000 hours. Weapons and equipment check. Every commando, British and American, would carry six hand grenades— two frag, two smoke, two thermite. The members of the Royal Marines Special Boat

Squadron would carry 9-mm Browning double action autopistols in special operations hip-extender holsters. For heavier, more rapid fire, half the SBS commandos would be armed with L70 Enfield Individual Weapon assault rifles, the other half with L2A1 Sterling submachine guns.

No "sissy" Sterlings for the DELTA commandos (except the five SBS boys with the Death Merchant's tiny but special force). The DELTAs preferred Colt CAR-15 SMGs, and for sidearms 9-mm SBF Beretta autoloaders.

In reality, no one knew how many handguns the DELTA boys possessed, for Colonel Ambule, in his combat wisdom, permitted his men to carry pistols or revolvers of their choice. His reason was psychological. A man's confidence increased when he carried a weapon he personally preferred. It was the same with knives. A DELTA commando could carry any kind of pig-sticker that struck his fancy.

There were 117 YO-41 all-purpose gas masks. All 117 men were dressed in navy combat cloth jumpsuits with combat harnesses and black LAW combat boots. Every man would also carry twenty-five pounds of Cyclonite in one-pound bars, wrapped in thick brown plastic.

2200 hours. The USS *Hawkbill,* the HMS *Warspite,* and the HMS *Resolution* hung suspended in the water. Eight submariner technicians in deep-dive suits now swam to and entered the four Whales. Their job was to prepare the Whales to rise to the surface of the Aegean Sea, unless they were ordered to remain submerged. To ensure VLF communications, two of the divers had pulled from the sub a four hundred-foot-long underwater antenna.

2400 hours—midnight. Still at a depth of 684 feet, *Hawkbill* and the two British nuclear submarines were now in the Sea of Crete, the "front porch" of the Aegean. The exact position of the force was eighty nautical miles north of the central northern coast of Crete. More important, the Death Merchant, DELTA Force, and the Special Boat Squadron commandos were only 58.7 nautical miles southwest of the island of Miskos. That meant they were only 58.7 miles southwest of the magnifying transmitter. . . .

Full stop. The only noise in the *Hawkbill* and the two British subs was the low sound of the turbo-alternators. The expectancy of danger crackled in the air. The men were all thinking the same question: What lay on the surface?

The USS *Hawkbill*'s SEWACO—sensor weapon and command system—was only effective underwater or if the submarine surfaced. There was another way to scan the surface electronically.

The antenna door in the afterhull opened and the buoyant antenna float rose slowly to the surface; attached to it was a Plessey Cormorant sensor with an antenna configuration that would give optimum resolution. If a Greek was moving the oars of a rowboat ten miles away, the PC-sensor would pick up the sounds. There were only the sounds of three engines far to the northwest. The PC's Sella computer estimated they were twelve miles distant and headed away from the attack force.

Commander Raymond Meyerscough of the *Hawkbill* gave the order to his exec. "Release the tow lines from the two Whales and reel them in. Radio the two other subs and the men in the Whales and tell them to surface. Then blow the tanks and we'll get the hell to the surface."

Meyerscough, who looked like he could be a model for a Marlboro advertisement, turned to Camellion, Ambule, and Burrell. "Your men are ready?"

"Affirmative, Commander," Colonel Ambule said. "The instant you say go, we go."

"The rubber boats are on the foredeck," Meyer-scough said. "We'll keep the long wire antenna out and wait here until seventeen hundred hours. Should your force not have returned by then, we'll leave. Those are my orders."

The transfer from the three submarines to the four Whales, by large, inflatable rubber boats, went smoothly, although several DELTA men almost let an FFV 84-mm shoulder-fired recoilless antitank weapon and its eight missiles fall overboard. The force had five FFVs and fifty missiles. The ten shaped charges of pentolite in their metal containers were easy to carry; their wooden crates had two handles on all four sides.

The men paddled the rubber boats to the Whales, the top hulls of which were only a few feet above the water. If the ballast tanks had been blown completely, each Whale would have been five feet above the water. Very quickly the men and their equipment, including the deflated rubber boats, disappeared through the forward hatches.

Ballast tanks were partially filled, air pressure checked, engines started, and the four Whales started in toward Miskos, their top hulls only a few feet above the water. Above them were trained Albaar sensors. Below, one technician steered each craft; the other technician listened to the sonar and the A-S.

This close to the surface, with their ballast tanks half empty, the Whales could move at twenty-two knots—too slow if the schedule was to be maintained.

The Death Merchant didn't like it. The time was 0113 hours and it would take slightly more than two hours to reach Miskos. As things were now, the four Whales wouldn't arrive until after the two RH-53D helicopters blottoed the sides of Mount Posso.

Camellion discussed the flaw with Colonel Ambule and Major Glen Camelback, the DELTA Force's second in command.

"I don't know what we can do about it," Ambule said. "These babies will go only so fast and no faster."

"All we can do is risk it—okay?" said Major Camelback.

The Death Merchant looked at Camelback for a moment. He couldn't stand the man, not that he had anything against him personally. It was just that Camelback could not speak two sentences without saying "okay" or "you know."

Camellion turned and walked the short distance to the technician who was piloting the Whale.

"How will this craft move on the surface, completely on the surface?"

The man thought for a moment. "Well, we have a sharp prow and a powerful engine. On the surface, I'd say maybe thirty-two knots."

"Then take it all the way up," Camellion ordered. "If we hear anything approaching us, we can always submerge."

"Yes, sir."

"We could be taking one helluva risk," Clint Ambule said, displeased with the Death Merchant's decision.

"But less of a risk than if the two birds opened up on the mountain before we were even on the beach." Camellion smiled. "How did Colonel Burrell phrase it? We don't want to do a burton, do we?"

Chapter Twenty

"Absolutely amazing!" breathed Dr. Lazar Marchenko, awe on his face as well as in his voice. "It—the device works!" He and the other Soviet scientists and a sad Dr. Stefanos Paspyrou stared at the magnifying transmitter, which had been turned on and had been operational for the past three hours, ever since midnight.

The device, resting on a round metal platform, fifty-two feet in diameter, did not resemble anything known to modern science. The main body of the magnifying transmitter resembled a giant stainless-steel drum, almost as large as a vat used in a commercial winery. From the rounded dome section attached to the end of the drum ran cables, some thicker than a man's arm. These were the power cables that led from the neutron klystron sweep to the magnatrons. From the magnatrons the power went directly to the magnifying transmitter.

From the center of the "drum" on the forward end of the mysterious machine projected what looked like the gargantuan barrel of a gun—forty feet long and several feet in diameter. Halfway up the barrel were two six-foot "arms"—steel girders—extending outward for nine feet. To these were attached two more barrels that protruded seven feet past the center barrel. From the rear of the shorter barrels ran thick cables, which entered the front of the main part of the magnifying transmitter.

The magnifying transmitter could be moved like an altazimuth. The main body of the machine was mounted to a giant U-frame, by means of which it could be raised or lowered, tilted either upward or downward. The electric motor that furnished the power was on the platform.

There were actually two platforms, the one on which the magnifying transmitter rested and one beneath it. The top platform could be rotated in a full circle. Six four-feet-high wheels similar to wheels on trains lay underneath the platform resting firmly on a round railing on top of the second platform. On this bottom platform was also the motor that effected the rotation of the top platform and/or the magnifying transmitter.

Surrounding both platforms were eight other wheels, each six feet in diameter, each mounted to a triangular steel framework. In the groove of each wheel was a steel cable whose end was fastened to a large eyebolt on the top platform. Each cable disappeared in a hole in the floor and went straight down 2,104 feet to the complex inside the base of Mount Posso, ending on the huge drum of an electric-powered winch.

Raising and lowering the platform in the shaft was an easy task, yet a lengthy one. First, in order for the device to fit inside the shaft, the magnifying transmitter had to be tilted back so that its three barrels were perpendicular.

The scientists and technicians gathered around the magnifying transmitter couldn't see the ends of the two smaller pulse amplitude converters—or barrels. The ends protruded four feet through the camouflaged canvas covering the entire crater. So large was the canvas that it had to be supported by numerous wooden poles, in the manner of a circus tent.

General Gregor Shchors hurried over to the L-Board that was being monitored by Stefanos Paspyrou and looked at the N-N-junction meter.

"Good! Good!" Shchors said, elated. "There is not the slightest neutron flux. We should not have any neutrino interference either. Do you not agree, Doctor?"

"Yes, General," Paspyrou said. "Yet I maintain we are taking a terrible risk. If the power were measured in volts instead of N-TEEs, there would be almost one billion volts flowing through the transmitter—and we're still not certain of the High-Q."

"You're being too cautious, Doctor," Shchors snapped, losing all his patience. "Do your work and keep your opinions to yourself. After all, it is because of your scientific achievements that the magnifying transmitter is a success."

Paspyrou would not be silenced. "We should have done more testing. For one thing, we should have consulted metallurgists. That much power? How do we know what it will do to the molecules in the metal?"

Giving Paspyrou a dirty look, General Shchors hurried over to Doctors Marchenko and Szamuely, both of whom were poring over numerous meteorological charts.

Marchenko glanced at Shchors and smiled. "Gregor, everything is going according to plan," he said.

"You are sure of the coordinates?" asked Shchors, a nervous ring in his voice.

"Da," Alexander Szamuely stated. "The F-particles are cutting through the ozone layer, the ionosphere E-layer, and the ionosphere F-layer—in fact, through the entire Heaviside-Kennelly layer."

Marchenko took a long drag on his cigarette and expelled the smoke forcefully. "It's almost impossible for American satellites to detect any standing waves. The thickest concentration before the reflection factor could even become a probable will be over northwest Turkey. There are the figures. See for yourself."

General Shchors looked at the formula:

$$\frac{\sqrt{4Z_1\,Z_2}}{Z_1\,Z_2}\ N = \log_E\ \sqrt{\frac{E_1}{E_2}}\ B = \frac{d\varnothing}{dA}$$

"Yes, I see it's correct." Shchors then tilted his head to one side. "Do either of you hear that sound?"

Dr. Marchenko listened for a moment. "An airplane?"

"It sounds like a helicopter far in the distance," Dr. Szamuely said.

Standing outside the operations building, Colonel Boris Malenkova, Major Valeri Fedchenko, and Major Sergei Diamov stared at the shaft that was used to raise and lower the two platforms that bore the magnifying transmitter. With the two Spetsnaz officers and the KGB officer were General Nikos Cyatorus and his aide, Major Adonis Brillakipolu.

The silent and uneasy truce between Malenkova and Diamov was holding up, due to the success of the magnifying transmitter, but Diamov could not resist saying "I believe, Comrade Malenkova, that even you will now admit that your fears about the Americans were groundless. All these weeks that the Americans have known about this base, and what have they done—nothing! Not even one whisper of protest to the UN. Having your men on full alert was a waste of time."

Colonel Malenkova refused to lose his temper. "Comrade, if your knowledge of security extended to the Soviet military doctrine of *vytalkivanie*, you would know that it is never wise to underestimate any enemy, particularly Americans. Your trouble is that you associate caution with cowardice and mistake carelessness for courage."

Fedchenko said easily to an embarrassed General Cyatorus, "Perhaps our Greek guests would care to see the magnifying transmitter in action. We can use the other elevator."

"There is another elevator?" General Cyatorus, dressed in a business suit, looked in wonder at Major Diamov.

Diamov nodded. "There is another elevator shaft around the bend at the other end of the complex. We placed the passenger elevator there because the rock strata was softer. The main shaft was built in harder rock to withstand the weight of the device. Would you and Major Brillakipolu care to go to the mountain top, General Cyatorus? We can—"

All five heard the series of explosions—six or more. They couldn't be sure. The blasts sounded far away, as if in the distance, but the three Russians and the two Greeks knew that the explosions had come from the east slope of Mount Posso.

A choking sound came from Major Diamov.

Colonel Boris Malenkova's eyes went wide, and anger and hate flashed over his face.

The impossible had become reality.

The Soviet weather base was being attacked.

Chapter Twenty-one

I

Difficulty is an excuse that is never acceptable, particularly if your boss is the United States government. The DELTA and the SBS commandos almost arrived after the two RH-53D Sea Stallion helicopters attacked Mount Posso.

That special kind of twilight that comes just before dawn was in evidence when the four Whales came to a full stop 2.4 miles south of Miskos island. The attack force crawled out of the forward hatches, inflated their rubber boats, and lowered them over the side into the water. Superbly trained, it took the 117 men only ten minutes to get into the rubber crafts and attach frames and small outboard motors to the rear of each boat and start the short journey to the south shore of the island. They were four-fifths of the way to the island when they heard the two RH-53D choppers coming in from the southwest, the *thub-thub-thub-thub* of the rotors becoming louder with each second. The force was still a thousand feet from the beach when the choppers roared overhead and attacked Mount Posso.

Each RH-53D chopper carried, in special extended pods, thirty Teledyne Ryan Firebolt air-to-ground missiles, which had twice the velocity of a shell fired from any antiaircraft gun, and a warhead of fifteen pounds of TNT.

The two large choppers—painted a bright white without a single marking—didn't waste time on a recon. The pilots had their orders and went about executing them, one big white bird attacking the north side while the second chopper went to work on the west.

The Death Merchant and the rest of the force didn't see the Firebolt missiles leave the pods, much less see them stab through the air. It would have been the same as the human eye trying to see a supersonic bullet in flight. All they witnessed were some of the explosions on the southwest slopes: BLAMMMM-BLAMMMM-BLAMMMM. Enormous balls of fire bloomed in the early dawn, the huge flashes making the rising sun pale in comparison. There were brain-crashing explosions, and tons of rock shot outward and fell downward. There were more rapid explosions from the north side of the mountain.

Most of the exploding Firebolts also triggered smaller explosions, those from the charges the Russians had planted on the slopes to trigger rock slides on any enemy foolish enough to try to attempt an invasion. The exploding Firebolts caused hundreds of tons of rock to roll down the west and the north sides—and the northeast side.

Firebolt missiles slammed into the northeast section of the mountain; however, the helicopters didn't fire a single missile at the southeast end. Any rock slide in this area would prevent Blue and White companies from first using the shaped charges, then blowing a small part of the mountain inward with the 2,992 pounds of Cyclonite.

The DELTA and the SBS commandos were almost to the shore when the two RH-53D choppers roared over them at four hundred feet and, flying north, fired off four Firebolts each at the lower south face of Mount Posso—BERRRUM-BERRRUMMMMM-BER-RRUUUMMMMMM-BERUMMMMMM!

The lower south side of the mountain exploded into a carpet of rolling fire and dislodged boulders that shot skyward and fell on the beach as far as three hundred feet from the mountain. When the smoke and gray dust had cleared away, the mouth of the caves had vanished. The rock slides had completely covered their entrance.

The pilots, their tasks completed, took their birds upward, turned and flew off, leaving behind them a still-smoking Mount Posso.

"That's one worry that's been eliminated," Colonel Ambule said. "The sons of bitches won't be firing at us from the caves." He crawled from the rubber boat into the water and, with the Death Merchant and some other ballistic-helmeted commandos, began pulling the boat through a space between the rocks to the smooth, wet sands ahead.

Each man knew what to do and precisely how to do it. He should. Monitored with stopwatches, the force had rehearsed a dozen times at the base in Poole. The rubber boats were deflated and repacked and, with the aluminum frames and outboard motors, concealed in rocks to one side of the main landing area.

The direction of advance was north. Some of the commandos occupied themselves with the rear; others guarded the flanks. The main body moved north, the recon in an arrowhead formation. Their destination was the bottom of the mountain's southeast slope. Twenty men carried the ten shaped charges in wooden crates. Many of the commandos kept a wary eye on the high slopes, for anything was possible. First the shaped charges would blow, then the Cyclonite. The final coordination line would assemble after the Cyclonite exploded.

Without difficulty, most of the commandos reached the area where the shaped charges were to be placed. In charge of the entire project would be Special Boat Squadron Sergeant Fred Tune, one of the best demolition experts in the Royal Marines.

After the shaped charges were removed from their wooden crates, Sergeant Tune went to each one, which was a sheet-metal case, one end shaped like a cone, the other end flat and resting on four metal legs. In each activator well in the nose of the cone, he placed an electric T-detonator that could be fired by radio control impulse.

"What about the legs, Sarge?" one of the men asked. "Are we going to take them off?"

"No, laddie. We don't have the time," said Tune, who had a shaggy mustache and was as spit and polish as any soldier out of Kipling's *Gunga Din.* He was also in charge of the four Special Boat Squadron commandos in the Death Merchant's special squad.

Tune turned on each T-detonator, then had the men place each shaped charge on its side and shove it into the rocks as far as possible, cone end inward.

"Everyone back," he shouted. "All of you! Back at least several hundred meters!"

"Earplugs everyone," ordered Colonel Ambule. He looked at Tune, who had picked up the blast box. "On what count, Sergeant?"

"Five, sir."

As soon as the commandos had moved to a respectable distance, Tune opened the MK blast box, turned on the "spark" switches, pulled up the short antenna, then looked around to make sure everyone was down. He yelled, "ONE, TWO, THREE, FOUR"—

and paused, giving everyone time, including himself, to shove the plugs into their ears.

"FIVE!" He opened his mouth, went "AHHH-HHH!" and pressed a finger firmly on the firing button.

BBBBEEEERRRRUUUUUUUMMMMMM!   The ten blasts, sounding as one, were of such magnitude that the ground shook. The forty metal legs shot to the east with the force of rockets, but there was little smoke, and no one could see any fire. In a shaped charge, most of the blast tears in the direction of the target. No one would ever know how much granite had been pulverized by the blasts. The Death Merchant and the others didn't care. Their only concern was that the pentolite do the job.

Sergeant Tune, Camellion, Ambule, Burrell, and many of the commandos rushed forward to inspect the results of the ten explosions. The commandos were more than ready for any kind of trouble—all of them, CAR-15 SMGS and I-W assault rifles waiting. In the meantime, the other commandos began taking one-pound blocks of Cyclonite—or RDX—from their kit bags.

Tune was pleased with his work. He got up from his knees and handed the flashlight to Richard Camellion, who was closest to him. "Have a look, sir. I estimate the length to be six to seven meters."

The Death Merchant could already see that the diameter of each horizontal "tunnel" was three feet. Why bother to look inside? He handed the flashlight back to Tune.

"There's no point in wasting time," he said matter-of-factly, and began taking bars of Cyclonite from his Gussett shoulder bag. "We can't lengthen the blast tunnels. Let's stuff them with the RDX and get on with it. We have to go inside that mountain as quickly as possible, do what we have to do, then get out of here and back to the Whales."

"Yeah, it makes sense to me," Colonel Ambule said heavily. "We don't want to have to waste Greeks. If any of them show up, we'll have to kill them."

Colonel Robyn Burrell concurred with a nod. "It does seem the proper action to take," he said. "The sooner we are inside the mountain, the better all around. Sergeant, prepare the Cyclonite for detonation."

"Sergeant, I'm curious about how you're going to do it," Camellion said, watching other commandos file by and place their bars of Cyclonite on the ground. "If you have to fasten hundreds of bars together, we'll be here until the Russians inside the mountain die of old age!"

Tune laughed politely. "Sir, you have much to learn about Cyclonite. Its sensitivity lies halfway between tetryl and PETN. The sensitivity is reduced a good deal by the addition of wax, but not to the extent that one bar can't be detonated by the explosion of another bar. I'll place a T-detonator on four of the blocks that go into each tunnel; they'll explode the scores of others. You'll see. The entire flaming mess will explode."

As Sergeant Tune and a dozen commandos prepared the Cyclonite, tossing bars of the explosive into the ten horizontal holes in the mountainside, the Death Merchant conferred with Burrell and Ambule.

"Tune maintains the opening will be nine meters wide and four to six meters high," Burrell said in a dry, dissatisfied way. "That's a bloody small area when one is facing concentrated fire."

Camellion correctly sized up the British officer's reluctance. "The Russians inside know the sound of shaped-charge explosions when they hear them. They'll be expecting us to come in from this side."

"We can't use smoke," Ambule said. He took off his gray ballistic helmet and wiped his head with a large brown handkerchief. "The ivans would concentrate their fire on the smoke. Those ivan fuckers would chop us down before we even got off to a good start."

"We don't charge, not right away," the Death Merchant said, spacing his words deliberately. "Instead we'll place several men at each end of the opening and have them use the Swedish missile launchers. A dozen or so eighty-four-millimeter missiles should keep the pig farmers down long enough for us to get in."

Camellion looked at the drawing that Colonel Ambule had spread out on the ground. "According to the old German records, from the opening to the ground level there will be a long slope, about one hundred fifty feet long—forty-five meters. Once we get past it—or *down* it—we'll have the initiative."

Colonel Ambule thought for a few seconds. "There have to be prefab buildings down there and all kinds of equipment. Once we reach them and have cover, we'll be able to effect depth penetration."

Unless the Russians blow up the complex and us with it! But all Camellion said was "That's about the size of it, Colonel."

Colonel Burrell's steady eyes remained on the Death Merchant. "Camellion, you and your own special force. How will you and they function once you're inside? I think it's time you told us your specific targets."

"My orders are to find Professor Paspyrou and his family and get them out of here," Camellion said. "I have to take photographs of the complex and grab important notes and progress reports. It won't do us much good to destroy the base if President Reagan and Mrs. Thatcher can't prove to the whole world why an attack was absolutely necessary."

"There have been some slight miscalculations," Burrell mused. "But I suppose the *Sam Houston*'s developing a slight problem with her engines is not exactly the end of the world. The *Hawkbill* served our purpose equally well."

The Death Merchant did not show his slight irritation over Burrell's mentioning the *Sam Houston.* The colonel had the annoying habit of letting the trivial flaws of the past project themselves into the present.

"Colonel, we are here on the island," Camellion said pragmatically. "Right now how we got here is totally unimportant. At the moment, my concern is our getting inside Mount Posso with a minimum of losses." Camellion glanced at Colonel Ambule. "Come to think of it, we'd better set up a couple of light machine guns at each end of the perimeter. They can open up—if need be—after the missiles are fired."

"A couple of M60 LMGs should do it," Ambule said with vigor. "We can rake each flank while we rush straight down the slot. There isn't any other way."

He looked past the Death Merchant at Major Charles Eastmore and Captain William McComb, both of whom were walking toward him. Behind the two British officers were Major Glen Camelback and Lieutenant Karl Pfister.

Major Eastmore stopped in front of Colonel Burrell and saluted smartly. "Sir, Sergeant Tune is ready to detonate the explosives. All he needs is for you to give the order—and you, sir, Colonel Ambule."

"Thank you, Major," Burrell said, wrinkling his nose. It disturbed him that Major Camelback and Lieutenant Pfister hadn't saluted Colonel Ambule. Privately, Robyn Burrell and the rest of the Special Boat Squadron commandos regarded DELTA force

as an outfit sloppy in protocol and military courtesy.
Why, the rank and file treated their superiors with an
unheard of familiarity, as if they were close friends
having a drink of bitters together in some pub! It was
a disgrace! But how the bloody blighters could fight!
And how they loved firearms. Whoever heard of permitting fighting men to carry any kind of handgun
they might choose? Damn it all, why couldn't they be
satisfied with standard issue? A case in point was Major Camelback. Other than the 9-mm Beretta in its
Bianchi universal military holster on his hip, he carried a mammoth .44 magnum Ruger Redhawk, with
a twelve-inch barrel, in a leather holster that rested
on his stomach. The Americans should be taught a
thing or two about regulations!

Smoking a cigarette, Camelback got down on one
knee and faced Colonel Ambule and Richard Camellion. So did Pfister.

"Colonel, you know no one has said a word about
cover fire," Camelback offered nonchalantly. "This is
one helluva important ruskie base. There could even
be Spetsnaz waiting in there for us."

"Mr. Camellion, what about your special squad?"
inquired Pfister, who had a square face and a slight
overbite. "Sergeant Minteargo wants to know when
to assemble Rushing, Troop, and the other two guys,
and I guess Sergeant Tune has the same question."

The Death Merchant got to his feet and placed the
palms of his hands on the butts of the two Steyr GB
auto pistols in their hip-extender holsters.

"Tell Tune that as soon as he blows the Cyclonite,
he can get his four men and meet me, then we'll
assemble—you know! Tell Monteargo the same." He
swung his gaze to a stiff-lipped Colonel Burrell.
"That is, as soon as Colonel Burrell gives the word to
detonate the Cyclonite. Then there's the matter of

the two M60 LMGs and the shoulder-fired missile launchers."

"Major Eastmore, tell Sergeant Tune to detonate the explosive as soon as our combined force has moved to the beach," Burrell said stiffly, knowing a hint when he heard one. "Captain McComb, have two of our troops ready with the FFV AT4 recoilless launchers and ten missiles. We're going to fire inside the mountain once the opening is made."

Taking out one of his little black twisted cigars, Colonel Ambule said, "Karl, have two of our men ready with their launchers. They can fire from the other side. Tell them to try not to hit any buildings. We're after files and records."

"Anything else, Colonel?" asked Lieutenant Pfister, who had a Kris dagger in its thick holster fastened to one of the chest straps of his Uzi battle harness.

"Move out," Ambule said, then bit off the end of his cigar and looked steadily at the Death Merchant. "We know you're CIA. Is there anything you want to tell us before we charge inside that damned mountain?"

The Death Merchant could appreciate Ambule's concern. He was a good officer and concerned for his men.

"It's like this, Colonel. If the CIA is withholding any information, they're also withholding it from me. I've told you everything."

Burrell gave a deep, amused laugh. "Except that the ivans might blow the joint sky-high!"

"That goes with the territory, Colonel."

The blast of the 2,992 pounds of cyclotrimethylenetrinitramine, better known as Cyclonite (or RDX, as the Americans called the world's most powerful military explosive), was so great that one could almost think that the foundations of heaven had collapsed. For a millisecond it seemed that the island itself was about to dissolve and sink into the sea, so violent were the tremors. But to the south there wasn't enough concussion to move a feather. The reason was that most of the titanic force had been directed inward against only twenty feet of granite.

Years earlier, when Soviet engineers had enlarged the base, they hadn't dreamed of anyone attacking, much less an attack with high explosives, and so they had used small explosive charges to "chip" away at the north, south, and east sides of the cavern. When they finished with the east side, there was only twenty feet of granite, for a height of sixty feet, between the underground Soviet weather station and the outside of the island. At the time, in 1983, the Russians had concluded that twenty feet of solid granite was more than ample—and it was.

Until the Death Merchant had arrived.

Until DELTA Force and the Special Boat Squadron of Her Majesty's Royal Marines had arrived.

Even as the triple echoes of the titanic blast were rolling over the waters of the blue Aegean, the Death Merchant, Burrell, Ambule, and the rest of the force were on their feet and racing to the side of the mountain. Hell was about to explode, and they didn't intend to be on the receiving end.

II

Except for Colonel Boris Malenkova and his 150 Spetsnaz Special Forces fighters and Major Sergei Diamov and his thirty-three Department-V KGB agents, the Russians were victims of fear and confusion. They had a right to be. Not only were they *not* professional soldiers, but what they had been told could not happen *was* happening. The base was under full-scale attack.

First, sixty Firebolt missiles had exploded on all sides of Mount Posso, washing the rocks with hellfire, the crashing blasts much louder to the scientists and technicians on top of the mountain, inside the crater, than to the hundreds of other Russians far below, at the bottom of the weather station in the base of the mountain.

General Cyatorus and Major Brillakipolu, in the crater with General Shchors and the other scientists, were the most terrified of all. Their intense guilt at the realization that if they were captured, they would be exposed as the worst kind of traitors, superceded even their fear of death.

When the first Firebolt missiles began exploding, Dr. Szamuely and Dr. Marchenko lost all interest in the experiment. Szamuely yelled, "Those missiles will kill all of us!"

"Soo-kyn syn!" cursed General Shchors in anger and disgust. "You damned idiot! They've guessed that the device is on the top of this mountain. They don't want to destroy it. Now they will try to climb the slopes in an effort to reach us. But we won't be here; neither will the magnifying transmitter."

General Shchors turned to the frightened technicians and ordered them to shut off the machine, then lower the platforms to the floor of the cavern far below. Shchors's utter frustration had not been born of his fear that the magnifying transmitter might be destroyed or damaged in any way but of his realization that the first part of the experiment had failed. The magnifying transmitter had to be fully operational for a minimum of nine hours in order for the N-beam to bring about very short standing waves in the jet streams and to generate electromagnetic impulses the exact opposite of the Nernst-Ettinghausen effect. Shchors was also forced to admit that there would never be another opportunity to repeat the experiment, at least not on Miskos.

It took seven minutes to shut down the magnifying transmitter.

"Stefanos, you will remain with me and help oversee the lowering of the transmitter," Shchors told Dr. Paspyrou. He then directed his attention to Szamuely and Malenkova. "Lazar, Alexander, take the passenger elevator and go below. General Cyatorus, you and your aide go with them."

"How—h-how are we going to leave the island?" Cyatorus blurted. "Major Brillakipolu can't remain here."

"I suggest you concern yourselves with staying alive," General Shchors said bitterly. "If the two of you want, you can leave with us in the *Stalingrad*. All of you, get below."

The two Soviet scientists and the two Greek intelligence officers were only too happy to comply with the order. All four turned and almost ran to the passenger elevator four hundred feet away, at the west side of the crater.

When Shchors saw that Dr. Stefanos Paspyrou was half smiling, he fooled the Greek physicist by smiling back at him. "Don't consider this a victory, Stefanos. The Americans might scale the mountain and reach the crater, but it will take them days to reach the main section of *Veliki*."

"But they will get inside," Paspyrou said unsympathetically, feeling that for the time being his wife and children below were safe.

"Yes, they will." Shchors smirked. "But by the time they do, we'll be safely in the *Stalingrad* and far from this island, and the magnifying transmitter will have been blown apart. Now, let's lower the transmitter on its platforms. We'll then go to the scientific building and transfer all the notes and records to the submarine."

Far below the crater, in the heart of *Veliki* experimental station, Colonel Boris Malenkova and Major Sergei Diamov worked with an efficiency unhindered by fear or thoughts of defeat. The men were well armed and ready to go to the crater, just as soon as the technicians were finished with the passenger elevator, which could hold only eight persons.

Malenkova and his aide, Major Fedchenko, had concluded that, since helicopters had missiled the sides of the mountain, the next phase of the attack would be for the Americans to scale the slopes to reach their objective—the crater.

"We'll let them climb the sides of the mountain and cut them to pieces when they're almost to the rim of the crater," Colonel Malenkova said, sounding pleased. "We have the advantage. They have to come to us."

Standing in front of the general headquarters building—five prefabricated rooms—with Fedchenko and Diamov, Malenkova and the two other men watched workers and technicians of all kinds move in an orderly and purposeful manner between the various buildings, erecting barriers and in other ways preparing for the invasion. Others, inside the buildings, were packing expensive instruments and loading weapons.

"We won't be able to hold them off indefinitely," Major Diamov said, a cagey look in his eyes as he watched the magnifying transmitter slowly descend in the huge shaft. "Instead of preparing for a fight, we should be getting ready to evacuate." Diamov proceeded to say exactly what he thought. "Everyone was in agreement that the Americans would not dare attack. They were too 'afraid' of what the world might think! But they're outside! They are attacking, and they're not stupid. They're not going to bother with climbing the sides of the mountain. I think they've found the fake wall in the water and will blow it up. I think they'll come through the water and surface in the sub pens."

Colonel Malenkova caught Major Fedchenko's eye. Both men smiled, showing a lot of teeth, and looked at Sergei Diamov as if he were an idiot.

"The Americans would be *chòr-vst-yiiéyi* if they attempted such a tactic." Malenkova laughed. "They know we'd kill them before they could even get out of the water."

Diamov was adamant, showing a stubbornness that both amazed and angered Boris Malenkova, the Spetsnaz commander.

"I'm not taking my men to the crater," Major Diamov said. "I'm keeping them down here where they'll be needed. I'm telling both of you: You're underestimating the Americans. I have been saying that all these weeks. You're doing it right now—assuming they're stupid!"

Colonel Malenkova and Major Fedchenko could not believe what they were hearing. How could Diamov utter such blasphemy when his orders were clear and specific: that in case of an emergency, Colonel Boris Malenkova would be in complete control of all defense and make all decisions.

Malenkova glared at Diamov, his eyes wild with rage. "Comrade Major Diamov, you will follow my orders or—"

The explosion to the east, cutting him off, made the entire mountain tremble, the blasts of such violence that many of the prefab buildings, made of aluminum and fiberboard, shuddered. Tiny rocks fell from the uneven rock ceiling 150 feet overhead.

Malenkova, Fedchenko, and Diamov swung

around and stared in disbelief toward the east, at the long slope of scree and small boulders that led upward to the solid granite side of Mount Posso. Everything looked normal. There were no cracks and none of the rocks appeared disturbed.

General Gregor Shchors, who had just left the passenger elevator and had run several hundred feet, hurried up to Major Diamov and the two Spetsnaz officers. Malenkova and Fedchenko were now completely frustrated and feeling stupid. Shaped charges! They knew the sound of shaped charges when they heard it.

"What was that explosion?" demanded General Shchors, out of breath. He reached out and touched Colonel Malenkova. "My God! Those damned Americans can't blast through the side. The granite must be hundreds of feet thick!"

"They're using shaped charges," Boris Malenkova explained angrily. "The main blast will come shortly."

"But we must move records and other data from the science building to the *Stalingrad*," Shchors said with as much authority as he could muster. He jerked a thumb over his shoulder toward the south, where Commander Korotchenko and his crew were boarding the huge OSCAR-class nuclear submarine, in preparation for getting the *Stalingrad* under way.

Colonel Malenkova, who never lost track of the pecking order, didn't want to anger General Shchors. He was not only a KGB general, he was also a very important scientist.

"Comrade General, I suggest that you and your people move the records with all possible speed from the science building to the *Stalingrad*," Malenkova said politely. "But my Spetsnaz can't help you. Within the next hour, we're going to be fighting for our very lives." He turned from a stunned Shchors—

who by now was feeling deep fear—and said to Major Fedchenko, "The *Amerikanski* will first use missiles or mortars. Move all our men to the middle of the base. Have them set up machine guns in convenient positions."

"We're going to let them come down the slope?" Fedchenko frowned.

"I want them to think the base has practically no defenses. Spread out the machine guns so that we can trap them in a crossfire. I'll give the order to fire."

"Where will you be?"

"You go to the radio shack; I'll meet you there." Malenkova turned his head slightly and glared at Major Sergei Diamov. "And Valeri, inform the regular KGB officers that Major Diamov said they are to take orders from you!"

Major Diamov laughed in his face. "Tell me, Comrade Colonel. Aren't you going to send men to 'defend' the crater?"

The Spetsnaz, KGB officers, and other personnel moved quickly. Armed with 9-mm Vitmorkin machine pistols, ARR and AKS-75 assault rifles, as well as scores of PPS43 submachine guns, they took positions at the west ends of a two-story barracks, the radio shack, the science building, and general headquarters. On the east sides of the four buildings, the Spetsnaz set up 7.62-mm *Rotnyi Pulemyot orb* RP46 light machine guns. Drum fed, an RP46 could fire projectiles at the rate of 840 rpm.

Colonel Boris Malenkova and his Spetsnaz and the rest of the Russians—the scientists, technicians, and construction workers—didn't have long to wait. Nor did Professor Stefanos Paspyrou, who had hurried to be with his family in the barracks in the northwest section of the complex.

Everyone was huddled down and waiting when Sergeant Fred Tune's finger pressed the button and thousands of one-pound blocks of Cyclonite exploded, the blasts running together in one millisecond so that the myriad explosions formed one monstrous fulmination, the largest that any of the Russians had ever heard.

To the east, a large section of the inside of the mountain bulged inward. No one saw it. No one could have seen it. It lasted not even a nanosecond. Then thousands of tons of granite, pulverized into billions of pieces of smaller rock—some the size of a thimble, many others as large as a small pickup truck —fell inward, the larger pieces rolling down the slope, thousands of the smaller pieces shooting west with the speed of shrapnel.

Veliki's buildings didn't have glass windows. Clear plastic was used in some. Other window openings were empty, for the openings didn't have to be sealed. Temperature in the cavern was constant, and there was never even a slight breeze.

Sharp rocks slammed into the sides of the buildings closest to the east, to the long slope—the repair shops, stores, and the spare parts building. The east wall of the KGB security building was almost torn down by a barrage of rocks.

In the radio shack, huddled down with Major Fedchenko and Major Diamov, Colonel Malenkova spoke into the Gez-UHF walkie-talkie. "Hold your fire. Let them make the approach. I'll give the order when to open up."

III

The hole in the east base of Mount Posso, 182 feet wide and 64 feet high, resembled a monstrous mouth frozen in a silent scream. The entire force waited below the lower "lip" while two Special Boat Squadron commandos and two DELTA Force fighters prepared to fire their FFV AT4 recoilless launchers—two at the north end, two at the south end.

There were several nice features about the launchers and their missiles. One man could load the launcher before he placed the tube on his shoulder and aimed through its wide-screen computerized-laser sight. The STRORR missile comprised a rocket motor, stabilizing fins, a shaped-charge warhead, a base fuse, and a nose-mounted crush fuse. The rocket motor of a STRORR used a bundle of "brush-type" propellant sticks, which assured an even burn far superior to older types. Because of the even burn, the STRORR had a flight time of only 1.2 seconds when fired at 1,115 feet and was considered to be one of the most accurate antitank missiles in the world.

The shaped charge had an aluminum core containing 16 ounces of HE explosive and could blast a hole through 910mm of armor or seven feet of reinforced concrete. In the extreme front of the "heavy" antiarmor rocket missile was a piezo-electric crystal that produced current to the base fuse when crushed by pressure of the impact against the target.

The Death Merchant and the British and American officers held an assessment conference. They were toward the center of the lower "lip" of the "mouth," ten feet from its top. Through binoculars, they had made a study of the Soviet *Veliki* base, which appeared quiet and peaceful. They had not seen one Russian. There were only the prefab buildings lying naked in the glow of Zenon gas lights mounted on tall steel poles.

Colonel Clint Ambule flexed his tonsils. "They're waiting for us. And I don't think they'll try to snuff us when we go down the slope. We wouldn't. If our positions were reversed, we'd let them come in.

Then we'd use a harassing ambush and then close the deal with a deliberate ambush. A mop-up would be easy."

"I daresay you're correct," agreed Colonel Burrell. "They're waiting in the forward buildings and more likely than not have machine guns set up. If we only knew how many of the bloody bastards are in there."

Major Eastmore offered, "It's a good hundred and fifty feet from the bottom of the slope to the first buildings." He let his voice trail off, but the implication was clear. In that 150 feet, the Russians would cut them to pieces.

Major Camelback said it plain out: "The ivans would blow our asses off before we could reach any kind of protection—after we're down the slope and on the level."

"Men, we're not going to missile the buildings closest to us," the Death Merchant said. The others noticed instantly that he wasn't offering an opinion or a suggestion. His voice was definitive; he was giving an order. "If I were the Soviet commander in that hunk of underground real estate, I'd assume the enemy would use the same tactics we've been discussing. I'd expect them to first use missiles. I'd evacuate all the buildings to the east and move my people toward the center, or maybe all the way to the west. I'd set up my machine guns toward the center and use them to stop any enemy advance."

Colonel Ambule had the sudden urge to tell Camellion to go to hell, then demand how he knew so much about military strategy. He didn't. The Death Merchant made sense.

He said, "Leave the forward buildings intact and lob STRORRs toward the center? Is that what you're suggesting?"

"Affirmative. The men at the launchers can lob missiles over us as we charge down the slope and not stop until we reach our first go-down positions—the first buildings. The explosions in the center will create so much confusion, we'll be in place before the Russians can reorganize."

Colonel Burrell, lying on his left side, peered closely at Camellion. "Yank, suppose you're wrong?"

"Send a missile into one of the forward buildings." The Death Merchant shrugged. "If the other buildings contain Russians, they'll retreat. They're not going to sit there and let themselves be turned into hash."

"I think Camellion is right!" Lieutenant Pfister looked embarrassed that he had spoken without thinking.

"And so do I," Major Camelback said emphatically.

"What do we do about the submarine?" asked Captain McComb. "We can't blow it up. Should we expose its nuclear reactor, we would all die from the radiation."

"We can put a missile through its conning tower, or 'sail,' as they call it on these nuclear babies," said Camellion, his tone as calculating as his eyes.

"What about all those giant magnet-looking deals to the northwest? Why don't we blow hell out of them right off?" Colonel Ambule pulled off his Facelet gas mask. Developed by the British Ministry of Defense, the RF mask came packaged with its own antifog, gas-sealed, shatter-resistant goggles and didn't resemble a conventional gas mask. The neutralizers were in a single, large half-square container that projected below the goggles and fit snugly over the mouth and nose, so that anyone wearing the mask looked like an alien with goggles and an enormous square lip. Each man also had a 117 YO-41 all-purpose gas mask.

"Absolutely not!" Camellion was trigger-quick with a reply. "I want to photograph that device as well as the shaft toward the center, which apparently goes to the top of the mountain. I suspect the machine in the elevator is the magnifying transmitter. Now, let's get to work." He stood up. "I'm going to gather my men. As soon as the men are ready to move, give the orders to the guys with the missile launchers."

Fired from the north end of the "mouth" in the east side of the mountain, the first STRORR struck the stores building and exploded with a thundercrash that quickly became five blast-echoes that bounced back and forth within the cavern. For an eyeblink there was a cloud of fire and smoke, followed by a lot of flying pieces of fiberboard and smashed canned goods. Then, nothing but total wreckage.

The second and third missiles—streaking thirty feet over the helmeted heads of the DELTA and the SBS commandos, who had come over the top of the bottom "lip" and were charging down the slope— erased the general headquarters building from the cavern floor and exploded the water purification tanks. Flying debris from the purification equipment killed two technicians and five construction workers, all of whom had wrongly concluded they would be safe near the plant.

A fourth STRORR exploded between the southeast corner of the radio shack and the northwest corner of the science building, the tremendous pressure caving in half of the north wall of the science building and shoving plastic filing cabinets toward General Gregor Shchors and Alexander Szamuely and Lazar Marchenko. The three scientists had been frantically taking research folders from the cabinets, determined to get the records on board the *Stalingrad*. The big blast knocked them to the floor and made them change their minds. Moscow was far, far away. Death was right here.

"T-this is hopeless," admitted General Shchors, getting up from the floor. Pressure made his voice sound, to himself, as if he were speaking inside his head. "We'll never reach the submarine."

"Gregor, listen," whispered Marchenko, moving close to Shchors. "Dr. Paspyrou is with his family in the far barracks. We would be safe with him. He's one of the objectives of the Americans."

"Da, you are right," Shchors quickly agreed. "Let's get to his barracks."

The Death Merchant, Sergeant Tune, Sergeant Minteargo, and the eight other commandos of Camellion's special force were to the south, the five Britishers armed with L2A1 Sterling submachine guns, the Americans with MAC-10 Ingram SMGs, with forty-three-round detachable box magazines. Glenn Broombaugh, an SBS commando, and Cecil Tenkiller, a DELTA man, also carried two shotguns called Strikers. Each Striker had twelve twelve-gauge shells in a drum and could be fired as fast as the trigger could be pulled. As a close-in kill-weapon, the Striker was ultra-lethal.

Camellion had another concern: He had to protect the two cameras he carried in a case lined with nine-ply Kevlar, which could withstand the impact of a .44 magnum slug. One camera was a 35-mm Nikon FA, the other a 35-mm Minolta X-700. Each camera had a 75-200mm f/4.5 zoom lens and was extremely easy to operate.

Camellion had already used two rolls of film photographing the entire complex from the rim of the lower lip of the gash in the side of the mountain. But he wanted another hundred or so photographs close up, especially of the magnifying transmitter.

The DELTA and SBS commandos soon reached the first buildings to the east—the two repair shops, the spare parts building, and the general meeting hall.

BERRRRBLAMMMMMMMM! The explosion came far from the southwest. An 84-mm STRORR missile had slammed into the front of the *Stalingrad*'s tall sail and had ripped off most of the top. Radar, hatches, and periscopes were gone. Unable to submerge, the giant nuclear submarine was helpless.

The Death Merchant reached the east side of the KGB security building, the other ten men of his personal strike force close behind him. With them was another Presence, one beyond time, beyond human conception, beyond human imagination.

Camellion pulled the fuse pin from an X-4 offensive grenade and tossed it through the middle window of the wall. The grenade exploded, showering the room and three KGB agents with thousands of steel needles, each 9.53 millimeters long.

With a twisted smile and a MAC-10 in his right hand and a Steyr pistol in his left hand, Camellion muttered, *"Dominus Lucis vobiscum!"* and started to crawl through the window.

The Cosmic Lord of Death went with him. . . .

Chapter Twenty-two

There are those times when Nature resents the interference of man—that puny and murderous two-legged obscenity who has the audacity to proclaim to the Universe that he—and he alone!—was made in the image of the Creator!

Nature becomes angry and rebels.

The very delicate balance of the thermosphere and the exosphere, formed above the planet over the billions of years, had been upset by the trillions of concentrated neutrons from the magnifying transmitter, the N-beam reversing the normal flow of the electrons in the ozone layer in the stratosphere, which begins six miles above the Earth.

A "hole" had been opened in the ozone layer, an aperture that was directly over north-central Turkey, four miles east of the tiny village of Artova. The instant the "hole" was created the effect was instantaneous and hideous. For only a second the "chimney," reaching from the damaged ozone layer to the surface of the planet, was only 2,710 feet in diameter.

The Turkish farmers within that ill-fated region, their wives and children, their horses, cows, goats, and all life that was outside in the open—even birds and insects—didn't even have time to suspect they were doomed.

If the men and women trapped outside had had only a few minutes, they would still have died horribly, but first they would have seen something that no human being had ever seen—something that hadn't occurred since the formation of the planet four billion years ago. All around them, extending from space to the surface of the planet, they would have seen an intense white illumination in which were scintillating flashes and swirls of color, intense reds, blues, greens, and violet, a Brobdingnagian aurora under even brighter lights in the sky, lights almost as brilliant as the sun now shining with full intensity through the hole in the ozone layer.

Human beings and animals had time only for short shrieks of agony as the hell-heat of UV burned them to death within seconds.

Unimpeded by the protective blanket of the ozone layer, the ultraviolet light had increased by a factor of one thousand. The UV (which is also the cause of snow blindness) produced instant blindness and turned human and animal bodies into charred, smoking things.

The people in houses, in barns, and in other kinds of buildings—especially those close to windows—were blinded. Screaming and dying more slowly from the intense heat, they were forced to endure the mental crucifixion of not knowing what was happening to them, or why.

Many screamed and begged for God's mercy, thinking that the end of the world had arrived. The dry roofs of houses and other buildings—those not tiled—burst into flame. Haystacks and fields of corn and wheat ignited. To any onlooker who could have made himself immune to the UV, it would indeed have looked like the end of the world. In only minutes the countryside had become a sea of fire and smoke, of acute white light in which flashed a billion zigzag lines and twists and spirals of vivid color.

The diameter of the hell chimney from space continued to expand at the rate of several hundred feet a minute. Within that large, round circle everything burned, everything died.

The opening in the ozone layer had been caused by a process called photosensitization. This is when a chemical acts as a catalyzer to effect destruction. The decomposition of the ozone layer would now be accelerated by the action of chlorine—close to the argument that ecologists had used for years: that if something was not done about certain types of pollution, in time the aerosol-carried chlorinated hydrocarbons would rise in the atmosphere and catalyze the decomposition of the ozone.

The magnifying transmitter had done the job fifty years ahead of schedule.

Other processes were at work in space. The solar wind was blowing through the widening "hole" in the ozone layer and going straight down the "chimney." Protons, especially alpha particles, and cosmic rays of all kinds were now extra strong and, joined by secondary radiation, X rays, gamma rays (electromagnetic radiations similar to X rays, but with a shorter wavelength), and infrared, poured down the chimney and struck the earth.

Within the expanding circle of death on the surface another phenomenon was taking place: Rocks and other objects were now glowing in all sorts of fantastic colors, a nightmare vision of waving and colliding colors. This was caused by the buildup of UV quanta (or blacklight beyond the blue end of the spectrum).

In only twenty minutes the hole had expanded to a

diameter of 6,710 feet; the hell area on the ground was 6,710 feet in diameter—for only a brief moment. It was then larger, and larger. Then still larger.

The expansion had now met with a factor that caused another occurrence to take place within the death circle—*wind!*

If the atmosphere, including the ozone layer, did not move with the earth, the wind velocity would be precisely 1,420 mph. The only part of the atmosphere that is absolutely and totally unmoved is the thin film held by molecular forces very close to the planet's surface. The rest is somewhat progressively swayful and slidy, but not enough to say that the earth moves independently *beneath* the billions of tons of air (or water vapor).

This natural law had now been suspended within the circular area of burning death. The ordinary atmosphere on all sides of the "chimney" rushed in and, churned by the solar wind and other forces from space, became super tornadoes that revolved at over 1,000 mph.

Because of its height, the tower of light from outer space could be seen by millions of people for many hundreds of miles, until the curvature of the earth made it impossible for anyone to view the terrible happening.

People in Ankara, in Istanbul, and in hundreds of other towns and villages in between, and in the western part of Soviet Armenia saw the gargantuan pillar of light, which could only be described as a shining, "solid," ever-expanding shaft reaching upward into infinity. Ships on the Black Sea saw the glowing cylinder and wondered, and began to pray.

Pure panic and total awe was the result of the phenomenon, which people knew had to be pure destruction, pure hell, pure death. All normal activity, everything, stopped. Even communists dropped to their knees and started to pray, asking, begging, for forgiveness.

Within an hour, newswires all over the planet were aware of the Hideousness growing in Turkey. In Rome, the Pope prepared for the Final Conflagration. Scores of millions of people watched the sky, expecting to see Jesus Christ—in all His glory and surrounded by singing angels and stern-faced "saints"—coming down on a white horse.

Hundreds of people dropped dead from fright.

Thousands rioted.

Hundreds committed suicide.

Inside Mount Posso, the Death Merchant and the commandos of DELTA Force and the British Special Boat Squadron prepared to attack the Soviet Spetsnaz.

Chapter Twenty-three

Huddled with his ten men in the KGB security building, not far from the three needle-riddled corpses of the three KGB officers, the Death Merchant pulled his Uniden VHF transceiver and contacted Colonel Ambule, who, with Colonel Burrell and some of the commandos, was in one of the repair shops. Other commandos were in the spare parts building. Both groups were pinned down by vicious RP46 light machine gun fire and occasional 5.45-mm slugs from AKS-75 and AKR assault rifles. The only protection the commandos had were metal parts in steel drums and shelving that they had turned over, for the steel-cored projectiles from the Russian weapons could tear through the fiberboard of the buildings with the ease of an icepick stabbing through tissue paper. By the same token, the Russians were in the same precarious situation, their own predicament equally as dangerous: 5.56-mm projectiles from Enfield L70 assault rifles and 9-mm SAA Ball slugs from Sterling SMGS were equally powerful, ripping with ease through the fiberboard.

"The ivans have us bottled up." Ambule's voice came over the walkie-talkie. "We're in what appears to be repair shops of some kind. The rest of the men are in a large building fifty feet south of us. What's your position and how secure are you?"

"We're in a building several hundred feet southwest of you and only a short distance from the big dump where the rest of the men are," reported the Death Merchant. "I'm not even sure that the pig farmers know we're here. We'll—"

A blast of machine-gun fire sent dozens of slugs tearing through the west wall of the KGB security building and forced Camellion to change his mind. "Yeah, they know we're here," he said into the walkie-talkie. "We can't—"

"Camellion! The bastards are attacking!" shouted Willard Troop, the only black DELTA commando with the Death Merchant's special squad.

"The ivans are coming at us too," Colonel Ambule said through the walkie-talkie. "Out—and luck, buddy."

Colonel Boris Malenkova didn't want a prolonged battle. Accordingly, he used two tactics that were practically sacred doctrines in the Soviet army. There were the tactics of *Massirovanie* and *Obrushit'sya na,* the first meaning the "massing of forces and means," the second "to throw oneself on the enemy with force," that is, a full frontal assault.

While two Spetsnaz gunners in the east end of the radio shack and one machine gunner on the north side of the partially demolished science building raked the repair shops, the spare parts building, and the west side of the KGB security building, fifty Spetsnaz troops charged from behind the elevator shaft that contained the magnifying transmitter, from the west end of the science building, and from the rear of the meeting hall. Each Spetsnaz, ducking and weaving, fired short bursts from either an AKS-75 or an AKR assault rifle, making a deafening racket.

Using windows and doorways, the DELTA and the

SBS commandos returned the fire, the roaring of L70 Individual Weapon assault rifles and of Colt CAR-15 submachine guns increasing the din and uproar. It was slaughter. Fifteen of Mother Russia's finest—and dumbest—were cut down within seconds, 5.56 by 45-mm CAR-15 and Enfield projectiles and 9-mm Sterling Ball slugs cutting some of the ruskies almost in two.

The DELTA and SBS commandos then tossed half a dozen deadly X-4 offensive grenades at the rest of the advancing Spetsnaz, all of whom charged into the explosions and thirty thousand rocketing needles that shredded them into bloody things that resembled nothing that had been human. Only four Spetsnaz were able to retreat from the kill zone.

Colonel Malenkova, Major Fedchenko, and Major Diamov, still using the radio shack as a makeshift command post, found it difficult to believe the defeat they had witnessed. How could a group of "soft" *Amerikanski* defeat the Spetsnaz, who were considered by the Soviet government to be the toughest, best-trained commandos in the world? In only four minutes forty-six Spetsnaz had been butchered. But there were still 104 Spetsnaz left, plus the twenty-nine KGB officers and maybe three dozen technicians and construction workers who could fight and were still able to defend *Veliki*.

Hunched down behind an overturned metal table, Malenkova said with a snarl, "We can get at them and they can't get at us. What we have to do is get around the damned *chernozhopski*."

Watching Malenkova pull the Gez UHF transceiver from its case on his belt, Diamov and Fedchenko remained silent. They both knew that it would be a miracle if they were still alive by high noon.

* * *

The DELTA and the SBS commandos had also suffered casualties. Six DELTA commandos and four SBS men had been killed by Spetsnaz slugs. The Death Merchant and his flying squad had also lost one man—Gid "Flaky Jake" Rushing. Two Soviet boat-tailed bullets had hit him in the head and chest.

Bee-bee-bee-bee. Camellion answered the call on his Uniden W-T.

Colonel Burrell said, "Yank, is there anything you can do from your present position? Colonel Ambule and I are thinking of having the four chaps outside the mountain present the ruskies with a few more missiles. What is your opinion?"

"Negative," Camellion said, speaking into the mouthpiece of the W-T. "We might have to use more STRORRs, but first I want to try a plan I have in mind."

Colonel Ambule interjected in his deep voice, "What do you want us to do over here, sit tight and wait?"

"You got it. The only thing the pig farmers can do is try to get around us. The best opportunity for such a tactic is to the south. We're going to stop them—out."

Rollie Elrose and some of the other Britishers kept watch on the north and the west sides of the KGB building while the Death Merchant, Sergeant Carlos Minteargo, and Joe Jerry Bianco pried loose a section of fiberboard from the aluminum frame of the room's south wall.

Earlier Camellion had noticed, by looking out of one of the west side windows, that there was a long barracks whose windowless east end was only fifty feet from the southwest corner of the KGB building. It was unlikely that the barracks would be empty. But, he reasoned, if he and some of his force could sneak along the south side of the barracks and catch off guard whoever might be inside, they might then be able to take over the building, in which case they would have gained more of their objective.

"The section is free," Camellion said. "All we have to do is lift it out and go on our way."

Cecil Tenkiller frowned in dismay at the Death Merchant. "Look, you must have boulders for brains! Fifty feet isn't all that far, but they can slam slugs at us from part of the south side of that building in front of us." Tenkiller, who was one-third Hopi Indian, shook his head. "Me, I don't think that committing suicide is going to help out the other guys."

"Cecil has a point," Minteargo said, looking closely at Camellion and scratching the left side of his neck with the end of the short barrel of a MAC-10.

"Yeah, he has a damn good point," Camellion said. "We'll give them a diversion." He looked wolfishly at Minteargo and Tenkiller as he pulled out his walkie-talkie. "Here's how we'll do it."

At the same time that Colonel Burrell and Colonel Ambule and the main body of the commandos opened fire and sent 9-mm and 5.56-mm projectiles at the science building, the radio shack, and at the sides of the tall elevator shaft that led straight up to the top of Mount Posso, SBS corporals Gerald Lodgebutt and Glenn Broombaugh began firing their Sterling submachine guns at the east end of the science building.

Simultaneously, the Death Merchant, three of the DELTAs, and one Britisher slipped through the square opening that had been made by the removal of the fiberboard panel in the south wall.

There were two window openings in the southwest corner of the KGB security building. Through them could be seen three of the windows in the southeast corner of the science building.

As the Death Merchant and the four other men slipped through the opening, Sergeant Tune cut loose with a Sterling SMG and sent streams of slugs at the windows in the southeast corner of the security building. No sooner had Tune fired off three-quarters of a clip than Milton Achersin leaned around the side of the other window and lobbed two thermite canisters at the corner of the science building. By then the Death Merchant and the other four were at the southwest corner of the KGB building.

There were two loud WHHOOSSSHHEEESSSSSS, the two thermite canisters bursting into brilliant blue-white flame that, for only a moment, was eight feet high and nine feet wide. Powdered aluminum and iron oxide had been ignited by black powder and had been turned into white-hot molten iron burning at a temperature of 4,000 degrees F.

The instant the Death Merchant and the four others heard the thermite explode, they ran from the corner of the KGB building to the southeast corner of the barracks. Camellion dropped to his haunches beneath the windows and began to duck-walk to the opposite end. The four other men had another task.

Sergeant Minteargo and Cecil Tenkiller flipped X-4 offensive grenades through the first two windows and dropped with Willie Troop and Rollie Elrose, the SBS commando. Both grenades roared off with concussions that shook the building. Troop and Elrose immediately reared up and began spraying slugs through the next two windows, Troop's broad grin a half moon of white teeth against a background of chocolate.

There were twenty-six technicians and construction workers in the long dormitory room, all of them at the north side windows. The terrible needles of the two X-4 grenades killed twelve of them, concussion leaving the others in a dazed, emotional limbo.

Before they could shift back to reality, Troop and Elrose's 9-mm Sterling and .45 MAC-10 projectiles were popping all over them, the impact knocking them to the floor and making them kick and jerk before the last breath fled from their lungs. Several of the Russians did manage to turn around and try to raise their RP46 SMGs, for all the good it did them. Two of Troop's flat-nosed .45 bullets hit one man in the chest and slammed him back with such force that his body almost crashed through the fiberboard of the north wall. The second ivan went down with blood pouring out of his mouth and his eyes rolled back in his head. Three of Elrose's 9-mm Sterling slugs had torn through his chest and had left bloody tunnels in his lungs.

For good measure, Cecil Tenkiller and Carlos Minteargo hosed down the corpses with their MAC-10 SMGs, the hail of metal tearing off tiny patches of clothing as they bored into the pig farmers, most of whom were total dead meat.

Willie Troop and Rollie Elrose hastily shoved full magazines into their weapons, then hurried forward to join the Death Merchant, who had reached the corner in time to see a group of Spetsnaz and KGB agents coming from two supply buildings 150 feet to the northwest, diagonally from the corner where he was standing. These Russians were part of the force that was making an attempt to move south, then east, and then get behind the British and American commandos. And they were trapped. They were too far from the buildings to retreat.

The Death Merchant triggered the MAC-10, the stream of FN .45 projectiles ripping into the forward ranks of the Russians and dropping them faster than a roller coaster at Disneyland. Spetsnaz and KGB scum, crying out in pain as slugs tore into their bodies, tumbled against each other like ten pins and went down, most of them dead before they hit the ground.

Other Russians managed to drop flat and trigger off AKS and AKR slugs at the Death Merchant, whose timing was perfect. Camellion pulled back and dropped down in time to avoid a typhoon of metal that ripped into the southwest corner of the barracks. Only one 4.45-mm spitzer-shaped projectile came close. It barely tweaked the combat cloth of his left sleeve on the outside of the elbow.

Realizing that Camellion was killing them from the corner of the barracks, the rest of the Russians made a desperate attempt to reach the door in the west end of the long building. This was their second mistake. After Tenkiller and Minteargo had reloaded their MAC-10 Ingram SMGs, they'd crawled through two of the south windows of the barracks and, wanting to save their own .45 ammo, had picked up two fully loaded Soviet AKS-75 assault rifles, which were the equivalent of Colt CAR-15 submachine guns. Minteargo had stationed himself by one of the north windows; Tenkiller had gone to the side of the door at the west end of the barracks. The Spetsnaz and the few KGB officers who were still alive rushed straight into Tenkiller's blast of 5.45-mm slugs made in the Soviet Union, chopping them down with all the power of an invisible blade. Those Slavic saps who frantically tried to run to the corners of the barracks were cut down by Tenkiller or by Troop or Elrose, both of whom had taken over the southwest corner of the barracks while the Death Merchant reloaded his MAC-10.

To the east, from the south side of the barracks and the KGB security building, came Sergeant Fred Tune, the three other Special Boat Squadron commandos, and Joe Jerry Bianco, the only DELTA Force commando who had remained with the Britishers in the KGB building. The five commandos rushed across the open space between the west end of the KGB building and the east end of the barracks. Their feeling was that the Russians in the science building wouldn't be able to fire at them because the southeast side was a mass of flame from exploding thermite.

The five commandos, reaching the side of the barracks, stopped, looked inside through the windows, called out to Tenkiller and Minteargo, then ran to the Death Merchant, Elrose, and Troop.

Once Tenkiller and Minteargo had left the inside of the barracks and were with the group, Camellion said, "Men, our next objective is those two buildings to the northwest. Once we have them secured, we'll be able to fire into the rear of the main group."

Having come this far west, the group could now look north into the bend and see the second barracks, a rock-scoop machine, and the shaft of the passenger elevator. The open shaft had three railings on only three sides, with the fourth side open. The passengers in the car were protected by a railing on the elevator car.

"Damn! Look at the size of it!" said Glenn Broombaugh. "Any larger and we'd need a bloody road map!"

The Death Merchant pulled out his walkie-talkie.

Corporal Harlan Blair, one of the missile men who had remained outside the mountain, was also the radioman. It was his job to monitor Greek government transmissions from the mainland and to inform the force if he heard anything in Morse code pertaining to Miskos. Now and then Blair tuned in to a commercial European station. What he heard from a station in France, and later from stations in Germany, England, and Norway, left him flabbergasted. The airwaves were full of a weird phenomenon occurring in Turkey. A "column of light" had come down from space and was constantly expanding in diameter. Already it had been estimated that the shaft was twenty miles in diameter and that millions of people were dead.

His mind whirling, Blair immediately contacted Colonel Clint Ambule and reported what he had heard.

Ambule didn't know what to say. He told Blair tersely, "Keep listening and keep us informed."

Colonel Ambule switched off the Uniden W-T and conferred with Colonel Burrell, who was as confused by the report as Ambule.

"What do you think it could be?" Burrell said curiously. "Some kind of optical illusion?"

"Blair said that millions were dead," Captain McComb said hoarsely. "And we're not that far from Turkey. If that damn thing is constantly expanding . . ."

"Bullshit! We have a job to do, and you heard what Camellion said when he called in," said Ambule, who was a practical man. "That joker is really something! Anyhow, once he reaches his objective—if the ivans don't blow his ass off—we'll have the damned ruskies where we want them. We have to be prepared to charge."

Colonel Burrell, secretly wishing he could remember Nostradamus' prediction about the end of the world, agreed in a calm voice. "Yes, you're right, Colonel Ambule. We have to attack."

Major Camelback said, "I'll contact Lieutenant Pfister in the other building. Okay?"

The Death Merchant and his nine men first lobbed six offensive grenades at the two supply buildings. Then they charged, zigging and zagging and jump-

ing over Russian corpses, all the while firing short
bursts from their Sterlings and MAC-10 Ingrams.
There were only five Spetsnaz and eleven of Major
Diamov's KGB agents in one of the buildings, and,
still in shock over the loss of their comrades, they had
lost all enthusiasm for a standup and slug-it-out fire-
fight. And while they didn't like to admit it, they
were afraid of the *Amerikanski*. Some of the Russians, however, did get off a few short bursts before
dropping to the floor and crawling to the north side
door.

Soaked in sweat, their breath making slight
whistling sounds as it was pulled in through the
square "lip" of their Facelet gas masks, the Death
Merchant and his group reached the closest supply
building. He and Tune and two of the Britishers
stormed into the building, their weapons tossing
slugs into crates and boxes. The rest of the force fired
through the windows of the second supply building;
it was empty.

The force had lost another man. Milt Achersin, a
Special Boat Squadron commando, had bought the
farm. He lay dead behind them, ARK slugs in his
chest and stomach.

Camellion and his men saw the small group of Russians who had occupied the supply building were on
the run, some headed toward the radio shack, others
toward the strange-looking magnetlike machines to
the north. There were fifteen of the machines, each
one thirty feet high, rounded at the top like a magnet, each connected to the next one in line by a series
of insulated pipes.

One Spetsnaz reached the rear of the radio shack.
The others were cut down by projectiles from several
general-purpose M60 light machine guns that Colonel Ambule and Colonel Burrell had set up, the

streams of projectiles knocking them every which way but up.

Camellion and his men had gained 230 feet. From their new position in the supply building, the Death Merchant and his eight men could now see the rear of the radio shack, of the large elevator shaft that carried the magnifying transmitter up and down to and from the mountaintop, and of the science building. Somehow the Spetsnaz and other Russians had extinguished the fire in the east end of the science building.

Gerald Percy Lodgebutt, a twenty-six-year-old, 231-pound SBS man, gave a low chuckle. "If we had shoulder-fired missile launchers, we could kill all them blighters within a few minutes. We sure could."

Sergeant Fred Tune, as spit and polish as ever, was not amused by the remark. He had other things on his mind. "See here, Mr. Camellion. We're wasting a lot of blooming time shooting at the rear of the buildings when we can't see the Russians. If you don't mind my saying so, I'm cheesed up with such tactics."

"I don't mind, Sergeant. I'm rather fed up with it myself," Camellion said affably, much to the surprise of some of the other commandos. "I'm open to suggestions. What did you have in mind? The way the plan is now, we open fire from here and the rest of the force charges."

Tune, also pleasurably startled by the Death Merchant's receptiveness, said quickly, "Sir, I'm not one to tell officers how—"

"I'm not an officer—thank God! And don't call me 'sir.' Call me 'Richard' or 'Camellion.' I don't care what you call me, as long as it's not 'sir' and as long as you call me for dinner."

"I meant the regular officers—Richard. It seems to me that if we would concentrate the fire of those light American M60s, we could blow some bloody damned holes in the walls. The walls are nothing but pressed wood fiber. I should think that such tactics might make those commie bastards do some rapid footwork, wouldn't you say?"

"Yes, Sergeant. I would say. Your idea is excellent." The Death Merchant smiled, pulled out the walkie-talkie, switched it on, and contacted Colonel Ambule. He informed Ambule and Burrell of Sergeant Tune's idea, adding "Personally, I think it makes a lot of sense, if for no other reason than the psychological factor. They've already lost a lot of trigger fingers. Such concentrated blasts could make them retreat to where we can really get at them."

The two colonels agreed, Burrell saying "Sergeant Tune is to be congratulated. I hope you heard that, Sergeant?"

Ambule then interjected, "Camellion, we received a report from Blair, our radioman. It appears that something god-damn strange is going on in Turkey."

Ambule then told the Death Merchant—and the eight men listening in—about the "pillar of light from the sky."

"What do you think it is, some kind of Soviet secret weapon?" asked Ambule.

I think it's the result of the magnifying transmitter. But Camellion, listening to pure intuition, said only, "I don't have an opinion. Too many unknowns are involved." *Could the ozone layer be collapsing? It's possible!* "How soon can you start the M60s firing?"

"Immediately," Ambule said.

Colonel Malenkova, the other officers around him in the radio shack, the regular Spetsnaz, and the remaining twelve KGB officers in the science building knew that the *Amerikanski* were preparing a full-scale attack when the small group of commandos to the southwest and the main group of commandos in the repair shops and in the spare parts building, to the east, began firing.

The firing from the east was especially vicious, the 7.62-mm NATO projectiles from the three M60 light machine guns a pure nemesis, the gunners acting as one trigger finger firing at the same target. An M60 fires at the cyclic rate of 550 rpm. This meant that in sixty seconds, 1,650 projectiles had all hit the same general area. The result of such synchronized and concentrated firing was devastating. In seconds whole sections of walls literally vanished. Then there were the ricochets, hundreds of them. Their screaming alone was enough to melt the iron in the backbone of even a well-trained Spetsnaz. Within minutes six of the Russians were wounded by the flying metal, some seriously.

Almost flat on his face on the floor, Colonel Boris Malenkova reviewed another Soviet tactic in his mind—*otkhodit!* RETREAT! To the Soviet way of thinking, there wasn't any such thing as retreat, not in the conventional sense. To the Soviet General Staff "Retreat is one of the moments in the general course of offensive operations." Along with this concept of *otkhodit* was the doctrine of *istoshchat'-sya*—"The enemy will wear himself out following a planned retreat in any offensive operation."

Colonel Malenkova yelled to Major Valeri Fedchenko, to make himself heard above the high shrieks of metal glancing off metal.

"We'll retreat to the magnatrons. They have been shut off. We'll be able to hold them off from there. Notify the men in the science building." In the back of his mind, Malenkova wondered if it might be possible to get to the passenger elevator and take it to the top of Mount Posso. A realist, he knew he was daydreaming and indulging in useless hope.

Fedchenko automatically pulled his Gez UHF transceiver. He and Major Diamov knew that *otkhodit* was only prolonging final defeat.

Unable to move through the west door because of slugs coming from the Death Merchant and his small group, Colonel Malenkova and other men cut out sections of the north wall of the radio shack, darted through, and, running for their lives, raced toward the long row of magnatrons, the first one of which was only a hundred feet to the northwest.

The Russians in the science building, fleeing through north side windows and the two doors, had a longer route to run—180 feet.

For the moment, the only thing in favor of the Russians was that the three M60 LMGs had stopped firing—for two reasons: because the gunners had completely exhausted their ammunition and because Colonel Robyn Burrell and Colonel Clint Ambule had ordered the entire force of DELTA and Special Boat Squadron commandos forward in a full assault. It was now either victory or defeat, life or death. There could not be any in-betweens. Man has always had more violence than reason. . . .

Racing in a crooked run, on a course that would make a pretzel look like a straight line, the Death Merchant and his eight men darted past the smoking wrecks that had been the general headquarters building and the water purification plants, their Sterling and MAC-10 SMGs spitting out three-round bursts.

Russians screamed and dropped from the deadly crossfire, from the streams of slugs burning air from the south and chopping into their bodies from the east. The Russians from the science building were particularly hard hit, losing twelve men before they had gained a hundred feet.

The British and the Americans also suffered numerous casualties. The Spetsnaz, now and then stopping to turn and fire, didn't intend to go down in defeat without exacting the best price in blood they could. Glenn Broombaugh cried out, jerked, dropped, and died. So did Joe Jerry Bianco, moments later. He had taken a stitch of slugs across his chest.

In the main force, charging from the east, SBS and DELTA commandos were hit by enemy projectiles in vital areas. Some died instantly, the final big blackness dropping over them with the speed of light. Others died slowly, still conscious as their life's blood leaked out of their bodies.

Yet all men die, some instantly from a heart attack, or a stroke, or perhaps an accident. Others linger for years, dying day by day, a little at a time, from cancer. Captain William McComb was one of the fortunate ones. A 9-mm Vitmorkin slug stabbed him in the left temple a moment before several PPS71 7.62-mm submachine gun projectiles popped him in the chest. Within half an inhalation of his last breath, McComb was stone dead, his knees buckling. Twenty feet to the right of McComb, Clay Shakvee, an SBS noncom, caught 5.45-mm AKR slugs in the stomach, which doubled him over before shoving him into death. DELTA Lieutenant Karl Pfister caught a 5.45-mm projectile in the right leg, the impact knocking him over. The FMJ bullet had ripped through the gracilis muscle, but the long femur had not been touched; neither had any important vessels or arteries.

Major Adonis Brillakipolu was turned into an instant corpse when he was only a few feet from safety. Two of Sergeant Minteargo's FN .45 slugs hit him in the back of the head, parted the parietal and occipital sections of his skull, and exploded his brain.

What remained of the Soviet fighting force reached the line of magnatrons, and right behind them came the grim and determined DELTA and SBS commandos. The ivans' retreat and the commandos' assault had been executed with such speed that no one on either side had found time to reload, except a few of the Russians who had first reached the metal safety of the magnatrons. The Death Merchant and the commandos pulled sidearms from hip-extender holsters. But not Cecil Tenkiller. He charged in behind the magnatrons with the special shotgun he had unstrapped on the run, the deadly Striker.

The main body of commandos had raced to the north side of the magnatrons from the east. The Death Merchant and his group of six, however, came in behind the Russians from the west. With commandos to the east of them and commandos to the west, and the rock wall of the cavern to the north of them, the Russians were bottled in—trapped.

Browning DA and 9-mm Beretta autoloaders roared, and so did Soviet 9-mm Stechkin and Vitmorkin machine pistols.

BLAM-BLAM-BLAM-BLAM-BLAM! In a low crouch and moving back and forth, Tenkiller pulled the trigger of the Striker, and each time the shotgun boomed a Russian went down from the shot of a twelve-gauge shell, the holes in their bodies large enough to shove a fist into.

A Steyr pistol in each hand, the Death Merchant shot a Spetsnaz who was swinging a PPS71 submachine gun toward Colonel Burrell. When the Spetsnaz fighter began to fall and another pig farmer tried to grab the PPS71, the Death Merchant put a 9-mm full-metal-jacketed bullet through the side of his neck.

In the meantime, Burrell wasted a KGB agent with

a slug from the Browning DA in his right hand, and an eyeblink later used a British para's battle knife to gut another Russian, the sharp blade ripping upward and cutting the man's belt in two in the process. The Russian staggered back, his eyes looking down in horror at his intestines oozing out of the huge perpendicular wound. But he looked only for a moment. Then he fainted from shock and fell against Evgenu Perlev, another KGB officer, who had just killed a DELTA commando with the last 9-mm bullet in his Stechkin machine pistol. Perlev was trying to pull a fully loaded Makarov from a hip pocket, but was shoved forward by the weight of the dying man. Perlev's pause saved the life of another commando and at the same time gave Jory Reelcur, a DELTA radioman, time to throw a Special Forces knife at the Russian. The big blade caught Perlev just above the hollow of the throat and slid in so deeply and with such force that an inch of the blade protruded from the rear of his neck. Jerking violently like a bug pinned by a pin to a board, blood gushing out of his mouth, Perlev sank to his knees, his arms flopping in an effort to reach the knife protruding from his throat. He succeeded only in falling flat on his face and shoving the blade in deeper.

Colonel Clint Ambule had found Major Valeri Fedchenko and was locked in a life-and-death struggle with the second in command of the Spetsnaz force. Ambule's left hand was wrapped tightly around Fedchenko's right wrist while Fedchenko's left hand was locked around the DELTA officer's right wrist. It was, for the moment, a Mexican standoff. Fedchenko could not lower his Vitmorkin and put a bullet into Ringo Ambule. Conversely, Ambule could not stab the Russian with his Special Forces dagger.

Ambule realized he would have to take the initiative—and fast—when he detected another Russian coming at him from his right, the man's hate-filled eyes on him, his intention clear. Ambule waited until Anatoli Nichenorenko was within range, then twisted slightly to his right and, with his right foot, kicked the ruskie squarely in the groin. Nichenorenko's eyes looked as if they were about to pop out of his wide Slavic face. A choked scream jumped from his mouth. His hands went to his groin and, stumbling back, he twisted halfway around and fell, losing unconsciousness from sheer shock.

A micromoment after he kicked Nichenorenko in the groin, Ambule opened his right hand and let the dagger fall to the ground. Almost simultaneously, he stamped his right heel on the instep of Fedchenko's left foot. The Spetsnaz officer howled in agony as bones snapped. Reflexively and without thinking, he released Ambule's right wrist.

Faster than a striking rattlesnake, Ambule used his right hand to grab the Russian's right wrist, placing it next to his left hand and violently twisting the pig farmer's arm. Again Major Fedchenko howled in pain. His fingers opened reluctantly and the Vitmorkin M-P fell to the ground.

"You commie son of a bitch!" snarled Ambule, who now had the edge and knew it. He ducked a very fast left knife-hand strike, stepped back, jerked mightily on Valeri Fedchenko's right arm so that the arm was straight out. Ambule then let the Russian officer have a high front snap kick with his right leg, the tip of his combat boot burying itself in Fedchenko's right armpit. The blow paralyzed Fedchenko's right side, the agony shooting all the way to the top of his skull. To further weaken Fedchenko, Ringo Ambule slammed him over the bridge of the nose with a right Seiken forefist, then finished him off with a four-finger spear-stab to the throat, the lightning TNT thrust crushing Fedchenko's thyroid cartilage. The Spetsnaz officer was as good as in hell. Hemorrhage was instantaneous. The Russian's windpipe started to swell shut and he started to make the sounds of a man being hanged slowly by piano wire, great gasping sounds that grew weaker and weaker. His nostrils flaring, his fingers digging at his throat, Major Valeri Fedchenko fell. He lay there, his legs kicking. Then he was still forever.

Each Spetsnaz had been trained in *Sambo,* the Soviet school of karate. One of the Spetsnaz, a noncom with an Oriental cast to his flat peasant's face, was confident he would be able to kill Rollie Elrose in only a few minutes. Why not? Elrose couldn't get away; he was backed up against the side of magnatron.

Very fast, Igor Gurva drew back his left arm in a fake knife-hand chop, then made his real move—a high, lightning-quick left-leg kick aimed at Elrose's face. Gurva was astonished when Elrose ducked the kick, and actually became afraid when he saw the speed with which Elrose could move. Gurva next tried a *zhdennyi* double-hand palm clap to the Britisher's ears. He then received another surprise. The SBS commando threw up his arms inside of Gurva's burly arms, knocking them outward and preventing his palms from slapping the ears. If the Russian's hands had clapped Elrose's ears, the intense pressure would have sent shock waves down the ear canals and ruptured the tympanums. The result would have been intense pain, dizziness, unconsciousness, and possibly death.

Cursing under his breath, Gurva tried to move closer to Elrose in an attempt to stun him with a series of right and left knife-hand chops. He was too slow. Instead he found himself in the worst kind of trouble. Elrose's left arm streaked out, his hand moving to the back of Gurva's head and holding it firm as he slammed his right elbow into the ruskie's mouth. Gurva's face exploded in agony as teeth were broken off and his nose was shattered. Igor Redenovitch Gurva didn't even get the time to cry out and taste blood. Again Elrose's elbow stabbed inward, this time straight into Gurva's throat. With his Adam's apple mashed into his windpipe, Gurva was finished and started to go the route that Valeri Fedchenko had taken.

The entire area between the north wall of the cavern and the long line of stainless-steel magnatrons became a bloody battleground of struggling men, men who cried out in victory, men who cried out in pain, men who died.

As the Death Merchant would later tell Courtland Grojean, "It was worse than a Saturday night in a Greek tavern in Athens."

Sergeant Fred Tune, spotting a Spetsnaz about to put a .357 magnum bullet into Major Charles Eastmore with a Ruger GP-100 revolver he had pulled from a canvas holster attached to the boot of a dead DELTA, took a chance and tossed a Gerber Survival III knife. The S-III was a very special knife; Tune had given it a solid lead handle. The S-III streaked through air heavy with powder fumes and caught Gurin Tchebotarev in his right side, the weight of the lead handle pushing in the surgical-steel blade to its full length of six inches. Tchebotarev cried out, jerked, and bent forward, his right arm dropping reflexively. His finger pulled against the trigger of the Ruger revolver and the weapon went off, the .357 magnum bullet hitting the stone floor, glancing off, and hitting another Russian in the left buttock.

Seeing Tchebotarev drop, Sergeant Tune muttered, "That will make you naff off, you damned bugger!"

Tune's elation was short-lived. The Britisher was trying to reload his Browning semiautomatic pistol when Lieutenant Vasalo Tagenrog came in from behind him and smashed him over the head with the the side of an AKS-75 assault rifle. Tune died instantly. A moment later so did Tagenrog. For a micromoment, the Russian's head jumped from his neck and hung there suspended—seemingly—in space. The head then tumbled sideways, hit the right shoulder, and fell to the ground, the eyes blinking once on the way down.

Willard Troop had used a machete to decapitate Tagenrog. Blood jumped a foot from the severed arteries in the stump of the neck, splashing all over the corpse, which fell forward in a giant spray of red.

It was now Willie Troop's turn to fight for his life. Three Spetsnaz—two even larger in bulk than Troop —rushed him, one from the front, the other two from the left and the right. Two were without weapons. The third, coming in from the right, had a long-bladed trench knife in one hand.

The three were very fast and very light on their feet. But so was Willie Troop, as Gregory Ralkoff, rushing in from the right, soon learned. Willie, acting startled and afraid, pretended to focus most of his attention on the Russian in front of him. At precisely the right moment, when Ralkoff was at just the right distance, Troop made a half turn to his right and stuck out his right arm, the hand of which was wrapped around the butt of the machete. Ralkoff was coming in so fast he couldn't stop, although he tried to. But his momentum carried him forward so that he impaled himself on the long eighteen-inch blade, which cut right through his green uniform, hurried through his stomach, and raced out his back. Ralkoff screamed, jerked, dropped his knife, and, continuing to shudder violently, dropped and began to die.

The other two Spetsnaz were determined to kill Troop. Reino Verkhne dove for Troop's legs as Antonin Patolik grabbed Troop around the neck and let him have a powerful fist blow to the stomach, the pain taking most of the strength from the black DELTA commando, who felt he was as close to death as he ever wanted to get. He was—and he wasn't! What saved Troop was that Major Glen Camelback happened to see him and the two Russians go down.

A crack shot, Camelback aimed at Reino Verkhne's lower left leg and pulled the trigger of his Ruger Redhawk revolver. BANG! The big revolver roared. The .44 FN projectile blew Verkhne's lower leg off below the knee and made the Spetsnaz release his hold on Troop. BANG! The next .44 magnum slug hit Antonin Patolik in the left ankle and sent his foot flying. He screamed and his arms went slack. Troop, getting his second wind, quickly rolled away from the two Russians who were in shock and bleeding to death.

Colonel Boris Malenkova was furious at seeing Willie Troop escape. He was even more enraged over the "murders" of the two Spetsnaz by Major Camelback. The Spetsnaz commander had two major hates. The first was the United States, an idiot nation he considered a gutless giant.

Malenkova's second hate was *chernozhopski*— "black asses." And there was one of the damned niggers right in front of him, only eighteen yards away.

Malenkova, snuggled down with Major Sergei Diamov behind two compensator drums of a magnatron, had three 9-mm cartridges left in his Vitmorkin machine pistol.

"I'm going to kill that damned *chernozhopy*," he snarled fiercely to Diamov. "That god-damn nigger won't kill any more of our people."

He started to get up and Diamov grabbed him by

the arm. "Stay down, you fool! This way we might have a chance."

Malenkova, his face demonic with hate, threw off Diamov's hand, stood up, and raised the Vitmorkin MP. He couldn't sight in on Major Camelback because three Spetsnaz and that idiot General Nikos Cyatorus were blocking the way. But Malenkova could see Willie Troop clearly. The damned black ape was pulling his machete from Gregory Ralkoff's corpse. Malenkova had another reason for wanting to snuff Troop. In his mind it was a sacrilege that any Russian, much less a Spetsnazopy, should be killed by a tree-swinging *chernozhopy*. By killing the savage, Malenkova would somehow rectify the mistake.

Malenkova fired. His first 9-mm projectile hit Troop between his shoulder blades; the second hit him lower in the back. Troop fell and started to slide into the Ultimate Elsewhere.

Boris Malenkova had made the biggest mistake of his twenty-eight years (four months and five days). By standing, he had made his position known. Among those who saw him were the Death Merchant and Cecil Tenkiller. They didn't know that Malenkova was the commander of the Spetsnaz. All they knew was that they had seen him kill Willie Troop, and both were firm believers in honest revenge, especially Camellion, who realized that the philosophy of turn the other cheek was an insult to the human spirit, a "rule" fit only for cowards and weaklings. Forgive and forget was Camellion's credo: *But first get even! Triple!*

"They've seen us!" Malenkova yelled at Major Diamov. Then he tossed his last 9-mm Vitmorkin slug at the Death Merchant, who had jumped to the right when the Spetsnaz leader raised the machine pistol. The projectile missed Camellion's left shoulder by several inches.

Confirmed atheists, Malenkova and Diamov were not afraid of death, nor did they intend to stand there like statues and let Camellion and Tenkiller have the advantage. The two Russians left the protection of the two compensator drums and charged out to meet the attackers, determined to kill Camellion and Tenkiller with their bare hands. After all, Malenkova had been an instructor in *Sambo*, and Major Diamov had won several competitions between the KGB and the GRU.

Malenkova believed in smothering an opponent with a devastating attack from which he could not recover. Conforming to this principle, he attempted a high roundhouse kick to the Death Merchant's face and, when Camellion ducked, rushed in closer with a rapid series of left-handed fish-head Seiken strikes and right-handed sword-hand chops.

The Death Merchant, who had obtained his first black belt (in *Tae Kwon Do Hyung)* when he was twenty-three, easily ducked every intended blow and retaliated with a right *Ni Hon Nukite* two-finger spear aimed at the Russian's eyes. He followed with a left *Shuto* sword-hand to Malenkova's right collarbone and a front snap kick that, if it had landed, would have turned Malenkova's sex machine into mush.

Cecil Tenkiller, an expert in *Kenpo,* the evolutionary pinnacle of *Kung Fu,* easily wrecked Sergei Diamov's attack—a right stab kick intended to land on Tenkiller's groin and a double punch to the throat. But Tenkiller was able to duck Diamov's next blow— a fast snap kick—only partially. The sole of Diamov's right foot connected with Tenkiller's left thigh, a foot above the knee. Tenkiller grunted in pain and almost went down. He was, however, able to block Diamov's next two strikes, a left bottom-fist to the solar plexus and a right middle knuckle blow to the nose. And that's when Major Diamov became overconfident and rushed Tenkiller.

Malenkova, enraged because he had failed to kill the damned American by now, tried an open knuckle punch to Camellion's face. Another flop! The Death Merchant jerked his head quickly to one side. Malenkova then countered with a right edge-of-the-foot kick aimed at the left side of the Death Merchant's neck. Camellion stepped easily to his right and moved a few feet backward to prepare for an attack of his own—and tripped! Losing his balance, he fell and landed on his back. With a snarl of triumph, Boris Malenkova rushed at him. Too experienced to jump on Camellion as a wrestler might, the Spetsnaz colonel came in from the left and attempted a heel stomp to Camellion's groin. In his excitement, he forgot all the moves an opponent could use to counter such a strike. Camellion used one of them.

Malenkova had attempted the stomp to Camellion's groin with his left foot. With astonishing speed, the Death Merchant used his right leg in a hard side-sweep that knocked the lower part of the Russian's leg away from his body. Malenkova's foot came down with the force of a battering ram, but it barely brushed the outside of Camellion's left hip. Disgusted with his failure, Malenkova let out a loud curse.

The Death Merchant, sitting up, used his hands to push himself backward and away from the Russian, who was ten years younger and outweighed him by thirty pounds. To Camellion, this meant that the Russian had ten years less experience than he. This also meant that Malenkova *Will now try to kick me either in the face or in the throat. Or he might try another groin strike.*

Colonel Malenkova was very confident and very

obliging. His next tactic was a right-legged snap-kick straight to the Death Merchant's face, a strike that would have broken Camellion's teeth, nose, and jaw.

Malenkova missed. He failed because Camellion grabbed the Spetsnaz colonel's right foot with both hands and twisted to his right with all the strength at his command. Boris Malenkova let out a high yell of pain. In spite of what he wanted to do, he didn't have any choice but to go with the turn or else suffer terrible, unbearable pain, pain already shooting past his right hip. Malenkova's entire body spun around to the left, so far that his back faced the Death Merchant.

Stupid pig farmer! Camellion raised his left leg and kicked Malenkova behind the left knee. Once again the Spetsnaz commander did not have a choice. He fell to his right, landing hard on his right hip. Before he could regear his thinking, the Death Merchant had reached him, his right hand flashing down in a *Shuto* sword-ridge strike that landed half an inch above the bridge of the nose. This is the glabella, an area often misidentified as "the bridge of the nose." If delivered properly by a karate expert, a blow to the glabella communicates directly with the front lobes of the brain.

In intense shock and only half conscious, Major Boris Malenkova was helpless. Camellion let him have another right chop, this one to the center of the throat. His windpipe crushed, Malenkova would be dead within seconds and would tiptoe through boiling lava into Hell behind Major Sergei Diamov.

Diamov had rushed Cecil Tenkiller, who had pretended to be weaker than he really was. Diamov had left himself wide open, and for his mistake received a snap wheel kick to the side of his rib cage that staggered him. Tenkiller leapt forward and killed him with a spinning wheel hook kick, better known in

Kenpo as the "Dragon whipping its tail." It was total catastrophe for Sergei Diamov. The side of Tenkiller's left foot had crashed into the right side of his neck and had crushed the carotid artery. Diamov's heart began to beat at a much slower rate. Blood flowing to his brain slowed. The arteriolar smooth muscle relaxed, pulling blood from the head. Diamov was dead before his body crumpled to the ground.

BLAAMMMMMMMM! Camellion, Tenkiller, and the commandos still alive jerked their heads toward the west. The explosion had been a STRORR missile. The first missile had exploded the barracks and had killed seventeen of the *Stalingrad*'s crew, who had been running close by. The second exploded, turned the science building into rubble, and changed ten members of the *Stalingrad*'s crew into chunks of bloody flesh that rained down over a wide area. The rest of the crew, armed with AKS-75 and AKR automatic rifles, turned and started to run back toward the large OSCAR-class submarine.

Commander Vorchinkovik, his officers, and the crew had decided to join the battle. They had been seen by the commandos watching with binoculars through the "mouth" in the east side of Mount Posso. Realizing that a battle was in progress and that they wouldn't have time to make radio contact, the commandos had acted instantly, afraid that the crew of the *Stalingrad* might affect the outcome of the conflict. The commandos had used STRORRs with total effectiveness.

The Spetsnaz and their officers were dead. The KGB officers and their chief were dead. Six Russians were still alive, but they were unconscious and dying. After the Death Merchant and the DELTA and the Special Boat Squadron commandos saw that the crew members of the *Stalingrad* were running back to their submarine, they gathered weapons, reloaded, and prepared for the assault on their last objective, the long, two-story barracks to the northwest, the one that lay past the bend of the cavern.

Colonel Burrell and Colonel Ambule contacted the commandos outside of the mountain, firing informing Corporal Blair that they had won and had only one more objective—the single barracks to the northwest.

"Corporal, give us a report on the latest news about that shaft of light in the sky over Turkey," Burrell said. His right arm was bandaged above the elbow, due to a knife wound he had received.

"The column has stopped expanding, sir," Blair reported nervously. "The last I heard was from a station in London. The announcer said that the shaft had swollen to four hundred eighty-two kilometers. Now it's growing smaller by the minute—that's what the announcer said."

Colonel Ambule spoke into the transceiver. "Have you seen any Greek aircraft, Corporal?"

"Yes, sir. Four fighter planes have flown over at only about a thousand feet. And two choppers at several hundred feet. The Greeks know something is going on, sir."

"Hmmmmm . . . four hundred eighty-two," mused Clint Ambule. "My God! That's three hundred miles." Shoving a full magazine into a .45 Colt Officer's ACP pistol, he noticed that Richard Camellion was busy taking photographs of the magnatrons while other commandos checked the bodies of the Russian dead.

A few minutes later Ambule, Burrell, and some of the other men approached the Death Merchant, Major Charles Eastmore stepping around the corpse of General Nikos Cyatorus, who lay dead with his sightless eyes staring up at the ceiling. His throat had been cut from ear to ear.

Richard Camellion had put away his Minolta X-700 camera and was talking to Sergeant Carlos Minteargo and Gerald Lodgebutt.

"They just did a recon on the barracks," Camellion said casually to Ambule, Burrell, and the others. "There are white sheets hanging out of windows—and it's not washday either!"

"And we saw one of the Russian blokes in one of the doorways." Lodgebutt laughed. "He was waving a white towel on the end of a broom and yelling something that sounded like *'zumasto,'* whatever that might mean."

"*'Zumisitu.'*" Camellion smiled. "It means 'surrender.'" The smile vanished. "But it could be a trap. I wouldn't believe a damned pig farmer if he said 'good morning.' And they love power, which to them is like sea water."

"But they could be on the level," Colonel Ambule said. "Maybe they do want to surrender."

"I speak Russian," Camellion said. "I'll call out to the pig farmer in the doorway and tell him that if they don't come out, we'll destroy the barracks with missiles." His eyes went to Ambule and Burrell. "By the way, how about the light over Turkey? What have you heard?"

"The shaft has stopped expanding and is growing smaller," replied Colonel Burrell, his close-set eyes surveying the Death Merchant with respect and admiration. "I should think we'll obtain more information on whatever it was once we return to the submarines. And Greek aircraft have been flying over the island. We're going to have to finish ASAP, Camellion."

Major Camelback finished lighting a cigarette and said thoughtfully, "About that light over Turkey . . . it makes a man wonder. I never was religious, but, you know, maybe it's better to believe in God and the Bible just to be on the safe side. . . ."

Pascal's Wager! thought Camellion. *As if anyone could force himself to believe—you know!* But the Death Merchant said, "Let's get to the barracks."

The Russians inside the barracks had not prepared an ambush. They hurried out both doors, all thirty-one with their hands above their heads. The Death Merchant and the commandos saw that many of them were women and included the family of Professor Stefanos Paspyrou: his wife, Irene, and his two daughters, Ione and Talisia, both of whom were in their upper teens.

The men were high-level technicians, the most important of whom were the Russians General Gregor Shchors, Dr. Alexander Szamuely, and Dr. Lazar Marchenko. All three Soviet scientists were almost trembling, convinced they would be chopped down on the spot.

With them was Professor Paspyrou, who immediately introduced himself and, in good English, said, "My family and I were kidnapped by the Soviet KGB and brought to this island. They and these men"—he pointed to Shchors, Szamuely, and Marchenko— "forced me to help them conduct very dangerous experiments in world weather modification, experiments with a device known as a magnifying transmitter."

The Death Merchant, a MAC-10 held loosely in one hand, walked up to the Greek physicist. "Yes, we know, Professor," he said mildly. "That's why we came here, to rescue you and your family and to stop the experiments. Tell me, could the experiments, could the use of the magnifying transmitter, have caused anything unusual to happen in the upper atmosphere?" He looked straight at Paspyrou, whose large eyes made him think of an owl.

Paspyrou's eyes widened and became mirrors of dread. "Why do you ask? Tell me, what has happened?"

The Death Merchant told him.

Enraged and horrified, Paspyrou swung on General Gregor Shchors, who stepped back before the sheer fury of the scientist.

"I warned you!" screamed Paspyrou. "I warned all of you. I told you that more tests were needed because we were playing with highly dangerous forces. But none of you would listen. Now millions of innocent people are dead! You, you—"

Paspyrou leapt toward General Shchors, his hands going around the Soviet scientist's throat. Major Camelback and Sergeant Ken Scollar of the SBS commandos quickly pulled Paspyrou from the terrified Shchors and held him back to keep him from making another attempt.

"Professor Paspyrou, is the device in the elevator shaft the magnifying transmitter?" Camellion asked.

Paspyrou stopped struggling. Camelback and Scollar released him.

"Yes, that's the hellish device." The scientist looked at the Death Merchant. "It should be destroyed and never rebuilt."

"It will be, Professor. It will be destroyed."

And it will be rebuilt. And you and the three Soviet scientists will help rebuild it. That's how the international game is played.

The Death Merchant and the commandos moved out. With them went Professor Paspyrou, his wife and two daughters, and the three Soviet scientists. With Camellion were seven rolls of film, including numerous photographs of the magnifying transmitter. To save time, the rolls of film would be developed on board the USS *Hawkbill* and ten copies of each frame sent to London on a fast jet. From London, nine copies of each photograph would be flown to Washington, D.C.

When Greek forces landed on Miskos, they could do what they wanted with the Soviet technicians left behind and with what remained of the crew of the *Stalingrad*. The technicians, the big OSCAR-class sub and its crew, the base itself . . . all of it would be proof to the world of what the Soviet Union had tried to do: change the weather—and proof positive that the USSR was responsible for the deaths of millions trapped inside the "hole" from space.

The last commando had just reached the outside and was in the bright sunlight when there was an explosion from inside Mount Posso.

Forty pounds of Cyclonite had been detonated by timer.

The magnifying transmitter was no more.

The Death Merchant and everyone else hurried toward the south beach. The rubber boats had to be inflated and then rowed to the Whales.

"Camellion, there's something that's been puzzling me," remarked Colonel Ambule, who was walking next to the Death Merchant. "You said that power to the Russians is like sea water. That doesn't make sense to me. What's the punchline?"

"There isn't any punchline, Colonel," Camellion said. "Power is like sea water. The more you drink the thirstier you get. . . ."

In the distance they could hear a helicopter. . . .

Chapter Twenty-four

The Death Merchant didn't expect to have a picnic from Mount Posso to the beach. He didn't get one either. The commandos on the outside had seen the four 321 Aérospatiale Super Frelon helicopters land on the beach and discharge sixty troops.

The Greeks were bunched up and moving toward Mount Posso when the DELTA and the SBS commandos ambushed them.

The battle that followed was necessary and short, essential because the Greek force was between the commandos and the rubber boats hidden in rocks to one side of the beach, short because it was a slaughter. In only five minutes all sixty Greek paras were dead.

The commandos headed for the beach. By the time the boats were inflated and the force had paddled to and boarded the Whales, almost three hours has crawled past. It took another two and a half hours to reach and get aboard the submarines. Total victory had been achieved, but it had not come cheap. Twenty-nine Special Boat Squadron and thirty-four DELTA commandos had been killed.

Commander Ray Meyerscough had all kinds of information regarding the hole that had been burned through the ozone layer. The circle of burning death from space had widened until it had swallowed even Ankara, the capital of Turkey.

"From what we've heard on world radio, an estimated ten to fifteen million people are dead," Meyerscough said grimly. He stared incredulously at Camellion, Burrell, and Ambule. "And you're sure that it was caused by that device you blew up on the island?"

"We're not scientists, but Dr. Paspyrou is," the Death Merchant said. "He won't be positive until he confers with other scientists and has the proper imput of data. That could take weeks, maybe months." Camellion paused. "By the way, Commander. Those three Soviet scientists we brought aboard the *Hawkbill*. I want them kept separated and guarded day and night. I want a guard with each man even when he goes to the head. Those three are better evidence for Soviet treachery than even the photographs we took."

"If they talk and tell you what you have to know," the commander of the *Hawkbill* said solemnly.

A strange glow flashed in Camellion's blue eyes. "Commander, before this boat reaches London those three are going to be singing entire operas for me—believe it!"

The USS *Hawkbill*, the HMS *Warspite*, and the HMS *Resolution* began the return trip to Great Britain through the Mediterranean at three times the speed they had used on the first undersea journey. The reason was that the four Whales had been left behind. After the commandos had boarded the submarines, the Whales were flooded, sent to the bottom of the sea, and blown apart with timed charges.

It required some time for a photographer aboard the *Hawkbill* to develop the seven rolls of film, enlarge each frame, and make ten copies of the hundreds of frames. Eventually the task was completed and the eight- by ten-inch photographs were placed in a large plastic case that was firmly sealed. The negatives would remain on board.

The *Hawkbill* was just southwest of Malta when it surfaced and sent a small white balloon 420 feet into the air. Half an hour later, a Lockheed P-3 Orion maritime reconnaissance aircraft from Torrejon AFB in Spain flew over and hooked onto the pickup line. In only minutes the case with the photographs was inside the Orion. Inside the case were also four one-hour tape recordings. On the tapes were the voices of Professor Paspyrou, the three Soviet scientists from *Veliki*, and a man who was identified on the tapes as Delmer Bobbs-Asir.

The photographs and tape recordings would be in England in two and a half hours. In nine hours they would be in Washington, D.C.

"The vital material will be sent to the U.S.," the Death Merchant told Paspyrou. "The Soviet government won't be able to refute such evidence. Nor will they be able to shout it's American propaganda. Shchors, Szamuely, and Marchenko are well-known scientists. Their faces are as well known to the world as your own."

Stefanos Paspyrou folded his hands on the small wardroom table. "It's the rip in the ozone layer that intrigues me," he said, a sad slant to his mouth. "I feel responsible for the catastrophe." He stared at Camellion, his eyes wide. "I tell you: Many times I warned General Shchors. He wouldn't listen. He was afraid of the bosses in Moscow and had a schedule to maintain."

"Doctor, you've got to stop blaming yourself," insisted the Death Merchant. "What happened wasn't your fault. You and your family were black-bag—

were kidnapped. The KGB forced you to work on the experiments."

"I could have killed myself. I d-didn't because I was afraid I might go to Hell. I know that sounds rather ridiculous—a scientist believing in superstition."

The Death Merchant's lips curled in a cynical smile. There were times when he felt he was the only resident adult in a house full of psychotic monkeys. "Not necessarily, Doctor. All of us are prisoners, more or less, of our early conditioning and religious training. Shucks, I sometimes get the impression I'm a human being, one of those puny, defenseless bipeds."

Paspyrou smiled for the first time since he had boarded the *Hawkbill.* "I do not understand your joke, Mr. Camellion."

"It's not important," Camellion said offhandedly. "I'm more interested in what happened in the ozone layer."

Paspyrou's eyes blinked rapidly, as if showing the speed of his thoughts. "The N-beam must have changed the flow of the neutrons in the layer," he said slowly. "Are you familiar with integral, differential, and infinitesimal calculus?"

The Death Merchant laughed. "To be honest, I've never even heard of the infinitesimal type, and I don't know too much about the other two."

"Infinitesimal calculus is only integral and differential calculus considered together. Infinitesimal calculus is the most difficult of all; however, the term is no longer in use. Today we scientists use it in conjunction with the orders of infinity, which involve accurate gradation of the sizes of infinite sets, for example, such as the set of real numbers.

"Unless you have an understanding of calculus, it is not possible for me to explain the dynamics of the forces that were unleashed in the upper atmosphere. It will be years before scientists will be able to understand. We know that a 'hole' was made in the ozone layer. We do not know how the hole was made. Let me ask you. What will happen now? What will your president do? I am told he is not a man of genuine peace."

"I'm afraid you've been around the Russians too long, Doctor." Anger flared in the Death Merchant's eyes. "And you should have more sense than to believe what you read in Greek socialist newspapers, which follow the Soviet disinformation line. President Reagan knows that it's weakness that brings war and that it's strength that prevents conflict."

"But what do you think your president will do?" asked Paspyrou, becoming more nervous. "Could it mean war, nuclear war?"

"It should be obvious. As soon as he receives the photographs and the tapes, he'll go on television and tell the world what really happened on Miskos, and why it happened. I suspect the world will hear first from the Greeks. By this time, the Greek government has troops on Miskos and has found the base. If they try to cover up the truth, they're fools." Camellion paused, thought for a moment, and rolled his tongue around the left side of his mouth.

"We'll also hear from the Syrian slime. The south section of the 'hole' expanded fifty kilometers into northern Syria, almost as far as Haleb."

The Death Merchant was wrong. The world heard first from President Hafez al-Assad of Syria. Assad denounced the United States for its "aggressions" and asserted that the United States and the Soviet Union "are superpowers indistinguishable from each other in the ethics which guide them. They are moral equivalents." Assad then said that when the cause of the disaster, "which murdered sixteen thousand innocent Syrians," was found, the world would learn that the United States had been conducting "secret weapons tests dealing with a death ray."

Before the world could fully absorb President Assad's ridiculous speech, Socialist Premier Andreas Papandreou of Greece appeared on Greek national television and proved that he had more common sense than the Soviet Union, which had first tried to cover up the nuclear disaster at Chernobyl, then had made the situation ten times worse by lying about it.

In a shaky voice, Papandreou told the truth. He said that, without the knowledge of the Greek government, the Soviet Union had been using the island of Miskos to conduct very dangerous weather modification experiments. As proof, he produced photographs of the wrecked Soviet base, of the technicians and the crew of the *Stalingrad,* and of the *Stalingrad* itself, and its wrecked sail.

Andreas Papandreou held up to the cameras the photographs of dead American and British commandos and explained that special forces of the United States and Great Britain had invaded Miskos and had attacked the Soviet weather-experiment base. He stated that the Greek government would protest the invasion of Greek territory at the United Nations and demand reparations from the United States and Great Britain, particularly for the Greek paratroopers who had been "brutally murdered" by "retreating" British and American forces. As a footnote, Papandreou said the Greek government would "protest" to the Soviet Union.

Some hours after Papandreou had made his speech, when *Hawkbill* and the two British subs were approaching the Strait of Gibraltar, President Ronald Reagan of the United States appeared on television and told the world that American DELTA

Force commandos and British Royal Marines, of the Special Boat Squadron, had indeed invaded Miskos and had attacked a secret Soviet base inside the mountain of Posso, an experimental station that had harbored a machine known as a magnifying transmitter.

"It was by using the magnifying transmitter that the Soviet Union hoped to change the weather of the world and use the change for its own advantage. The United States has proof."

The proof was not only the hundreds of photographs of the base itself but Doctor and General in the KGB Gregor Shchors, Dr. Alexander Szamuely, and Dr. Lazar Marchenko, the "three scientists who were captured inside the base, which the Soviets called *Veliki*, a Russian word that means 'friend.'"

The President then explained that further proof would be the voices that would follow from a tape recorder. The interrogator was a man named Delmer Bobbs-Asir. The other voice would belong to General Gregor Shchors, the scientist in charge of the experiments.

QUESTION, by Mr. Bobbs-Asir: What was the purpose of the *Veliki* station hidden in Mount Posso on Miskos?

GENERAL SHCHORS: To complete the construction of the magnifying transmitter, which would be used to effect a change in world wide weather patterns.

QUESTION: Directed at what specific nations?

ANSWER: The United States, the nations of Western Europe, and Great Britain.

QUESTION: Be more specific. What kind of changes did the government of the Soviet Union hope to bring about in the United States?

ANSWER: We wanted to turn your Midwest

into a barren desert and bring intensely cold winters to your industrialized region in the east.

QUESTION: Did the Soviet Union arrange for the kidnapping of Professor Stefanos Paspyrou and his family?

ANSWER: Yes, the KGB kidnapped Dr. Paspyrou, his wife, and their two daughters.

QUESTION: Please explain.

ANSWER: It was Dr. Paspyrou who perfected the magnifying transmitter. We needed him to help us with our weather modification experiments, and we knew he would not help us willingly. We had to kidnap him.

As a clincher of his indictment of the Soviet Union, which President Reagan referred to as a "bandit nation of sadists and paranoiacs," the President presented a fifteen-minute interview between Professor Paspyrou and Mr. Bobbs-Asir.

In the interview, Professor Paspyrou thanked the Americans and the British for rescuing him and his family from the Russians and confirmed everything that General Gregor Shchors had said.

He added, "It is my belief that it was the misuse of the magnifying transmitter that caused a 'tear' in the ozone layer, this hole resulting in the terrible burning which occurred over Turkey."

"Do you have a scientific basis for your opinion?" Bobbs-Asir asked. "Are you speaking as a scientist or as a lay person?"

Paspyrou answered angrily, "As a scientist. For months I warned Dr. Shchors and the other fools of the dangers. I told them that the magnifying transmitter, in its present stage of development, presented a clear danger to the upper atmosphere of this planet. None of them would listen."

Bobbs-Asir said, "Assuming you are correct, Professor Paspyrou, can you tell us why the 'hole' stopped its expansion and why, apparently, the ozone layer 'sealed' itself?"

"I don't know," admitted Paspyrou. "We had the magnifying transmitter in operation for almost four hours. It is possible that we shut off the machine in time, that is, before the destructive forces were large enough to overcome the layer's natural repair abilities. There is much about the atmosphere we don't know."

"Professor, do you mean that if the magnifying transmitter had been left on for a long period of time, it might have completely destroyed the ozone layer?"

"Yes, that is what I mean."

"What would the result have been if the entire ozone layer had been destroyed?"

"The surface of the planet would have been scorched by intense heat. All plant and animal life would have died. Every tree would burn. Eventually the oceans would boil. One could say it would be a slow end of the world—by heat. . . ."

President Reagan concluded his two-and-a-half-hour presentation (which the Voice of America broadcast in thirty-one languages) by saying in a firm, warning voice: "This nation will protect and defend itself against any enemy that might try to destroy us by back-stabbing means, such as changing our basic weather patterns. We invaded the island of Miskos, which is Greek territory, because we had to. We could not tell the Greek government what was taking place on the island. To have done so would have been to warn the Soviet Union. It was this man"— President Reagan held up a large photograph of General Nikos Cyatorus—"who made it possible for the Soviet Union to establish its base inside of Mount Posso on Miskos. He is General Nikos Cyatorus, the head of the Greek intelligence service. It was he and many of his officers who betrayed their own nation and sold their services to the highest bidder, to the gangsters in charge of the Soviet Union."

A monitoring of world broadcasts convinced the men on board *Hawkbill, Warspite,* and *Resolution* that President Reagan had scored a great victory. And so did Mrs. Margaret Thatcher, the Prime Minister of Great Britain, when she went on the air and told the world the same story.

The world condemned the Soviet Union. Reports began coming in of Soviet embassies being stoned all over the world.

Reporters in Washington, D.C., London, Paris, Rome, and in other great cities of the world demanded to talk with Soviet ambassadors. The ambassadors were "not available." Neither were spokesmen for the Soviet government in Moscow.

The official Soviet word? Nothing. Neither a confirmation nor a denial.

The return trip to Great Britain was almost over. The three submarines were 120 miles from Land's End, the southernmost point of England, when Courtland Grojean contacted the Death Merchant by shortwave, scrambled and in code.

Congratulations, Camellion, Grojean said, the dots and dashes coming through the headphones on Camellion's head. *You pulled it off.*

The Death Merchant was more than a bit surprised. The Fox never congratulated anyone, ever. It was not his style.

Camellion, with two of *Hawkbill's* radiomen watching him, tapped out: *You didn't call to give me any congrats. We're practically on British soil. What's up?*

I didn't get a chance to listen to the tapes after they reached England, Grojean replied. *We sent them on to Big Uncle as soon as they reached us. How did you get General Shchors to admit everything so fast? I assume you had to use intensive interrogation?*

I never touched the pig farmer. I merely told him that if he didn't cooperate, we'd ship his tail back to Mama Russia and leak word that he was a double, that it was he who tipped off the CIA to the location of the base. He talked faster than a politician caught in a lie. But you didn't call just to ask me that. Out with it.

Grojean's reply was instant: *It's possible that your wish about the Soviet Union is about to be fulfilled, very possible.*

The Death Merchant felt a chill crawl down his back. He knew that Grojean was well aware of his wish, his desire to see the entire Soviet Union turned into a sea of nuclear glass.

He tapped out, *Explain fully.*

Courtland Grojean did. *I thought I'd let you know in advance. In another hour our forces and NATO will go to Alert One. The* Hawkbill *and the other subs —in fact, all subs—will be notified shortly. The Soviet Union is already massing its forces. Our satellites have picked up intense activity, not only in the Soviet Union but also in East Germany and Czechoslovakia. I have more news for you. Rebellions have broken out in Poland and in Rumania.*

Anything else?

The Hawkbill *and the two British submarines will not be returning to England, not yet. There are two Soviet subs in the English Channel. If the Big One comes, those two subs have to be taken care of. As I understand it,* Hawkbill *has both acoustic and rocket-boosted winged torpedoes. ASROCs.* Warspite *and* Resolution *also have ASROCs. Commander Meyerscough has already been told.*

Even if we get the Soviet pig boats, there might not be a London for us to come back to, Camellion tapped out.

Exactly. In case I'm vaporized and we don't see each other again, God bless you, Richard—out.

The Death Merchant switched off the set, removed the headphones, and got up from the chair. He thanked the two radiomen, left the compartment, and started down the corridor, passing half a dozen submariners who rushed by him, going in the opposite direction.

Camellion couldn't help but smile. The only real enemies of the world were the enemies of beauty and reason. The Universe could not care less about billions of bipeds crawling around on a speck of "dust" that revolved around a quite ordinary star on the main sequence scale. The realism involved Time and Cycles. Death had to feed on Life, and from Death always came Life. It was all relative. Like the man who won a dog named Hugh in a crap game and later lost the dog in a poker game.

You win a Hugh, and you lose a Hugh. . . .

A klaxon began to ring loudly throughout *Hawkbill,* and a voice called out over the intercom:

"BATTLE STATIONS! BATTLE STATIONS! BATTLE STATIONS!"

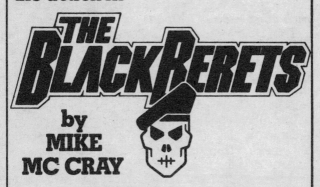